W9-CBU-344

"So much of American fiction has become playful, cynical and evasive. *Preparation for the Next Life* is the strong antidote to such inconsequentialities. Powerfully realistic, with a solemn, muscular lyricism, this is a very, very good book."

—Joy Williams, author of *The Quick and the Dead*

"An illegal Chinese immigrant meets a broken American warrior, and the great love story of the 21st century begins. The intersection of their paths seems inevitable, irrevocable. Their story: tender, violent, terrible, and beautiful. Atticus Lish's prose, lyrical and taut, sentences as exact and indisputable as chemical formulas, is trance-like, evangelical in its ability to convert and convince its reader. *Preparation for the Next Life* is that rare novel that grabs you by the shirt and slaps you hard in the face. Look, it says. It isn't pretty. Turn away at your own risk. In case you haven't noticed, the American Dream has become a nightmare. Atticus Lish has your wake up call. He has created a new prototype of the hero, and her journey provides us with a devastating perspective on the 'promised land' of the post 9/11 U.S., where being detained is a rite of passage and the banality of violence is simply part of the pre-apocalyptic landscape."

—Christopher Kennedy, author of *Ennui Prophet*

"*Preparation for the Next Life* is a masterwork. A love story for the lovers—but also our first true great-American tale of the new world qua terror in the mighty city of New York."

—Luke Goebel, author of *Fourteen Stories, None of Them Are Yours*

PREPARATION FOR THE
NEXT LIFE

Tyrant Books
676A 9th Ave. #153
New York, New York 10036

www.NYTyrant.com

Copyright © 2014 Atticus Lish
ISBN 13: 978-0-9885183-3-9
Third Printing

This is a work of fiction. All of the characters and organizations portrayed
herein are products of the author's imagination or are used fictitiously.

All rights reserved, including the right to reproduce this book or portions
thereof in any manner whatsoever without written permission except in
the case of brief quotations in critical reviews and articles.

Cover design by Erik Blair
Author and cover photographs by Shelton Walsmith
Interior design by Adam Robinson

PREPARATION FOR THE NEXT LIFE

ATTICUS LISH

Tyrant Books
NEW YORK, NEW YORK

*For Beth
in this Life and the Next.*

Part I

1

SHE CAME BY WAY of Archer, Bridgeport, Nanuet, worked off 95 in jeans and a denim jacket, carrying a plastic bag and shower shoes, a phone number, waiting beneath an underpass, the potato chips long gone, lightheaded.

They picked her up on the highway by a plain white shed, a sign for army-navy, tires in the trees. A Caravan pulled up with a Monkey King on the dash and she got in. The men took her to a Motel 8 and put her in a room with half a dozen other women from Fookien and a liter of orange soda. She listened to the trucks coming in all night and the AC running.

They gave her a shirt with an insignia and a visor, the smell of vaporized grease in the fabric. Everyone told her you have to be fast because the bossie watching you. They didn't speak each other's dialects, so they spoke English instead. Her first day, her worn-out sneakers slipped on the grease. She dropped an order, noodles popping out like worms, and that night she lay with her face to the wall, her jaw set, blinking.

The Americans parked out front, their pickups ticking in the sun, and came in slow and quiet in bandanas and tank tops. They would lean an elbow on the counter and point a thick finger at the menu and say that one there. The blacks came in holding what they were going to spend in their hands, the wadded dollars and change.

Is y'all gonna let me have them wings? Y'all tell me what I can get with this then.

She knew how to say okay. When they pointed at the menu, she got it fine. In Nanuet, they wanted the all-you-can-eat. She could understand that. You need to get some more of this. Okay. She knew how to hurry up and get something, to work because she had to, to work fourteen hours a day every day until the tenth or eleventh day, until they got a smoking day, as the boss called it, because it was better than picking through the trash in the brigade field south of the river.

In the motel, they kept the TV running to practice English. They squatted on the carpet, moving their mouths in the blue light, seeing the grocery store aisles and the fast cars. Unbelievable, they said. This Tuesday on Fox. A grim day in Iraq. She watched goggled soldiers and radio antennas driving past adobe houses in the desert, which she had lived in.

Camel, she pointed. The animal, it's very good.

Too hard, they said. It can't be absorbed. Mind is a wooden plank.

Someone yawned.

Have to practice it a lifetime.

When they had finished their work at night, they crossed the parking lot to the one car still there, the Caravan waiting to take them back to the motel. They gave the man his takeout, and he put it on the newspapers open to Hong Kong stories. She watched the large sweeps of the night go by as they drove home, the black areas of the forest, the slate highway and sky. He had a gold chain and a green card and he drove with the lights off, watching for cops.

The women were from Begin to Celebrate, Four Meetings, Connected Mountain, and Honesty Admired. She told them she was from south of the river.

But you're from somewhere else, they said.

I'm Chinese, like you.

You don't look it.

In the sun, you could see Zou Lei's hair was brown and not black. There was a waviness to it. She had a slightly hooked nose and Siberian eyes.

Our China is a big country, she said.

You sound like a northerner.

Northwesterner.

She's a minority, one of the women said.

You can teach me your language.

That's meaningless. You've got People's Terrace, Peaceful Stream, Placid Lake, Winding South, Cotton Fence, Zhangpu, Convergence of Peace, Swatow, Common Tranquility, Prominence, Samyap, Jungcan, Broad Peace, Three Counties, Next-to-the-Zhang-Family Dialect, and a hundred more. Which one we teach you?

Zou Lei thought for a moment. Then tell me how to say heaven is high. She smiled and pointed at the stained ceiling. Heaven is high and the earth is wide.

Some of them nodded, a few smiled, revealing bad teeth. That's true, that's true, they agreed, and one of the women sighed.

What she learned instead was how to take an order. The fortune cookies were in the box under the Year-of-the-Goat calendar and the little plastic shrine. The napkins, straws, and chopsticks were all together on the shelf. Give everybody plastic fork no matter what. When a customer came in, you asked him what you having? Then you shout his order in the back: chick-brocc, beef-brocc, beef-snow, triple steam, like that, to make it fast.

No one had to teach her how to mop and take the trash out and go through a sack of greens, chopping off the part you didn't eat. They saw she was a hard worker. Most of what you did was something she already knew. Squatting, she washed her clothes in the bathtub, wringing them out with her chapped, rural, purple-skinned hands, and hanging them up on the shower curtain rod with the others' dripping laundry, the wet sequined denim and faded cartoon characters.

At the counter, she put a piece of cardboard in the bottom of a bag, stapled the lips of a Styrofoam shell together, and set the shell in the bag on top of the cardboard. The other containers went on top with cardboard in between. She stapled the menu to the bag and handed it over the counter to a lean guy in a red baseball hat and long blond hair. Taking an extra menu, he said, You're gettin a whole lot better. I timed you.

The boss said the women needed someone to supervise their well-being, a big sister who would report to him. He gave them a phrase to memorize—It's not a matter of time, it's a matter of money—that he wanted them to repeat a thousand times a day as fast as they could say it.

What does it mean? she asked.

It is not significant. Its significance is unknown.

One of the women was mentally imbalanced, given to bouts of silence, and then saying the police had given her a forced abortion in Guangxi.

When the weather turned cold, some of them slept together. They squatted in front of the space heater, their wet clothes hanging in the shower, all of them sick, coughing and spitting up in the wastebasket.

On TV, she saw girls surfing, driving trucks, boxing, and marathoning in the sun. When deliveries came in, she ran outside and carried the sacks of rice in on her shoulder. The women disapproved, saying let the men do that, the cook and his cousin. Don't go licking the boss's piles. Zou Lei told them that she liked to move her legs. At night, she did sit-ups. She took a paper from the van and read the classified ads for jobs in other states.

She left for Riverhead and worked the rest of the winter there, staying in a La Quinta with a group of women who spoke Three Lights and country Mandarin. They had a hotplate, which they shared.

America is a good country, an older woman said. We took a fishing boat across the ocean. The ocean police caught us and closed us up on an island near San Francisco. I almost died on the voyage and that was what saved me. That was lucky. The others were forced back home, thirty people, but not me. My cousin applied me for asylum. Some of these other sisters have been deported once already. Now they come back, once becomes twice, twice becomes three times. They go to the Yucatan Peninsula, cross the border in Arizona. Now that's hard, of course. That's the desert, not for us people, river people. My village language is Watergrass. We're fifty kilometers from Old Field and they don't know a word we're saying.

She spent a year in Archer and six months in Riverhead. Swine-flu season was over and the World News was carrying stories about the war on terror and the difficulty of getting a green card. She turned the page and saw a photograph in black and white of a naked prisoner lying on the ground with a sandbag on his head. She turned the page again, studying the words: construction, seamstress, restaurant, beauty, pay depends on ability.

She went to Nanuet and got another shirt with an insignia and another visor. The women lived in a trailer on cinder blocks, which rested on pine needles, and hung their washing on a line. On their smoking day, she hiked up to the mall, running across the highway and hopping the divider, and looked through the glass at the sneakers made in China.

The boss wore a jade bracelet and drove a dirty Astrovan. He had Zou Lei wash it out back where there were loading docks and dumpsters, a fence, and then the woods. She let the hose run, gazing past the dumpsters, and imagined herself running through the woods.

The next year, in another state, she was in a motel room with eight women who talked in code even in their own dialect. When she asked what village they were from, one of them said, Cinnamontree. The others turned on the woman who had talked and said, What are you doing telling secrets to an outsider?

They had a big sister called Sophia who determined when they could watch TV. They weren't allowed to open the door when someone knocked unless Sophia was there and said it was okay.

In the women's rhyming slang, Zou Lei eventually realized that a sailboat meant money that they were sending back to China. A shout was a phone, a crow was an illegal alien, and Andy meant the police.

A man arrived in mirrored shades with a dragon on his wrist, bringing them a pack of Stayfree. The boss loved music, he said. Everything I do, I do it for you. You know the song?

Once, when Sophia wasn't there, Zou Lei let the maid into the room and asked her where she was from and what her job was like.

Honduras, the maid said, a tattoo of a cross on her hand. They were about the same age.

Zou Lei ran into the bathroom and came out with the wet towels in her arms and put them in the hamper. The Honduran girl smiled and said gracias.

How about you job, is the job money? Zou Lei asked.

No, no much money. Poquito money. You has working papers?

Zou Lei said, Take a guess. You think so?

No. They both laughed.

Maria taught her a handshake. Zou Lei showed her the ad in the Sing Tao where it said you could buy a social security number.

By knocking on a steel door, she found a job working eight-hour days putting clutch plates in cardboard boxes, the best money she had ever made: $9 an hour minus taxes. At lunchtime, she ate rice and turkey from a Tupperware container, while the Americans in Dickies and bandanas lined up at the lunch truck. She carried all her money with her all the time, clipped around her waist, cell phone, fake ID, the things she couldn't lose.

One day in mid-autumn, she went into a bodega and got caught coming out the door.

Just relax. Do you have anything in your pockets? Anything sharp? It's okay. Just relax. A Spanish guy in a football jersey lifted up her arms, looking past her as he turned her pockets inside out. He unclipped the belly bag from around her waist and handed it to a guy with a pistol half-hidden by his sweatshirt. She had just cashed her check inside the bodega and she followed the bag with her eyes. Do you need a translator? I feel your heart pounding in there. Just cálmate. Tranquilo, okay? You speak Spanish? What are you, Chinita? Chinese?

Why I didn't run?

They felt through her clothes and took her money, zip-tied her, and put her in a van with a Salvadoran prisoner. It took all afternoon. Hey, mama, you shy? They had Fookienese, Cambodians, men from Guatemala. She was taken into a glass tank with a stainless steel bench and a cement floor and the fluorescent lights on, and other girls kept coming in and out all night, until they moved her. She rubbed the dents on her wrists made by the restraints.

A white girl with mascara down her cheeks said, These niggas better let me out for my boy's birthday.

In the middle of the night, they ordered her out. Through the reflection on the glass, she saw someone looking at her, an American with a mustache. The intercom came on. Yeah, you. Stand up. She did as she was told. The door opened. He beckoned with a finger. She exited the tank. The corridors were dark throughout the jail and she didn't know what they were doing. There was no one there except the deputy and, down the corridor, a head-down figure mopping the floor with a strange, self-denying patience, as if he wasn't there, and she realized he was an inmate.

Take one. The deputy pointed at a laundry bin of fraying orange jumpsuits. She had to ask him where to change before he showed her. She locked herself in the bathroom and, for a moment, was alone with the sink, the mirror, the porcelain toilet, and tile. A radio was playing a car commercial on his desk. She hurried taking her jeans off, avoiding the mirror, pulled on the jumpsuit, discovered it was sleeveless, and zipped herself up, and hurried out, her arms colder than the rest of her, holding her jeans out to the deputy like a gift. He took them.

Then he took her elbow and walked her deeper into the facility, his weight compressing his shoes into the waxed floor, the heels of her shower shoes tapping rapidly next to him. They turned another corner. She could not hear the radio anymore. There were no lights and there was an animal smell. They came to a large black window and the deputy stopped. He unlocked a door. Inside was a big black room. He took her elbow and put her in. It felt like an indoor basketball court. She could just make out the numbered cells across the concrete floor. She turned to ask what she was supposed to do. That one. Seventeen, he said and locked her in. She felt him leave. Holding her blanket in her arms, she squinted her eyes and identified her number and started towards it. Above her was a second tier. In her tiny numbered cell, behind a heavy wooden door painted with marine paint, she felt a steel shape with her hands. It was a bunk. She lay down. Her eyes adjusted. She saw the graffiti on the cinder blocks. She got up and pulled her door shut. It did not latch. She lay there listening with her eyes shut.

I will stand this, she said when the lights came on and she saw where she was—the steel thing on the wall that was the toilet. In China, the conditions would have been worse.

She left her cell and saw the others shuffling out, fat, puffy-faced, hostile, acne-covered, their afro hair standing up, taking over the picnic table in the center of the room, milling around the stairs, wandering to the glass window and back. They played with each other's hair. A black girl farted and said, You heard? There were rural women with Indian blood in them and crosses on their hands who stayed together. You could tell who had been picked up in an immigration sweep. It was obvious who she was. She squatted by herself, as all the migrants did.

The deputy came and let a trustee in with a food cart. Everyone got up. She stood aside and let the blacks and Americans go ahead of her. When she received her tray, she took it to her cell and ate her boloney and cheese sandwich, looking resolutely away from the toilet.

She spent the day walking back and forth to the window in the big room, keeping along the wall, until the lights went out in the facility.

She had been there two or three days when she realized she wasn't sure if it had been two or three exactly, which. It could have been either, or it could have been more. She tried to count the days, but there was no way to tell them apart. There were no clocks. She briefly thought of keeping a calendar, but she didn't have anything to write with. There was nothing at all except themselves, her and the other females, in the loud, dirty sealed room.

She tried to say to a woman, a white woman with a crushed nose, did they ever have a chance to watch TV in here?

TV? Oh, yeah, sure, we got one. It's over by the Jacuzzi.

What there was was a payphone by the window. It had a bail bondsman's card taped to it with an 800 number on it. She had watched people calling from it. Silvio, a voice said after she put the number in and the line clicked. She did her best to tell him who she was. He asked her where she was calling from, and she didn't even know that. Well, no problem, he could call around. It would be one of two places if she had gotten herself picked up in Bridgeport. Do you know what you're being charged with? No? It could be from the sound of it, they got a thing now where, if you entered the country under the radar, so to speak, you're not eligible for bail. That's the Patriot Act. He repeated it for her. Yes, she nodded. I know it.

Do you have anyone who can bond you out?

No, she said. I am just me in this country. I will work for you when I get out, if you just get me out, she struggled to express. I am honest. I pay everything. She said this into the receiver gripped in her hand, half bowing her head.

Oh, he said. I don't doubt that. But if it's like that, there might be nothing I can do.

She listened.

That's the way it is.

He had to go.

To keep her spirits up, she went back to walking up and down along the wall and distracted herself counting miles.

She started doing walking lunges every three steps, counting in her head. There was yelling, but she didn't think it was directed at her. It surprised her when someone got off the picnic table and came over. She went around them. They followed her, getting louder. Now they were really yelling and everyone was looking. They were yelling at her to stop. Don't be doin that in here. I ain't playin with you. She stopped doing lunges. The yelling stopped. You could hear the person who had been yelling at her breathing hard.

Fuckin monkey-ass bitches playin like they don't speak English.

Something troubled her and she pushed it out of mind. No one told her anything. There were no lawyers. Then in the night, she dreamed her father came to the jail, short, tan, sharp, in uniform, saying nothing. The Americans deferred to him. He picked her out of the rest, and they had to let her go. The dream returned in a second version in which he had made a terrible mistake by entering detention and now he couldn't leave. She sat uncertain on her bunk.

She watched a woman who was being released walking away on the other side of the window, sashaying with one arm out, following the deputy towards the front of the facility, where she would be given back her clothes and let out on the winter street.

Zou Lei ate a boloney sandwich and did knee bends in her cell next to the toilet.

They were lined up to see a social worker, who asked her if she had STDs. This concept was explained. She thought it meant AIDS. No, she said.

Are you pregnant?

She shook her head.

Do you know what day it is?

She shook her head.

It's Tuesday. Do you speak English?

She nodded, then shook her head.

Are you gang-affiliated?

She didn't know. No.

She said she wanted to know if she was going to get to see a lawyer. No one had told her what she had been charged with or on what basis she was being held. When she tried to ask what was going to happen to her, a deputy ordered her to move away and return to her side of the room.

The Latinas had a gang they called the Niñas Malas for self-protection. And what are you? the white women with their stringy hair wanted to know. Someone said Al Qaida. I'm Chinese, Zou Lei said. She wet her hair in the sink and tied it back to make herself look another way.

She did not like exercising in her cell. When she was alone, her mind turned inside-out like an envelope. She would drift and come back and hours would have gone by. Once, her mind traveled to the clutch plate factory where she had been working, and she saw and heard them working and talking about this and that. They were saying, Remember that girl? What happened to her? And she knew they were talking about her. In her mind, it was a day of blue sky, and she could smell the asphalt and the field and the lunch truck.

Some Latina girls asked her, Are you with it? Hey, yo, you wid it? And instead of ignoring them, she stared back at them and said, I don't with nothing. She pretended she didn't see them, but she was scared. The fear came in and out like a radio signal. When it faded out, she went back to being sick. She picked up the phone and listened to the dial tone and put it down, stared out the window and waited for anyone to walk by. Her sickness came from this sealed room. I cannot stand it, she thought. Deputies walked by from time to time in their green uniforms. Sometimes a male trustee would come by, a certain expression on his goateed face because one of the females would jump off the picnic table and rush the glass and pound on it and make signs at him.

There was an aching in her eyes from loneliness. When she closed them, tears scattered down her face.

Later in the artificial day, she stood by the others, who were talking on the stairs, gathered around a composed young woman emphasizing what she was saying by socking her fist in her hand. Zou Lei got as close as she could and tried to listen. The speaker was saying that she had been given thirty years for armed robbery.

He had the gun and I was with him.

Ninety-nine problems.

For real. He doin life.

You stay here? Zou Lei spoke up.

The others looked at her, then at the armed robber to see what she would say.

Will I stay here? No, I'm going to state prison.

After a minute, the woman, as if vexed with children, lowered herself off the stair where she had been sitting and moved apart from the others. Zou Lei approached her and asked her what she had been waiting to ask.

Deport you, the woman said. I don't know. They might put your ass in Uncasville.

This was the answer Zou Lei finally received: No one knows what will happen to you.

Well, what would she probably be facing?

Probably you're talking a year. Zou Lei got a look of concentration when she heard this. A year and then? A year and then they decide what to do with you.

Okay, she said. And what they do with me?

That's the thing. They can do anything they want, because of your status.

I can be my life in here?

A good part of it. Look at Gitmo.

But there was more, she learned. This was just the beginning. Any deputy could take you by the elbow on a long walk through the jail to the other side. He could show you to a laundry room full of male trustees and say, Here's your new helper. Howbout I leave her here? He would wait just long enough for your blood to run cold. Just kidding. You shit yourself? You wanna check? And he would march you back to the female wing. Along the way, he would say, Bet you feel like being nice now. He would lock you in the bathroom and come back for you later. If you fought him, he was authorized to rush you like a man, tackle you, pound your head on the floor, Taser your backside while you crawled, drag you out by the leg while you screamed under the cameras recording all of this in black and white, strap you in The Chair, put the spit bag on your head and leave you there for up to twelve hours while you begged for water. And he could count to twelve any way he wanted. You could see a social worker who would look at your blackened eyes like plums and say, Why were you fighting with staff? and write Antisocial on her form. They would add time to whatever sentence you got, whenever you finally got a sentence, so they could help themselves to more of your life. All you had to do was give someone a reason. They were going to rape you unless you carried yourself a certain way, and even then, they could nail you anytime, misplace you in the laundry room. They did it to the small half-Indian girls in the Mexican gangs. If you cried too much afterwards, you got Trazodone. Then they wheeled you upstairs strapped to a folding bed and left you in a hall.

Anyone who was here on immigration sweeps was in violation of the Patriot Act. If you were suspected of terrorism things got really interesting. There was a cell on the upper tier that no one ever left. Or had she failed to notice that?

They showed her what was going on on the top tier, in the cell that no one ever came out of. They had a project they'd been working on. It was a woman lying in a bunk. The deputies gave her to us. We take care of her. Right after 9/11 they put her in a cell with like fifteen guys. She was in Al Qaida for real. I don't know how they could get it up because she's so nasty. Look at her. She's old. Zou Lei looked at the woman. She couldn't tell if she was breathing. They told her she was Lebanese, a mom. Her husband had been flown from New Haven to Syria for interrogation. Dried feces on the walls. Her feet were black, hair tangled wild over her face, going gray, going white. They threw wet toilet paper at her. Used tampons. A black girl screamed at her. Ugh. You stink so bad! and ran out cackling.

The woman would not speak or move. The Americans had uncovered her head and she lay with her hands clutched over her face.

Zou Lei wanted to leave.

Scared? an inmate asked. I don't blame you.

In the northwest, she used to see men lying under the saplings on the medieval street in the desert town where she grew up, the dome of the mosque visible above the mud-brick houses. The men lay directly on the stone, face-down against the curb, faces sunburned, skull-caps still on their heads, their sandals sometimes having fallen off and lying a few feet away. The street where they were lying went uphill to the mosque, and when she was a little girl, before she knew what heroin was, she thought they had been climbing the hill to the mosque and had gotten tired along the way and laid down to sleep.

God be with you, she said to the woman.

2

IF YOU TURNED AND looked downhill from the mosque, you saw the end of the city, the last stones of the wall, then the gravel on the ground and the red sand and the desert descending away from you. The land rushed out and away from your feet and opened out into the vast distance, to the snowcapped mountains on the horizon. There was a great desire to launch yourself out into that distance and fly out to the mountains, which were in sharp focus in the brilliant air.

Until the call to prayer sounded from the mosque in the evening, the only thing you heard was the desert wind. It was quiet in the orchards. A donkey cart wheeled by, clop-clop-clop, with a suntanned old man sitting up front holding a lash, carrying melons, peaches or his daughters in the back. In some parts of the town, you could hear the hammering of tinkers, and if you went down west of the orchards, there were stone sheds with a fire roaring up and a bare-chested boy in a white skullcap working a bellows who would look up and grin at you, his face carbon-blackened.

Her mother picked watermelon in the orchard by a ditch near a half-built section of roadway. It was so quiet you could hear the flies, the thump of a melon rolling into the cart, the creaking of the cart when the long-eared donkey shifted. The women worked in earrings and skirts and headscarves with flowers on them. At noon, they prayed on a rug. They worked slowly in the immense dry desert heat and their sweat dried immediately. They would go to the spigot by the mud wall and drink from the tin cup and you would hear them laughing with each other as they drank as a group.

The city was on a route that came out of the desert and went on to the west. Trucks came in from Aksu and went back with sheepskins. She remembered the smell of animals and dung and wood fire, everyone putting out whatever they had to sell on the roadside, the pink plastic sandals her mama bought her, her dirty feet. Playing soccer on the clay behind the bus station.

When the trucks came in, she ran out on the shoulder to see who it was. Someday it would be him, she knew—she hoped and prayed—her mother told her. God willing. Sometimes there were live sheep in a flatbed with a blue cab. Sometimes a soldier or a Mongolian, in ragged army surplus or bellbottoms, climbing down and squatting in the half-shade, eating lamb kawap, while Zou Lei hung around watching.

Have you come from far away?

A grown man ignoring her, squinting. Sometimes grunting, lifting his greased chin, at the distance. Shaking his head. Nodding. Waving the flies away or ignoring them. The sun reflecting on the mud houses on the roadside, the one thing built by man, and everywhere else the tremendous soaring vastness.

The northwest was a territory of tribal nomadic herdsmen who did not recognize the borders between nations. They traded sheep and horses and spoke each other's languages. In the vineyards, they grew their fruit. The word for man was adam. Apple was alma. Silk, yurt, camel, and khan were pronounced the same in Uzbek and in Uighur. Tibetan women hiked up from Qinghai, carrying blankets and silver things to sell, wearing black cowboy hats and sheath knives. They would not let you touch them. Her mother's family's ancient dead were buried in Siberia.

The songs were the same. The girls sang them turning around, looking over their shoulders, coins around their heads.

The sun reverberating on the golden land, the snowcapped mountains—Afghanistan in the radiant air—no clouds—ram's music—purely wondrous blue over this part of the earth. Her mother's God above, causing the streams to flow from the snowcaps and make green the pasturelands and vineyards—the Kazak horses grazing!

In Gulja, the Russian architecture was European, with white columns, like a palace in France, and then, over the tops of the conifers, you saw the blazing dome of the mosque. Her mother's people came down from the steppe, before they were collectivized by the Chinese, who came from the east.

The Chinese closed the border. They paved the highway and put up red banners and billboards for the good of everyone. In Altai

Province, they established cotton plantations. The nomads were forced to curtail their trading. Now they were peasants, according to the Chinese, who found work for them picking cotton. Everything was being done for their own good. We are all one family. To prove that this was true, nomad girls were eligible for one hundred dollars if they divorced their husbands and married Chinese men. The new loudspeakers attached to the medieval buildings in the desert towns announced that we are very happy. Ration cards will be issued. Splittism is a serious offense.

A convoy drove through the desert. The center of it was a massive flatbed trailer hauling a section of pipe for the oil pipeline. The other vehicles were camouflaged, soldiers sitting in the back. The convoy drove at speed, sending up a column of dust, bearing down on a settlement, not slowing. The people selling bread and water by the roadside moved out of the way. Zou Lei, who was five years old, opened her mouth and said oh and advanced, looking for the soldiers as they roared by and watching them as they sped away, packed in the back of the trucks in their steel helmets.

An older girl ran up and pulled Zou Lei back from the roadside and held onto her until the convoy had passed and its dust had blown over them and settled. Then she took her by the hand and led her over to one of the adobe dwellings roofed in gray desert driftwood.

She was playing too close to the road and I scolded her. A big truck came by.

I heard it, Zou Lei's mother said. She was standing at a table in her doorway, half in the sun, making laghman. The sun sliced across the table. She was kneading the dough, wetting it with water from a blue plastic tub.

It was the biggest truck ever. And she wanted to get squashed.

What's that?

She wanted to get on it. She was running and if I hadn't grabbed her, she would have run right to it.

Zou Lei's mother peered at Zou Lei.

What did you do? she asked Zou Lei. To the girl, she said, Did you give her a swat?

I gave her a swat on the leg.

Give her one for me right now while I'm watching. Not to the ear, just the leg.

The girl hit Zou Lei on the leg of her faded orange pants.

You've got to put more pepper in it than that. That's not going to do anything with her.

The girl hit Zou Lei hard on the bottom and Zou Lei was driven forward two steps and put her hand back there to protect herself.

Don't do it again! the girl said.

Listen good! her mother said.

I tell her, her father is away in the steppe with the army. He isn't on the truck. If he was on the truck, he would come down. Even if he was working, he would ask the officer for leave to see his family. If they couldn't give him leave, then he would wave at least so you could see him. They would at least let him do that in the army, to wave.

Her mother wet her hands and began forming the dough into a rope.

Play a game with her, why don't you? Or sing something. Can you sing anything yet?

I can't sing, but I know a little dancing, the girl said.

The girl made movements with her hands, pressing her fingertips together, rotating her wrists, undulating her hands.

That's all I know.

She tried to teach Zou Lei, who did not want to learn.

Pretend I'm a wolf, Zou Lei said.

In the afternoon, after the girl had left and Zou Lei's mother was resting on the rugs, it was just the two of them in the dwelling while the noodles boiled. Zou Lei crawled over and played with her mother's hair. Her mother waved a fly away from them. For a time, they played made-up games where they would hold hands and her mother would say, where's the bread and salt? It's in the mountains. It's in the river. It's in the pasture with the horses.

The light turned golden orange and the heat eased. Another truck went chugging by on the road and they both listened to it passing. Her mother took the noodles out to let them cool before they ate them with a green pepper and an onion.

The shadows fell over them and through the gaps in the drift-wood roof, the sky showed. In the doorway, the sun was setting on the mountains and its rays were coming in a straight line to their eyes, passing from rim to rim across the vast blue-shadowed desert basin.

All we had was soup when I was picking cotton, her mother said. That was before you. You were still being carried around in your father's cotton sack. He asked if I would like to have you. I said I would, and he gave you to me. Come here and take a bite of this— her mother had peaches that she had picked up from the roadside— let's brush it off. Don't eat sand. Sit here now. He'll be home soon, God willing. Now let me tell you something nice. Let me tell you why you should be happy. Do you want to hear? Now, listen.

Did you know that there is a place that is better than any other? Okay, I'll tell you about it. First of all, it's out there, past all the bandits and wolves. It's a long way off out there, a good three months on horseback at least. The officials don't tell anyone about it because they want it for themselves. Still, people know it's there. Now, look, everyone there is full of joy. They spend all their lives feasting and singing, so why wouldn't they be? No one goes without. Everyone has what he needs. Everyone has shoes, clothes, and a fine cap. It's a place blessed by God in a green valley protected by mountains and rivers. The herds graze and the grapes grow in the vineyards and, in the summer, they ride up to the larch forest, where it's cool. They hunt as much as they like and then they ride back down where the sun shines on the green grass. You need only put out your hands and blackberries fill your arms. The air is filled with the sweet music of finches in the trees. Everyone gets yogurt, cream, milk, bread, and meat—as much as the heart desires. The fire is singing and the fat is frying and the pots are tipping their lids. To have a whole roast goat is no great thing there. You don't have to be rich. If somebody wants it, it will be theirs. All they have to do is say I will have bread! and the bread leaps out straight from the oven. That's how eating works there.

The women are as beautiful as sun and moon, as the saying goes— cheeks red like apples and a brow fair like milk. Arm in arm, sister and cousin, they go picking flowers, while the men gaze after them with longing, hearing them laughing like nightingales. The men cannot stop singing to them, courting them. A girl will only have to throw her comb on the ground and twenty men will fight to pick it up. If she yawns, the men will make shade for her and call the wind over to cool her, saying: here, Breeze, blow! Well, that's well, but who will peel potatoes for my mother's supper while I am lying here? she says, and the men will trip over themselves peeling potatoes.

While everyone is eating and having a good time, there's music and dancing and singing, lifting everyone's hearts. All day long, the men hold contests of riding, running and wrestling. Any one of the men could be a prince for looks and bravery. They go galloping back and forth on the steppe, making one thundering pass after another, and each time they go by, the people rise up and huzzah with one voice. The steppe is filled with cheering. You have to imagine that great sound coming from thousands of us at one time, how it echoes out around the world. It makes the red and yellow poppies bloom everywhere on the green mountainsides and the rivers melt with admiration and flow from the snowcaps.

If an official demands taxes, you tell him next week! and he'll take that for an answer and put it in his book. If he doesn't, you show him a hair on your head and say, not even this will I give you! and he goes away knowing he's met his match. The prison gates are flung open and the prisoners come out singing and giving thanks, and go back to their families.

Zou Lei's mother touched her face in the dark.

Are you awake?

She was. They could see the stars through the roof but they couldn't see each other. At night, the rugs disappeared, the very surface they were resting on. It was easy to imagine they were on a precipice and that it wasn't wise to move until the sun came back and brought the earth back with it. At night, Zou Lei would wake up and figure out the house was empty and then she'd hear a sound and see a ribbon of the night sky appear and her mother would come back in, having gone out to the roadside, having thought she had heard a truck stopping.

She told Zou Lei a story about a girl whose father was taken away by a witch and the only way to be reunited with him was to travel west. Zou Lei's mother shifted, talking with her hands, describing the witch's long nose like a sausage. Outside, a sandstorm turned the darkness cloudy. In the morning, they would sweep the rug off, shake the sand out of their own hair, go down to the spigot and wash their feet before praying on the rug, hands to face, her mother's eyes closed, lips moving.

Her mother told her Clever took seven mulberry seeds, one seed to live on in each of the seven deserts she had to walk through. In the dark, Zou Lei saw the gravel hills, the gorges and caves, places like the moon, the river running dry, the scrubland going on forever, the golden desert. The bandits took a liking to her. There was one desert of glass and one of iron, her mother gesticulated. Clever wore out all her shoes. A journey of seven years. The seeds were gone, no more water in the sheep's bladder. The iron desert tore the soles off her feet until the fresh blood ran out and boiled to steam on the hot iron. But she kept on, believing in God until the sun blinded her. With death coming, she stretched the bladder over her knees to make a drum and chanted I am a ghost now. She drummed for seven days. A bird came out of the blue blue sky and cast his shadow on her. As long as she sang, he flew with her, running above the steppe on wolf's legs. They came to a pure blue river and she leapt in and when she came out her sight was restored and she beheld the Fergana valley.

Her father came home—no one saw him coming—they heard his voice at the door and there he was—it didn't seem real. He picked her up and hugged her. Mama dropped her basket, Oh, God! She pulled him inside. He smelled like gasoline. I'll cook for you. Thanks be to God! She gripped his arm, wiping her eyes with her dirty sun-tanned fingers.

Don't cry. Don't be hard-up. Look! he smiled, taking ration cards from the pocket of his military blouse and giving them to her mother. Flour, oil, potatoes—for us, eh.

He dragged his sack inside and Zou Lei watched his forearm flex.

They did his washing in the ditch next to the orchard. Zou Lei and her mama wrung his dark wet green uniform out.

Her mother gave her a knife and a potato to peel.

Like this, her sunburned Chinese daddy said and showed her how to cut the skin off in one unbroken spiral. He dug a pit out back with his army shovel and killed a goat. Bring me a bowl from mama. He hung the purple chalky meat up high behind the house—always working, even when he was on leave, a cigarette on his lip, the salt drying on his shirt.

It was summer in the Taklamakan. They would let the tea cool in the kettle overnight. In the day, the sky was clear, magnifying the mountains in the distance, the snowcaps that never went away. The speed of evaporation made the desert seem less hot. The grownups sat on wooden squatting stools in front of the door and drank their tea from the day before in the afternoon. A wind came, picking up curtains of dust that moved down the street like giants in dresses.

Zou Lei ran back from playing. It's kicking up!

Looks like it.

Her father picked up his chair. Come on. They went inside and she helped him shut the door.

It's a bad one! her mother laughed.

The door banged and her father moved the table in front of it and it still banged. Dim blue night fell as the sandstorm swept against houses. They lit the lantern and moved their dinner away from where the wind was getting in. Her mother tore the bread in three pieces.

Eat so your hands don't ache.

The bread was warm. Zou Lei leaned on her father's tan arm.

In our army, we say don't be slow. Slow one cleans the pot.

Are you slow? her mother asked him.

Me? No. What do you think?

I don't know. I was thinking about my husband cleaning the pot.

Your mama likes to think.

Yes, I like to think. I think all the time.

I don't think so much myself.

Oh, you'd be the first man who didn't think so much.

No, I just follow orders.

Oh, you're the first man of your kind!

The door had stopped banging. It got later at night. The lantern kept up its glow, red through the hanging curtain. Her father looked like a tiger with his crewcut and muscled limbs, talking about his job to both of them. In the mountains, it was flat and strange, a tarn. His regiment had camped where the Yellow River ended. We carry rifles, but we carry shovels too. The pipeline work is like mining and, though it's dangerous, we're committed to it, because we want to make the country go forward. A Kazak wanted to give him his horse for settling a dispute over livestock, but her father, a soldier, couldn't take it. We're here to serve the people. He didn't know he was part of us, but he is. The people includes everyone. So then he brought out his daughter in a pretty dress, and all the boys laughed at my embarrassment. Was she very pretty? Zou Lei asked. Her father put her on his lap and she listened to his voice through his chest. Her mother half-lay on her side, listening to him, the flowers on her skirt becoming birds on the rug beneath her.

Zou Lei jogged with him—she was running, her pink sandals slapping—he turned around and jogged backwards downhill, serious about teaching her. The land panned out, past the lot where the bus came in.

Her father balanced on the parallel bars, swinging his legs, holding them out straight, pressing himself up and down. He jumped down. She remembered the sound of his boots landing. Everything he did was correct and simple. He brushed his hands off, helped her up on the bars.

She was lifted. His sunburned face, his crewcut, the smell of his cigarettes, his sweat dried by the desert—a white crystal salt in the center of his chest. One of her pink sandals fell off. She looked down and saw her dirty feet waving. Don't look down, he said, steadying her. She was scared, but she could hold herself with his help. Her headscarf fell off. Use your arms. He lifted her up and down—she pressed herself. Ha! she laughed. You did it. He lifted her down. Hopping to keep her bare foot off the hot concrete, holding onto daddy. He put her sandal on her little dirty foot. Good soldier work, he said. He went and picked her scarf up off the ground.

Things are coming along, he said. Little by little. Her mother's hands were covered in flour, baking bread in a clay oven, which her father had wrestled in front of their house singlehandedly.

Melons, peaches, apples, almonds, dates, Uighurs waiting in the shade, waiting for jobs, waiting for a drink of water, minarets above the rooftops. A hot wind blew across the highway. Zou Lei squinted. She had a plastic bag with bread in it. The bus came in and the cloud of dust drifted away. Sunburned women climbed down in headscarves, holding their money in their hands. How much for bread? Zou Lei put the fractions of a dollar in her pocket.

She saw the red banners getting hung across the medieval street and the army drive through and the shoeless children come back out when they were gone. Chinese cadres in glasses and worker's hats and black plastic shoes posed in the desert with their hands behind their backs, having their pictures taken by other men who looked just like them and nothing like her father, as proof that they had been here and that everything was a success.

The loudspeakers said, Strike down backwardism! and played triumphant music. She saw a fight over livestock. A man hit his neighbor and threw a sheep into a truck and the other sheep jumped up after it bleating. The smell of wood fire blew across the road from the lamb kawap. Her mouth watered. She broke her sandals kicking a soccer ball and mama hit her.

Russia's that way, her father pointed. Those are the Muslim countries. The other way is China. He lit a cigarette. The Russian soldiers are good, they have advanced equipment. To protect this frontier from the Russians, that's why we are here. The Muslims have backward conditions. They don't make good soldiers because they are too independent. In the middle of the war, they'll decide to leave and go tend the herd. America has the best equipment, the richest country. In America, a private owns a car. Here, only the general has a car. We have equipment in the middle range, but it is not very advanced. What we have is the size of the population. Conditions will slowly, slowly improve. Everything has to be balanced to win. It's just like wrestling. If I'm too weak, you push me over. If I'm too strong, I push myself over. You have to be in the middle. China is in the middle, which is just right. In thirty, forty years, we will be able to beat America or Russia.

The buses brought Uighurs from the west, some of them from Fergana. A barber put a chair out on the roadside. Zou Lei watched the open razor moving up the back of a man's head, fluffs of hair dropping, drifting against the stone curb when the breeze came. The men were sitting in a circle. They raised their sunburned forearms and held out coins to her. You are from the land of milk and honey, she said. They were wearing skullcaps, staring off, clean-shaven, eating her mother's bread. Who told you that? All of us pick cotton in Fergana. They make us. Now go and tell your mother that.

How far can you run, Dad? she asked her father.

Run or jog? he said. It makes a difference.

Well, to those mountains.

Not running, you mean, but could I get there on foot?

Could you get there? Could anyone get there?

I think so. With determination, yes. And enough water.

The decade ended and, all of a sudden, there were crowds in the streets. Their neighbors disappeared. Alani didn't come to school. Soccer was considered fundamentalist, so they stopped playing it. They tossed it through the basketball hoop. Her father was mobilized and left them.

———

Take this, her mother said and handed her the plov to carry out front where their customers were eating.

In the back streets, the boys tried to wrestle each other down. Tyson! they yelled. Arabic graffiti carved in the mud brick. I am Rambo!

A girl threw rocks at her. Your mother is married to a filthy pig-eater.

Truck drivers came in from Gilmet talking about what they had seen. They ordered cold noodles and beer. A Karamlik bit the bottlecap off with his teeth. Smugglers get decapitated over there. Opium paste hidden in bread ovens, usually. On this side, they just put you in the gulag, nothing more than that. Gang members and separatists. Imagine not being allowed to talk for five years. Haven't you seen the oil-drilling in the desert? I saw them hauling a piece of pipe out there big enough to live in. They have the army camped all around out there. They have everything they want. They get village girls. There's a tent for them and a doctor to keep them healthy.

She brought them out more beer. A sandstorm hit and they went inside and sat on the rugs. They called for yogurt, vodka. They called her mother over.

How old is she?

Get in the kitchen and stay there.

When they received a notice from the regiment, they waited in the sun from 11:20 to 14:40, which was the official rest time for post office employees, while the Chinese woman and her coworkers in nurse's hats ate dumplings and fanned themselves and chatted behind a gated window. Her mother sat on the curb holding her head. When the gate lifted, they went inside. The woman in the nurse's hat said the notice meant that someone had died in the regiment.

But it doesn't have a name, miss. Maybe it's not him.

Maybe nothing. It's the name of whoever you have in the regiment, the woman yelled. If you have somebody else in the regiment, then it's them.

Her mother began crying out.

The notice had to be stamped, they were told.

Where do I get it stamped?

The woman snatched the paper away, pounded it with her stamp, and took it.

Why aren't you giving it back to me? her mother cried.

What are you going to do with it?

But her mother banged and shook the bars and yelled until the woman gave it back. On the street, someone told them to go to such and such an office. No one told them how her father died. It was a seventeen-hour bus ride to the provincial capital. There, they found out that the notice was essential to collect the death benefit, a little pile of pink banknotes with heroic profiles on them, some of them ethnic minorities. Her mother rolled them up and put them in her stocking, while Zou Lei hung her head.

Now they lived in a big western city, the truckstop gone, failed, they had not made a go of it, her father gone. The banknotes flew away. She was fifteen, sixteen, and she was hungry. She wrote to him. She cut her hair like him to remember him by. A soldier in everything I do. No more school. There were no ration cards unless you bought them from kids in tracksuits, orphans who dealt hashish. She sold things on a blanket. Cassette tapes. A tarnished horn from someone's Tajik wedding. The street was wired with lights to keep the market going after dark. You could smell the whole roast goat at another one of the tables. There were more Chinese here. Do you like disco? She was into soccer whenever she could play it. The American president was Clinton. On a garbage-strewn field behind the market, she picked up a broken knife and threw it as far as she could.

Sunburned, red-cheeked, her face peeling, she was seventeen years old. They were all sunburned, playing soccer at the extreme end of Liberation Road, dust getting knocked out of their army castoff clothes. Tariq had the ball and she ran way out in an arc, as if something very thin were keeping her here. He kicked it and she curved in to meet the ball. She never stopped moving. She had her elbow in a boy's face, the two of them fighting for the ball like praying mantises with their legs. The sun was a bright, purifying sun coming out of winter. Everything smelled like leather, a sourness, charcoal dust and manure. This was the end of the city. The wall was four hundred years old and beyond it was the desert.

There was a wild woman in the small shade beneath a juniper tree, her baby on the curb, a tiny filthy boy digging his fingers between the crumbling blue hexagons, trying to prize one up and find a scorpion.

The road began from nowhere, out of the desert, built so that tanks could roll down it four abreast. Now she traveled down it, dribbling a ball. Things were being built or broken down and the stones they were made of lay in piles, huge wedges of concrete with rebar coming out, a tooth extracted from the earth, excavations in the dust. The edges of the road were crumbling. A highway went overhead and stopped in midair. In a vast ditch was a sea of tires and a man climbing through them, examining the treads.

The spaces were wide and long, extending to the busy part of the city by the train station, a carnival of tan buses where the tunnel ended, the signs in Uighur and Chinese, migrants seeking work, sleeping wherever there was shade. In among the old adobe houses was the public security building and detention house made of tile, like a bathroom turned inside out. The sun sparked off the spire of a mosque above the construction sites. The dome was down below, but you could sense it, a bubble rising.

They were going to move again, this time to the interior, to one of the factories that always needed migrants, in Shenzhen. A subsidy would be promised, an incentive for Uighur women. They would be told it was a fruit juice plant, but very little would be as advertised. The humidity of the rice-growing land south of the Yangtze River would be their first inkling of a mistake. A different heat from what they were used to in the desert. Haze everywhere, no horizon, the dull fields smudged into the sky. The factory produced polyethylene derivatives, without safety equipment except for surgical masks. If you put your head up, the Taiwanese bosses would make sure your head got pushed back down again. He did not have to pay you. You were an illegal immigrant in your own country, you found out. That's how big China was.

They would be sick, their own food would make them sick, bacteria in the water, unidentified meat on the tables along the surfaced road, flies and blood. No imams in the countryside; there was avian flu, malaria, and schistosomiasis. The whine in your ear whenever you dropped off. You smacked yourself. Scabs all over from scratching the bites. Her mother would not eat pork. They would squat in the wet village latrines next to the other girls. Fish in the scummed ponds. They would eat fish when they could get it, a farmer stepping on a live bream on the mud-covered floor of the bus. Her mother would have to ride the back of a motorbike with her arms around a mototaxi man's waist. There would be dogs in the roadway, a dead goat lying in the trash pile where she hunted for paper and plastic. They would eat lamb sometimes, mainly cabbage, cooking with round coal bricks, which they would gather, the half-burnt ones, whenever they found them. Mustard greens and potatoes and white rice and the bones of anything besides pork.

From the factory, where they could not tolerate being locked in for their own protection, it was a short step to having nothing, to living in the brigade field, collecting paper and plastic for recycling. There would be no way to pay the fee for her mother to go to an infirmary. A lot of girls would have gone to work at the KTV bars to sing and drink with Party cadres, but at two in the morning, Zou Lei would gather beer bottles amid the litter of Styrofoam bowls dripping with chili oil and the throwaway chopsticks under the woven plastic tenting and the still-burning light bulbs strung over the unpaved street, then travel a kilometer back on the mud road with just a sense of the walls and huts in the blackness, turning into the paddy fields. Piles where the farmers dumped their shit. The horrible shit-stink in the dark. Stopping to set the clanking weight down, all alone on the mud lane that led out into the giant squares of water.

If you wanted heaven, they would say, maybe you shouldn't have come. There's always America, if you think your feet will carry you.

She met her mother in the crowd coming out of a mosque. They went to Liberation Boulevard and there were peasants, the sons of nomads, pulling enormous wooden wagons through the broken street. Desert people with gold teeth and leathery hands and faces. Men in white skull caps and dark suit jackets holding up flatbread, saying it is for sale. There were tubs of dates and nuts, watermelons cut open, the red flag of a butchered lamb hanging up, the spokes of cartwheels interlocking through the legs of people walking through the square, interlocking and scissoring, a hundred crossings. The late afternoon sun reflected off something bright at the edge of a mosaic fountain, one side for men, one side for women to wash their feet. A pair of cops with large oiled heads like seals went by.

Her mother was recounting to her what the imam had said in his sermon. The loudspeaker said, If you suspect fundamentalism, tell your leaders. Zou Lei nodded at a group of young men and boys in tracksuits. One had a boa constrictor hanging around his neck, mirrored sunglasses, no shirt.

Who are they?

The children of the police.

She saw razor blades and hypodermics in a bucket under a cart where her mother was buying apples. Zou Lei went up to the snake and touched it, the smooth, beaded surface slipping under her fingers.

You cannot ask for the things of this life, her mother said.

They went back to where they lived in a stinking concrete room next to a latrine, lay down in the same bed and couldn't sleep. She was going to learn to march. She was going to practice in the field.

In the night, she woke up. The bare bulb was on and her mother was turning in circles. She was chanting into her hands, her hair undone and swinging out, almost touching the wall. Zou Lei watched her mother spin, get dizzy and stagger. I'm on my horse. I'm in the larches. Zou Lei tried to get her back in bed. She claimed to have seen a stag. Zou Lei reached for the switch. They'll charge us for the light.

I went a thousand miles, her mother said. I should be weary, but I'm not.

She got back in bed, fending off her daughter with her thick strong hand.

———

They went to court. It had a brown carpet. Someone told her to stand your ass up. A white woman in a pinstriped skirt with a manila folder said, The people have no objection. No one told her why. Later, they just told her she was leaving. Pick your things up there, the deputy pointed. A paper bag with her jeans in it sat on the counter. She took her clothes and changed under the fluorescent light, not counting her money until she got outside. They buzzed the glass door open and she went out past the bulletin boards, the thumb-tacked notice that said To See Your Prisoner in four different languages, and out towards the open space of the small city—it was seven in the morning—the train tracks, barbed wire, and the water.

On the bus, she leaned her head against the glass to watch them leaving town. They traveled past the peeling houses, His Grace of Healing. It was cheaper than the MetroNorth. The driver, on the PA, looked in the rearview. There's no smoking, thank you. The drifter in a black cowboy hat, a swastika on his neck, said, Ya got a light? At Roy Rogers everyone else got back on eating except for her. She closed her eyes on 95, hearing someone's headphones. When she opened her eyes, they were rolling through projects, and there were cops with web gear and soldiers with assault rifles in the Port Authority.

3

HE GOT PICKED UP before it was light, down where there were trees dark and arrow-shaped along the highway.

You goin AWOL? the driver asked.

That's what I should have done, Skinner said.

The sun broke and irradiated them in the cab. It painted the endless forest along the highway in cherry light. He watched it happen. Slowly the highway curved like the arc of a planet. Sitting high over the road in the cab. The big steady noise.

He was not a big guy, but he had a large skull and hands, which made him seem bigger than he was. He put his boot on the dash without asking if that was okay. The driver had the interior of the cab upholstered in velvet and chrome.

You live in here?

Only when I'm away from home, the driver said and went through the production of showing him a photograph of his kids and his plain blond wife posed in front of a swirly background. That's Kyle and that's Connor. I live for them. My boys are my whole life.

Skinner dropped the photograph on the dash. The driver picked it up with his pale red-freckled hand and put it away in his folding wallet.

You plan on stopping at all?

For what?

For Mickey D's or something?

I don't eat until I get where I'm going.

Must be a hardass.

Call it what you want, the driver said.

Skinner had bothered the driver somehow. The driver told him: You got two ways you can do this. I can either keep going or I can stop. If I have to stop, you can thumb a ride with somebody else.

Whatever, Skinner said. Do what you feel.

Skinner put his other boot on the dash and watched the road. Lit a cigarette. He put his shades on. Behind his shades, his eyes went from the cars to the roadside to the side mirror and back to the cars. The traffic increased as they travelled north. He put his feet on the floor and sat up. The landscape changed to bare trees and brown hills. He lit another cigarette. Both he and the driver smoked, the radio playing country.

A black car overtook them, cut around in front of them, and went speeding on ahead, weaving in and out of other cars. Skinner's jaw flexed. He started jiggling his foot.

You need to take a piss or something?

On the radio, a woman sang: she's got family pride.

No, said Skinner.

He put his boot up on the dash again.

Are those things comfortable?

Pretty much.

He stuck his thumb in the stitching, pulled at the laces.

They're holding up all right. But these aren't my last pair. My last pair got someone's brain all over them.

The driver looked at him.

Fuckin army took half a year to give me a new pair. Where are we?

Virginia still, I think.

Skinner took a white hexagonal pill with Gatorade. He watched a McDonald's sign go by. There started to be snow on the hills and it got colder in the cab. He wrapped himself in his green poncholiner, his large tan boots sticking out, his head bent against the edge of the seat, shades still on, pallid sunburned face, large hands with broken nails. He looked unconscious. The driver glanced at him. The sun went in and out like shadow play, like time-lapse photography, something with the clouds.

He slept through Pennsylvania, where his mother and brother lived, and woke to rap music. The sky had changed to gray. He rubbed his face.

The driver turned the radio off.

Slumped, Skinner watched the road, catatonic.

How long you think we've got?

Could be a while.

He looked in the trash underfoot and found the Gatorade bottle. That's all right. Used to do this all the time. He turned sideways, filled it up. I better not see that, the driver said. You won't. He capped it, put it warm and beer-colored in his assault pack.

They were in the approach to the city for a long time, an identifiable feeling, the road getting worse, fast and narrow and crowded, thudding over breaks in the surface. Graffiti began popping up, a flash of it here and there, and then it multiplied. Skinner lit another cigarette and sat leaning forward, jiggling his foot.

I think you overshot it, dude. It's gotta be back there.

They swung around west when it was almost sundown. The sky had cleared and they were driving fast along fences, houses, the adjoining highway tapering, disappearing, coming back, dividing. He was searching up ahead. There it is. He saw the famous skyline minus the two towers. It was very distant still and when the highway dipped it went away. Then he saw it again, a precise silhouette, the lava sunset behind it.

The city disappeared behind the roadway, gravel pits, a mountain of sand, the sideways ladder of a crane. A glimpse of a sheet of water. The New York skyline came back. They were close now. Blond hair and tan tits on a billboard. Gentleman's Club. He rubbed his hands. You catch the address? The driver said nothing.

They barreled down an off-ramp, tenements rising around them like curtains, graffiti on the bricks. The piers of the highway flashed by outside the window. The elevated highway rose above them like an airplane lifting off over their heads. They were subject to the g-force pull of the big rig angling across the lanes, downshifting, cruising, decelerating neatly into a gas station. Airbrakes. Their bodies rocked forward. The driver thumped into low gear and made the rig crawl in next to the pump and when he killed the engine, there was a momentary quiet, though the engine seemed to continue running in Skinner's head.

This was as far as the driver was taking him, he was told—which was fine, he could see where he was going from here—and they climbed out. While the driver gassed the rig, Skinner went into the convenience store. He went directly to the jerky and pulled a bag of it off the metal tree and got a Red Bull out of the drink case. On his way to the register, he stopped at the magazines. There was a Haitian with blue-black skin reading car ads. Skinner reached across him and took a copy of Ironman, the bodybuilder on the cover holding so much weight the bar was bending and veins were webbed around his screaming neck. Skinner went up to the bulletproof window and dropped his bank card in the tray.

Gimme a pack of Marlboros too.

He went back outside and pulled his bags out of the cab. He shrugged into his camouflage field jacket and flipped his black hoodie over his head. The piss bottle he set by the curb for someone else to have. The driver, in nothing but a t-shirt, was still gassing the rig up. Skinner went over and asked him if he knew the way.

That way somewhere.

Skinner adjusted his pack straps, glanced at the highway. Then he picked up the military duffel at his feet, shook it, held it, gripping it. He looked at it. He did a curl with it. Then he slung it on.

All right. Thanks for the lift.

I don't mind.

The driver stuck out his hand at the last minute and they shook hands.

Good luck.

Later.

Skinner went around the truck and disappeared.

Now he was cutting through monumental project towers, his silhouette distorted by what he was carrying, a burdened figure moving steadily across the great barren landscape of giant shadows and building structures and cold lights filtering down. A single car was parked against a line of gated storefronts exploding with graffiti—huge, wild, blazing—the letters pumped up like muscles about to burst, like smoke bulging, billowing, swelling in a bubble over the steel and concrete walls, like everything was on fire. He crossed the open area, a solitary figure carrying his gear, and reentered the shadow on the other side.

He was hiking by tenements so small you could reach in a window and put your hand out the door. They were burned-out and boarded-up and there were trash lots. Some of them were lived in. As he traveled, he was feeding jerky into his mouth and chewing. The Red Bull, which he had emptied down his throat and thrown at an oil drum, had frozen him to the core. Now his heart was pounding, his boots were whopping the concrete, steam was coming up from his face, and he was sweating in the cold.

Hey, he said, when he saw somebody and tried to ask them where to go. Papi, they called him. Go there—and pointed towards the traffic lights ahead. Liquor store, groceria, Iglesias de Dios. From somewhere, there was Spanish music. Taillights shot by him and over a bridge. He crossed beneath the highway, in a great tall vault of dark, the steel being knocked by vehicles going over, and climbed pigeonshit-splattered stairs, coming to rooftop level, billboard level—cash for your car—and then he was looking at Manhattan across the black water, a postcard view with all the lights and just the sheer scale of it, the sky violet with energy.

He took his cell phone out and took a picture of it. Steam was rising from his head from charging up the stairs. Then he turned around and took a picture of himself with the Empire State Building lit up laser green above his shoulder. His face was white and distracted in the phone flash.

On the other side of the bridge, which spiraled down into a field, he came to a place where an avenue began, littered and dark, going long and straight for miles and getting brighter as it went, until it became dense with clustered lights in the distance, and he started down it, bent against his weight.

He came to a wall mural of brown people working in the fields, wearing white dresses and straw hats, babies slung on their backs. He passed another mural of portraits of young men and their years of life and death. You Are in Our Hearts. There was a Salvation Army. A block later, he overtook two young women pushing baby carriages over the broken sidewalk, sparkling with broken glass. The Kingdom of the Almighty on a light box sign. A guy came out of a liquor store, wearing a cell phone earpiece, saying: Come uptown and check out what we doing. See how we provide. Skinner passed a fried-chicken restaurant. People moseyed into his way and he went around them. He was remarkably mobile despite the weight he carried, always slipping away and barely noticed in his faded, dusty-looking camouflage and boots, as if he had been doing farm work, head hidden under the black hood.

A grand white car pulled up and a big woman climbed out wearing a short red leather jacket. Five guys on the corner in ski hats were looking at her. Damn, one of them was saying. Skinner stopped and spoke to them for a minute. They told Skinner where the action was.

Forty-deuce.

Is that where the hotels are at?

That's where the action at. Over here not really. It's mad action down there. A hotel, I don't know about. Beers, bitches, weed, good shit, I do know about, and they got it all downtown.

An SUV with halogen brights drove at them and Skinner flinched.

They got everything, yo. Mad shit. Hotels, motels, pussy, chicks with dicks…

Chicks without dicks…

I could go for some pussy maybe.

You got money, you can go for whatever you want.

He caught the train and rode it with his feet planted, watching the stops. People stepped around him when the doors opened. He got off and took the escalator up to the street, into a spectacle of silver stadium lights and monitors.

For half an hour, he went up and down Broadway, looking in the bars before going into one. He took one of the high tables in front where the drinking was going on. There was a flat-screen TV, a male server. Let me get you started with something to drink, get you started with some appetizers, get you started with some guac. He drank a series of shots. All right! He drank a margarita like he had something to celebrate. When he was done eating corn chips, the waiter took his bank card and electronically removed forty dollars from his account. He continued sitting, moving his eyes back and forth between the bar and the TV. Being drunk wore off. A blond came in, but she came in with two guys. They all had briefcases. Her voice carried. She said, You have to capitalize on that. They changed the channels on the flat-screen. Someone clapping. Someone pouring orange juice. The golf report. Skinner picked up his bags and went back outside.

Somewhere there was music pumping behind blacked-out windows. A pair of limos cruised by with laser ground effects, black lights, a Filipina with ultraviolet lipstick sitting in someone's front seat, and he turned his head and watched them go around the corner, amid theaters.

After hunting through Times Square north-south, he tried east-west, stopping in front of bars or places that he thought were bars, backtracking, going on again, staring in the window of a porn store just for a minute, then moving on again, the weight strapped onto him, hanging off him, bouncing when he marched, the strap creaking like a saddle. He was smoking a cigarette, which occasionally he left in his mouth in order to use his hands to hold the duffel bag, which was getting heavier.

On 11th Avenue, he threw his butt away and went into a sandwich counter where the chairs were upside down and a Mexican was mopping. There was no sign of food. A young woman with ringlet hair and a green and blue uniform shirt and a gold chain and earrings was down under the counter going through the stock of cups and napkins.

Are you closed?

She stood up and finished jotting down what was out of stock on her clipboard before she spoke to Skinner. Her hair was worn pulled back giving her a high egg-like forehead and she had a hefty bosom and a narrow waist under her uniform shirt.

I can give you whatever's out, she said, but we can't make you nothing.

Do you know the hotels around here?

There's a lot of them. Like which one?

Just like a basic motel.

She mentioned the Marriott.

Isn't that like that super big one?

So, like, smaller than that.

Yeah.

She told him to wait and went to the back. The Mexican, who was broad-shouldered, stood aside for her and watched her going by.

Skinner sat down while she was gone, pulled off his watch cap and itched his head. The wall was mirrored and he could see his short wet dark hair, the tattoo on his neck, and sunken eyes looking back at him, multiplied a million times. He seemed not to recognize himself and looked at other things.

She returned carrying a page torn from a phone book.

This is them. Call them or you could go right over. She pointed to the address which she had circled in ballpoint pen. The penmanship was feminine. He could have imagined it signed Love with a drawing of a heart. So how do I get there?

Down and over, she made right angles with her hands.

Hey, thanks. That was going the extra mile.

No problem.

Yeah, look, I'm just thinking, he said. Why don't you let me return the favor? He kept talking, trying to turn it into asking her out. Like when you get off or whatever. Just kickin it, he said. No attachments, you know? I'm basically a good person. He was watching her face with his sunken eyes to see how he was doing. I just got here, literally like an hour ago. Two hours ago. We could have a drink or something and you could tell me about yourself.

Thank you, no.

You sure? I just got out of the army yesterday. I literally just got here. All I want to do is buy you a drink to say thank you. Howbout it? I mean, you're not talkin to a bad person.

I realize that.

So how can you say no? I'm just asking.

And I was just answering. Now you got what you need, go to this place.

Damn—he shook his head—I didn't mean to sweat you. I'm not that kind of guy. I'm just confused. You know, like, there's nothing bad there. What about if I could call you some time? Some other time, you know? We grab some drinks… I mean, life is short, you know?

That's not going to happen. In the mirror, he saw the Mexican watching him.

Aw, come on, he laughed, revealing nicotine-stained teeth.

Thank you, no.

I just walked like ten miles with all this. I just fought for my country. Are you sure?

She did not smile.

Why not? Is there something wrong with me?

That's something for you to ask yourself. That's not my issue.

Wow. Ouch. I mean, like, a little harmless date.

That's not my issue. I don't go out.

All right.

You have your answer. You need to accept it.

All right. Roger that.

A sign above a bank said it was one a.m. and fifteen degrees Fahrenheit. He had been drinking and the bar was closing. He headed down Broadway with his eyes squinted shut. The wind was blowing the vapor off the manhole covers.

An all-night McDonald's was operating beneath a neon theater marquee. He bumped through the door and flipped the duffel bag down. This'll work. It was warm. The backs of his hands were flaming red. He dragged his duffel up to the counter and gazed up at the menu. A skinny female with ragged hair and narrowboned hips waited for him to order, jiggling her leg. She rolled her eyes up at the ceiling. Supersize? she asked. Yeah, he said and wiped his nose. She looked around him. He got out his bank card. The speakers were playing Cherry Baby. He slung his bags into a booth and went back for his tray, sat down and pigged out with dirty hands, stuck his feet out—he belched—he burned his tongue on the coffee. The fries were cold, he dipped them in the coffee, and ate them a handful at a time.

After he was finished eating, he pushed his tray away and sat there looking at his Ironman. His eyelids closed and he opened them again. He stood up. Taking his gear, he went down the line of homeless people at the tables to the restroom and urinated in the shit-smeared toilet.

The door banged. In a minute, he said.

He pulled off his jacket, hoodie, and polypro, and laid everything on his bags. Beneath his clothes, his skivvie shirt was stinking and sweat-soaked. He peeled the skivvie off, revealing his upper body, and wrung it out in the sink. A metallic smell came off him. He had a farmer's tan. His torso was grayish white and there were zits on his skin. He started giving himself a canteen shower in the sink. He had vertical tattoos down his forearms. With a handful of paper towels, he washed his armpits. His face and hands were covered in half-healed cuts. Then he undid his jeans and wiped himself down. Lifting his scrotum, he held a hot towel between his legs, his eyes half-shut. Crotch rot. He winced. On his tricep, there were Chinese characters.

Across his back, above his scar, he had a tattoo of a skull and death wings, spanning his shoulders. He had a star on his neck, which predated his enlistment, and a U.S. flag on his shoulder, the original idea being for it to look like he was wearing his uniform even when he took it off. He pulled the skin down taut over his abdomen and flexed his stomach, trying to see his six-pack. He raised his arms and flexed his biceps. You could see the Chinese characters wrapping around the tricep. He could also see the bright pink scar wrapping around his ribs. Turning, he looked at his back in the mirror. The area of the scar was of a color that did not look like flesh at all. It looked like a melted plastic toy.

He got himself organized, changed his shirt. The new one said Army Strong. In his assault pack, he had a handgun wrapped in a faded green army towel, a Berretta nine-millimeter, and he took it out and checked it. He released the magazine, locked back the slide, checked the chamber with a finger, dropped the slide, squeezed the safety, decocked the pistol, reinserted the magazine, and switched the safety on. He wrapped it in the towel again and stuck it back in his bag.

Someone banged the door and he ignored them.

They banged again.

Chill, he said.

Back at a booth, he untied his desert boots and changed his socks, rubbing his peeling feet one at a time. The music had been turned off. You heard them cleaning in the kitchen. He put his head down on his arms. Someone rapped the table with a billyclub, a man in a navy sweater with nylon elbow patches and sergeant's stripes, handcuffs attached to his belt and what could have been a Smith and Wesson.

Skinner pushed himself up. Sighed.

Don't tell me you don't know about the rules, the guard said. You oughta know all about the rules. These other ones don't, but you should.

Skinner looked at him and looked away.

There were derelicts everywhere. A guy in a Mets cap with a triangular unshaven face strutted over to a feminine boy in bellbottoms, and said, Yo, homegirl, give me a quarter.

The time on the wall was three-something in the morning. The lights were half-on, as if in energy-saving mode, and the black and amber field of the street was visible through the glass. A vehicle went by, just one, and litter got sucked up and flew after it, spinning.

He took the magazine out again but couldn't read.

At four, the guards told everyone they had to leave. The whole McDonald's was getting to their feet and shuffling to the door in a moving column of piss- and b.o.-stink. He picked up his bags and shuffled outside with them. The cold was vicious. He had to take a piss so badly it was stimulating. The wind lifted a sheet of newspaper from the gutter and blew it against his calf. He had heard someone, possibly the guard, saying that there is another location down the street that stays open. The sky was black and, at the corner, there was a surreal in-the-mountains feeling from the giant silent buildings in the silver-dust light.

No one else came with him. Maybe they went down into the subway station or waited on the street. But he found the other McDonald's and the door opened when he pulled it, and when it shut behind him, he was warm. He dropped his weight. The Men's was being cleaned, he used the Ladies and drained his bladder, one of those endless rich-smelling pisses. He bought another coffee, blowing over the plastic lip of the cup, tongue scalded. A Spanish guy with a broken nose, tattooed forearms, and a bop walk was mopping the floor in sections. The stairs leading up to the second floor were chained off and no one else was present.

You think you could let me crash up there?

Come on, the guy said. He unhooked the chain, took him up. Lay your shit on down there. You don't gotta go nowheres till nine. You got all the way until then.

Fuckin A. Thanks, bro. The ex-con slid off and Skinner piled his gear on the floor and stretched out on a bench.

4

WHEN SHE FIRST ARRIVED, she had tried to stay awake all night in the Port Authority, trying to avoid being seen by the police. She sat on the floor with her forehead on her arms across her knees next to the humming vending machine. They patrolled through, she heard their radios, and she got up and moved. In the restroom, there was toilet paper unspooled across the floor and a black woman was bouncing off the walls, rubbing liquid soap on her arms and legs like lotion. Zou Lei went down through the tunnel and waited in the empty station for the subway. It came and she got on and sat at the end of the car holding her plastic bag with her clothes in it.

At two in the morning, everyone was black or Mexican and they were men, sitting with their knees spread out, sleeping with their mouths open. The door between the cars opened, letting in the roaring at full volume and a column of men came easing in, swinging along the bars, their jeans low and bunched around their ankles, rags on their heads, towels hanging from their pockets.

She crossed her arms and stared straight ahead, seeing the lights flick by.

Her back kept slumping forward and she would prop her chin up with her hand. When she woke up, her bag had fallen off her lap and her clothes were showing. She picked it up and stuffed her clothes back in, the train blasting through the tunnel.

She saw the dawn begin on the elevated tracks, water towers wheeling by against a dark blue sky. Her face was creased from trying to use her clothes as a pillow. Construction workers started getting on, their boots and jeans covered in dust. She sat up straight and crossed her legs and then her head sank forward again as they rocked along. People got on talking. She stood up and read the map, keeping her balance, leaning over someone else. She traced her finger along the colored line beneath the plastic.

This one the Chinatown?

A Salvadoran woman in a white ball cap and gold earrings, whose sneakers barely reached the floor, took her headphones out and said, Qué? Sí.

Zou Lei sat back down. She took a comb out of her bag and combed her hair, tying it back in a ponytail. A man in overalls watched her from across the car, then closed his eyes again.

She took the subway to a station with overflowing trash cans. You could hear the splattering, when the train had gone, of a soda getting poured out on the concrete. She saw someone in multiple coats but no shoes digging through the garbage, taking out the bottles.

The street was lined with dumpsters. She passed a city building for pain abatement that had benches splintering out front. A block later, she saw the Manhattan Bridge arched up over the tenements into a boiling dry-ice cloud ceiling. Framed under the arch, there were fire escapes and clotheslines, brush calligraphy coiling down the ironwork, graffiti booming off the rooftops.

She went into a coffee place and stood to the side, holding her plastic bag, and watched them fixing a coffee, putting condensed milk in it. Do you have the paper? Not here, they said. The subway crashed by on the bridge above their heads. It was a very small store. Someone pushed by her, holding out a dollar. Where's the best place to get a job? she asked. They lidded it and handed it over the counter. Outside, they said. Outside is the best place.

A chain banged against corrugated steel on the cold street. The locks were coming off, the steel shutters going up, the stands opening. She went door to door down the line of kitchens with candied ducks on steel hooks in the grease-smeared windows and the shrines behind the counters, and asked if they were hiring.

Sometimes the boss was the man standing right next to the person she was talking to and he wouldn't say anything unless she asked him directly, are you the boss?

They were not hiring, but try the paper.

On East Broadway, there was a condemned building where you could stay for ten dollars if you called the number. When she pushed the buttons on the intercom, she heard nothing. She looked past the notice that had been partly scraped off the glass and waited for anything to happen. She bounced on her toes, her face ruddy, hitting her arms and thighs through the denim. A bus pulled away behind her and revealed a sign for New York to Virginia across the street. She stared at it and thought about it.

In a basement, where she had gone to get warm, she heard a hollow clattering and down a hallway that smelled like beer found an underground mountain of aluminum and crushed glass where they were buying bottles and cans from the people who found them on the street.

She read the handwritten notices taped to the traffic lights, the ones with the bottom edge cut in fringes with a phone number written over and over, so you could tear one off.

In the dusk, she saw an open flame burning on the sidewalk and old women in quilted jackets feeding spirit money into it with tongs.

Her second day out of jail, she looked for work as far as the Imperial Dragon Kitchen in South Jamaica—the wide empty avenue with the clothes strewn in the street, pigeons on the stop lights, early on a Friday morning. The long wait, freezing—hugging herself, hitting her legs, blowing on her hands.

Three males in ragtops looked her over.

The street smelled like hair oil and dryer sheets. The pigeons were seagulls, she realized. The front page of the Sing Tao was a blue square. It looked like the sky of western China, the same color as the sign over a Uighur restaurant with the pastureland rolling and a steer superimposed in the foreground and flaking gold Islamic script. It looked like the sky today in New York.

She watched them taking the locks off and pulling the shutter up before she crossed out of the winter sun and leaned her head in. There was a rat in the center of the floor.

Not open yet. The speaker had black plastic shoes and acne.

What about the job?

What job?

The job in the paper.

Two other women pushed inside, complaining about the cold, carrying their lunches in plastic bags, and went behind the counter with the money cat on it.

It says apply in person.

He read it while picking his nose. There was a long hair growing out of a wart on his chin. He took his long nail out of his nose, looked at what was on it, flicked it, it clung, put his nail on the classified ad, tapped it. This, he said. The number. You call this number.

She called it and voicemail picked up and all she got was music, and so she started walking in the pale winter sun, not stopping when she came to the subway. Instead she picked up her pace, strode beneath the tracks, crossed a road with a median, and walked along the median, looking out at the wide open space and started hiking north by the sun. She went past all the places where you could buy a coffee and a roll and kept going until there were no businesses, no people, simply buildings and the sky. She walked rapidly, her plastic bag swinging in her fist with her clothes in it. A bus drove by her and she let it go. She carried on into the afternoon, migrating along the backdrop of the buildings with parapets connected together like one great fortress wall. The graffiti repeated for miles. Stigz. Luni. Blip. Crew. Tire and wheel. Audiotronic. A dog got up and shadowed her on the other side of a fence until it reached the limit of its enclosure while she kept going.

Her shadow changed, the graffiti changed. She crossed Metropolitan Avenue and a thundering underpass. When she had found her way onto another northbound road, a plane flew overhead like the hawk leading the drum girl out of the desert. The sun snuck behind her other shoulder, it only fell on half the street. She sensed woods beyond the houses. In the windows, there were flowers, broken blinds, a Puerto Rican flag, a stone statue of a saint in a glass case in someone's yard. On a garage, there was a poster for Tito Swing a la Semana.

At 110th Street someone said Chinita and blew kisses. It was evening and there was music.

She went into a pizza place, a handwritten sign on the door saying baño sólo para clientes. One of the short barrel-chested men behind the counter with their hats on sideways, thumping out the dough, asked if she was frío.

Tire, she said. I very tire.

She leaned her elbows on the glass and looked down at his hands dusting out the flour on the dough.

Por qué?

You know Jamaica? I walk from this one, very far.

No, he said, too far. She hadn't done that.

I come very far.

Really? he asked in Spanish.

Yes. I don't lie.

Maybe, he allowed.

Before, I in jail.

This he believed from the way she looked, a short woman in jeans, hatless, with the plastic bag in her fist.

They let her use the bathroom. Okay, mamacita, they said. She ran hot water in the sink and washed her hands with the coconut soap, used the paper towels. Closed her eyes. There were plastic flowers. It was a nice small room. The pizza baking out there, in the narrow store, the ovens.

On the phone, a man told her where to come in Queens. He called it Queensie. He picked her up at a gas station on Roosevelt Avenue in view of the projects, the train yard, and the stadiums and derricks across a river. They accelerated down a boulevard that roughly followed the water. She was warm in his minivan. She hadn't slept and had a headache. She watched building supply warehouses going by outside her window, thinking she could fall asleep.

He turned into a back street and she sat up. He was a fat solid man in an expensive parka, his stomach touching the steering wheel, turning and accelerating, taking them zipping past graffiti-covered walls and courtyards. Slowing at a construction site, he said, Building. She reached for her bag, but he put out his large soft hand to stop her, not quite touching her. No. Not yet. He slowed again. Building. Everything new. There were weathered boards and scaffolding. Maybe I buy. Maybe the investment property. He insisted on speaking English with her in a soft delicate voice that back home would be called sweet, causing her to wonder if he was from Taiwan.

They parked in an alley near the expressway surrounded by faded brick walls. She climbed out of his car and stood in the cold with her arms crossed, the wind blowing strands of her unwashed hair across her drawn face, waiting with her bag over her shoulder while he went through his keys. She saw people's laundry hanging outside their windows. He got the paint-peeling door open and led her in, up a stair, close quarters, stale cigarettes, concrete-colored light filtering in from an angle. Nobody home, he said. She heard the dead silence of two-by-fours and wall board, his breathing after climbing the stairs. They were alone and she hung back, letting him go ahead. On the second floor, they picked their way among shower shoes and plastic sandals. It was a standard illegal apartment divided into sheds to accommodate eight or more people. The first kennel was made out of a shoe rack and plywood and see-through plastic film. The jury-rigged door was held shut with a bike chain. Through the plastic, she saw somebody's mattress. She put her eye to the film and looked: a can of Kirin Afternoon Tea.

The kitchenette was an alcove. In his parka, he filled the space entirely, turning in place, looking at things so that she would look at them too—the cupboard hanging open, the frozen explosion of clutter. No walls visible, just cardboard boxes, garbage bags stuffed with clothes, luggage. Mushrooms floating in a wok.

Refrigerator, he said. He tried to open it and bumped his leg. Sink, he said. Everything very complete. He turned on the tap and put his large fingers in the water, rubbing them together like a man feeling silk. He looked at her. Lifted his fingers to his face and tasted the water, brushed the water off his brown lips, leaned in and drank from the tap, came up with his cheeks full, spit in the sink, brushed the water from his lips, twiddled his large fingers to shake the water off.

Water, he said. Hot, cold, everything.

Bathroom, he pointed. Laundry dripping in a doorway.

He came towards her, his arms whispering on the body of his parka and she stepped back. This is it. He pulled open a pleated screen she had not noticed and pointed inside at a blackened mattress.

It has everything, I think. Take a look. You have window. He pushed himself inside and pulled the chain on the bare bulb to show that the light went on and off, tugged the shade and it went up. She saw the gray houses tumbled down the slope outside, the clotheslines and antennas and tree branches. The sides of the shed were plywood construction barricades. There was no lock on the screen door.

The mattress a little dirty. You put a sheet, I think. Turn it over. In the summer, put a fan. You don't need much, I think. It is okay for you. You don't have husband, he smiled. You don't have baby.

He was waiting for her, standing over the broken mattress.

She shook her head from the doorway.

It's good, she said.

She put her hand in her tight pocket and felt her money.

You give me key.

———

When she heard the door close downstairs, she went inside her shed and sat on the mattress, thinking she would finally sleep. She took her sneakers off, her socks off. She turned on her side and one of the hard rusted wires coming through the canvas snagged her jeans. She shifted. She kneeled up and checked what was left of her money, rubbing the bills apart with her shiny calloused fingers to make sure she counted them all. Her lips moved, counting. She took the classifieds out of her bag and spread them out and concentrated on what they said.

She went back out to Roosevelt Avenue and, walking briskly with her arms crossed and her shoulders hunched, headed to the intersection where the subway was. People were teeming off the subway. She saw Pakistani women carrying their children outside a Dunkin Donuts. Then she lost sight of them. People bumped her. She started moving with the crowd, looking above their heads and seeing that she was going into a Chinatown, a thicket of vertical signs, the sails of sampans and junks, too many to read, a singsong clamor rising. No English. There were loudspeakers and dedications and banners for Year of the Dog. Voices all around her, calling and calling. Here, here, here, come and see! Someone spitting in the street. Crying out and running along next to her, pushing and pleading, grabbing the sleeve of her jacket. They put flyers in her hands and she dropped them. Missing teeth, younger than they looked. Illegals from the widow villages. Body wash, foot rub, Thai-style shower, bus to Atlantic City. A neon sign for KTV turned on in the dusk. She saw the endless heads of strangers, the crewcut workmen, running crates of rapeseed out the back of a van. The feet coming, the sneakers everyone wore, the work boots, the spike-heeled boots worn by the women. The square-faced workmen smoking Golden Crane, wearing

Gortex, wearing military castoff. The women had black hair, black leather jackets, black purses, lion's manes of hair dyed orange, teased and split and tinted. Faces glazed white with photo developer. She smelled the buckets and the hose. They were shoving by the scales. You give me a pound. You give me two for one. Give me three. Be honest a little.

The crowd was a river with girls coming through it like flower-boats sailing along. The mothers were looking at the oranges in the market stands. The girls were pretending to be good. They had to let their mothers talk. They were looking at other things, at things that were happening on the street. The girls were part of a different society. She saw a Chinese girl with no one, with a scabbed ear and breast implants, her face flushed and sweat-greased and strung out.

The crowd went under the train tracks. Billboards carried hepatitis warnings. Tall blue-black Africans gesticulated, selling something in the street. The way was narrow because of the vendors. A block of squid gelatin hissed on a grill. She smelled coal fire. Chicken skewers cost a dollar. But you can't buy anything until you get a job, she said. In the crowd, she saw one American face, a guy in cornrow braids, looking sideways, sliding through the crowd, looking back at her. Then he was gone, headed for the projects, which were here before all these Asians like herself, the boat people and country people with gold teeth, the ones who grew up under communism, who took out loans and built something. The wet black bags of garbage were piled up in walls along the curb forming a channel that they moved through. There was too much to see and she noticed small things. She saw a hairstyle, a black mohawk, the brown scalp shaved on the sides, and when she saw his face, she was right, he was from Mexico and now he did deliveries for a man with a jade bracelet who had learned enough Spanish to tell him what to do. She passed ducks on steel hooks behind the grease-smoked windows of kitchens where she would ask for work. Everyone was like her, she thought, and she did not see any police.

She was here in New York for a reason. She was never going to get arrested again. She was going to stay where everybody was illegal just like her and get lost in the crowd and keep her head down. Forget living like an American. It was enough to be free and on the street. She'd rather take the scams, the tuberculosis, the overcrowding. She knew how to get by. On the street, she watched for undercovers. The paper carried stories of deportations, secret detentions, prisoner abuse. A Morristown cabdriver of Syrian ancestry was thought to be held in the Metropolitan Detention Center in Brooklyn. The Federal Bureau of Prisons had a list of detainees, but not all its detainees were on the list. A lawyer hired by the family said a person cannot simply vanish.

Zou Lei stopped reading and started doing sit-ups.

I'll be fast, she thought. They'll never get me.

All she needed was to make some money. Pay her rent. Eat shish-kawap. The fresh air was free.

What you want? the girl said in English, in McDonald's. I doesn't speak Mandonese.

The hot water. No tea, only the water.

What?

One cup the hot water.

What does she want? the boy in a visor asked.

Forget it, I got it now. The girl made a hand gesture, hooks on her fingers, acrylic tips, filling and lidding the Styrofoam cup.

Zou Lei put her hand around the cup and drew it across the countertop.

You give me the spoon?

The girl gave her a plastic spoon.

A dollar nineteen.

Thank you.

No, a dollar nineteen.

Thank you. Zou Lei stepped back holding the cup.

The boy, who had wet-looking spiked hair above his visor, came over. What is it?

She got a water—I supposed to ring a tea. Now she ain't—whatever.

Void, the boy said. Void, void.

She got a job on Main Street in a basement food court hidden under a 99-cent store, hidden among nested Chinese signs. You would never know it was here unless you were looking for it. Zou Lei ran down the steps in her tight jeans and went from one mini-kitchen to the next telling them she was looking for a job.

A woman asked her if she knew what she was doing. Can you make this noodle? Do you understand this flavor? One bowl sell one dollar. Nobody buy the cost, nobody has money. I don't make money, so what I pay you with? You don't make nothing working here. This the miscellaneous, pull the trash and dump it. We don't use meat. Waste the money. Everything vegetable, you take a look, kabocha. Not like the one they have at home. Customer don't care anyway, so I don't care. He pays a dollar, already he knows it won't be anything special. Just to hurry, eat, goodbye. All they care about is the dollar. We sell the southern taste as thin as hair—the noodle—you see that one. One hundred, I get fifteen, make right here in Brooklyn. By the time I sell, maybe three times the cost, I still make next to nothing. How cheap you work?

The boss-woman wore a baseball cap and was shorter than she was and talked with her mouth flexed in a tight O around her over-lapping teeth. I learn business on the Mekong River. Between customers, Zou Lei picked up a rag and wiped the food service steel, the woman pretending not to see her. She wore a gold pendant, talking on her cell phone with the hands-free earpiece in. Eleven hours later, when the propane tank had been turned off and the flame was out, Zou Lei asked her, Am I coming back tomorrow?

You can, the woman said.

When deliveries came in, she said, Look, to Zou Lei, I show you, and pointed with her ladle where the man had left the Goodyear Farms boxes at the top of the stairs. Zou Lei carried them down two at a time and stacked them behind the counter. When they slipped, she caught the boxes with her knee, grinned and regrabbed them.

She went back to the stairs and reappeared hurrying this way between the pillars, taking fast steps, leaning against the weight of a bucket, one arm out to the side, the other arm pulled straight down, the wire handle cutting into her fingers. Halfway, she set it on the rubber mat with holes between the fused strands so water could drain through to the linoleum and flexed her hand. Something thumped the plastic. Then she went around the bucket and picked it up with her other hand and carried it the rest of the way. The boss-wife popped the lid and poked the frogs with her ladle.

Look, still living.

On her break, Zou Lei would go upstairs and look at the merchandise in the bins, while the vendors talked in their own dialect, pieces of what they said coming through to her and making a half kind of sense. She saw a denim-jacketed figure with a ponytail on a TV screen and it was her. They sold battery operated radios, the pink and blue words on the plastic package meaning Happy Sound. This is practical, the vendors said. And cheap. And you can learn English from it. Or she went out in the alley to be in the fresh air to do lunges under the fire escapes, but Fookienese teenagers with rat tails watched her, tried to get her attention, and after failing at this, began laughing at her. She get her ass big to fuck more tight.

Later, she tried another door and wound up in the shell of the building between the basement and the street, where she could be alone.

Mekong, that's in the south, the boss-wife told her. On the Chinese side, I live. I live in South America, Ecuador. I see everything. They have a war there. I make money in the war, better in the war, better than here. Because people want to buy DVD, they want to drive away their life.

With her calloused hands, Zou Lei put frogs in a pot and turned the propane on. She kicked the cardboard boxes flat and stacked them in the trash. I'll include you one meal a day, the boss-wife said. When Zou Lei got paid, she did her laundry and came to work the next day eating a twisted piece of bread fried in oil and drinking hot milk. Business is a joke, the woman said. They played Cantonese radio. Zou Lei took condiment packets home at night.

On her break, she did a handstand against the wall and tried to do a vertical pushup, even just an inch. First she took her phone out, which she had felt slipping out of her back pocket, and laid it on the stairs. Then she went back to the wall and kicked up into a handstand, holding herself on her hands. Her hat fell off her head and her shirt fell down to her armpits, exposing her flat stretched abdomen. She rolled down to her feet to a squatting position, dusted her hands off, and tried again.

She went for a jog around the block, but there was no block. The neighborhood around her house was full of levels. Walls and fences. You went down the street and it closed behind you, it screened you off, the courtyards and the back alleys, straw in the frozen mud. The bricks were faded on the buildings, turning to pumice, grayed-out. The boards and barricades in the alleys were gray-weathered, the piles of leafless brush were gray, husk-dry, piled under the windows, woven into the rusted wire fences. You could look up from a back alley to an old wall, a tree on the wall, another tier starting, a building, one of the new condos, the foundations at eye level. You could climb it. The houses and walls were stairs. It was a terraced hillside, a maze on a slant.

Dirty white houses were tucked in under other buildings, red blessings on the doors, Chinese New Year's just behind us. On the dashboards of their Caravans and Quests, there were Buddhas. You could always see their laundry hanging out to dry. They made projects. Plants of ascending sizes, little designs, a money cat, plastic bags woven together to make ropes, the ropes tied from beam to beam, a contraption, you never knew what for.

You might smell joss in the tumbledown alley. You might see a stolen Corolla. You might see it going up and down if a girl was in it. In the back, where the rust was dripping down and the grills were weeping black on the bricks, everything was tended, an arrangement of boards and plaster buckets, a small pyramid design. If you heard voices coming from a window they were saying... what were they saying in Zhejiang dialect?

The workmen coming home—they might be exhausted or look sly with a smoke, smoking out of the side of the mouth, paint on their hands. They talked on cell phones, waited in pickups. Orange extension cords coiled in the back, a crew of five or six, drinking coffee, vapor coming up from the manifold, idling—bachelors, cousins, one last name.

In the evening, they came back to the apartment and ate their takeout and she heard their battery-powered radios tuned to Voice of Mainland, speaking the common language. Singing ballads. The moon is round, the moon is round.

Along with the Chinese, there were Guatemalans and Hondurans and other Central Americans, having left behind what they called the problems in their countries. They were here and everywhere, here to work, across the expressway, beyond the globe from the world's fair in Flushing Meadow Park and the stadiums over the river. Especially in Corona, except for the hole in the donut, the patch controlled by Italians. In the summer, in the park, she knew she would see the homeless Salvadorans burned black, see them playing soccer with a beer can, their shopping cart staked out under a tree like a horse grazing, the flags of their shirts hanging from it. The Chinese in jeans and jean jackets she saw here and now, coming home covered in plaster dust, or the odd one stoned, down here in the labyrinth of back streets.

There were people from India, the help desk people, the IT people. They had a string of businesses on the main artery: video, hairstyle, Punjab grocery. Neon signs, second-story porches and satellite dishes. Pakistanis living above their stores on the other side of Cherry, next to the tattered awning of Little Kabul.

You could take a wrong turn on Franklin, by the next lane over, by that courtyard with the cats in it, the trees with cancer, the ones that looked boiled, melted, cooled-off and hardened like that. The kind of high gates you see at a tow truck lot. The trash in the shed, the back of the building, an American flag with holes in it. Each unit had a steel door painted the color of Crest toothpaste. It said Nutty in spraypaint. On the chest-high foundations, Wreck, Remy, Slugz '92. The graffiti was faded. Asians lived in the low rises, but it said Murder in fresh paint and where did the alley go? You could climb into the windows, which were low on the first floor and unguarded, but you wouldn't want to.

The streets had what some people called culture, one that preexisted the Asians. Franklin don't quit, they said. It kept going, all the way from Hillcrest to Woodside to Sutphin. They were Spanish, black and Irish with their heads shaved and they compared their level to yours. You could follow it to the Rockaways, to South Suicide Queens. They meant street genius, notorious block parties, the deep five boroughs.

From here, the bus barreled downhill and the terrain opened out onto a field, a cemetery, into a wider form of shadow. You saw women in black burkas waiting for the bus, unwilling to speak with strangers. Or not waiting, taking whatever they had with them and getting farther away on foot, traveling with girls in burkas, pushing a grocery cart with a twenty-pound sack of jasmine rice in it. They had WIC, asylum. Whatever skin of theirs was visible—the hands, around the eyes—having been tanned in a burning oil field.

The field was far more extensive than you might imagine. She ran and ran, under trees, bypassing ditches, areas where the ground was stamped with tire tracks of Bobcats, in the subliminal winter pre-dawn, the gray grainy ground lapping under her feet, the houses a presence beyond the trees. In front of her, however, there was only distance. She crossed a street, the park kept going. As she ran, there was a transformation in the sky: dawn. At length, she stopped, some-where in a baseball diamond, apparently no closer to the apartment towers that rose like mountains on the far horizon, exerting the same magnetic effect on her with which she had been familiar as a child.

Her tracksuit sweated through, she ran back, the sun behind her. The Chinese did t'ai chi in the botanical gardens.

5

HIS BODY JERKED. HE moaned. The bench was slippery and he moved his legs on it in his dirty jeans, one of his socks coming off, the denim and camouflage and the American flag, his body and gear strewn out.

His brain was on but he was not awake. The plate glass window was lit up with white sunlight coming through his eyelids. It was very hot. They were driving and he was seeing the road go by and feeling the vibration. Metal was hot to the touch. It was loud and the vibration surrounded him and filled his ears like the heat. There were palm trees in the ugly desert panning by.

He was watching the side of the road as it kept coming towards him, bouncing over his iron sights, the dark poor sunburned people by the side of the road, their animals and goats, the little white goats, the tents and rugs for selling whatever they had, bread, souvenirs, hashish, and then the stretch of nothing, the table land.

In his dream, he knew what was happening. When they had first arrived, they hadn't known, having yet to learn. Their unit had provided security for a colonel on daylong sector-assessment missions called SAMs that lasted into the night, and they had seen very little action. If this is war, I'm disappointed, Nowling said, pulling security in the spectacular heat. They looked up the line of vehicles at the senior men clustered around the colonel in his crisp camouflage pointing at features of the landscape. Occasionally, they heard battles being fought and at night they watched the lightning flashes and felt the thudding in the ground. It was hard to sleep. People said I miss my girl. I wanna get some. They manned a checkpoint and shot up a car. Their doc from Opa-locka poured a bag of clotting factor in an Iraqi's chest. Mom's head was gone. White-faced, Sconyers ran and got a beanie baby for their daughter. They poured canteen water on doc's hands and it smoked on the road. Someone took a picture of the front seat.

They saw contractors and Special Forces guys wearing boonie hats and carrying different weapons, long-barreled sniper rifles. Dominguez said he had talked to them and they were British. The colonel was gone. Rumors abounded, what was being planned, what was said on CNN. They crossed paths with other units, soldiers who had been in heavy house-to-house fighting and there was a bad feeling, like they wanted to hurt somebody and you were it. Captain Friedman told them to take a knee. He briefed them on who the most wanted people in Iraq were at this time. Then they were ordered to each write an official postcard home. They found a corroded hangar in the desert that was supposed to have contained chemical weapons. The Special Forces men drove away smoking cigars and they moved into it. Rotting drums stood in the heat. The company was divided. They built shitters using the drums and burned their shit with diesel fuel, wearing their gas masks.

It was revealed that they were being held responsible for an area of four hundred square miles. Things started picking up. They got broken down to platoons, and the platoons got broken down to squads, the squads into sticks, the sticks to bricks. At night, they went out on raids, out into the villes along the canal. Before they mounted up, they turned each other in circles checking each other's gear, put their chew in, banged their helmets together and shouted Get Some! In the day, they drove through the sector, seeing Iraqis running along the road calling out to them. They found adobe houses burning, black smoke rising, clothes in the street. The mosque was trashed. You know what that smell is. Out of nowhere, someone yelled contact left! and they unloaded at the rooftops. They went cyclic, burned a barrel on the 240. Afterwards they checked each other, but there was no evidence that they had taken fire. Adrenaline is real, said Dominguez.

In the basements, they found electronic equipment, stiffened rags, a crumbling prayer book. Children stared at them. The corpses were few at first, but then they started finding bodies every day. Some were mummified by fire. A bomb went off and spit a person out of a doorway. That smell is burning hair. A truck drove by them full of men with beards and satisfied expressions. Why are we letting them go? Sconyers asked. I don't get it—Sconyers who carried a copy of the Report of the 9/11 Commission in his assault pack.

Because this is the army. Because this is their country. Because this isn't supposed to make sense.

They swam through a sewage trench at night to provide security so that Special Forces could snatch someone important. The mission got called off and they had to go back the same way. At the hangar they stripped and washed the shit off with their canteens. Then they cleaned their weapons. They did not sleep. They took Ripped Fuel. Whatever that sound was in the city they could always hear it. Nowling opened his mouth and let the chewing tobacco fall out with a long shining strand of drool and then he threw up. What day is it? Fourteen, I think. The Hells Angels sergeant said, I'm countin on you guys to suck it up. The soldiers all said hooah. Going into the city, they took fire and it was not their imagination. It was a hit-and-run. The fire fights proliferated. You could tell there were people on the roofs. They got shot everywhere, in the armor, boots and Kevlar helmets. Sergeant Rogers got shot in the arm. I can still move my fingers. That's a medal, goddamnit. Gimme a smoke. Hey, Jones, I beat you to a medal.

Hold still, their doc said.

Doc's mad at me. Think I'm goin home?

Fifteen days after they had arrived in-country, they drove over an IED in a soft-skinned vehicle and lost Chidester. The explosion leaped out of the road and rose like batwings. In the following vehicle, Skinner's ears popped and cut off like overloaded speakers. The process of evacuating the casualties did not go smoothly. There was a mound of dried black lava on the ground and his mind kept focusing on it instead of on tasks he had been given. When they got back inside the wire, the platoon was in a shambles. Someone ordered Lawson to clean the blood off and Lawson said I don't feel the need to do that. Skinner's ears were ringing still. They were ordered right back out again and spent the night on overwatch, seeing the land in infrared. The word was that we will bomb the city from the air. Dear Lord, please let me kill someone tonight. For days inside the wire, they sat around with their shirts off, their chests pasty and macerated from their armor and covered in heat rash, wearing shades, smoking cigarettes, examining their peeling feet.

Bomb the living shit out of them.

That's not going to happen.

Burn them all alive with Willie Pete. Yes, it will. That's why we're getting downtime.

It turned out there was an argument going on between Captain Friedman and the battalion. When he came back, he said there's been some discussion about survivability with the kinds of attacks we're getting out here. He chose what he said carefully. We will be adaptive. They were dismissed. At the end of the month, a second memorial got set up by the rotting drums. Well, it turned out Lugo hadn't made it either. Why'd you have to tell me that? Lawson demanded. He pushed the chaplain's arm off his shoulders. The colonel showed up and spoke about the viscous medium of combat. Did he say vicious? When he was gone, their captain told them the best way they could honor those they had lost. They rigged the trucks with hillbilly armor and went back out in the city.

It now stank like something you could not imagine. They rolled by villas with ironwork terraces and Skinner looked for the families that had been there. Instead, he saw bearded men with cell phones, shiny watches. One had had his eye cut out, you could tell. In some sections, walls were perforated like lace. Through the holes you could see movement and hear noise and then see dogs ripping at something in the rubble. A freestanding staircase led up to nothing. Sarge, who do I get to kill today? Lawson said. They came upon a bus without wheels resting on its axles. A woman with her head covered came out and emptied a bucket into the shit lake on the ground. The day never ended. Skinner shifted in the glare, holding the weight of his gear on his body, turning back and forth, looking around, touching his safety with his thumb, standing in rubble, feeling watched, chewing on his Camelbak hose, sucking water, tasting warm bacteria plastic.

Time jumped or crawled. How long have we got left? Nowling said and guys told him to shut up. Let me see. He counted on his short fingers but came to no conclusion. For a week, another unit bivouacked with them. Skinner watched their dark-skinned zip-tied prisoners, on their way to Abu Ghraib, eating MREs like contortionists. The outside world seemed far away and less than real. He watched them praying, whispering with their eyes shut, foreheads pressed to the dirt. A scratching loudspeaker in the city was playing the call to prayer.

Allah can't help you, a soldier from down south said. Now you got me.

They shot a farmer's goat and Broadbent cooked it over a drum, Jamaican style. It was meant to be Chidester's wake. The translator could get you hash. It was a celebration after a fashion. They told stories about Chidester, about the man he'd been.

In the middle of the night, Captain Friedman came out of the hangar and came right at them.

Would those motherfuckers of you who are drinking fuckin haji booze like to join me when I notify the families of the buddies you're going to get killed?

Skinner hung his head.

Have a nice fuckin party.

Their captain left and they stared into the dark orange glow evolving in the drum. Their translator sold them pills. Dominguez's trousers fell off. I must of lost like twenty pounds. Everyone was thin.

Two guys got in an argument and started threatening to frag each other. Here's the deal, the squad leaders said. Anybody who's a problem child, the whole unit is gonna beat their ass next time. All of us. And if that don't work, you will get fragged. By me.

In broad daylight, they snuck up on a boy hiding an explosive device on the side of the road under a plastic bag and they photographed him.

I just can't take the anxiety, Jones said to the doc. I'd rather do whatever and get it over with.

Then you need to talk to a combat stress nurse, not me.

A rumor went around that they were going to be sent somewhere else, but they knew it wasn't true. They didn't believe anything they heard. They got resupplied. Y'all make a chain, the driver said. I gotta turn and burn. The ammunition boxes formed a cube nearly ten by ten by ten. The Texan with the radio cleaned his battery contacts with a pencil eraser and checked his fill three times before going out. The heat intensified, if that was possible, and they had a heat casualty, Pomerant. The consensus was that he was bullshitting. There were fewer and fewer of them. A building exploded when they were in front of it and Danzig, a high school wrestler, disappeared. Skinner's mind interpreted a piece of twisted metal as a person who had been burned and crucified, but it was not. A sniper shot their staff sergeant in the head. Their staff sergeant scrambled after his Kevlar like a fumbled football, caught it and put it back on. Guys jumped away from him as if he were covered in hornets.

They did IED sweeps on foot, down the roads along the canal. He kept thinking this is the last thing you are going to see, the red earth with the sun glaring off it.

A man wearing brand-name knockoff sunglasses and tight jeans came walking towards them through the heat shimmer. He was pulling along a dirty little boy by the wrist. The boy was filthy and his hair was full of powdery dust. The man ignored the weapons pointed at his chest. Gesturing at the blasted dwellings, he said:

These people are enemy. I am friend. You will come to me for cooperation.

He was wearing perfume, a heavy, cloying, womanly, boudoir fragrance.

I don't know you, Graziano said, rubbing his black-whiskered jaw.

You will know. Believe me.

Skinner saw the inside of a green room that had been a school. The furniture had been piled against the windows. You saw the charred buildings across the street through interlocking table legs. Flies were clustering on the eyes and mouths of the children on the floor. He held his rag over his face to breathe.

When they were driving and the hot wind was blowing over them, he tied the rag over his face to block the sand. He used the rag when he took apart his weapon and rubbed his firing pin, leaving black streaks on the cloth that smelled like cordite and CLP.

Cross-legged, he dumped the rounds out of his magazines and, taking his time, cleaned each one of them individually using the rag, the cigarette hanging out of his mouth, fingernails black with cordite, and loaded each one of them back in one at a time, taking them from the candy bowl of his helmet and putting them back in his magazines, which he rapped against his helmet when he was wearing it, before he shoved them in his weapon.

They called their captain Freebird. At ease, he said. He had a whiteboard on an easel and a dry erase marker in his hand. Lessons learned. We know they talk to each other. We know about the cell phones and the loudspeaker on the mosque. When you are in the same location more than five minutes, you are getting in the red zone. There needs to be a countdown in everybody's head. The roads that are soft, that they can dig under, obviously those are our danger areas. Anytime you've got a road going over a culvert or a stream, they can emplace something under there. You've got the sides of the road to look at. If the sides are hidden, it means they can get to the road without you seeing them. We're talking about bigger and bigger munitions. He drew a circle on the whiteboard. We're getting inside the kill radius before we can even see anything, so we need to look at that. We're looking for trigger hides, anytime you see piled up rocks, little hooches, whatever. Det cord sticking out of the ground. Trash, plastic bags, anything that covers something else. I need you talking to each other. This is everybody's ballgame. Our safety zone is here. He tried to draw it on the whiteboard but the marker was out of ink. Fucking thing. He threw it. Let me see your Ka-bar, Staff Sergeant. Thank you. All you men in the back stand up so you can see this. The twenty-year-olds stood up. He drew a line in the sand. This is Tomahawk. Here is Hogan. He drew another line. This is the no-go line. The ammo can is Town Hall. The rock is the Post Office. The eraser is the Goat Farm. He took his G-Shock watch off and put it on the ground and squatted over it with the knife. Can everybody see? This is what we want to do. We can't do everything we want to do, so this is it.

A tanker truck came in a convoy and brought them diesel fuel. The dull landscape rippled in the fumes. They unloaded thirty pounds of broken cookies from the USO. Sconyers, whose colorful full-sleeve tattoos included carp and long-throated birds, received a book from his parents, who were schoolteachers in West Virginia. He put his shades on and went behind the hangar and held the book in his hands. A great cloud of dust lifted up behind the tanker when it went away. Skinner drank warm Gatorade and read Muscle & Fitness and went in and out of sleep.

He woke up confused and disoriented. Something's different, he insisted. Yeah, it is, they said. The other squad had had contact and it was serious. They waited up smoking until they came back. This sucks, they said unshaven, staring at the red horizon. It was dark and the truck didn't turn on its headlights until it was inside the wire. They saw blood and pale skin in the light of their diesel generator. Dominguez shoved his way in saying no, no, no, dude, as they lifted Lawson's body down. Give me the fucking needle. I'm type O. They reached to cradle Lawson's head and unintentionally put their hands inside the cavity in his skull. Someone jerked his hand away and Skinner felt wet matter hit his boots.

Freebird got relieved. I'm reevaluating my lifespan, Sconyers said. The new commander parroted the colonel on area denial. Graziano said if you're in a forward unit, you're living on borrowed time anyway, and stared at them in a challenging manner. They stuffed spare flak vests all around the interior of the vehicle, in all the holes.

Saddle up, the Hell's Angels sergeant said.

Having checked the fill, the Texan gave Graziano his radio.

His call sign is Battleaxe.

Skinner walked away from the others. No one said goodbye, they pretended he wasn't leaving. He climbed up in the truck with all his weight. He gave his hand to Sconyers and heaved him in. Short, independent Nowling, who was from Georgia, got in alone. The Hell's Angels sergeant took the wheel. Graziano slammed the creaking armored door. The engine started up and everything began to shake. He stared at nothing. They rolled out between the guns. He turned to look. Behind them, the road paid out and the black mounds where the sandbags and the 240's were got smaller. Having nothing else, he ate the instant coffee from his MRE.

In his dream, the yellow land wheeled by too bright to look at. He saw a woman in a black burka on the road. They drove at speed for several miles and their dust drifted out behind them. They blew by a road sign in Arabic. Nowling shouted up front, Wasn't that the no-go line? Obviously it was. No one answered. They entered a zone of burned-out gutted houses. Sconyers mouthed what the fuck? You looked in the window holes and saw the sun shining inside, no floors, no roof, just a shell. Sometimes darkness, metal wreckage white with ash. They weaved around a dead truck. A turn was missed. Graziano keyed the radio. Interrogative: Was that Omaha? The sergeant stopped and backed up. They jumped out to pull security, pointing their rifles up at the roofline, blinded by the sun, and mounted up again to make the turn into an alley, the walls nearly touching them on either side. Skinner covered the terraces above them, craning his neck. They bounced over rocks and he held his Kevlar on. There were intersections full of sunlight. They drove into the continuation of the alley, which kept getting tighter until they were scraping the sides. No one was saying anything. The voices on the radio spoke all at once and Graziano said: Battleaxe, say again your last.

Wait one.

The Hell's Angels sergeant started slowing down. The way ahead of them appeared to be blocked by a car spun sideways, the front sheared open, wires and metal things spilling out. He braked and they rocked forward. Fuck me. We're stuck. Something moved in the corner of Skinner's eye but it could have been the caffeine. He looked through the holes in the building walls for movement.

Put it in reverse, Graziano said. I'll guide you.

It was impossible to steer inside the alley. Every time the sergeant touched the gas, they went a foot or two and dug into the wall. It took them three minutes to go two vehicle lengths.

How deep in are we?

Nowling ran back and looked.

Two hundred meters to the last intersection.

What if we just power right through the car up there?

It's got nowhere to go.

Okay, the sergeant said, steadying his voice. Gimme some security while we unfuck this.

Skinner climbed out, his insides feathery and weak. In his sleep, Skinner tried to say I cannot do this. In his dream, someone punched him hard in the chest—he did not know who—and said: You awake in there? Good to go—and handed him a grenade. It was almost impossible to lift his chest to breathe. He took a knee on his catcher's kneepad and aimed at the trapezoid of sun between the walls. Behind him, he heard Graziano's low voice saying straight back, straight back. Straight. Stop. Left. Little left. He heard the humvee dig into the mud stone and the engine revving up. The sergeant cursed, fuck. He wiped sweat out of his face with the green gun-oil rag. The countdown in his head had run out more than once already. The trapezoid changed shape and he blinked and stared downrange, but he could not tell what he was seeing. However, the eye sees shape, shine, and movement first and it was one of these. He looked around for anyone. His nearest friend was hiding in an alcove. Am I seeing them down there? he screamed. His face was a white oval beneath his helmet.

They've been there this whole time. We're dead.

In his sleep, Skinner yelled and hit the bench.

When the firing began, he couldn't tell how bad it was. The not-knowing lasted one second. Then the air started getting shocked by him and it was obvious he was close to getting killed. He thought someone was grabbing his harness. By this time, he was shooting back. Somebody should be on the 240 in the vehicle, he thought, but that never happened. He kept looking to make sure he saw at least someone in his uniform. As long as I can see them, we're still here. By this point, when he put his hand on his chest, he was still feeling magazines. But there was not enough fire from us and, the whole time, you could hear the balance sliding like a scale, and it was just getting heavier on the other side. He felt the whole thing was just falling apart, that the enemy had fire superiority. Then he looked again and he couldn't see uniforms. He couldn't hear anything when they called him and they had bounded back. So then he had to run by himself, and the closest he came was when he almost ran in front of them while they were covering him—and it was almost another terrible accident in the middle of a giant disaster.

They took cover in a building that they shouldn't have been in. The enemy was so close, they could be seen as individuals down to the details, pointing out where the Americans were. A fire mission was on the way and then it wasn't. Seeing tracers was the first he knew how long they'd been there, that an unbelievable twelve hours had passed. That and thirst.

He heard a crack that echoed. Then another crack. Crack. Crack. Crack. Crack. Pop pop pop pop pop. Then silence. There was nothing to see. Pop pop pop. A string of lights. Then a boom that traveled through the earth and he felt it in his legs, ears, chest. A strange wave that disrupted his pulse.

Graziano low-crawled over and hit him on the helmet and shouted in his ear and pointed from one black jagged formation to another sticking up out of the battlefield. See your field of fire? And crawled away.

Sconnie, he croaked.

Skin, that you?

Are we gonna get air or what?

I think they're waiting on it.

You got any water?

Then green lights streamed up out of the earth. They spewed up, streams of them, incandescent. The sound hit—roaring screaming earsplitting. In the arc-weld light, solid forms appeared to shift—the hanging dust. Shadows were running. The drilling deafening thundering never stopped. The razor lights leapt straight across the black, flashed past—he whipped his head around—and they went away and went arcing slowly down like baseballs. The ground and the air were being shocked. He forgot what he was lying on, whether it was the roof or the ground. The reverberating detonating went on. In the pockets of the sound, there was deafness and blindness in the sudden total black. Everything that was not massive was obliterated. The shock-shock thudding got louder and louder like an exercise to destroy the hearing. The green stars were streaming back this way like a garden hose. He felt them in the ground. Hypnotic and kinetic. The zipping energy and acoustic snapping getting nearer.

Then the spot where Sconyers' voice had been exploded and they were buried in sand.

He scrambled to the floor. When he came to, he was trying to hold his body together and his heart was revving. The McDonald's made no sense to him at first. He was hyperventilating and attempting to dig into the tile floor with his hands.

His heart kept slamming as if he had been injected with atropine.

When his friend exploded, something had struck Skinner in the back. After the pieces stopped raining down, he scrambled to his friend, he felt him in the sand, and tried to pull him up. Skinner couldn't lift him. Instead his weight had pulled him down with all their armor. The sand was filling up with Sconyers' blood. He was letting him die. He was trying to lift Sconyers, and Sconyers tried to help. The sand became a sucking, sloshing pit that soaked them both and overflowed with blood. It soaked his trousers, his PT shorts, his legs, and socks, which squished. The blood wet his hands and arms, it got on his weapon, and got in his face and mouth and eyes, and he tasted it, his friend's blood. And the blood itself had weight and the sand had weight, and they combined as a blood mud that dragged them down.

Then the others helped him, and Jake's body came up, and they ran with him swinging between their arms. They put him on a poncho. Skinner had to be ordered to pull himself together. He was sent back stumbling over the thundering wasteland, barely able to run, to get the rest of his body, and ran ducking and stumbling, wheezing with exhaustion, at a loss to find where they had been. And he collapsed because his body finally realized that he had been wounded too. Graziano ripped out plastic from his butt pack and stuffed it over the hole in his chest cavity.

He stopped.

There was no one here—he huddled frozen rigid, waiting for things to fall into place. Limb by limb, he unclenched himself, dropped his head back against the plastic seat, let out his breath, sat there on the floor blinded by the white fresh sunshine. It was bright and still among the clean, modular tables. A regular, soft, sweeping sound coming in through the thick sealed glass.

Could be a dayroom in an army hospital.

The sound outside was cars going by, in America.

He made the decision to put on his filthy sock, the one that had fallen off. Then his boots. He wadded up his poncholiner and stuffed it away again with his shaking hands, which were going to fly away on him. He used the restroom faucet and took a pill.

After a minute, he picked his gear up and, balancing the weight, climbed downstairs. There was a sea of people surging in the doors and he pushed his way out through them.

He dropped his bags on the sidewalk, stood and smoked a cigarette in the cold sun.

Skinner and Jake had been evacuated and saved. They were alive when they made it back inside the wire. Both of them had heartbeats in the sandbagged field hospital in the battalion camp out in the desert. Skinner in unbearable pain, the convoy delayed for tactical reasons, gunfire pop-pop-pop thudding in the street, a calm voice speaking on the radio as searing hot shell casings spewed on them, the gunner yelling, everyone in panic, Skinner screaming and groaning—the driver shouting that they had to back up and try a different route because they were taking too much fire. Other soldiers were killed outright. They heard death on the radio. They were all going to die. Then they made it to the battalion, and their bodies were dying. Jake, a half body, was thrown on a dripping canvas cot in the green field hospital, generators running, his genitals exposed between the meat cross-sections where his thighs had been, his flesh being worked over by a spinning brush while a jet of water sprayed at the wound to clean it. The army sent them back to a giant military hospital on the east coast. Jake was kept alive in Walter Reed.

Six weeks later, Skinner joined a rehab platoon in Georgia and stood formation with guys in wheelchairs. He raked sand in the volleyball court and took painkillers for the headaches and shuffled through the chow hall putting gravy on his meatloaf, watching the war on TV. The summer days were dark and storming and the trees blew down on base.

A doctor, a Coloradoan who looked like the captain of a college wrestling team, told him he was better. You're four out of five. Your unit will be glad to have you back. Good news, right? He called Skinner hard charger. Now you can go strap on an M4, hard charger. He had brown hair, a muscular athletic physique, sunken cheeks, and the insincere niceness of a frat boy. He tossed the file onto the desk in the consultation room, called Next!, and Skinner shuffled out.

No one told him the results of his cranial scan. He had unbearable headaches and double vision. The army gave him reading glasses. There was no mention of PTSD or TBI. When he got back to the war, he was considered a discipline problem. In the cold season, in the blue desert night when the steppe winds came down from Kurdistan and his squad was sleeping bundled in the hangar after an 18-hour patrol, he squatted alone outside smoking a cigarette butt and staring at something-nothing beyond the wire. His speech was affected. He did not know how to diagnose himself. He was disciplined for having a round in the chamber of his weapon when weapons were supposed to be clear. They caught him walking around with his safety off. He was ordered to perform remedial calisthenics in NBC gear and a gas mask.

On leave, he went to see his family and got physically violent with his little brother. His mother threw him out. He went back to base and thought things will be better when he got out of the military. He apologized to his brother and his brother forgave him even if his mother didn't. The army let him believe he was eligible for the Warrior Transition Program, and he was already planning to buy a car and go visit Jake, when they stop-lossed him. It was fairly devastating news. His mother cried on the phone and said she was sorry.

The battalion was handing out antidepressants like free candy on your way to the PX to get the magazines and iPods and protein powder and energy drinks you were taking with you back to war.

Back in Iraq, he deteriorated as a soldier. He was in a new AO, hard by the Euphrates, and car bombs went off at mosque time. The civil war had started. He could not function. He fell asleep on watch. A rugby playing sergeant known for being hard smoked him in MOP gear in the noon heat, called him a shitbag, a bottom feeder, a retard, etcetera.

Skinner drank five canteens of water and the water kept running out of him, his eyes unfocused, the sun blazing off his sweat, the rubber suit lying on the sand at his feet like the empty shell of himself, a human skin.

Everyone in the war had changed, the war had changed, and Skinner's strangeness barely showed. It was chalked up to the war, as if it were logical. The war itself was always ever stranger. Within his unit, he became identified with a group of soldiers called the Shitbag Crew. A shitbag was a wag bag, which they called a wookie bag. They said Wookies, Yo, when they bumped fists, and it was like saying we're staying alive. They had superstitions, rituals, which became ever more involved. A tribal life began. Some of the gangs within the infantry were involved in murder. They dropped wire or weapons on corpses. A gunny from Akron, Ohio, was the capo of a death squad.

Skinner was mentally ill, logging day after day in a combat zone, compounding the damage: cuts that wouldn't heal, back pain, diarrhea, hearing loss, double vision, headaches, pins and needles in his hands, insomnia, apathy, rage, grief, self-hatred, depression, despair.

People laughed at him, watching him trying to lift the water bull.

Two Iraqi men came up to Skinner, ostensibly to try to tell him that they were not insurgents. Feeling threatened, Skinner began kicking out, his foot connected and a man fell back and Skinner fired his M4 and shot him. The other was trying to hold onto his weapon. Skinner's buddies came running. They forced the barrel of the weapon around until it was on the man, who started writhing and shouting. Skinner triggered the weapon, killing him in cold blood.

His war went by one eighteen-hour watch at a time, feeling the jump of his own adrenaline-fed heartbeat, thinking how many more of these heartbeats he would have to wait through to get through the next minute, the next hour, the next eighteen. His thinking was flattened by drugs, fatigue, repetitive thoughts. But the war led you into the mystical thinking of someone in a psych ward. He added time in new ways. Today he wouldn't die if he did ten deadlifts with his rifle.

When he was rotated back to the United States, he ran into Freebird outside a mall with his family, and the man wouldn't return Skinner's greeting. He just looked at Skinner and spat on the asphalt and stared at him aggressively until Skinner walked away.

Jake emailed him:

Skin my friend it been a long time. i wanted to write but had to learn first. this device i use my mouth. u should c me. i seem retarded b/c my mind trapped. frustrating to be thot of as broken. especially for us grunts the doc talks to me like 5 yr old. !!!! let me c him do our job guy..

i cant stand when people use word brave hero ets. i would do all again

all my wheelchr, computer comes from donations made me cry

my plan to go to nyc w/ u – negative for reasons obvious. ive decided college is next war for me – want to untrap my mind. so focused on therapy havent had time think big picture. worried am i going to quit lots of thoughts of what we saw - surreal. yes anger. alos a gift something nobody else knows

i love you my brother

jake

Skinner went to an exit meeting in the base auditorium where GIs were told how to make their military service sound useful on a resume. It was a sunny winter day and the demobilized soldiers wore fleece tops over their leaf-patterned cammies and black watch caps like bank robbers in the movies. The blue sky was clear and cold. The bare trees poked up into the sky like bundles of wicker. During the intermission, the soon-to-be civilian soldiers stood smoking in groups, some with canes, holding glossy pamphlets bearing the words Once a Warrior, Always a Warrior.

The news came that Jake would not be making it to college. He'd had too many surgeries and, at last, an infection he had thrown off previously returned with renewed ferocity and attacked the sheathing of his spinal cord. His parents came from Virginia to be with him for the last ten days while he existed in a coma. The machine that breathed for him moved its piston up and down. His parents slept on chairs in the waiting area by the elevators past the nurse's station. They stood over Jake's bed and touched their son's tattooed arm and examined his yellowed face for signs of returning life. He had become aquiline. He had been given a tracheotomy and a hose went into a gauze-packed hole in his neck and was held in place by tape. The room smelled the way skin smells when it is covered by tape for months and starts breaking down. He was not coming back, and they made the decision to let him go. The nurse turned off three switches and they waited at the bedside while he stopped living.

We love you, Jake, his father said, still wearing the tie he taught high school history in, loosened, over a plaid shirt. He emailed Jake's friends.

This was the news that Skinner received before he went to New York alone, holding to the idea that if he partied hard enough, he'd eventually succeed in having a good time and would start wanting to live again.

Broadway in the daylight. People streaming out of the subway, moving in clusters that broke apart into fragments and passed through other columns of people like a strainer. He smelled pretzels. A black Denali with the driver's hand visible, resting on the steering wheel, an athlete's hand, an expensive watch. All the girls wore Eskimo boots. Their hair bounced behind them. There were so many it was unbelievable. There were office chicks smoking outside the entranceways and there were guys in shirtsleeves coming out to smoke with them, young guys in slacks, just ordinary guys who had not drafted themselves after high school, and he heard the normal sound of their voices as he went by and the whole thing sounded strange.

He stayed at a hostel by the Port Authority, drinking and surfing the web. There were drag queens staggering sideways across the broken pavement when he went out for beer. He bought a bag of weed and smoked it with the window open wrapped in his poncholiner listening to the sirens. He checked his email, typed Hey dud whatsup, and hit send. No one wrote back from his unit. A block away, next to the peep shows and the Foo Ying Kitchen, he found a strip bar, the same blond hair and tan tits he had seen on the highway coming in. In a few days, his bank account was down a grand already. Awesome, he said, and toasted himself with a Red Bull. His clothes lay all over his bunk—jeans from American Eagle, shirts to go out and get laid in—bought with hundreds of dollars in hazard duty pay. He got dressed and went out drinking. At the Blarney Rock, where there was an American flag behind the bar and a memorial to the Towers and the faces of the fallen, a few guys bought him beers and clinked bottles with him and called him family. That's it? he thought. But he stayed pleasant, watched the game. When he was falling down, they tried to offer him a ride. He left without speaking. Take it easy brother, they said. Let him go. Let him go. His mother emailed him from Pittsburgh to tell him he was wasting his life. He took his meds with beer and lay on his bunk with his tattooed arm over his face and his tan boot on the wall, the Chinese characters saying No Pain No Gain, and watched Sconyers convulsing in his head. The others at the hostel said, You were making noises in your sleep.

6

ONE DAY, THREE OR four days after arriving in the city, having just taken his meds, he went back down into the subway and sat down on the first train that came and didn't move until after it had risen up out of the tunnel into daylight onto elevated tracks, passing the backs of billboards, train yards, and water towers. After a couple stops, he went up to the window and stuck his face against it and watched the rooftops coming. The stops kept coming. He had gotten a long way out. Across the field of rooftops, he saw cranes. Down below, he saw a car turning on the littered street and heard a burst of the hammer drill from an auto repair.

In theory, it might have been possible to figure out where he was from the map and how he could get back. Instead, he said to himself, No, let me go all the way to the end.

When they got to the last stop, he got off because he had to and went out on the street.

It was crowded and a woman bumped him with her shopping bags coming out of Caldor. He raised his hooded head and looked at her and she apologized. Along the curb, he noticed people sitting in the Asian squat, selling wallets, belts, New York hats, backpacks, and DVDs. It was very loud with people yelling. A truck was idling blocking the intersection, the engine spinning, and he could hear the diesel exploding in the shaking block of steel. Someone honked and Skinner twitched.

He lit a cigarette and watched pigs being offloaded onto the shoulders of Mexicans. They were carrying the heavy cold white carcasses through the crowd and in through the hanging plastic strips into the back of a Chinese market.

Vertical Chinese signs were everywhere. Someone tried to give him a flyer and he said, I don't understand you, and dropped it. He went into a newsstand and got a Red Bull. In the back of the store, he stopped and stared at the magazines. All the metal slots were filled with porn. He saw a tan girl with her wet hair plastered to her face and her mascara streaked.

He kept getting pushed and it bothered him. He forced his way out through the people coming into the newsstand, and, once outside, drank his Red Bull moving with the crowd.

Another four-foot woman handed him a flyer.

Ma-sa-jee, she said.

The piece of paper said Bodywork 1 hour.

Awesome, he said, and stuffed it in his pocket.

The garbage on the street had a peculiar smell. In the windows, he saw red roast pork on steel hooks. A mother was squatting helping a boy urinate in the gutter. When he flipped his empty can into the garbage, an immigrant in flowered sleeve guards came behind him and picked it up with tongs. He heard a chanting, which was all their voices overlapping. The women wore black leather jackets and spike-heeled boots with buckles and fringe. One of them looked at him directly and she had eyeliner and a mane of dyed reddish hair and then he lost her in the crowd.

He went down the avenue, crossing under a railroad bridge, and searched down an alley, passing right by a doorway where each tread of the stairs said Table Shower, leading up to a massage parlor on the second floor. At night, the stairs would have been lit up like a runway and he would have guessed what it was then, but in the daytime you had to read Chinese to know what you were seeing. He came to the projects behind the train tracks. From here, he saw the bridge and the water and he went back down another alley until he was on the avenue with the crowd again.

He took the flyer out of his pocket and checked it. The crowd was taking him like a conveyer belt past everywhere he had already been. After he had gone beneath the railroad bridge a second time, he saw a group of men hanging around in front of what looked like a condemned building, smoking cigarettes. There was a dead gray neon sign on an upper floor that spelled KTV. Skinner tried to see inside through the thick smeared glass doors.

The men eyed him. What's the foreigner doing? Look at this clothing of his. A cop? A health inspector. A person with time on his hands. Pay no attention to him.

Skinner pulled the door open and went inside.

The building was occupied and there were utilities functioning inside it, he could feel them right away. A back door was open and a young male, by the sound of his voice, was in the alley talking on the phone in a rough loud Asian language. Stairs led up and down. When Skinner began checking the first floor, he discovered a maze filled with ninety-nine-cent-store-type goods. Backpacks and umbrellas hung from the ceiling. The vendors, eating noodles out of Styrofoam bowls and talking loudly, went silent as he moved down the aisle. When he looked back, he realized they were watching him on closed circuit TV.

What's down here?

They ignored him to his face. He saw them exchanging looks, and a woman stared at him as if he were a monster. A man in a gold chain circled behind him, pretending not to look at him. When Skinner repeated his question, a thick-faced woman of about forty, who was knitting, shook her head. Then she turned to the others and said, Impotent.

No speakie English, huh? Good to go.

He stuck his large, broken-nailed hand in a cardboard shipping box, took out a padded bra and chucked it back.

Clumping upstairs in his boots, he found nothing but a locked door on the second-story landing and a table covered in takeout condiment packets and other trash. He jogged back down to the first floor and stuck his head out in the alley, catching a whiff of garbage, seeing fire escapes, and hearing exhaust fans. Whoever had been on the phone out here had gone. He went back inside and checked down the stairs, this time descending to the basement.

In the basement, there were food stands packed in together. Fires were hissing and it was loud. Napkins were soaking on the floor, the linoleum was rotting down to the wood beneath. He went around the rusting folding tables where Asians sat in jeans with keys on their belts, looking fixedly at their phones.

What you want? a woman yelled.

Where's the massage at?

Where the who?

Where's the massage spot at? The girls?

No! No girl! she yelled. Noodle!

Skinner tried to see inside her metal pot.

Well, what kind of noodles is it?

She pointed with the ladle at the sign overhead. Up there, she told him.

The sign said:

Feld poultry w/ family flavor northern hot $2.75.

He kept walking through the maze of tables and pillars holding up the bowing ceiling and the gas hissing and the yelling and the banging of woks. When there was nowhere else to go, he returned to a steel fire door with a half-lit exit sign askew above it, which he had noticed earlier, and checked it again. The alarm contacts were painted over. There was no handle on this side, but he could see the latch was not engaged. After glancing briefly over his shoulder, he wedged his fingers in the gap and pulled it open. Nothing went off. He held the door open and leaned inside, seeing a cinder block hallway.

The ceiling was half-ripped-down and there were acoustic tiles buckled, rotted, water-stained, and lying broken on the floor. He stepped inside. The fire door banged shut behind him. For a moment, he stood there listening. The air was cold. A sheet of plastic hung over a window in the cinder block wall and it puffed in when the air pressure changed. Through the plastic sheet, he could hear the street.

Something was humming, barely at the level of hearing, and his head turned towards the sound. He took a step, concrete shards popping under the heel of his boot. The humming was electricity, he thought. He moved down the hallway, past standpipes rising through the floor, the humming growing distinct. He went through a doorless doorway and began to see fluorescent light. Then the hallway angled and when he turned the corner, he saw someone.

She was sitting on the fire stairs in tight threadbare jeans. She had work-discolored hands and her dark hair was in a ponytail and he could see her thighs curve down to where she sat. A muscle ran up the side of her neck from her collar to her jaw. The brim of her hat tilted up and she looked at him.

Hey, he said.

She watched him coming towards her.

I'm cool. I just took a wrong turn.

You get lost, she said.

He came a little closer.

Yeah. I got lost.

She had not taken her eyes off him. At first, she had thought he was a cop. Now she was examining his camouflage.

You are army?

He glanced at himself.

Yeah. I just got out. I was down south until a couple days ago. I just got here. It's my first time in New York.

She listened to this, put a lock of hair behind her ear.

You live here?

I live? she asked.

Yeah, you—do you live—he pointed at the ground—here?

New York? Yes, I live New York.

You like it?

Yes, good.

It's supposed to be a good place to party.

Party?

You know, like beers, jamming out to music, whatever. Just partying…

He sang dahn dahn dahn da-dah and did a little goof-off dance.

I like, she smiled. This is very good.

Their eyes met and they looked away.

He took his cigarettes out.

You smoke?

No.

Good girl, huh?

I am runner.

Runner? Like running?

Yes, runner.

Why'd you want to know if I was in the army? Skinner asked.

Why? Why I ask?

Yeah… why?

Because in my family, we are the army.

You were in the army? What army?

Not I am. My father. In the People's Liberation of China. My father is the sergeant.

No way! Is that why you're strong? You look strong.

Strong? Yes! She stood up and stepped forward into a deep lunge. Everyday I am doing running, gymnastic. Like this one—and she dipped up and down, touching her knee to the floor.

Skinner watched her legs flexing.

I do many of them. And… and yangwotui.

What?

Yangwotui, she said. Pushing, like this one—she mimed doing pushups.

Most girls can't do them.

Yes! I can do.

I don't know. I have to see this.

I show you.

She got down, brushed concrete shards away from her hands, and hooked one foot behind her ankle. Skinner gazed at her cell phone outlined in the back pocket of her jeans. She did a perfect pushup. Then she took a breath and did a series of them.

Wow, he said.

She got up smiling, dusting off her hands.

Ten, she said.

That was awesome.

Please! she said, stepping back with a sweeping gesture, offering him the floor.

Who me?

Yes! You are push! Please!

How many you want? he asked, pulling off his camouflage.

Oh! One hundred! In China army, boys can do one hundred. If you will be better than them, maybe, I think, one hundred twenty!

Is that all?

He got down and started pushing.

She watched the nape of his erect short-cropped head, the ridged plates of his shoulders going together and apart, his kinetic energy as he threw his body up and down. He counted off in a rapid mild voice. Her eyes went from the star on his neck down to the fulcrum of his boots. In the center of his spine, his shirt was getting damp. He paused with his tattooed arms locked out and his triceps twitching, sucked air and kept going. His neck turned red. He kept his voice even as he counted off the hard ones. Finally, he grunted, and his back bent and he came up slowly.

Fifty okay?

You are good! She gave him the thumbs up.

I don't know. Used to be.

Yes, strong! Very strong! she said.

It's nothing great.

She felt his arm. He flexed for her and she gripped his muscle.

You have Chinese word?

He pulled his sleeve up and showed her.

It says No Pain, No Gain. Can you read it? Is that what it says?

Somethings like this, she said.

Want to try this? he asked pointing at his chest. Soberly, she felt his chest.

How about you? You show me?

Yes. She flexed her bicep for him. They both looked at her bicep as he felt it through her long underwear shirt.

What about the leg?

Leg? Okay.

She took a step forward with a bent knee and he placed his large hand on her thigh. Man, he sighed. She let him slide his hand around to her hip. Good? she asked. She flexed for him.

Damn.

After a second, she hipped away.

Skinner stared after her.

I go to work now.

You have to go?

Yes, I go.

He grabbed his camouflage off the stairs and hurried after her. She led them back through the derelict hallway and pushed out through the fire door.

Hey, wait.

Zou Lei slowed for him.

I want to ask you something, Skinner said.

———

In the morning, on a steep side street lined with bushes and fences with the feeling of a mountain trail above a highway, Zou Lei sees a woman in a conical straw hat with her hair divided into three black rivers, one down her back and one over either shoulder, hanging down to her waist. She is pushing a laundry cart with her bottles laid up pointing in opposite directions, the necks interlocking. The forked hair hangs like a ragged black shawl. A thin woman whose age is hard to tell without seeing her face, just the romance of her hair, as if she has prepared herself for a lover and was waiting years for him, a lifetime.

The cell phone rang in her pocket while she was in a tile-walled sink room, chopping. She dropped her cleaver, wiped her hands on her apron and took her phone out.

Wai? she said. High-lo?

She checked the bars and listened but there was nothing there.

When she got her break, she went into the back alley and tried calling back again. Phone pressed to her ear, she walked back and forth beneath the fire escapes, hugging herself, looking up at the sky. It was bizarre and incandescent, like magnesium burning behind boiling yellow clouds. The line clicked and Skinner's voice said hey.

Hai! she said. I call you back. I can't pick up before. You call me, right?

A piece of squash was stuck to the heel of her work-swollen hand, and she wiped it off on her thigh, laughing at something he was saying. She leaned against the alley wall and rested her sneaker on the bricks behind her. He was saying we could get together. She was nodding.

If you're free, he said.

Yes, I am free. As soon as work finish, I am free.

Listening to him talking, she tucked her hair behind her ear and smiled, dimples appearing below her cheekbones, her strong teeth visible, the paper-thin smile lines around her mouth.

7

THEY WERE SURROUNDED IN neon and headlights, striding through
the darkness, going in and out of darkness and light among the Chinese signs and lights, Skinner almost shouting. Asians went around
them. Zou Lei was marching with her arms crossed across her chest
and her hair blowing around her face and she was laughing.

It's funny story!

I'm like, no, dude!

This animal.

I'm like, do not do it! I'm like, think again!

Their combined momentum moved people out of the way. Or
people didn't move and Zou Lei and Skinner went around them and
rejoined on the other side, Skinner saying:

I'm like, take a breath!

—continuing to talk through the silhouettes of people like paper
targets who got between them.

He halted suddenly and she halted and someone bumped her and
she didn't notice. She waited, pulling her hair out of her eyes as Skinner lit a cigarette.

A puff of smoke lifted out of his cupped hands and rose up into
the black and disappeared and when he dropped his hand, he had a
lit cigarette in it. They started marching again.

There! I need that for this story.

She laughed, It's funny. Unbelievable.

Look at it, I tell him. Look at what you're doing!

It's the crazy!

Somehow, you get it. I don't know why you do. He didn't.

When they were on the other side of Chinatown, he said:

I have no idea where we are. Do you?

He stopped again and looked around and she joined in looking
around at the projects, train yard, the highway and cranes.

Fuck it! he started walking again.

Fack it! she laughed and made a fist.

Fuck it. It don't matter. It makes no difference. We're gonna force-march this way as hard as we fuckin can. It don't matter if it's a bridge or a hole in the ground. We're gonna do things the army way. It don't matter if it takes fifteen hours. Let's just be stupid.

We will be crazy!

Oh, yeah, we're gonna be crazy! We're gonna shoot donkeys!

Oh my God!

I'm feeling the guy's arm and he's all shaking and terrified.

It's funny.

It's so stupid. We did so many stupid things. I really hope you're not working tomorrow, cuz the two of us are not coming back.

They were hiking up over a bridge that went over the water and down to an industrial area on the shore where there were derricks and containers. She looked back at the small Chinese signs behind them.

I think we can just turn around and go back.

That's true, but, see, that's the problem. You ain't thinking the army way yet.

I have to be more crazy.

Crazy! You gotta get with it. Don't worry. I know you're scared, but I'm here and I'll help you.

He patted her back. Then he tried to put his arm around her.

Oh my God. We are so crazy. You are killing me with this arm.

It's okay. I'm here to comfort you.

It's too heavy. This arm is crazy. My God, I can't walk. Go the normal way.

Okay, but I have to comfort you later.

We come far.

It's the boonies.

They were walking by the stadiums and parkland. The sky was a slightly lighter shade and everything on the ground was black. The red ember of his cigarette appeared and disappeared as his hand swung. Then it rose up to his mouth and glowed and then went flying off in an arc and bounced.

Stop a minute, he said.

What?

Just stop a minute. Come on. Come here.

Why?

Come on. Closer than that.

What for?

Cuz I'm crazy. I want to feel your leg again.

No, not now.

Come on, you were so chill before. I want to remember what it feels like.

It's cold now. It's too cold. Now it's too cold to stop. Come on. We has to march.

A car came driving toward them and Skinner's white face was crossed by the extended shadows of his outstretched fingers shielding himself from the glare.

Come on, we go.

Yes, ma'am. Roger that.

Soon we come to a place.

You know where we are?

It's not far.

After they crossed 111th Street, they encountered more headlights coming at them, bouncing along underneath the elevated tracks, and they began keeping to the sidewalk. From far away, they heard a rumbling that grew louder and louder until it reached them and the subway came thundering over their heads and screeched and slowed and came smashing to a stop. It exhaled and all the doors opened and the cold white light from inside the cars was cast down from high up above and the intercom spoke. Before they reached it, the subway went away, making blue sparks, and a little group of quiet men with Indian faces and string knapsacks and work boots was coming down the Z-shaped flight of stairs to the street.

Is this where you were talking about?

The intersection smelled like sweet fried plantains and chicken.

I come here before.

The men appreciated Zou Lei and one of them clucked his tongue at her as he and his friends crossed the intersection, passing in front of a truck with its engine gurgling and headlights spotlighting the men, flinging their shadows on the cement wall of a lounge.

There's bars here, Skinner said. Will you drink with me?

Up to you.

They went into a windowless one-story building filled with Spanish singing and red light. There were men standing almost motionless swaying in the dark in cowboy hats and belt buckles. One of them staggered and his friends picked him up. You could not hear him in the music but you could see his mouth open and his eyes shut, shouting or crying out.

Skinner and Zou Lei waited at the bar until the short woman who tended bar in a cowboy hat came down to them.

Two beers, he said, holding up two fingers. Coors.

Coronas, the woman said.

Skinner picked up his bottle and drank off half of it as soon as it was put in front of him.

Zou Lei was talking to him, but he couldn't hear her. She held up her bottle and they tapped their bottles together, then she drank. He put his arm around her. She shifted slightly, making it awkward.

I'm comforting you! he yelled, but she shook her head and he let his hand drop.

We're still crazy, he said. I know we're crazy.

I cannot hear.

I know, it's nuts.

There were rainbow lights flowing around the jukebox, which had the image of a saint in the center of the songs.

You love music?

He was looking around them in the loud dark. At the sound of her voice, he looked in her eyes and said oh yeah.

He got her attention and pointed at the high-definition TV over the bar, which was showing a professional boxing match between Mexican fighters in tasseled shorts and boots. He watched her face in profile watching the match.

Nice TV, he yelled.

She nodded seriously, the blue of the ring reflected on her face.

Skinner noticed a man wearing a bandana staring at him. The bartender set another round in front of them.

Hey, let's see how fast we can drink these. Hey, look!

He drank his beer straight down while she watched.

Now you.

He watched her lean her head back and her throat working as she swallowed the contents of the entire bottle, then she set her empty bottle on the bar next to his.

I don't drunk.

But you're getting there.

They had created a little forest of clear glass bottles on the bar.

In the China, the beer is much bigger—this big, big one! She held her hands apart to show their size. I cannot drink them. Here, this small one it's nothing.

All right. Then go again with me.

I don't get drunk still.

The man with the bandana had come over to them.

You got the prettiest girl at the bar.

Thanks.

She's the best one here. Believe that.

Skinner clicked bottles with him. The man leaned to Zou Lei and touched bottles with her.

I told him you're the prettiest girl at the bar.

She raised her beer and he raised his.

God bless you both, the man said. Beneath his bandana, he had an earnest face, and, although he couldn't have been over the age of twenty-five, fat on his chest and stomach. She could see that he did not do many pushups.

For half a minute, all of them directed their attention to the TV, where the match had ended and people other than the athletes were milling in the ring. Shortly, the earnest man eased back and stood with his friend.

The Spanish music was loud enough to swim in.

Zou Lei pointed to her ear.

What? He's crazy?

No, the music!

She imitated the cowbell. It sounds like the animal is coming! And she imitated the feet of an animal with her hands.

Don't remind me!

You shoot this animal!

I didn't. It wasn't me, I swear!

He threw his arm around her shoulder, squeezing her to him briefly and letting her go before she could object. A minute later, he reached up behind her and tugged a lock of her wavy hair.

In the center of the floor, a man in a black cowboy hat was dancing with a woman who looked as if she had given birth to many sons and daughters and they would all be drunks together forever. She was in her fifties perhaps, and wore a very short black skirt. In her high heels, she was taller than her partner, whose shoulder she rested her hand on. When she moved, you could see the thicker section of her nylons.

I didn't kill it, Skinner said. Another round?

You are crazy.

I've got trigger control.

You are strong boy.

He pulled her to him and they stood swaying with his arms locked around her waist and his face against the back of her skull, smelling her hair.

Okay, it's enough.

The bartender, in her cowboy hat, collected their empty bottles into a tub, bending forward, her breasts hanging in the red light.

Another one, Skinner yelled to her, still trying to hold onto Zou Lei, who was beginning to wrestle him.

Here's to us!

Here to you!

To getting shitfaced in a strange place!

To America! she cried out. Your country!

They drank.

You're okay, he told her.

Zou Lei's face had gotten alcohol-flushed to the point that it looked as if she might be sunburned.

My country is the friend of you country. It's like one. The brother to one another, we come here to make our life. No matter what happen, we are still brother.

I feel you.

He twined his fingers in her hair again and she let him do it.

When he tried to give his bank card to the bartender, she gave it back and pointed behind him. They journeyed across the bar, wondering what they would find. They found an ATM padlocked to the far wall. Zou Lei went to the bathroom while he paid the bill. She held herself on the sink in the tiny green room. Scratched into the paint on the stall, it said Cholo BCB. Mi Corazon. A pierced heart.

They were outside now, taking reeling steps under the subway tracks and laughing. He did his dance.

Run! she yelled.

She broke away and started running and he chased after her, all the way up the stairs and through the turnstile and up the stairs again. They shoved on the train laughing and gasping.

Thanks a lot. I was in the mood for that. Are we gonna PT when we get there?

I test you.

You test me? I guess I better hope I pass.

You has to work hard.

What happens if I don't pass? More pushups?

Pushup, one thousand!

The subway took them back the way they had come, through a sense of rural emptiness, as if they were riding in another part of the world and there was nothing but desolation beyond the houses under the widely separated streetlights.

At the last stop, which was underground, they climbed up the stairs to the street. On the last flight of steps, they passed three males in hoods jogging down in sagging jeans.

What you lookin at? one said.

Skinner stopped on the steps and turned around. The males were looking back at him.

What, you wanna try it, nigga?

I'm right here, Skinner said.

Then do something, nigga.

There's a gun in the bag, nigga.

Zou Lei came back down and took Skinner's arm and pulled at him.

Test me, nigga.

The male with the knapsack started coming up the stairs. He had long black braids swinging from his head like an Apache Indian. Skinner didn't move but didn't say anything.

Listen to your bitch, nigga.

Test me, nigga!

Fuck this nigga scared. Walk, nigga, walk.

Your bitch saved your life, nigga.

The males pulled each other down the stairs.

I'm right here, Skinner said.

Zou Lei pulled him and he followed her up onto the street.

Don't do that, she said.

They shouldn't mess with me.

Come on.

He was silent as they made their way across the intersection, which felt like a vast empty stage set, handbills littering the sidewalk, Chinese signs in the dark.

Don't pay attention to them.

I don't.

He caught up with her as they walked along. She noticed he had lit a cigarette.

Hey! she said and hit his arm.

Trust me, I don't.

They heard a vehicle coming and he put his head down until it broke out of the background of the stage set and came speeding at them, floodlighting them, and soaring past them. Their shadows, flung on the metal shutters of storefronts, seemed to rise up and lie down again.

Look at that, he pointed. Mickey D's is still open. You like them?

Of course I like.

Well, let's go.

Okay! We go.

He grabbed the door for her and threw his cigarette in the street and she went in rubbing her arms and wandered towards the counter and he followed, standing behind her, close enough for her hair to tickle his face while they stared at the menu sign with bloodshot eyes.

She wanted to treat him, but he told her to put her money away.

I got it. She's not paying.

It's together? asked the girl behind the register, who was not Chinese this time.

Yeah, but she's not paying. She's just all happy.

Next time I treat, Zou Lei said. The real Chinese food.

They waited while the girl went over to the chute and put her hand up and waited for a sandwich to fall out of it into her hand.

Macky D you say. It's the name Macky D. It's so cool. The cool guy say Macky D. You are cool? I teach you one in Chinese: maidanglao.

My. Dong. Lao. My-dong-lao.

It's mean Mack-don-al. You say perfect. I think you are Chinese, maybe one half.

How do you say be my girlfriend?

Girlfriend: niupengyou.

New-pong-yow.

They had their food now and they were sitting at a booth unwrapping their sandwiches.

So, like, if a guy likes a girl in China, he goes new-pong-yow and that's how she knows?

He will give her some present, maybe just to show his feeling. If they the rich people, maybe he will buy her the TV or refrigerator. Sometimes the boy buy the small animal, rabbie.

Rabbit?

The ears goes up tu-tu-tu, the nose is red, the hairs is coming from the nose like cat. Yes, rabbit. You can keep it in a jail.

Like a cage?

Yes, the cage, and give it vegetable. When it get more fat, even they will eat it. Cut the head—piiyah—and cook.

Do they make like rabbit sandwiches?

Maybe. I think you can make the sandwich if you want.

Can you go into a McDonald's in China and get a McRabbit?

Maybe soon, I think. Next week.

He put his burger down, fished out his cell phone and moved over to her side of the booth.

Get next to me so we're both in it. I have to remember tonight.

He reached around her waist and pulled her in. He took the picture and then turned the phone over and looked at it. In the picture, her head was tilted sideways resting on his camouflage coat. She looked old and beautiful.

Under the table, her legs looked young but she would not release his hand and let him feel her.

Go back that side.

You're a hardass.

I told you, I test you.

And if I pass the test, what happens? You'll be my girlfriend?

Yes I can, maybe.

What do I get when you're my girlfriend?

Girlfriend.

Yeah but what do I get? Like, exactly?

She ignored the question.

Don't ask this question.

Aw, come on. I'm sorry.

Eat you food or you will be hunger.

Here, he said and put his large fries between them. Get some. He set his burger down and wiped his face. I could use another Coke. Twisting around in his seat, he looked at the counter to see if there was a line. She saw the tattooed star on his neck and his jaw scraped red from shaving.

You want one?

She shook her ice. I have, she said.

He watched her putting fries in her womanly mouth with her chapped, calloused hands, her back straight, her legs crossed under the table.

I don't know what time it is, he said when they were outside again. It was darker than before, maybe because some of the streetlights had timed out. She said she didn't need him to take her home, but he said there was no way I'm not going with you, and they began to walk up the long incline of the avenue. They went under the railroad bridge and past the dead signs, seeing the tarps over the stands, the empty wooden trestles that held vegetables and fruit during the day. Skinner stepped on fruit mashed into the sidewalk like glistening organs.

They turned a corner by a parking lot and went down a narrow way between buildings with arched entrances. There were names and numbers written quickly in dripping spraypaint repeated on the concrete foundation, which came up to chest height before the bricks began. The street doglegged. They went around another corner, going downhill now. She led them under trees. There were clotheslines on the second-story decks. Hanging in the dark, he saw a flag with a crescent moon. The hill was very steep. A blue flickering light showed in a window and they heard gunshots, sirens and muffled music.

Somewhere down the hill, they turned again, onto a long block of row houses going out to the expressway. There were large expanses of blackness. They walked past carports, satellite dishes.

You live here?

She had stopped to get her key out.

Yes. I go home.

Let me come in with you.

No.

It'll be cool, I swear.

No. We say goodbye.

He tried to reach for her and she caught his forearm.

What? I was just holding the door.

She let him hold her hand.

You don't know what it's like, he said.

I know.

Let me do this. That's all I'm doing. That's all I did last time.

Okay, it's enough. Be a good boy.

Okay, he said.

8

SHE TOOK HER JEANS off and squatted on the mattress, barelegged beneath her t-shirt, and poked in the plastic bag which contained her things. She changed into tracksuit pants, hiking the ankles above her knees like shorts, her muscular calves flexing as she walked, bent, squatted. She took her jeans to the bathroom and turned on the water in the tub. A box of detergent had been wedged behind the toilet. She took it out and slapped it to knock the powder loose and poured out a handful of blue and white gravel and mashed it into her wet jeans. A cockroach decorated the wall. Humming, she grabbed the denim in two fists and rubbed them together.

The cockroach waved its antennas at her. You're not so formidable, she told it.

She turned the faucet off, wrung her jeans out, hung them on the shower rod.

Still humming, she dried her arms, threw her peelings out in the wet bag in the kitchen. She rinsed her hands and looked outside at the expressway. It was the middle of the afternoon, the traffic sounds seeming to come through cotton wadding. She took the trash out and swept the grit up off the floor and put their sandals back in front of their respective sheds. She went back to check her jeans. When she squeezed the ankles, water ran down her wrists. She took them down and went outside.

Yesterday, she had bought a sweatshirt on the street for three dollars from an African. I'm cool guy now, she said, pulling the hood over her head like him, speaking English to herself as if he were here to hear her.

She went down a road beneath trees arched overhead, passing low-rise buildings in the trees, an American flag nearly shredded, the colors washed out, an old wide rectangular car beneath a rusted gate. The foundations were tagged with spray paint. At the end of the tunnel of trees a bus went by. Then the sound carried back to her.

At the laundromat, she spent her last quarter drying her jeans, leaning on the dryer, feeling the warmth through her side, hypnotized by the ticking and the lifting, falling, and lifting and falling of her clothes as the drum turned.

A Puerto Rican woman said do you mind? and Zou Lei moved.

A male wearing a massive down coat came in walking with a cane. His pitted face was very white. He sat down with his legs out, the only adult male, eyes hidden by the brim of his cap. The Puerto Rican pulled her kid over to him. Hold him. Don't let him run.

When the drum stopped, she opened the door and put her hand in to feel.

Well, that's not bad. And if they shrank, then even better when you put them on. Oh, you better not be crazy! I am a little bit. Fold them, smooth them out. Make them sharp. Everything military spirit.

In his shorts, his calves were white. He had low-bodyfat calves, which striated when he walked in the gym, across the corrugated rubber floor. From the back, he had a V-cut torso. Without his black hoodie and camouflage jacket, just in a skivvie shirt, you could see the apelike way he held his arms out, his stiff-legged jock walk, which resulted from his injured back.

They gave him a white towel and he carried it around with him from machine to machine, his image rippling along the mirrored wall, an olive drab torso with a yellow insignia on the chest. On his back, it said Third Battalion – Desert Tour – Playing in Ramadi – We Bring the Heat. He loaded plates on the leg machine, one at a time, as if pacing himself for untold hours of labor. He sat down in the sled, put his boots up on the black sandpaper treads, and released the brakes on each side. The plates clanked. Sharp ridges appeared in his white calves as he let the weight come down onto him and, straightening his legs, pressed it up again. When he was done, he swung up to his feet and changed the weight. He took a plate off and carried it over to the steel tree and slid it on. In the mirror, you saw his thick tattooed forearms, his head carried forward and down, as if he were sullen, but that was not exactly it. There were things he did not see. His towel fell and he walked on it.

How many more you got? he was asked.

A bunch. I got a lot of work to do. His attention seemed to spin off sideways following his uncentered eyes. Go ahead and work in.

That's okay. Is that your towel?

What?

Possibly he had been angered by the question and he was left alone. He did leg presses for an hour. When he changed the weights around, he went back and forth to the weight tree, stepping on the towel, which he left where he could step on it. Eventually, he kicked it with his boot without looking at it as he carried a forty-five-pound plate in front of his chest and it went where he wasn't going to walk on it.

Then, when he was done with the leg machine, he picked the towel up and threw it in the laundry hamper on his way into the locker room. His clothes were tossed in the bottom of a locker with no lock. There were other individuals in the locker room behind him. When he took his skivvie shirt off, revealing his ribs and spine, there was a catch in their conversation. Their discussion of good places to go bicycling on the weekend—up the Henry Hudson to the George Washington Bridge or even over to the Palisades where you could do a good ten miles if you were feeling strong—hung fire for a moment.

He put on his Army Strong shirt, the black one. Flipped his hood over his head. He looked like a monk. The pills rattled when he dug in his jacket for his Velcro wallet. He clumped out of the locker room in his boots. Noticing that they weren't tied, he took a knee on the corrugated rubber mat and did up his laces.

He went to the supplement counter where they sold protein shakes. Sweat was welling out of his bad skin. He was asked what he wanted. The mass builder, he pointed. He circled the weight room floor, drinking from the paper cup with the heavy chalky liquid in it.

He went to the preacher bench and set his shake down on the floor. It was the middle of the afternoon and there was hardly anyone in the gym except a Caribbean woman folding towels. He leaned forward for the bar and started doing curls. Between sets, he poured the mass builder in his mouth and swallowed.

A manager appeared across the steel and white room and came over to him. Skinner, who seemed to be watching several things at once, kept curling the weight. The manager was over six feet tall.

He had muscular arms and wore his jeans pulled up in a way that divided his butt cheeks.

Excuse me, sir.

It was not clear whether the manager had his attention. The hooded sweatshirt concealed Skinner, draped him, radiating clammy heat, and the stink of sweat and metal, rubbed off the weights, came off him.

Excuse me, sir.

Air hissed out of Skinner's teeth. He dropped the bar in the rack. Yeah.

The manager, who outweighed him by perhaps sixty pounds, said: We don't allow boots on the exercise floor, sir.

I'm almost done.

Finish your next set, and then you have to change into sneaker attire.

I've got like five more, then I'm done.

But the manager insisted he change immediately. So he went into the locker room and pulled his boots off and tossed them in his locker. Then he went back out and worked out in his sock feet until he was spoken to again.

They were wrestling in a doorway. She pushed him off and pulled her sweatshirt down. Come on, come on. It's cool. I won't. He backed her into the door until she pushed him off. No wait no wait just trust me. It was cold. He tried to grind against her. She raised her knee. He jerked back. She put a finger in his face: I am you sister. I don't have a sister. She held his wrists and when he broke her grip, she dodged away laughing. He hugged her and she took his hands off and forced them to his side. No touch. Just let me go like this. No. What's wrong? They look at us. He turned to see who she meant, but there was no one there.

That's funny. Come on. He leaned into her. He got his hand inside her sweatshirt and managed to touch her breast just barely as she struggled.

Stop! she ordered. She shoved him off and kicked him in the leg. He turned sideways and she punched him in the arm.

Let's not fight.

She grabbed the fabric of his clothing as if to choke him with it or rend it. The strap of his assault pack got caught in her grip.

Wait up.

He stepped away and readjusted his pack behind him.

All right, game on.

No. You are bad boy.

Aw, come on. Come back.

No.

Seriously. Come back.

No. You are the wild boy. Out of control.

He followed after her as she went out onto the main avenue where there were people and lights. She acted as if she were browsing the markets, surveying this and that. She clasped her hands behind her back.

Look at this apple.

He had caught up with her.

Are you mad for real?

She looked at the crowd of people buying things.

Look at this peach. Pear. Melon. No.

They stood on the edge of the light from the bare bulbs that had been set up in the market so that people could see the produce, him in his pale loose camouflage gear, both of them unhooded, with their strong heads like two animals who had wandered in from the dark out of curiosity.

I carry maybe one hundred thousand or two hundred thousand of this melon, she said. Me and my mother.

She knocked one with her knuckles.

He rubbed it.

Feels like somethin to me.

Look at this fish, she pointed.

The fish were large and heavy. She read the cardboard sign planted in the ice. Six dollar. Hm, she said.

You into fish?

It's expensive.

They wandered along the margin, shoppers streaming around them out into the night. He took a chance and put an arm around her. She said, No, like this, and took his arm in hers.

Wanna hit a bar?

But she said, No, we go up here.

At the top of the hill, there was a silver cart with a minaret spinning on top and smoke billowing out almost invisibly in the dark. You could smell the smoke. Painted on the side of the cart were the words Xinjiang Shaokao One Dollar. The vendor, who had a bag of charcoal by his cooler, wore a surgical mask and military fatigues. He was fanning the grill with a piece of cardboard. They watched the coals glow like red teeth. One by one the vendor turned the skewers over.

Liangge yang! Zou Lei sang out.

Two lamb, the vendor repeated in Chinese, from under his surgical mask.

What'd you tell him? Skinner asked.

I order the lamb kawap. I tell you before, I will invite you the real Chinese food.

Lade bulade?

Lade.

What'd he say?

He ask if he make it spice or not spice.

The vendor took a pinch of spice out of a cup and sprinkled it over the grill. When the meat was ready, he snipped the ends of the skewers off with meat scissors. Two lamb! He handed Zou Lei the skewers like a bouquet and took her money.

Your nanpengyou? the vendor asked.

You could say that.

American fellas have money, don't they?

I wouldn't know.

Everyone knows except you. Why don't you have him pay?

You're so concerned!

The vendor pulled down his surgical mask, revealing a lean face. He addressed himself to Skinner. You, he said, rubbing his fingers together. Money.

What? Skinner said.

The vendor went on with tending the fire and turning the meat and checking in his cooler.

You concern yourself with a lot, Zou Lei said.

Just looking out for you, sister.

Oh, that's how it is.

That's how it is.

Keep your eye on that fire. Don't burn your little sticks, Skinner said.

The man made a tolerant sound, as if he were humming a lullaby, placating a child.

Zou Lei took Skinner's arm and walked him down the block. There were condominiums and trees. They left the avenue behind. The concrete sparkled where it was not in shadow. They leaned on the scaffolding to eat.

What's with him?

Maybe he is angry. The Chinese is poor people. Maybe he don't have enough money to get the wife, the family.

He can't afford a girl.

Or they cannot afford to live together. A lot of family is apart.

So he's a hater.

Yes, maybe. Maybe he is jealousy.

I get it, Skinner said.

They were eating, their chins covered in grease.

You ever have this one before?

Yup, he said chewing. At like haji shops and stuff.

You like?

Hell yeah. It's good. Messed me up a little.

How it mess you?

He chewed.

Like digestion or whatever.

You are not used to it. But if you can be used to it, it is very healthy. The people who eats this one grows up up up up.

She put her hand up in the air above both their heads.

This one is not the best. In my home, it's the best one. You cannot believe. The lamb is kill very fresh. In the morning, he is alive, run around. In the afternoon, he is hanging up. Cut the meat, put the fire.

He nodded.

You never eat so good in you life. The bread, my mother bake.

She went on:

In my home is the mountain, forest. River. Everything.

He watched her silhouette. She started to say something else and stopped.

What?

You guess.

Then give me something to go on.

I am not the Chinese.

I thought you were.

No. One half.

She leaned forward, the bottom half of her face coming out of the shadow. He stared at her chin.

What are you?

You guess.

He didn't know.

The Muslim people. Eats lamb.

She grinned and bit her skewer and slid the meat off with her teeth.

Are you messing with me?

She walked around in the dark smiling at him.

He shrugged.

She poked his shin with her sneaker toe.

You surprising?

No. I knew there was something different about you.

Maybe you don't want to play games anymore.

That's not true.

To hug.

Yeah, I do. Quit movin and I'll show you in a heartbeat.

————

They were in a KFC in a chaotic Spanish and black neighborhood. They had walked here, having travelled down a rolling stretch of tall trees and small houses, a narrow strip of sidewalk to go on, sometimes going in ranger file with her in the lead, stepping over sodden cardboard which could have been where people camped. The restaurant's windows were steamed over, and gangs of teenagers in matching red colors and blowout afros were calling back and forth across the place. She saved a booth, her face windburned, eyes bright. He came back from the counter carrying their dinner, his boots just missing the feet in red and black Jordans which were extended in the aisle.

He set the tray in front of her. She clapped her hands.

We has everything!

I know. Here's your Coke.

He sat down and something heavy in his pack, which he had again worn to see her, clunked the seat. He shrugged out of it and set it under the table between his boots. They reached into the chicken bucket. She leaned forward, eating with both hands. The skin came off his chicken and he put it in his mouth and wiped his face. He wiped his hands, which, even when washed, looked as if he had been handling charcoal, the nails outlined.

At the next table, a female voice was hollering, Is you ready to stop bullshittin? And a gale of hooting went up around the place. In ecstasy, one of the teenagers screamed and stamped the floor with his Jordans.

You want ice cream? Skinner asked Zou Lei.

Ice cream! Maybe, she nodded. Maybe it is nice.

I know I'm feelin it.

He got them cones. When they were halfway done, he moved around and sat next to her on her side and reached under the table and squeezed her thigh. There was no resistance in her leg, as if the warmth of the restaurant had relaxed her joints.

How's that ice cream, baby?

Good!

She licked the side of the cone. He watched her, his mouth a flat line. Slowly he slid his hand up her leg. He swallowed. He put his hand all the way up between her legs and squeezed.

How's that.

He glanced at her.

She nodded, concentrating on her cone as if he wasn't there. He swallowed again. She kept her eyes straight ahead. His arm was working under the table. Heat through her jeans. He pretended to eat his ice cream. A minute later, she sighed and shifted forward, hiding her face from the loud restaurant and from him. She flushed, as if in mortification, and opened her legs. He heard her breathing. Her jeans damp. He kept working, glancing sideways again. Then she tremored—it was distinct. She swayed and went weak and pressed against his arm.

Outside, he held her around the waist, saying to her:

It don't matter where we go, we just gotta go somewhere. You feel that?

He pressed against her leg.

Yeah, I feel.

He was scanning around for a black car that might be a cab.

You bring the thing?

The what?

The... the biyuntao?

What, a rubber? Yeah, I got that. There's one. Let me flag this fool down.

A Lincoln Town Car pulled up in front of them, aerial waving, and Skinner and Zou Lei got into the leather backseat, a wooden cross dangling from the rearview with the air freshener and reggaeton ratatatting from the speakers.

Dude, I want to go to a hotel near here, like not too far away. You got me? Like what hotels are there?

The driver, who they could barely see, said he would take them to Queens Boulevard.

And we can't go to your place, right? Skinner asked Zou Lei.

No, they could not do that, because she had roommates.

Good to go, Queens Boulevard.

But right when the driver put his foot on the gas, Skinner had to tell him to wait. Just hold it, thirty seconds. He jumped out and Zou Lei watched him run back into the KFC. Then he came out carrying something, and it was the assault pack with the pistol in it, which he had left forgotten under the seat where they were sitting.

The first time he had taken his shirt off in front of her—this was in the motel they went to in Rego Park—she had seen his yellowish gray torso in the lamplight, which cast a warmer color on him, giving his skin a life it didn't have on its own. She had not been paying attention. But then her hand had moved from his shoulder and touched his back. She withdrew and they stopped kissing for a moment. She gave him a little push to turn him so she could examine him in the lamplight. He said oh that.

She hadn't known what it was, had not connected it to the war. She had thought it was a birth defect or a contagious disease.

You can't like catch anything from it.

She said okay. She touched it. The tissue felt cold.

It hurts?

Not really.

She laid her palm on the dented puckered slick bumpy knotted flesh.

You get in the war?

He said yeah.

She made a tsking sound.

They shoot you in the body?

Shrapnel, he said, his back to her in the lamplight.

She examined him for a moment longer. Sighed. She moved her hand up above the damage and smoothed her palm across the death wings spread across his shoulders.

9

He found a room on Craigslist that was in her area, one stop further out on the Long Island Railroad. From Chinatown, he took the bus up Franklin and got off at 160th Street. They were all small houses under the power lines, with sneakers tossed over them. The curbs were worn-down, creating the illusion of pooled water sheeted over the ground, as after a rain. Through the trees, you could see the train tracks and the graffiti on the rocks.

One of the houses had its postage-stamp yard filled with statues and figurines—of elves, wise men, the crucifixion, leprechauns, animals, plastic flowers, a sleigh, a whirligig that spun in the wind. There were wind chimes on the porch and an American flag bumper sticker for 9/11 on the house. This was where he was going. Behind the lace curtains in the windows, the house had a dead appearance. There were angels too. In the upstairs window, the venetian blinds were broken.

Circumnavigating a pickup—there were no bumper stickers on the pickup—that had been left parked on the cracked sidewalk, he went to the side door and knocked.

When he didn't hear anything, he pressed the bell, but maybe he shouldn't have, because right then he heard somebody say, I'm coming.

The door was answered by a giant young woman in black, a head taller than he was.

There was an instant mood of cold dislike between them and they averted their eyes from each other. She did not greet him. All she said was, My mother's in the kitchen, and turned her back on him, becoming nearly invisible in the dark doorway in her huge black shirt. She was there and then she wasn't.

He heard thump-thump-thump and saw her cold bare white feet running up three steps, as if she were escaping from him, escaping to her apartment door with an outline of light around it. She pushed through it, giving him a glimpse of the interior before it swung shut:

a yellow lamp, a wooden table. In his boots, he tramped up the stairs after her and followed her inside.

Sitting at the wooden table, there was a woman with a cigarette in her mouth.

That wasn't the most polite thing in the world, that's all I'm saying.

He's fine, the giant girl said, not looking at Skinner.

You shut the door in his face.

No, I didn't, the daughter said, skirting the big wooden table and the circle of yellow lamplight and disappearing down a hallway with old dark pictures on the walls, and, when she was no longer visible, uttering something else in that indifferent voice of hers, but it was impossible to hear what she said and was she even talking to them.

Yeah, right. The woman rolled her eyes. Come in, she told Skinner. Don't be shy. Come in, come in.

She was enormous. He figured three hundred easy. She was wearing a purple velvet housedress and she had beefy shoulders and puffy hands, and from all the way across the kitchen, he could hear the air going into her lungs and coming out as cigarette smoke. Her skin had been sand-blasted. It was pitted, gray, and rough. Her hair was styled close to the sides and rose above her head in a kind of pompadour which rotated like the keel of a ship when she turned, her eye half-shut against the smoke from a cigarette, watching him as he approached.

Uh, hey, he said.

Hey, she said. Then she gestured with her eyes. She was directing him to the place across from her where she wanted him to sit at her table.

He drew the chair out and dropped into it, slouching with his knees spread. He looked across the table at her.

She stared back at him.

How's it goin? he asked.

It's goin. She was holding her cigarette up by her cheek, resting her thick elbow on the table. You made it here okay then?

You mean like finding the house?

Coming here and finding the address, yes.

Yeah, obviously, he said. That was nothing.

Well, I ask because it sounded like it was going to be a problem. It's a long way for some people.

Not that long.

Well, good. You're here.

As long as I know where something is, I know eventually I can get there.

Well, like I said, you made it.

Not a problem.

Good.

Once you've humped twenty miles a few times, getting to Queens isn't so hard.

Once what?

Humped. Humped a pack on your back for twenty miles. Army infantry?

Is that what you do?

That's what I did, yeah.

You were in the army?

Yeah, I just got out of the army I want to say like three weeks ago.

You just got out.

Yeah, I just got out.

I saw the garb, your coat—I thought you were military, but I wasn't sure if it was you or someone else I spoke with.

No, it was me.

Well, she said. Well, we owe you. That's my belief.

I just came back from three tours in Iraq, he said.

Three tours?

Not one. Not two. Three.

She shook her head. Goodness. My word. She looked over her shoulder in the direction of the refrigerator. I'd give you a beer if I had one. If I was still tending bar.

They stop-lossed me.

Where they don't let you go.

Yeah, they don't let you go, even though you're supposed to.

We've heard about that. It's been on the news.

You might have a doctor saying you need to get out, a med board or whatever, or a baby on the way or some shit, and they don't let you go even though, on your contract, they're supposed to. Legally, they're screwing you over. Legally, they're just saying screw this piece of paper, you're going back in.

They don't have people for the war.

I was supposed to be out a hell of a lot sooner, but they kept putting me back in. I had to do thirty-six months of combat duty.

Well—

That's supposed to be okay.

Well, you're out, thank God.

He shook his head.

You're out and in one piece, she said.

Yeah.

You served, thank God, and you're in one piece, and now you're out. She reached out and tapped her cigarette in the ashtray in the center of her table.

The woman said, We have a friend, a friend of my daughter's, the Gambias—down the block—they have a son in the army—the army or the marines, one of the two—and he's going over, over to Iraq. He's there already, come to think of it. It's the 82nd wing, the 82nd something.

Airborne.

That could be it. They're an elite, I know that much. It's a special platoon that they only take the top. I couldn't believe what these men do, when she told me. They have running and pushups and the usual, bad enough, but then she says they put rocks in the backpacks until the men start throwing up. The highest number of battles or wins, she was saying.

I wouldn't know.

They're famous outside the army, but I can't remember the name. They have a saying. His mother wears the t-shirt when she comes. Barbara. In her glory. I guess you wouldn't happen to know the saying? I wish I remembered it. She was telling me. I'd tell her to get me a shirt, but I don't think it'd fit me.

He didn't say anything.

Like I said, I'd offer you a beer. She raised her head to project her voice down the hallway and called out, Erin! and when there was no answer, she twisted her head around over the other shoulder, trying to turn herself towards the refrigerator. She pushed the table, which jolted on its legs, but her chair didn't move. He heard her take a breath and prepare to turn her body. Her foot slid on the linoleum.

You wanna do me a favor? Check the fridge, I should have a beer in there, at least one.

He got up and went to her refrigerator, which had the look of when a lot of people share it. It smelled like mayo turning hard. There was a cardboard case of Michelob, a twenty-four pack, dominating an entire shelf. He stuck his hand in the ragged hole in the cardboard and felt nothing in there until he had his arm all the way in and felt a single cold can all the way on the inside.

He cracked the can open, fell into his chair, mumbled thank you, slung his head back and drank off half of it. Wiped his chin. A belch snuck up on him—a loud one.

Better?

Whoops.

Don't mention it. I've raised two sons and a husband. You'd think it was prehistoric times.

Yeah, he said.

Believe me, they think it's Conan the Barbarian.

She grinned. A missing canine tooth.

Don't get me wrong, they're good Irish men, she said gravely.

He lifted his beer can six inches off the table and set it down. I hear ya.

Anyway! she said and stubbed her cigarette out. You're here for the room. She began to describe it in her strong, hoarse voice. It was clean, she told him. The paint was new. The neighborhood used to be Irish. Now it was take-your-pick.

He swallowed the rest of the beer, which mixed with the medication in his bloodstream, creating a tightening effect at the base of his skull.

Chinese, he said.

When she told him to go take a look at it, he said he didn't need to. I'd prefer if you did.

Hey, if it's got four walls, that's all I need. Is it a room?

Just go and look at it already. See what you think.

So he said yes ma'am and got to his feet and went down the stairs in the pitch dark to the basement, palm stroking the wall until he felt the switch.

There was a flat click and the lights came on, recessed inside acoustic ceiling tiles. He smelled Pine Sol. It was so quiet he could hear the refrigerator, the boiler ticking. His footfalls. The dried white Ajax in the metal sink next to the stove with the four electric coils. He opened the bedroom door and his shadow stretched out across the floor and touched the patterned sheets. The space was neat and empty. There was a plastic broom and dustpan in a corner.

Still carrying his beer can, he climbed back upstairs.

The woman acknowledged his return by reaching for her Slims and taking another one out.

Okay, so what's the story? You've seen it, what are we doin here?

It's good to go.

Is that a yes? Okay. Put your can down, for goodness sakes. Put it there—the trash is there. Siddown. Take a seat. She lit her smoke and tossed the Bic lighter on the table like a poker chip. Looked at him. Told him what the room was going for. He already knew. I know you know, I'm just going over it. When we get your money, you get the key.

He was like, no problem.

The smoke ribboned up from her cigarette. He noticed it was night outside the window.

She went over a few things. This was a family house. She didn't get involved in people's business. I don't expect men to be angels. That's not what I'm looking for, but there are limits. I'll put a man out—not that I would, unless it was an unusual situation.

Skinner said, I respect that.

She said good, and he was like no problem, whatever you say, to everything she said.

10

He would come to her job and wait until she was done and take her back in a gypsy cab because the bus took too long. She made her way down the carpeted stairs into the basement, Skinner behind her, saying Go on. She saw the bare walls in gray shadow, the empty kitchen. They went into his room and he turned on the light for her. The boiler smelled like copper in the closet. She went to the bed and sat and crossed her legs and leaned back on her hands, watching him kicking off his boots and tearing off his camouflage.

Here comes a wolf. I am afraid.

Much later in the night, they would open his room door and let out the heat that had been generated. Wearing only her t-shirt, she followed him out to the kitchen where it seemed cold by contrast. The light felt blinding and a reflection of the room covered the black rectangle of the window above the sink. He checked the empty cabinets for food. Negative, he said, perspiration shining at his temples. She drank water from the sink. We will eat water, she smiled and wiped her chin. No, we're not down to that yet. He ordered pizza and they ate it sitting at the small round table next to the fridge. I was starving, weren't you? She let him feed her. She licked his hand. They ate it all and he leaned back in his boxers and lit a cigarette, his hard white knee against her thigh.

When she went back into his room to get her jeans, she saw what they had done to the bed, the mauled sheet. His camouflage gear and clothes were all over the floor. He slept in his poncholiner. On the bedside table were his pills and his lifter's magazine and a strip of four condoms with blue wrappers. The room smelled like him and her, their sweat, latex, and tobacco. All about the room were empty beer cans he used as ashtrays. Under the bed, there was a used yellow wet latex condom. Another one was twisted in the poncholiner. Her eyes scanned over his cigarettes, his jeans. His boots were lying where he had kicked them off. A pair of blue faded cotton panties had fallen on them, hers.

He came up behind her and put an arm around her waist and put his face in her neck. She held his hand. His face smelled like tobacco. They rocked back and forth like that.

Oh, it makes me want to sleep, she said.

But she made herself put on her jeans, her hoodie and her denim jacket, tie her hair back with an elastic band, and tie up her worn-out sneakers. She checked the time on her cell phone and stuck it in her back pocket where it was outlined against her muscle.

Okay, I go.

I'm coming with you, he said. Wait up.

They went out into the quiet night and started hiking down Franklin Avenue until the small American houses gave way to ghetto buildings and then the huge cathedral of Chinatown, over the hill through the dark trees and down the long block that extended out to the freeway like a jetty.

Now you have to go all the way back, she said.

That don't matter. I can't sleep anyway.

She told him to be careful. They told each other I'll see you tomorrow. He stood guard until she was inside and the bolt clicked.

Then she crept upstairs, convinced that the other tenants were awake and monitoring her arrival. If she lost her balance taking off her sneakers in the dark, they would think she was drunk. As quietly as she could, she opened her accordion door. The sheds were built open at the top like changing rooms, and when she pulled the chain, her light disturbed her neighbor, who muttered behind the plywood. She switched the light off and kneeled down on her broken mattress, on her coverlet bought in Chinatown, showing teddy bears in bowties. By feel, she plugged her cell phone into the charger, her link to him, and the screen lit up indigo in her hands for several moments shining through her fingers.

hi mom im fine here in NY as planned. nothing going on/wrong remember fox news been wrong before I know your right about school, gi bill etc. i have enough maturity to know when your right just not mature enough to do it yet. my time well spent - one thing i learned in the army

    brad

———

You has the dish? The cooking pot?

Wearing only her t-shirt, she opened the cabinet beneath the sink. The only thing in the cabinet was a container of Ajax. She opened the refrigerator, seeing nothing but their pizza box, and closed it.

The bathroom door was open and he was standing with his back to her, his legs apart, the cigarette in his mouth moving as he talked. He was urinating loudly and she couldn't hear what he was saying. When he was done, he shook himself and turned around, still shaking himself and flipped himself back inside his boxers as he came walking out to her.

Pots and pans?

I check but I don't find nothing.

He went through the kitchen opening and closing the cupboards one after the other and banging them shut.

She stood up on her toes to look inside the cupboards, her full bare calves flexing. Her t-shirt, which said I'm Fallin' for Juicy, rode up to the edge of her rear.

Does that answer your question?

She tsked and folded her arms.

The typical boy. No dish. What you will eat? Maybe I will buy for you. Pot, dish, bowl.

During the day, he bought beer and condoms at a gas station on Northern Boulevard and they drank together at the round table in his kitchen. He did not buy groceries. She got drunk and rubbed his hair. So cute. She pointed at the empty shelves. No cooking pot. No nothing. You are just like man. Make your muscle. He flexed his arm and she felt it. Like my father. How's that? Acts like man. She leaned in and stared fixedly at him, her eyes thick with liquid. Good man. Skinner agreed the way you do with someone drinking. He give everything to me. To us. To my mother. Everything he will do for us, even he has nothing. He is poor man. She told Skinner one of her small stories about things her dad had done. There were just a few to share because he hadn't stayed with them very much.

He give everything to me.

I know, Skinner agreed.

Tears ran out of her eyes.

It's all right.

She took another drink from her can and finding it empty, cracked open another. Whoa. Skinner stuck his cigarette in the side of his mouth and took it away from her. She took it back and took a slug out of it. Okay, he said. There's always more beer. He took it away from her and put it as far away as he could reach.

She had started sobbing, her face in her arms crossed on the table. He reached over and squeezed her shoulder and shook it gently. You're gonna be okay. She said something he couldn't hear. She repeated it:

I never going to see him again.

It sucks. I know.

He helped her into his room and put his poncholiner around her.

But she was happy after all. It was a long time ago, losing him. I drink too much. She indicated their empties all around the place. Shed blood, not tears was the rule in the northwest—except if you were drinking. Or you could show yourself through a song. However, she did not sing. She sang Skinner's name at work and the boss-wife said, What are you so happy about?

Frogs, she said.

She showed herself through her actions, by coming over to his basement every day after work and then going all the way home at night. I have energy a lot. She did not buy him pots and pans. She was not the mother type. When she collected their empties one day and took them to the redeemer, it was because she was enterprising, not because she felt she should clean up after him. With the dollar and change she made, she bought a chicken skewer and saved it for them to eat together, half each, the meat cold by the time she had walked there with it through the small houses covered in Spanish graffiti. She was logging all these miles and it was good. Spring was coming, the big wheel of the city starting to turn.

I can't get rid of you. Maybe it's the pizza. Or maybe it's something else you're getting from me, he said.

It was his camouflage, she told him. His army jacket. It was his poncholiner. It's your boots. I love your boots.

Howbout this? he asked and pulled his shirt up. Is it the shrapnel in my back? Is it my war?

I love your war, she said.

11

WHEN I AM A little kid, my father tells me all about it how to be the soldier. There is a lot of duty that you must perform. All the men live in poor conditions, but they must not mind it. The people live in poor conditions, so the soldier has to be the same. He cannot have more than they do. He will work to give them a better life. So they say: we are like the out-of-town cousin. When he comes to town, he comes to stay with us and we feed him. Only after he is fed does the army eat its dinner. So the army is skinny and society is fatter.

A long time ago, the whole country is in disaster and we have enemies inside and outside the border. United States, Soviet Union, Japan all attacked because our country is weak. Criminals take advantage of this weakness to steal from us. The army saved us and punished the criminals.

The people and the army are joined together, though they are not the same. Everyone when he gets to be eighteen is supposed to serve the army. I want to serve the army when I am eighteen. Actually, I cannot do it. There are so many Chinese, it is hard to join the army. Even though it is very hard, it is a good job and everyone wants to do it.

I don't know about the American army, but in the People's Liberation Army, it is very strict. The soldiers come from poor places and they are all used to it. Some of them have never seen a toilet before in their lives. Don't know how to read.

But in those days, the quality of the soldiers is very high. They can survive on just a small ration of food. I don't know about the American army if it can do that. The Americans have big bodies and I think they would be too hungry. But in China we are used to it.

The situation is changing since I am a kid. Before, we don't have any technology. Now, the technology is getting stronger. We can use cyberwarfare—it's very popular now. And we have many nuclear weapons, almost equal. We depend less on the individual soldier. Maybe, as we become greater, the individual is getting weaker.

Whenever disaster happens to our country, the army can do its best to save the people. If the river floods or the land slide. It happens countless times in our history. When it happens, no one will save us but the army.

Really, all the people must thank them or we would not be able to exist. When a farmer drives a truck filled with vegetables, the oil to run the motor is coming from the pipeline. I think if you are a woman in the market and you buy vegetables, you must thank my father.

I don't think anyone remembers this. Even I forget, but I shouldn't. Everything comes from somewhere.

I'm saying my father, but of course it wasn't him alone. I mean the Lanzhou Regiment and the Western Development Project are responsible for providing oil. They made sure we got it instead of Russia.

They built the pipeline in the beginning with no equipment except shovels, picks, and baskets. The oil is covered by a mountain range called the Onion Mountains. If you can imagine, they dug through the mountains. It's a little bit like when the Chinese built the railroad here, only in this case, they were serving their own people. So much dynamite was used that the herdsmen were superstitious. They believed a devil is trying to terrify them. Then they got used to them after a while. They called the soldiers the Thunders. This gave my dad an idea. He named me Thunder for good luck.

In China, if you ask what is the most dangerous job, everyone will tell you the job of coal miner is number one. The truth is, this job was even worse. Sometimes you can be working and someone is putting dynamite right next to you, and you don't even know it until it goes off. The mountain can collapse at any time. Once, it fell in and trapped a lot of men. My father is lucky that he went to drink some water. Just at that place where he was before, it fell in.

Immediately, they all try to save the ones who are trapped. I think in a rich country, someone would bring some special equipment. Today, maybe in China they can have this equipment as well, but at the time, it is impossible. All that they can do is dig with tools in their hands. Of course, there's no way it can work and the friends of theirs die. Actually, they have to let them die. The leaders cannot waste the time to save them. They were ordered to go back to work.

It's the same as war. The country is in a war to modernize, and many people have to give up their lives.

Including my father had to give his life. So, by what he did, he taught me what it's all about to be a hero.

Look, it's me and you.

Yeah.

Macky D.

This is my screensaver.

She reached over his arm, her breast against his arm, and clicked to the next photograph. It was Skinner with New York behind him at night. Empire Building, she said. She studied the solitary white face in the camera's flash, surrounded by the black sky and galactic skyline, a week before she had met him.

Then she clicked again and saw dull land and sky, blue over brown, dark palms, a blurred shadow of a vehicle, a striding figure in a robe. She clicked again and saw a haze of dust hanging over mud buildings. A mosque, a truck driving by in the glare. A goat lying on a rubble of bricks in a ditch, the blur of a child carrying a bucket, and a soldier looking the other way.

He had gotten silent. She kept clicking.

Those are the guys.

An angry face in a helmet. She clicked. Someone giving the camera the finger. A laugh. A picture of a military vehicle with the hatches open and gear everywhere as if it had been torn apart in a hurricane. The soldiers' heads were down. They looked confused and disorganized. A focused man spoke on the radio.

The next picture was of a soldier sitting in a wooden latrine closet holding a roll of toilet paper in his filthy coal miner's hands. He was speaking at the camera.

Damn. That's Sconnie.

There was a picture of what was a human foot lying on the sand and another picture in which the object was shown from a greater distance and you couldn't tell it was someone's foot. But you could see something else, a pile of drenched clothing at a distance. In the pile, she made out a beard, a face—she thought. Blurred soldiers smoking. She saw animals, dogs. A woman covered in a nun-like robe, except for her fearsome face in mid-yell, her thick hands lifted and about to come down in the act of hurling curses at the picture taker.

She tapped the key again. She saw a platoon all sleeping like homeless men in shallow graves that they had dug in clay, lying in a spill of camouflage, each man's boots next to him.

As she kept clicking, the disorder of everything seemed to reassemble itself in reverse. She saw them in shades, posing with their weapons, dressed as if for the beach in flip-flops and towels, sunglasses and guns.

There was a photograph of a young man asleep with his mouth open and someone holding a hotdog in front of his crotch and putting it to the other's mouth.

Neither she nor Skinner laughed. She murmured, kept clicking. A photograph appeared of a young man, shirtless, in motion, close to the camera. He was extremely fit. Lines separated all the muscles of his torso. A gold light surrounded the subject. He bore a likeness to the man sitting next to her on the bed. A cousin, she thought. But his tattoos were the same.

Yeah, that's me, he said. I know I'm not as good now.

Seeing a magazine under his bed, she said, Hm, what's this? And she picked it up and started flipping through it. It contained pictures of people having sex in high resolution. There were two women having sex with one man, and two men having sex with one woman.

Aw that's nothing serious. Well, you know what that is.

She knew what porn was, yes, she did. Chinese men had these kinds of magazines, showing Japanese women tied up with clothesline, men's hands pinching their breasts. They included educational articles on the mechanics, significance, and health requirements of various sexual acts, such as so-called flute-blowing, which was described as the ultimate way to show appreciation of the man's yang force by a devoted female on her knees. Bachelors read these stories when they came home from restaurant work and needed to relieve themselves. That was just men for you. The sound of them masturbating came through the plywood walls when she was trying to sleep.

The Western magazine she was now looking at was a Club International. With a raised eyebrow, she examined the scenes of double penetration and gazed long and skeptically at a woman sticking out her tongue with a proud and satisfied expression showing that the men had ejaculated in her mouth.

At length, Zou Lei tossed the magazine back on the floor. This kind of thing was fine for other people, but it was not for her.

You sure? Skinner asked, and she hit him. But he was serious.

You might not always know yourself.

Well, anyway, he said, take a look at this. Check this out. He stuck his cigarette in his mouth and rummaged on the floor, eyes slitted against his smoke, and found his Ironman and opened it for her. See this is what I'm doin now. And she joined him in looking at the lifters: athletes dividing their anatomy into logical sections and applying resistance to each section in accordance with a disciplined schedule. The lifter on the cover was straining and bulging, his skin straining and flushed red, his teeth bared in a grimace of ultimate effort, his face flexed and flushed and bulging with veins as if even his forehead were yet another slab of muscle.

Good, she said. How much is the weight?

He's got like 650 on the bar. See it bend. You don't get like that on MREs.

How can he do it? He use drug?

He showed her the pages of supplements. Creatine, glucosamine, mass builder—that's a protein bomb. When it goes off, you just get big.

She pretended to stick a needle in her vein and made a popping sound with her mouth.

This is the shit I'm talkin about. He tapped it with his cigarette. I gotta remember to get this.

You will look like him?

I probably won't.

She took the magazine from Skinner and turned the pages until she came to Ms. Fitness Arizona, in turquoise spandex and white Reeboks, doing donkey calf-raises on a Cybex machine. There she was doing barbell squats, her dark eyes on the ceiling. She looked Mexican or Middle Eastern. And there she was on the beach in a bikini—hooking the spaghetti strap with her thumb—and just a touch of lip gloss, the waves around her thighs.

Zou Lei flexed her legs and looked at herself. Hey. They laughed. Not bad.

I like her.

You look like her.

She has very beautiful clothes.

———

One day when she wasn't working, Zou Lei had Skinner meet her on Roosevelt Avenue. His grown-out hair rose up stiff and uncombed from his head, no longer military. It was a clear day after a rain and the trash was pulped on the street.

They hiked out of Chinatown until they were far enough away to see the red lacquered Chinese eaves and the fire escapes and then kept going. There was no plan, they just walked, walking down by the expressway and the autorepairs whose signs were in Chinese. The road took them by a cemetery, then a stretch of little houses with pitched roofs and falling-down siding.

The air was bright and cool and warm—a deceptive day, since they were still in winter. She thought she could smell the springtime in the street, in the air rising from the asphalt and from the soil in the broken bricks.

They fell into a rhythm, going for miles, and she lost herself, their hoofs beating the drum of the earth as they marched.

When they made it to the rise where Jewel Avenue crossed over the fields and they could see in all directions—the old condominium towers, the sheets of water, the rooftops and the distance—they stopped and looked at it all. They were at the center of a wheel. Skinner put his arms around her.

That's a view, he said.

In it, she beheld what was possible. The city was uncontained. It covered a massive area and graded out into the world. There was no definite end at the horizon. There were more buildings, miles of them covering the earth on into the distance. She saw the areas of trees, the shade of wood, the intricate fuzziness of the branches from this distance in among the houses. The highways—massive, industrial, and lonely—were to her left. To her right, there seemed to be still another city and then, past it, the skyline of Manhattan, which she identified by the Empire State Building, which she could cover with the tip of her finger. And she had a view between tenement rooftops of one of the suspension bridges that connected Manhattan to the other boroughs. It was ten cities all together. She saw things from this elevation that were normally hidden from her. In the direction of the water to the north, she saw a green dome, which had to be a mosque. She saw the spire next to it among the confused rooftops, fire escapes, and water towers. It was blocked and revealed again by the centipede of a subway pulling by. There were splinters of metal embedded in the blue stratosphere to the south: planes coming head on. Passing over her and Skinner, they elongated and became commercial jets, tracking towards the airport on the water. She saw the complicated shape of the shoreline, the lack of contrast between the brown city and the water, as if it were all part of one thing, which it was, the geography of the earth, which you could move across as you lived.

She asked him where he had been on this disk of territory that they were overlooking. You go there? It's a Bronx.

I came in there. I went like this, he said, pointing out the trajectory he had walked across the brown horizon. Down to right around there where all them buildings are at.

I goes like this: down, down, down to Chinatown. You cannot see. I start up there—she turned thirty degrees to the east—where is Connecticut, all the way. I been out, out, out to there, to Long Island, Riverhead…

She squinted in the sun. Look! She patted his arm and got him to look where she was pointing to the west. I work there, where it's Nanuet.

What'd you do out there?

Restaurant. She held his camouflage. If you keep going to that way, west, west, west, you will be the ocean, then China. No one will understand you. Everyone will be confusing. Maybe it's different for you. In the morning, get up early to get the water. Burn the fire. The people is a billion. It is more big than here. Ride the bus. The train. Truck. Camel. Sleep the ground. See the mountain.

12

She looked at him in his roughed-up boots and the American flag on his sleeve—and began looking for another job to increase her productivity on days when she wasn't working at the noodle stand. This demanded that she ride the subway with the cops, but she felt that she could risk it.

Among the jobs she tried, she collected bottles and cans and redeemed them at the Beer Center, a recycler on Parsons Boulevard across from a factory that made fan belts and timing belts.

On two occasions, she distributed coupons for the Western Beef grocery store, tossing the rolled-up booklets onto porches of row houses above the Grand Central Parkway. The rolled-up booklets were fitted into plastic sleeves. She pulled armloads of them out of the back of a van and heaped them in a shopping cart and rattled up and down the block, the only one who ran.

The other guys were homeless drug addicts in True Religion jeans. The man who operated the crew wore a gold chain and had no voice. He was completely and permanently hoarse. She outworked the others, but he didn't pay her any more than them. He talked on the same level with the other guys. On the way back in the van, they would talk about buying a bottle.

Pointing out the window at the liquor store, they'd tell him, Lemme out here! and he'd pull over.

She got out too and didn't go back. She got a number out of the Chinese paper and shortly started selling DVDs.

The man who gave her the DVDs took care to avoid arrest. He would not give her his name, so she couldn't rat him out if she got caught. All she knew about him was that he was from Wenzhou in Zhejiang Province and people from Wenzhou knew how to survive. On the phone, he would say to meet him in the doorway and she would go to the place he meant. He would drive up in an Expedition, his ball cap on sideways, and give her the goods. He looked like a manager from a Chinese factory in wintertime—all dark clothes, down vest, fingerless gloves, smoking Mild Seven cigarettes. His face was lopsided, the result of ingesting pesticide as a child, which gave him the knowing look of someone who wasn't going to be fooled again.

When she went out selling, she rode the train in her navy tracksuit, the satchel over her shoulder, holding the bootleg movies fanned out like playing cards in their clear plastic envelopes, murmuring:

Deeweedee, deeweedee. Hello, deeweedee.

What you got? the truants asked.

Nah, they said and gave her her movies back. A working man in corrective glasses shook his head, uninterested in kung fu comedies like Dream Return to Tang Dynasty.

Having made one sale, she got off at Tremont Avenue in the Bronx, turned her back to the platform, counted the cash, and hid it. The graffiti on the station tiles said Ca$h $mells. Beast. LLL. Byron. Ruthless AKA Jie Burn.

She caught the train going the other way and took it all the way to Brooklyn, getting off downtown by the federal court buildings. There were cops in neoprene gloves and balaclavas and Arabs selling shishkawap, coal smoke blowing in the street, police barricades in front of the wide white buildings that looked like the White House.

For a time, she strolled casually, watching the cops to see if they were writing tickets to street vendors.

Then she went into a Wendy's and went table to table flashing her movies. Big black couples told her no politely. A woman whose child was dressed the same as her boyfriend down to tiny sneakers and a denim hat told him: Jamal, stop playing.

A man asked if she had any kung fu.

They looked through what she had together. This one is kung fu, she told him. He said this is all right, but I want Jackie Chan.

Jet Li is good, she tried to tell him.

Jackie Chan is my man.

Howbout this one?

She held up a Hong Kong movie called Black Society in Chinese and Buttonman in English.

Gotta be Jackie Chan, he said. Let me tell you what's wrong with this here. They doing side effects in this movie. Jackie Chan don't have no side effects. He do all his own stunts. Look here—and he made a sudden flurry of blocks and strikes, smacking his own arms and shouting: Hut!

He wheeze-laughed. You see that, baby? Look here! He showed her his knuckles, which were calloused like the palms of his hands. All this here is from my Shaolin style. He took her hand and had her touch his hand. I never took no shit off these gunslingers out here.

Okay. I get for you. Next time.

I tell them, if you bad, bring it, thundercat!

She went back outside the restaurant. There was construction hammering in the street, a giant truck with cable on a reel. A man from Lahore, Pakistan, a city at the end of the Karakoram Highway which came out of western China, was selling fruit on the corner of Fulton Street. His beard was red. He had a piece of cardboard that he prayed on. She watched an NYPD patrol car drive by him and the driver look at him, but they didn't look at her. She felt throughout her body that she was protected.

The broad-shouldered American blacks rolling along Fulton Street looking in the windows of Jimmy Jazz wore big leather jackets with wings and eagles and griffins engraved across the shoulders in much the same pattern as Skinner's tattoo.

He's with you, she believed.

The NYPD would not stop her. If they scanned her, they would see an American flag on the scan. She beat her drum and his shadow flew before her. He raised her above the iron ground so her feet would not be torn. He kept her from being destroyed and defiled in a shitsmeared cell.

On Pennsylvania Avenue, there were low buildings, the huge space of the winter sky, a fence with a faded basketball behind it. She climbed through a hole in the mesh, stepping over empty twenties and forties, and cut downhill in the dead weeds, a figure in a hood and jeans, convinced she would not fall, and stood on the median beneath the interchange. When the cars stopped for the light, she went out to the driver's side windows holding out her movies.

A woman bundled in a hat and hood and plaid jacket was selling roses. The light changed, and they went back to the median.

Con cuidado, the woman told her.

Yes. Sí.

And you watching la policía. Siempre.

The woman had a pretty face and conspicuous blackheads dotting her cheeks. She said she had a shopping cart that she could push away if the cops came, and she seemed to be saying that she had a van that she could put it in, but Zou Lei didn't see one. The cops wrote her fines: one hundred, one-fifty, maybe two hundred.

Yes. Sí. But what about that?

The woman looked at herself where Zou Lei was pointing. She had a vendor's license in a wallet strung around her neck. She held it in her mitten and said something about it. Then she tucked it in her plaid jacket pocket.

It cost money? Dinero is a lot?

The woman shook her head, talking Spanish. It was not a real license.

Zou Lei bounced on her toes, waiting for the cars to stop, rubbing her hands.

Mucho frío.

Zou Lei nodded, Yes, sí, she knew.

She was saying to herself: I will sell one more.

You could do anything—sell toys, oranges, ice in the summer, phone cards so that people could call home. Singapore. Philippines. Yemen. Iraq. Ivory Coast. Salvador. You could give out flyers for all-you-can-eat, compramos d'oro—get a cart and roll it over hill and dale now that he is with you.

She could take out a loan and buy a truck and then be truly free. And she fantasized that she and Skinner lived on the road together traveling from city to city, selling what they bought and traded. She saw them wearing sheath knives and cowboy hats and riding horses in a sun-filled land outside the reach of the authorities.

13

HE WANTED HER TO know that he was working too. I'm gonna follow the program that they got in here, start doin two-a-days. Doin my protein. All he had to do was find a gym without stupid rules and it was on.

He was from a place called Shayler, which he described as pretty basic. There were bars, Lutheran churches, and a 7-11. When he said home, he pronounced it hoeme. The houses went up a hill, like a mining hill, close to West Virginia. Under the highway going into town were mountains of gray gravel. A lot of bars, a lot of drinking. Steel Town football was big. People were pretty racist. But they were open about it. They could be friends with anyone. That's just how they were. Real patriotic. His house had a raccoon under it. They were poor. It was a poor area, basically. His mother, a lean energetic woman with short blond hair, had sat in their trailer reading a Reader's Digest and drinking vodka out of a blue plastic cup. She was really big on anything unusual. Nothing unusual ever happened for the most part—except drinking. When he was five, probably his first memory, his mother showed him a picture of a two hundred-pound dog in TV Guide and said, Look at that. You ever see anything like that before? He would have signed up even if the recruiters hadn't come right to his high school. 9/11 was the big reason, but he would have gone anyway, just to do something.

As he talked, he had his tattoo-lettered arm around her and held his burning cigarette away from her while he smoked. He had played high school football, he said, and he remembered the stadium and the numbers on the score cards and the all-black team they played from the gangbanger area up the hill. A gas station outside the stadium was where they turned. All the white cars went down the hill to the white bars, and all the black cars went up the hill to the black bars on Lafayette Hill.

Did you have a lot of boyfriends?

No.

How do you say that?

Nanpengyou.

Nan-pong-yow. Did you?

No. I fight with boys. What about you father?

What about him?

You don't tell me about him.

Skinner told her that once when he was seventeen, thereabouts, he was in a bar across the river and he realized the guy taking a leak at the urinal next to him was his father. He pictured him: Carhartt jacket and pants, incredibly hard hand when they shook hands, drinking with two women at the bar. That was his father. What about yours? Oh, yeah, I forgot. You told me all about him. The Chinese soldier. But girls? said Skinner. There'd been this one girl he'd liked, and the whole school had known he liked her. It had become a story that everyone talked about. It was the closest he ever came to being famous. When he would see her in front of school, they'd stare at each other with all this social pressure on them. She would just say hiiiiiiiii, Brad. Nothing more than that ever happened. He never told her, I like you. There was no point in saying this since everyone else already knew it, including her. It was fifth grade and it was the beginning of the rumor mill.

Did she break your heart?

Oh yeah. She tore it in two.

She weighed whether to tell him she had been to jail. You know, I am surprising that you like me.

Why's that?

Because I am old.

No, you're not.

The immigrant.

So?

You can have American girl. The yellow hair. The tall beautiful woman.

I don't know if you noticed, but I'm not that tall. Nobody like that's gonna go out with me.

Yes, she would. Of course. She will love you.

Love's what makes the world go round for some people, Skinner said.

What makes the world go round?

To be honest with you, war.

War?

Actually, I'd say money first. Money, then war. Everybody's all, like, patriotism, the flag, all this happy horseshit.

Society need brave men and women to fight.

At her request, he rolled over so she could look at his scar again. She said she saw it getting better.

She put her foot behind her on a park bench and did one-legged lunges, carrying her weight on the working leg, hands clasped behind her head, eyes looking up at the sky over Queens, whispering the repetitions, seeing if she would do them all today. She had strong legs. She did not have a gym, she had the park. She had a schedule of exercises, days, sets, and reps, a page from Skinner's magazine with Ms. Fitness on it folded in her bag at home. And she would learn from anyone she saw, and there was a lot to learn that people had invented when they had nothing else but their imaginations. The Latins brought work gloves to the park and did calisthenics routines learned in correctional facilities, different kinds of chin-ups, pushups with the hands wide, hands out front, lat pushups, diamond push-ups, one-armed pushups, Cuban pushups, incline pushups with the feet up on a bench. And then they jogged around, arms beefed-up and swollen. She did pushups and step-ups on a bench and back extensions by the bars and then she got down on the concrete and did a splits, holding herself off the ground, and then jumped back up, her thighs tight.

Dirty guys kicked through the weeds looking for dope bags, swinging their legs like scythes. Women in sagging sweatpants walked their pit bulls, talking to men from the houses on Elder Avenue in rasping voices, smoking while they talked. He's a Red-nose. Half Rednose, half American Pit. They're twins. The other one is Lucky. This is Flash. He wants his mommy. Be careful. He's a sweetie, but he bites.

Through the diamond fence, a woman with a hospital cane and a purse began yelling at an old stooped woman half her size. You lost my keys! You lost my keys! I can't get in without my keys.

The Chinese arranged themselves in military ranks and played waltz music. A recorded voice said: yi... er... san... si... They spread their arms and lifted imaginary handfuls of water, earth, raised their arms and spread their fingers and let it rain down on their upturned heads, to cadence. In the cities of China, travelling monks climbed off grain trucks and performed in putties and slippers. They broke bricks over their shaved heads and hit each other in the stomachs with sledge hammers. They directed their qi to a point over their hearts and bent swords against their chests. Feral teenaged disciples walked on their hands for a furlong, performed handstand pushups, did them clapping with screams of effort. Villagers watched open-mouthed, the roots of their teeth showing in sun-wizened faces. The Chinese police watched the villagers to make sure that not too many of them were gathering in one place at one time and that all their activities were healthy, politically healthy.

For the first time in her life, Zou Lei saw the members of a banned sect, the Falungong, in Kissena Park. They were wearing matching white tracksuits and stood in a ring and they turned the dharmic wheel to New Age music playing on an audio player. This wheel was an orb that existed in the cosmos, and they also had miniature wheels in each of their abdomens. They believed that the act of turning the wheel would bring them health, cure their cancer, and change history. In Queens they were free to change history. In China they went to detention centers, labor camps. Ultimately, through their exercises, they would be able to throw the business-suited men, those bestial criminals, in Beijing right out of power, they said. The sect members had a great deal of literature and photographic evidence of what the Chinese authorities did in the name of state security—the kidnapping, sexual torture, organ harvesting, and so on.

14

On Cantonese radio, she heard an ad for a shopping center called the Flushing Mall, located on 38th Road behind the Sheraton LaGuardia. The boss-wife said that's where they're making money. After work, Zou Lei went against the crowd towards Roosevelt Avenue and cut through a parking lot. She crossed the street and went inside a building—a general purpose office-retail space—with gold characters on the roof next to an Indian-run Holiday Inn.

It was mobbed with kids, fifteen-year-old girls shouting, marching with their arms straight, screaming, telling off boys. They sat on the tables texting, wearing Eskimo boots, their jeans riding low. Adult men lifted their heads like horses, their long, hollow-cheeked skulls, staring. Putting their faces back in bowls, eyes over the rim. Plastic bags, black hair, and sneakers, eating with their long sharp fingers. The counters were spot-lit. You could see the wooden faces of the women in aprons, standing, waiting, waiting to serve somebody, and, behind them, the kitchens steaming like public showers.

She went up to the first counter and said she was looking for a job.

Talk to him. To that one.

The boss had his hair Brylcreemed back. He was sitting in front of a tray of soaking wadded paper napkins, tendon, lotus, coughed-up tripe, wearing a pink shirt with the collar up. In the open V of his collar, he had a piece of jade. My name called Polo, he said. Coughed. Wiping his mouth and reddened nose. He had bracelet of wooden beads, the large hands of a northerner. He was slim and tall and placid.

Where you work before?

I work everywhere before. From here to Carolina. Fast food. I learn everything, work very hard. I'm fast, running. Open gate, light fire, pour oil, put the kettle on, dice meat, mince meat, parse meat, make rice, make sauce, pick greens, make dough, make dumplings, make french fries, carry in goods—because I'm strong, even though I'm female. I've had military training. Take order, shout order, deliver takeout, count the till, dump trash, sweep floor, mop floor, wipe counter, wash dish, bowl, pot, dipper, cleaver, shovel, chopstick, spoon, turn out the fire, shut the light, lock the gate. Every day, work hard, sleep sweet.

You understand Cantonese?

Of course, she lied.

He stood up, leaving his tray. She picked it up and dumped it for him.

That doesn't matter, he said.

I like to work, she said.

He led her in past the counter. The other women stared at her. She had a glimpse under the lights of wolf hair, eye shadow.

I need people who can handle the big menu. We expand the item. His voice was drowned out by the exhaust fan as they went through the kitchen. Someone, his forearms pale and wet with sweat, jerked a wok, heaved it, and a burst of flame came up.

They went out the back into a corridor that smelled like garbage, barrels of it, guts and rice. Kick marks, shoe treads on the walls. The caramelized filth, the dumpster. She followed him inside a storeroom where he started digging through papers in an empty Sun Disc vegetable box.

You want the job, right?

Of course.

There was a health inspection certificate taped-up next to the Han May calendar. The typed-in name was Eugene Cheung D.B.A. Fong and Associates. Through the walls, she heard the people working on the other side.

What is your surname?

Zou.

Given name?

Lei.

She watched him write it on a piece of paper that already had handwriting and phone numbers all over it, underlined, circled, and crossed-out.

Not that Lei.

Not flower-bud Lei?

No. No grass top.

This—lightning-thunder Lei? He wrote well.

Yes.

That's not right for a girl. Are you a boy?

That's the way they named me.

They want the son, I think. Or they do not recognize literacy. Many Chinese don't recognize literacy. Right?

She didn't say anything.

The Chinese people want a son. In America, girl power, right? You hear about it?

Man-woman equality.

You believe the girl power?

Yes, she said.

I think so, he smiled. The business expanding. This area getting bigger. A lot of money comes in. This just the beginning, so we try to change, capture the new wave. We import the ocean flavors, beef, eel, everything sa-cha. We want the team, like the army. He made a claw to show what he meant. Take over the market, make the market share bigger, bigger, bigger—

spreading his fingers wider each time. He seemed to be conducting music. This is the time opportunity, real opportunity. You look: the Olympics will be to China. How great!

What is the pay like?

It is rational, he said.

Minimum wage?

Of course. That's the law. I have to obey the law. You have to obey the law. Everyone has to obey the law in society.

He asked for her working papers, knowing all along, she thought, that she didn't have them.

This is a very severe problem, he said. If I hire you, I have risk.

Right? he insisted, when she remained blank.

I have risk. Very serious. If I have risk, who is responsible? You have to be responsible. If I give you the break, you give me the break. Only fair. So the salary will be adjusted. He wrote it on the paper, circled it. This salary.

She did the math in her head.

One more dollar, she said.

He smiled, no.

I give you break, he said.

Really. Do not be disappointed. I tell you something, the truth. This a lot of money.

15

Her first day, Zou Lei arrived in the food court early and had been waiting for half an hour before she heard the exhaust fans come on in the kitchens in the back. Then, with a snap, the lights came on. She heard a rustling plastic bag and someone banging things around and then saw a woman with a mask-like face moving around under the lights.

Good morning, Zou Lei said. I'm here to work.

The woman snorted and took a drink from a plastic tub of yellow liquid. Zou Lei looked around. She waited. She couldn't see the man who had hired her. She ducked in under the counter.

Nobody invite you, the woman said, a wonton hanging from her lip.

I'm here to work.

You just remember that.

They made her wait. The register girl came in and said, Could you move? Flung her purse on a shelf under the counter. In the back, a wok was getting beaten with a shovel. They brought the fish-tofu out. Stinky tofu is mad good, the register girl said, glitter in her wolf hair. She held the skewer between her acrylic tips. They talked in slang she couldn't follow. Everything was number nine. She would learn it meant cock or dick. You can't stand there. Zou Lei moved again. The cook came out and slammed another tub into the steam table, purple burn marks on his arms.

Go hang that up. You can't work like that. They meant her jacket. The peg was under the security camera. The woman threw away her soup. I the supervisor. She had a glazed white face, slanted eyebrows painted on her forehead—a Cantonese. Where your apron at? Come on. She showed Zou Lei the fryers, the salad dressing, the congee, meat paste—she flipped the metal lids and pointed, whacked it with a ladle—custard! Don't forget it! Yanked a crate from underneath a rack. You need a garbage bag, you get it here. Kicked it back. Fried leg, she pointed. There was meat bobbing in water. Fishball. They stepped around a bucket. The exhaust was going. The cook banged a wok over the gas fire. Sink, wok, knife, scrubber. You chop at this table, not over there.

Come on! she said. She took Zou Lei to the storeroom with the hanging rags, the gallon cans of starch.

Time schedule, she pointed. A clipboard with a ballpoint taped to a string. You check it every day before you go.

What did you say?

What?

I don't understand so well, Zou Lei said.

I say already.

Say what?

Ask somebody else if you don't get it.

She was given a uniform shirt, a visor, and an orange apron. You have to pay for that.

When she asked what? they thought she was putting up an argument.

Because we all did. Nothing free in this life.

They sent her with a cart to go and get the trays. The basement was roaring. She collected everybody's trays in the food court. No, only ours! they said when she returned. Basic common sense. No one had told her. She was sweating. There was other people's food all over her hands. It's okay, the little one said, the one called Sunnie. Just separate them and put the other ones back.

She made up for it—she tried. She hauled the dishware off in tubs. There was Chinese techno playing overhead. Watch out! the register girl snapped at her. Okay. She stepped around the bucket. The tub weighed almost more than she could take. Her fingers slipped—she caught it with her knee—and swung it down into the sink. They were yelling orders from the front. Sa-cha. The cook repeated sa-cha.

You know how to wash? She nodded. She stuffed the chopsticks in a vented can. Some stuck through the vents. She shook them and rapped them in place and blasted them with the sprayer. It threw water on her orange apron. Steam came up. The cook snatched the sprayer from her and blasted the dishes. Water thudding off the metal sink. He squeezed the soap, and bubbles came out floating sideways, quivering, heavy, rainbows on them. He wheeled away. She took on the dishes with a scrubber. Fast, fast, fast! he shouted. He was slamming pots around, wiping down the stainless table, whipping back and forth with his rag. She was pulling out the plates, one, two, three, water raining off. Her arms were wet. The blast of the water thrummed on the steel sink. Everything was wet, the rubber treads on the floor were wet. She could smell the black muck being worked out of the fissures and moldings, silted in the drain trap.

The rush was over. In front, they were standing around drinking cups of soda.

No one said anything to her. She poured a full-sized Coca-Cola, no ice, and drank it straight down, gasping. Now that was good. The sugar flashed inside her like sunshine in the desert.

She took meat from the steam table and made him a care package. She filled a Styrofoam shell with rice, beef, dumplings, and put it in a plastic bag and hid it on the shelf by the cornstarch and took it to him after work. She had only one plastic fork and he said, no, you keep that, and he ate it cold with his fingers, having done this all the time in the infantry. When it was her turn, she leaned down and ate in her own way like any Asian working person using the fork as a shovel. The two of them had to take turns at the trough or their heads would bump. She prodded him with an elbow and he looked at her.

Tongkuai.

Is that good?

Yes. Tongkuai is warm. We are very warm here. She gestured at the purple-walled basement surrounded by the cold black night outside the window.

The insignia on their uniforms said Ah Genuine and there were two kinds of people working there. There were the twin register girls, Angela and Kay, who had been to high school in New York and who spoke a hybrid slang, in which DG meant to masturbate. Immigrants were called fleas or fence jumpers, boat people, or saiwooks—cargo—a reference to how many of them died in trucks crossing the border. The register girls' parents had come here legally. They would defiantly admit they couldn't read Chinese for real. When they texted, they used a mix of Cantonese ideograms and English acronyms. They wore fishnet tights and bras to emphasize their chests.

Sassoon, who was older, had been here fifteen years already, having arrived when Asians were still a minority on the streets, at the beginning of the current wave of immigration, around the time of the First Gulf War. Black people had made fun of her for how she spoke English. She lived around them and called them jiekwans when she spoke to other people like herself, people who understood her Cantonese, who had green cards.

Back in Guangdong, she had unacknowledged relatives living in Wide Net and Watergrass, where they went barefoot with their faded pants rolled up to the knees, laboring with water buffalo in the wet fields, their peasant faces seamed and puckered from man-years in the sun. The fields were fertilized with human feces. She carried hepatitis, but she had family in Hong Kong as well, and she applied Beauty White to her face. Even in winter, she would shield her face from the sun with her copy of the Sing Tao. In the summer, she carried an umbrella. And she went to the beauty parlor and had her hair highlighted red and had her skin massaged with cream and had ovarian rejuvenation.

She was single, having been married to a husband she did not like, who had gone back to China. Her brother had his own business installing windows with another man, a cousin. Once a week, she cooked them fish in brown sauce with the bones in and left it for them in the refrigerator in a blue and white bowl covered by a dish.

She did not like talking to people who didn't understand her, because then she would have to rely on Mandarin or English, which she did not speak well, which meant she wasn't educated. But she didn't resist any opportunity to be addressed by Polo, who sat alone at a table in the food court, reading his paper with his headlines facing out, the paper held in his large, healthy, well-oiled hands.

When they got their break, Sassoon and the register girls would go and sit at Polo's table. They helped themselves to food off the serving line, taking the same food the customers ate. Angela was picky. She said meat was disgusting. Sassoon was on a soup diet for her figure. The cook, Rambo, would sit with the boss as well, eating hot piles of rice. Rambo had a gold chain and a shaved head and doughy muscular forearms with purple burns all over them. He had a couple gold teeth and a tattoo of a dragon on his forearm. There were one or two other men in some way involved with the counter and they would either eat with Rambo or by themselves.

These other men, who were from a selection of places in the northeast of China where the coal mines were, were paying off mortgages on properties in Queens. One of them had a background in private security for a coal mine. They spoke of going back to China, where it was now possible to make a fortune, and, in fact, they did go back and forth regularly, as did Polo, for business.

Polo demonstrated his English with them, and Sassoon, chewing with her mouth open, her face glistening and reflective from skin-whitener, gazed at him. Rambo didn't speak except to men. Polo spoke to various people in different languages depending on who they were. He crossed his legs and positioned himself at an angle, speaking at an angle to them, explaining. He was rational and informed, speaking just above their heads. Then he would laugh with understanding. You will learn. It takes time. Ability comes slowly.

Or he opened the paper and read it and the entire table would be silent.

This was the first kind of people at the restaurant and they were in charge. The second kind of people, a subordinate class, did not eat at Polo's table. In the cacophony of the kitchen, one of them would look at the time and holler: jie bun! and a group of them would fetch their bowls. They ate in shifts. They would go out into the food court, one of them carrying a family-style pot of bean sprouts that they would share out of. They were all allotted rice from the twenty-gallon rice cooker. A member of this second, subordinate class, Zou Lei would eat when it was her turn. All of them were illegal women. They ate hunched over, heads down, at a table by the exit.

Two Mexican men who had deeply tanned faces and arms even in wintertime would come out from the kitchen where they had been cutting vegetables and share their meal with them from time to time. They wore their old red baseball hats backwards. Or they would go sit at another table, also by the exits, and talk in very quiet Mixtecan.

The women were older, or they simply looked older, and were small, because of poor infant nutrition. Some had big rough rural voices. What they had in common was that they did not have working papers. Most were from the south, Zou Lei being the exception.

A woman who washed dishes in a head-rag said:

You don't understand me because I'm from Mineral Spring Prefecture, very country. Soil-dirt. Soil-dirt. We were dirt and we lived in the dirt and it gave us our lives. We used to have fields. Used to have food to eat without end. It was country there. Then they destroyed the fields and put buildings up everywhere. There are no fields to plant anymore. They put up factories and nothing grows. The life gets pressed down. There's no work to do. People fish, if they can. The factories, you can't get work there either. The jobs get given to minorities, to Dai people and Wey people in their turbans, to what-do-you-call-it's.

What what-do-you-call-it's?

Uighur people.

What's a Uighur?

Out-of-towners. Backward people. Grab food with the hand, without chopsticks, eat it wa-la-wa-la. They carry knives. The government lets them have all the children they want. We can have one, they can have many. Then they give them jobs in the factories because they'll do it for nothing. Presses down the standard for everyone.

They wear turbans like so.

No, they don't, Zou Lei said.

Yes, they do. Osama bin Laden-style, they wear turbans. I've seen them in Buddha Hill at the factory there, a great big foreign factory there, a big one with two big buildings, foreign bosses, big money men from Taiwan. Big wrists. They let off poison all over the field. We couldn't live, and we ordinary people held them up with a protest. Their Uighurs had turbans this big, and three-four times a day, they had to shut down the whole thing for them so they could pray to Mecca—hooligooli-hooligooli superstition. No money got made and it ruined the whole thing, no economy.

No, they don't.

And how do you know so much? Look at you, the way you look, like you've got something you're not saying—doesn't she? You know something, don't you? I bet you're a Uighur! Oh, you are? See, I knew it!

What's a Uighur?

You tell them. Teach your new coworkers. You're the expert.

The imam wears a turban. The men wear a doppa. The women wear a scarf.

Are they foreigners?

They're from Afghanistan over thataway, but they belong to our China. Tell them! So, where's your scarf?

Why do I have to wear a scarf?

You probably don't want people to know who you are.

I'm half Han.

See, you're very tricky. Just like them. You're half Han now. I bet you're saying that because you're scared all of us will discriminate you.

But most of them couldn't remember what she was. They did not see that she ran when others walked, that she got there early and left late, that she pretended she was in the army. What they noticed about her, what got around was that she was different: she was a northern minority, didn't speak Cantonese. They put it down that she was a Mongolian or Russian—whatever might explain the difference in the way she looked and talked. The main thing they saw about her was that she was built differently from the Chinese girls. One day Polo reviewed the women on the line and said Zou Lei is different. She is healthy. American style! He laughed hahaha. He told the register girl she looked skinny. Why you don't do Jack LaLanne? And the Cantonese women made foul faces.

They gave her a box of cellophane baggies and had her fill each one with one packet of duck sauce, one packet of soy sauce, a napkin, and a plastic fork. See how fast you can do five hundred. Like this—you blow and pop the baggie open. Time to stop. You can do that later. She hauled the dishes in. They were chopping cabbage.

I try, she said.

No, said Rambo, You are dishes, garbage, dumplings, mop.

She filled in for Sunnie on the line, a ladle in her hand, on the balls of her toes, looking out past the lights at the kids wearing their hats sideways, bigger than their parents, hearing them talking: He my nigga, he my homeboy. Zou Lei watched them going by—she watched them as they watched her, examined her, checked her out, and talked about her, staring at her until she looked someplace else.

They talking about you. They say they seen you doing some exercise in the parking lot. Like was that you? No way. She's the new employee. It was her. I gotta tell someone.

The register girl began to text her sister.

Like, what kind of exercise? Oral exercise?

Gymnastic, Zou Lei said.

The register girl let out a piercing laugh at something she was reading on her phone.

16

THEIR CANTONESE WAS HARD to understand, it echoed off the tile. They had their backs to her. Her back was to the sink. Get the gwat, they said—she thought they said. It was like hearing someone talk through a prism. The dialect came in different versions, depending on whether they were from inland or the coast. Sunnie went around the corner. They were pulling boxes out from under the metal table legs. Sassoon's hand went inside and came out with the organs from a chicken, sliding in her fingers. Take the jewels. I cook the jewels, they said, and peeled the membrane off. Take the silk, they said. No need to waste. Take the hand of Buddha. Give me the way. A hand with fat greased over it picked up a knife. She heard something getting cut in coins and thought they called it gwat but it was carrot. What are we doing? We make the hairy crab, wealth of the entire family. Way is very dull. Sunnie came back with bowls and set them on the table. The one is here to put the fat, the jewel, tendon, lotus, umbrella, jewel, fetus chicken. They pointed with the knife at Sunnie, you don't count arithmetic. She said, I'll get another one. Three more one! See? She don't count arithmetic! Sunnie said okay and left again. One times three was three. She realized they meant a bowl. The women kept handling the meat. A monthly smell. I smell you having monthly tension, they said, wearing little bits of yellow gold, small eyes. They went into the dirty boxes on the floor and took out a radish, coined it with the knife. Gills stuck to the metal surface from the mushrooms they were cutting, mud clinging to a root. The lotus, when cut, resembled the cross-section of a pig's sinuses. Dirt is on it still. Better make it neat or you embrace the Buddha's feet. She used the cardboard as a dustpan for sweeping underfoot. Dirt clings to it like a country girl.

He say you mess his order up. The order come in stringy beef, chicken, pork, and oyster. Turkey separate. When order, whether the combination plate, that's a question. You can have the combination of the congee or the rice. If meat, you ask the sauce. The oyster only has the combination with the rice. If they want the chicken with oyster, you tell Rambo so he add it in the back. When she say order, she say the order first and the combination second. If it combine with noodle, she say beef and noodle. To save the time, she say only pork. She say a hundred time a day, don't say again, everyone go crazy. Just one word, that's it, everybody know. Simple! Congee another one. If they want the vermicelli, if they want the tendon, don't keep the secret. You tell in back.

On her break, she did not exercise. There was no time anyway. She put her chopsticks in the shared tub and lifted out a wet nest of greens and dropped them on her rice and sucked them up into her mouth and kept sucking rice and chewing with her head down in the time allotted.

When deliveries came, she unloaded boxes with the Mexicans, and outside of work, she did double distance, sometimes running west in the evening towards Corona. Then she might get on the train and head back towards Skinner, getting a free transfer on the bus when she was tired. Her sneakers were falling apart, the soles completely flat. She looked in the window of a Footlocker.

A broad-shouldered black youth wearing the store uniform spoke to his friend and came outside to see if he could help her. He licked his lips and said, What you lookin for? She was standing hipshot in her jeans, reading prices. Can I be of service?

She got smile lines by her mouth. But she was calculating days until they paid her.

Yeah, I see you. Would you care to step into my office where it's warmer?

Even then, with rent, she would be leaving herself with next to nothing.

Now, now, now—no need to go. I'm here to give you the service you desire.

Before letting her go, he insisted on shaking her hand, which he kissed, and she yanked her hand away, laughing. He called after her as she went down the block:

I see you! Think it over, ma!

In the morning, she ran farther out in the park, crossing a road after which the park continued on in the direction of the tall isolated buildings that she thought of as mountains. She came to a basketball court where Afghan men and boys were playing soccer in leather sandals in twenty-degree weather. The men had imam's beards and the boys had loosely jointed running styles from birth defects, depleted uranium.

When she got paid, she bought an off-brand pair of sneakers in a 99-cent store. They tore her heels and she put tape in them to make them better.

When no one was around, she went beneath the steam table and took out a plastic shell and then, after looking around first, picked up a stainless steel cover and checked beneath it. There was nothing under it but water, and she let it go—it sounded like a symbol when it dropped—and wrung her burned hand. She grabbed a dipper and flipped up the next one with the handle. Steam flowed up. She heard someone coming and put it down and stood aside. The cook, Rambo, was coming out, bent over fast-walking as if trying to catch up with a tub he was carrying in front of himself, gripping it with rags. She backed out of his way. He heaved it down, flipped up a lid, and slammed it home. From where she had retreated to, she watched the heat coming off the rice. He took her dipper and flipped the covers up and caught them like a juggler of spinning plates in an oriental circus. She pretended to be organizing drinking cups. He squatted and dialed a flame up. She put the shell back and went and got her rag in the closet with the jackets and purses and the starch. They had shopping bags with their own greens in them sitting on the floor. Box thorn, Shanghai cabbage sprouts. Someone had come in with coffee. She went back out and saw the girl at the register eating a pastry—crumbs on a napkin, coffee rings on a napkin—you could smell the milk and sugar.

What you doing? Hiding back there?

She had wanted a piece of stringy beef.

When she went into the kitchen to wash dishes during the rush, Rambo saluted her.

Leaving work at night, she was cutting through the parking lot to Roosevelt Avenue. In the projects across the street, someone was running across her line of sight. She watched a figure in sweatpants vault over a railing and run up to a steel door and start bouncing her ass back and forth. The door banged open and others came out in ball caps, laughing and making noise. The girl jumped around and clapped and another girl jumped into it with her, clapped at exactly the same time—they slid sideways on cue, danced a couple steps in sync together—the whoop came to Zou Lei from across the avenue—and then they dropped right in step with everybody else, the group of kids passing under the streetlight and becoming a squad of shadows, just their energy moving out into the nighttime and the voice or two that carried back.

Then Zou Lei had a stroke of luck on the street, on Junction Boulevard. She found clothes out front of a thrift store, everything on the rack three dollars. She bought a pair of jeans at the Colombiana. The label, which she could not read, said Euphoria, but they were good as new and cut her way. She did three hundred squats one night at home and put them on and they fit her nice and tight.

Polo was speaking to Sassoon.

Everyone has their own characteristic. You look: One, two, three, four... One the style of Taiwan, one the style of Hong Kong, another one Japan. Polo paused for reflection. Another one Thailand, another one Singapore, another one Korea. More and more, on and on. The more modern style.

But we, we, what are we? You think.

Sassoon waited for him to tell her.

We provide the modern flavors, he said. The front line. That is our characteristic. You look: Sa-cha. Thick soup. Oyster. Everything is leaning to Hong Kong-Taiwan. This is the front line. Not just smell. Flavor. Also culture. The big plate. Why a big plate? Because this is modern. Look, someone is eating—he pays money, he is eating, but the plate is small! Just like twenty years ago! Just like village! I feel so poor! Why do I pay? I am unsatisfied. I want a big plate. The big plate generates the atmosphere of freedom. The modern culture. Ah! Now I am so free, so magnanimous, so relaxed.

You understand this? He observed his listener, before going on.

You know sushi? Haha! He hooked his fingers towards his mouth. Sushi is advanced. This one—he pointed at another counter—provides sushi. You love to eat sushi? How do you know it? I am your senior and I just found out about it. I will invite you. You can taste it. What do you think? Hahaha.

You have to study the meaning. This meaning is very deep, this, this characteristic. If you understand this characteristic, you can advance, you can expand your market share. This is your capital. Otherwise no one will know you.

Little by little, you are learning. You must keep working. You will have your own business.

Too old, Sassoon said.

Maybe hair style? Maybe beauty? You will have your own business and be my competitor! He raised his pompadour and laughed hahaha.

Too old. I'm looking for a husband. A rich one. Let the husband work.

What will you do?

Bodyfit!

Bodyfit! What? The disco, aerobics… He smiled, raised his arms up, to the sides.

Lose my weight. I love to lose my weight, Sassoon said. She danced in her seat.

Ah, the boss said.

A boy from Cardozo spoke to Kay or Angela across the register. You scared about you image. There's no girls here. Don't be afraid. I protect you. I got to protect mines own image. Yeah, right. Yeah, right, he said. Yeah, right. Yeah, right. I told you first. Uh huh. Uh huh. Yeah. They let you touch the money. Let me touch the money? Don't even think about it. KC. K-sahp-C laaaaaa! They the one who crazy. Mou aaaaaaah! Talk less. You boyfriend in the gang. So why you talking? I know you take it. Speak about the thing you understand. You take the money. Shut up already. You at the register all day… so much temptation for girl like you. Let me get twenty. Let me get a hunnie. Lemme get a knot. Seriously, chill with that. I'm on camera. There are four camera on me all the time. X film. For real. XX film. Watch the porno of you. Mental illness. He must suspect you. This place does mad good. How much is mad good? Twenty dollar? Phat knots? Try like way more. You got stacks. Word? Bossie got mad dollars. He live in Jersey. What kind of car he drive? He push a Escalade. Escalade… The big black one. You likes the Escalade. Ahh yeah. She smirked and curled her tongue up over the front of her teeth. You on his shit. She hummed a little tune. Never know. No way. I could get behind the wheel. She put her fist up and steered, rocking her narrow body from side to side.

The men said, She is healthy.

The three of them were sitting at a table at the far end of the food court from the counter and they had a view of the women clearing trays in their orange hats and aprons.

You give her steak and she eats it, that kind of girl. Our Chinese girls are not like that. They have a modesty, that is their characteristic. When they show their flowers and branches it is different.

Miss, miss, don't be angry. I sit on a chair, you sit on the ground. I eat watermelon, you eat meat.

It rhymed in their dialect from coal country. They had been discussing real estate, taxes, and how to beat a traffic ticket in American court.

She'd make a good bit of goods for Polo.

His blood isn't red enough.

He's a man of higher quality. He wouldn't be interested, I'll tell you.

If he did, you-know-who, the ghost-face one, would do away with herself.

He's frightened of that leopard.

The former security man, whose name, Qing, meant Whisper in classical Chinese, told a story. There once was a labor organizer in our mine. He was connected to a clan, so we stayed clear of him. But he had a girlfriend we knew about, a fiancé. They weren't married yet, you see. She was taken off the road, invited to a quiet place.

We offered her a seat. Told her to get comfortable. We had made a hot fire. We helped her off with her coat and her pants. It's too warm for that, we told her. Be careful of your health. We don't want you to catch a fever. In our village, we grow beans, the product our village is famous for, besides coal. Now we prepared a funnel. This will remind you of your lover, we told her. Your tears are tears of impatience. A kilo of beans was heated till they were smoking hot in a brazier. They were put inside her using a funnel.

One of the men, whose name meant Bell or Clapper, wanted to know if that was a true story.

I don't know, said Qing. Is it?

That's why we don't have 9/11, the third one said.

We have had 9/11. A nation as big as ours, we've had more than one 9/11, but you don't hear about it. But that's why we are catching up to America. Because we don't allow backward people to slow us down. Here they have blacks, everywhere the blacks—taking drugs, playing with guns. If an iron fist were used with them the way we do back home, America would be a much stronger opponent.

An open country.

Too open. The women are open. Buy them a soda pop and they open their legs.

Some of our Asian girls are getting like that too.

Society is changing gradually, as the quality of life increases, the material level increases. People have levels. You can't confuse a low-quality person with a civilized person. If people are not confused, then society will not be confused. But some people confuse society, telling lies, that kind of thing, and it holds the country back.

Skinner listened to her voice on the phone while he smoked a cigarette, sitting in his boxer shorts, his hard white legs apart and his bare foot bouncing up and down, listening to her, looking around, listening to her, nodding occasionally in his empty room.

Come over and kick it with me.

She talked in his ear, her voice saying she could not.

Aw, come on. Yes, you can—he laughed, his teeth yellow.

I have to work. After work I'll come. She had to work. After she had said no again and said goodbye, he rolled a spliff and went out on the avenue and smoked it. He paced under the naked trees and power lines.

Ahead were the liquor stores and Chinese takeout counters on 162nd Street, Dutch-looking houses and shuttered storefronts and Mexican graffiti. Before he reached them, he turned back. He went back into the basement, the ripe smell of weed smoke clinging to his camouflage. He took a pill and sat there drifting.

Sassoon started throwing things and yelling and demanded that Zou Lei come with her. They went into the hallway with the dumpster and she screamed at her. The Fookienese men working in the adjacent kitchen opened doors and watched.

Everyone have to be careful, right? You know the saying, every man for self. The man, woman, kid, also. This is the life. You want me take my time, what you give me? Think about. That's America. Everyone come here the same story. The one who take the boat, the fishing boat, the one who take the bus, get inside the truck, hiding, smuggle the people, Mexican. They die in there. Pay a lot of money the whole lifetime. The one is legal, the one is not legal. Everyone has the problem, the tears they cry—you no hear about it? I am the Cantonese. This one, she from my hometown. The same family. Don't ask me for nothing, right? I don't know you. This the life. You do the same to me. Don't explain it, right? Just do it. America. The things is dead, the people is live. Everyday same thing, the things is dead. Chop the vegetable, chopping, peeling, washing. Maybe I tell you cut the meat, you cut the piece this big, supposed to be smaller. You get it wrong. That why I put you on the dish. You suppose to learn, daily, daily, the people is alive, supposed to change, right? You can't get it right, basic common sense, I don't need you. That's fire. Fire. Hire the new one. The smart one get ahead.

He cleaned up some of the garbage in his room. He checked his pistol, put it back in his assault pack. He arranged his boots neatly next to his bed.

They had snow. When you looked up, you saw a plain of snow like an inverted image in the mountains. The snowfall covered the lots and rooftops and car tops and the fields adjacent to the highways. The plows came rumbling out at night. She stepped through the slush-filled gutters wearing plastic bags on her cheap new sneakers, which were already coming apart. Work had made her tired. She fell asleep on his bed—in his room, the boiler in the closet—water puddling on his floor beneath her plastic bags.

He pulled her socks off and laid them out like bacon strips on the floor. The ankles of her jeans had snow crystals on them. He unbuttoned her tight jeans and pulled them off. Even with the phone in her pocket and the water in the cuffs, they were light. He put the poncholiner over her.

She felt it snowing in her sleep—enormous heaven making snow above their heads, falling on the grate above his window in the sidewalk.

He sat next to her, plugged into his laptop, listening to anthem rock, and a sound—barely more than a premonition—reached him through the music. His eyes narrowed and he looked sideways at his door. Something was happening. He pulled the wires out of his ears like someone pulling off his EKG and listened to the house.

She had heard it too. She was waking up, her brown hair in her eyes, confused.

I hear somethings.

Then, overhead, there was a burst of running pounding feet. A man's voice shouting. Another voice yelling faded and came back. The pitch of the yelling rose. They heard furniture legs. Then there was an impact to a stud and the thud vibrated the frame of the house. Zou Lei sat up and pushed the cover off. The yelling turned into the sound of a woman screaming.

Skinner got up and stood listening in the doorway. She tiptoed over to listen with him. The woman was screaming and screaming and screaming—and now they could hear that she was crying. They stared up into the dark at the origin of the sound. The man continued shouting at her. He had a brogue. Skinner cocked his head, trying to understand him. The man was shouting:

I don't keep whores! I don't keep whores!

The Murphy's kitchen door smashed open and someone came running out breathless and slammed out through the side door of the house. At the bottom of the basement stairs, they heard whoever it was running away from the house and out into the snowy street.

Their daughter, he said.

They remained there, listening for whatever else would happen. They heard a voice say this:

All the rent is is another four hundred dollars a month drinking money for you.

Zou Lei asked what was being said.

That's my landlady. She's telling him off.

This was the last thing they were able to make out and then the voices faded.

17

His episodes of weeping had not started yet, but they would. Her love, something he was so unused to, seemed to hasten the emotional outpouring. The not-sleeping and irritability were already there, were familiar. Her love was not to blame for any of it. But he looked around for something or someone to blame, and that was typical. He did not understand the process he was going through. He did not have a medical degree. It was not a healing process. The breaking down was the opposite of that. It was not catharsis. He didn't know enough to be as scared as he should have been, or he might have gone to the VA.

The day he moved in was a Saturday. His duffel bag and his assault pack lay on the floor of his new room. Skinner was sitting on the edge of the bed. In his hand, he held the keys Mrs. Murphy had given him. The door of his room, which he had opened with the keys, was half-open, and through it, he could see the stairs that led up to the street and the March afternoon.

He spun the keys on a finger and caught them with a click. Yawned and rubbed his face. He dragged the duffel bag over to the edge of the bed and unzipped it and started digging through it, the insides coming out like the wadding of a car seat punctured by a round. He put the twisted jeans and t-shirts by him on the bed. Then he felt the significant dense weight of something L-shaped and the pistol tumbled out from a green army towel and thumped down on top of his socks.

For a while, he pretended not to see it. He pawed through his clothes, hunting for his hygiene bag and other things. There were pills he had that were supposed to knock him out and help him sleep and he could take one now, he thought. Maybe that would be the best thing. Or he could go out. Was it raining? He looked behind him at the window above his bed. It didn't look like it. He could see the grating in the ground and the gray white sky above it. He squinted. There was no rain.

But his attention returned to the weapon. His foot was jiggling. He could hear the weight of people walking on his ceiling. This was their house. He listened to their voices, forming a picture of who was who, the woman presiding over her kitchen, smoking a Slim the same color as the gray white light coming in the window.

He picked up the nine, compressing the grip safety, and pointed it one-handed at the bedroom wall. The front sight wavered. He reached out with his weak side hand and cupped the grip to steady it. With his thumb, he switched the safety off—now you could see the red dot. He thought he heard the giant daughter talking, a male he didn't know, maybe others, and the smoker's voice of the woman. How many? Maybe four. Put his finger on the trigger. Gave it pressure. Just enough to make the hammer move.

Bang, he said—and his heart was beating.

He experienced a sense of wrongdoing. Took his finger off the trigger, extending it straight along the outside of the trigger guard, where it was supposed to be. Thumbed the safety back on. But his mind did not have a safety and there was no way to shut it off.

Part II

18

THE WHITE LOOKED LIKE a long-legged biker, as if, instead of being inside these razor-wire-topped walls, he should be leaning back on a chopper going down the highway, with his long legs extended and his boots on the chrome footrests. He had soft brown hair and thin eyes. His mustache made him resemble a wolf. He was pale and large and when he walked, he rose up on his feet like the piston in a motor—up and down—chin always up, an eighth Cherokee, last name Turner.

He was in the yard with gang foot soldiers who said you could get transferred anywhere in the gulag system, from state to state, and wind up in the SHU. The Abu Ghraib prisoner-abuse scandal had just come out on CNN. They said you've declared war on the State of Indiana, we've declared war on the United States. This organization is bigger than the United States. We go to the outside, two thousand, three thousand miles away. This is a structure. We're like Al Qaida. They give us life, double life, life without. The state has our commanders in max segregation units, no human contact, twenty-four hours a day, and they're still calling shots as far as politics, operations, whatever the case might be. Who goes in the hat. The state takes everything they can and we're still going on like magic.

We control the drugs, we control the individuals. We control ourselves. People fear us, in here and on the street. We control the nicotine, they said.

Jimmy, smoking a cigarette under the blue sky, nodded.

He had a laconic New York voice from Queens. He hadn't always been here, he had started his bid in Rikers. I built up to it, he told his social worker. I passed through there, Rikers, doing skid bids. I had a life more or less. I didn't see my opportunities.

What about your behaviors do you need to watch out for?

The drugs. Definitely the drugs.

The social worker was an obese blond woman whose facial features were confined inside a small area in the center of her face.

I ain't like these other guys, he told her and glanced to check if her features relaxed and spread apart slightly.

Positivity, he said.

He had been a fifteen-year-old kid with an electric guitar slung across his pale flat torso, strutting back and forth in his bare feet, hair long, throwing his long leg out in a kick, making faces, making sounds with his mouth while the stereo played Led Zeppelin. He drew designs in blue permanent ink on his jeans, took his jeans off and drew directly on his naked legs. When asked why he had done it to himself, he said, because it's artistic.

Erin told her homegirls, I know he stole that thing.

He didn't know how to play but claimed he was teaching himself the way some musicians do. The symbols meant he would never do alcohol like his parents.

Jimmy grew up wearing a plaid shirt, standing brooding silent with his mouth shut, the trace of a mustache over his lip, waiting for Patrick to say, Let me have the spanner. Then Jimmy would take the spanner out of the red tool box and hand it to him, in the basement of someone's house in the neighborhood, down with the boiler and the risers.

Patrick was a heroic-sized man. He looked like a man from a WWII movie. First of all, he was big. He had a big slab face like a sergeant-major with a cigar in his teeth. The word was that you could go into any bar in Belfast and they would tell you that Patrick Murphy was a mighty, mighty man. He was a hurler. He had the strongest hands of any man that you would ever shake hands with—he had a crushing grip, thick hands that came alive and turned to rock generating merciless compressing force. He must have gone about two-fifty, in his boots, more. You did not want him angry. His iron black-and-gray hair was combed back flat and handsomely on his head with a little obedient bend in it where it had been trained by the comb to bend back on itself, a little bit of a bump, a pompadour, but trimmed and barbered tight over his ears and at the nape of his brick-red neck, giving him an old-fashioned look.

He had been through the Troubles of course and had been starved when he was young. Now he did plumbing and medium-sized things and the like, nothing too grand. As he crawled on the floor looking into a pipe, a lock of hair fell forward over his forehead like Elvis.

Jimmy got a tattoo of a clover on his hand when he was fifteen. But his hand was not as strong as Patrick's. His hand would slip off the wrench, then Patrick would take the wrench from him and turn it further until the pipe opened.

A woman teacher in Cardozo told him in front of the class, you're not registered as Jimmy Murphy. I don't know what to tell you.

He thought he was on the edge of understanding a mystery in the lyrics of a song, so he played it over again in his small room, looking out the broken venetian blinds.

The house was full of curios, bedding, scratch tickets, yard equipment, and vinyl records. Wearing a robe, his mother sat in the lace curtain living room, her feet up.

Why am I registered as Turner? he asked her.

She turned her impressive face towards him and said, Come here, I'll tellya a story. She had a bag on and the story was about something else completely.

The house was two houses. On the first floor, there were the lace curtains and plastic on the couch, the kitchen had a cuckoo clock on the wall, and there was a velvet picture of Elvis looking handsome above the couch his mother sat on. The saints and elves were in the yard. The rooms upstairs were a mess of clothes and junk where his mother and Erin lived among bottles of perfume and shampoo and tarot cards and curling irons and maxi pads and beer can empties and cigarettes and photo albums. You could open a drawer in a broken dresser and find a stack of Polaroids of people and scenes you did not recognize, then look at yourself in the mirror and wonder who you looked like. A seventies barbeque, sunshine and green fields and motorbikes. You might recognize your mother as one of the faces cutoff by the camera, eyes bright, lifting a beer, fifty pounds younger.

Patrick was bigger than his real father, who had spent his life in prison and was now dying of AIDS in Morristown.

I'll give you carfare if you want to go to see him, if you should want to do that, his mother said. I wouldn't stop you. Don't ask me to go, though. Her voice broke. That, I'm not up for. She pressed her hand to her eyes and checked her palm for tears. She heaved herself up in her robe and t-shirt and massive drawstring shorts and moved from the living room to the kitchen for the whiskey bottle. After she took her belt, she steadied herself on the countertop and searched the room for him. She located him. He was not looking at her.

My eye socket, she said, drawing a line along the side of her face with her finger. Cheekbone. Jaw. This tooth—she hooked her lip and pulled it back to expose her missing canine.

What's your point?

My point is don't ask me to go with you.

But if she was implying that it had been Jimmy's father Jerome Turner who had battered her, Jimmy remembered it differently. He remembered Patrick fighting with her right in this house not more than three years ago. They fought like two bears on their hind legs, leaning together gripping each other's heads, until he knocked her down.

They were going to renovate the basement and turn it into an apartment where someone could live.

19

ERIN ALWAYS SAID SHE was the priestess. Her thing was magic. She drew a picture of a woman who looked like Elvira with a cape standing in the wind under the moon with a wolf at her side. She showed her homegirl and reported back, Maria thinks it's fresh. No man can touch her, Erin said of the woman in the picture. Because she's got spells, nigga. And, standing on the corner of Utopia in the autumn with her homegirls, she said, My father can bite my dick. At sixteen, she said, I quit smoking. I don't party no more. She listened to L7 on a Walkman. A year later, she talked about how after this, she was going to go to art school for my drawings. She spoke to a kid from LaGuardia who was going to FIT. She had a copy of the Chalice and the Blade. She had gotten very big and tall and there were things she never tried. I'm the high priestess, she said. She did not go out no more. A boy she knew was having problems with another girl and she provided a friend who cared. Once she lit candles for him and told his fortune in the dark, holding his hands. She knew that nothing would happen because they had to respect their friendship. I'll kill you if you let her dog you, she told him. She avoided Patrick, her father, even when he was sober. The television played in the middle of the day, speaking for her, her back to him, the female on Jerry Springer screaming, screaming, crying and screaming: You're a piece of shit! They bleeped it and kept bleeping. Jerry said, Oh wow. We can't have that. She pretended to be absorbed in black magic, white magic. She ran into Maria after not seeing her for a year and she was a mother, she was married to a fireman, Kevin, and they were moving into a house at nineteen. I'm not good with kids, said Erin, who wore black, weighed roughly two-twenty in her cold white bare feet on the scale in the back of the house. The tight, depressing, spring-loaded silence that she lived in, decoding sounds, the way the boots sounded coming in the door, how drunk was he, and how enraged. She was her mother's friend, but not her best one. She helped her put the figures in the yard, for the season. She put up Christ with his shirt off. She got the subs or cake from 162nd Street if something special was happening to someone else, if they were going through a change of life. She knew other people's news. It was part of Wicca, it was part of her mastery. She told her friend once, There's another side to life, another dimension. How did she know? Because when I was younger, I tried to kill myself. So I saw it. She hung a wind chime—wire circle, a circle within a circle—from the eaves of the house. When she was young, she came home from school high one day and something was not right. She was alone. Finally, she realized that she was not. A person came up from the basement. His footsteps came up the stairs, and she said: What the fuck were you doing, Jimmy? All she saw was the long hair covering his face so that there was no face and the pentagram he had drawn on his white chest. She was just a fat girl. Her father called her a whore. Her brother's rock thundered from the upstairs. The cars came and went outside, she heard the engines and the yelling. The threats and the scuffling and then the fighting that could be felt in the street even when it could not be seen. People would be standing outside looking up the street. You heard echoed yelling, an energy. Something's goin down. Sometimes you ran to see or help. She fought a girl in the middle of a mob of kids when she was in school and they all wore Raiders jackets. The red emergency lights whap-whapped through the windows. Sometimes someone banged the door, said, Hello? Police. And she heard them coming in to arrest one of them, or take her mother's blood pressure, give her an ice pack, to look inside her lip with blue gloves and a flashlight, and say, You lost a tooth. The ceramic ornament her mother put on the porch said Take a Deep Breath, You're Home. The violence came in cycles with the moon.

But her brother came out of nowhere. He nearly got in serious trouble once when she was young. Charges were never filed, but they said he did something to a girl. The girl was one of Erin's friends who had come over to the house. Jimmy played his guitar for her at her request, nothing more. Later when Erin heard what she was saying, she said, You're lying about my brother. She was going around claiming he sexually assaulted her. Supposedly, the story was that she was so devastated that she had told her priest. Rather than reporting the incident to the police, out of a concern for privacy, the priest had called the girl's mother. The girl's mother called up Erin's mother crying and screaming on the phone, and now it was all over the neighborhood and everyone knew at school. In the office at St. Andrews, the victim described her assailant's body to the priest. Erin's mother said she would talk to Jimmy. All she wanted was a fair hearing, not a lynch mob. She talked to him and now she was satisfied there were holes in the girl's story. The girl had asked him to take his shirt off when he was playing. This she told the girl's mother on the phone.

The woman drove up outside with some men in the car and screamed fucking rapist scumbag and threw things at their house.

I never liked her, Erin said. I never talked to her after that. She was a ho and I never trusted her no more after what she said about Jimmy.

20

JIMMY BECAME A UNION man in rubber coveralls, boots, and a World War I helmet, going down into the ground for the City. He's made his bones, his mother said at the bar. The sandhog's intricate patch depicted the figures of men inside a cutaway view of a multilevel excavation. The same families worked for generations on a dig. You would have father, son, and grandfather in the pit. At Feeney's, Patrick had a shot with him.

Good luck down there, lad.

What began as grounds for celebration became his daily life. Autumn after summer, Jimmy drove a wide, dull gold Buick Skylark through the houses with gapped siding and the leaves turning to soil bounded by rusted fences. The irrelevant sun rose and fell over his windshield, as he drove to work and back, Led Zeppelin playing on the stereo.

He had a confined space certificate. The sandhogs changed into coveralls in a low-ceilinged trailer with beige lockers and an OSHA poster tacked to the fake-wood-patterned wall and trooped out into the sonic drone. The drilling equipment, which moved on train tracks, cost 30 million dollars. You could feel the rock being pulverized seven times per second. Under the noise frequency, an Irish voice and a West Indian voice sounded identical. They ate their lunches underground, by lantern light, Jimmy's blackened hands leaving fingerprints on his white bread.

He wore death's head silver rings on his fingers. After work, his eyes hurting in the daylight, he put his rings on again and put the Zeppelin on again, a mysterious version in another language of the great underground music of the drill. The excavation site was in Midtown Manhattan by the river. He drove through the flickering channel formed by the suspension cables of the bridge and headed back to the rusted fences and dilapidated houses to a bar where there were union bumper stickers on the wood and the brogue was distinct. Still more music was playing. When he entered, Jimmy! they said.

How's your father? they said.

Fine.

Jimmy went to play Keno.

He would go from the cave of the dig to the dark peat-hollow of the bar. Drinking opened tunnels in his head that led into the third tomb of the night.

He watched an amateur video of guys doing stunts on bikes, set to hip-hop by a white DJ crew. They did wheelies, burnouts, endos. The backdrop was a heavy tree line. Jimmy put his hand in the plastic bowl of Doritos. The guy whose house it was came in from the kitchen and sat down in his chair and said to the TV, She's making hotdogs. They watched without speaking. Not taking his eyes off the screen, Jimmy rubbed his fingers together to brush the salt off. A helmeted rider tilted his bike forward, elevating his rear wheel, and drove past the camera balanced on his front wheel. Dismounting, he pointed to the Wheelz logo on the back of his jacket. That's dope, the guy whose house it was said. In the kitchen, you could hear a woman boiling water.

The TV was an enormous sleek cabinet-sized piece of equipment. The picture was very bright and sharp. A set like that cost fifteen hundred dollars, assuming you paid for it. The three men watching it were Jimmy, a plumber, and the guy whose house it was. The plumber was the intermediary who knew both of them separately. To Jimmy, he had said why don't you come out? We'll hang out, smoke a bone... He sat between them now, wearing a black-and-white sweater over an iridescent green shirt, having placed his beer on the carpet next to his feet in white Nikes.

One of the riders lost control and wiped out and his bike flipped over. It landed on him and went sliding down the road. All three men said, Whoa! That'll leave a mark. Holy shit. That hurt my balls from here. Hahahahaha.

Where do they do this? the plumber asked.

Bay Shore. That's my boy filming it. He gets money from like the promotion.

The money these guys can get in Vegas is unreal.

Watch this. He's gonna wipe.

Oh shit.

Hahahahahaha.

Oh shit, my man came down hard. Homeboy's out.

Here they come. They're gettin him up.

What you gotta say about that, Jim-bo?

He got messed up.

Here's the next one.

The guy whose house it was's woman brought out a tray of hot-dogs and set it on the coffee table, which was behind them. The plumber turned around and said thank you, hon.

There's relish, she said.

She sat down on the couch, which was behind the coffee table, and spooned relish on a hotdog and bit into it with her hand cupped under it and chewed.

You want one? she said to the back of her guy's head.

No.

The video was ending. The words Strong Island Wheelz scrolled by on the screen. The guy aimed the remote at the TV and the game came on.

Who is it? she asked.

Philly, he said.

The plumber said: Darius Johnson, number 44. Fastest man in the NFL.

Yeah, but Capslock would go right through him.

Not if he can't touch him, bro.

The woman, who had high hair and a judgmental nose and lips, had left the room. The plumber took out a flask of Captain Morgan and they all drank Dixie Cups of it. The guy whose house it was lounged in his chair with his knees open, the ceiling light reflecting off his eyes. His clothing was clean, like his house. His jeans, with a loop for a hammer, appeared freshly laundered. Speaking to the ceiling, he said:

I'm getting the phattest street bike... There's a chapter right here... Take it to Virginia Beach...

The plumber remarked that he used to ride in the Air Force. Vegas, Lake Havasu. I used to meet a lot of women, boy. I wore the mirrored shades... They called me CHIPS.

We oughta all ride together. He looks like a biker.

My man Jimmy's got the look.

It's how you carry yourself, Jimmy said.

Straight up.

The men regarded him, their eyes at half mast. He took a hotdog off the tray with his silver-ringed hand, his jaw opened, and he bit it in half. He licked as his teeth chopped together, resembling a wolf eating a camper's rations surrounded by twilit snow.

My man Jimmy over here. Look at him. Them hotdogs don't stand a chance. Don't worry about it, my man. He'll tell his old lady to cook more. Hahahahahaha.

He's union?

My man's a sandhog. He's on the biggest dig in the city after the Holland Tunnel.

There's a lot of money in that.

There could be, Jimmy said.

Like with tools and shit.

Yeah.

A lotta shit walks off the job.

It could.

Do you have any idea what a Bobcat costs? A boom? The kind with the thing that telescopes? A hundred thousand easy.

The kind of money you go up to any broad you want and tell her I'm the Kid.

You need a truck that can carry equipment, a flatbed thing.

The guy lit a Newport and crossed his legs, resting his shin across his knee, as if setting up a planning table. Indicating Jimmy, he said: And he's our guy on the inside. The plumber said, We gone be rich mothafuckas… Jimmy reduced his movements to a slow speed, made sure to drink from his bottle of flat beer in the coolest possible way. They made statements with a significant air. Speaking slowly, Jimmy repeated a line he had heard in a movie: Security's a joke. You're lookin at it. The plumber glanced at the guy whose house it was as if this was indeed a very significant statement. No one had a problem with the line's being stolen from a movie, apparently. I can feel it, the guy said. They did not get into specifics. The conversation stayed abstract and then wandered into notions of what could be done with the money from a score and debates about what criminal charges would be faced. The plumber suggested they get high. They passed a joint and watched the game. Female voices could be heard. It was the guy's daughter, a brown-haired girl of seven or eight, being brought home. She said something about the funny smell of the smoke and the woman suppressed a laugh. Can you close it? the guy said. The woman pulled the sliding living room door shut, and they heard her saying, They're watching the game, in the kind of voice you use with a child.

They never stole heavy duty construction equipment—Bobcats or lifts—and loaded them onto interstate flatbed trucks. When Jimmy was arrested, it was for DUI. He had a couple of bags of cement in his trunk and a Ryobi that retailed at six hundred dollars. He wasn't raised to steal, Mrs. Murphy said. I know he knows better. Up in the Bronx, the local received a call about him and in the bars they said he was going to get bounced. In the meantime, he kept working. He had his supporters. Keep your head high, Jim. He went to the rectangular building with many windows on Queens Boulevard near Union Turnpike and went through the metal detector, found his Part.

His defender, a sarcastic man with a double chin, did not seem to understand that they were both Irish and what this meant or that Jimmy was a union man and what that meant. Jimmy stood outside the Part waiting for him against the dirty marble wall with the other people who were milling and waiting. The defender showed up late after the case had been called, pushing through the crowd with his briefcase, sweating and distracted.

They called me already.

I'm sorry, I had another case. The judge talks too much. But you don't need me today. They're dropping the vandalism, aren't they?

What vandalism? That wasn't me. I'm DUI.

DUI, right. You're Turner. I thought you were Rodriguez. Are you sure this is where you're supposed to be?

They looked at the names under the glass.

That's you. Let's go in. I've got another client here. Wait for me while I go talk to him.

The case was continued. The next time he got arrested, they impounded his Skylark and locked him up and he stood before the court while wearing sneakers minus the laces. In court, they referred to him as Mr. Turner. He turned to his defender: I thought you were getting me off. His defender said: Nobody can get you off. You're guilty. Right or wrong? You did it, didn't you? Yes or no? So take the plea and next time learn to call a cab.

Then they led him back out to the bus after waiting eight hours in the holding area behind the courtroom where you could not use the bathroom. He sat pushing against the individual shackled next to him who pushed him back. They drove through Jackson Heights, they looked out the windows at the taillights, the Spanish women getting off the subway. He looked ahead at the front of the bus, the transport officers behind the cage, at where they were going. They were surrounded by industrial buildings and the airport. He heard the vacuum cleaner roaring of jet engines going over them and saw the shadow of a plane come rushing over them, swooping down, and landing, and the dark water going by, the lights on the fences in the dusk.

Rikers could make you deaf. It made him smell. For weeks after his release, he shouted. It turned his volume up. He somehow found himself in exchanges with other men on the subway or on the street who had passed through the jail as well. In hoarse rattling voices, they shouted about the mayhem or the riots or the way it had been worse five years ago, before the reforms. They found each other by the way they spoke out in public, in the line outside the unmarked entrance in Ozone Park where Jimmy waited with the other offenders wearing sweatshirts over their heads and blowing vapor in the cold, shuffling upstairs to give his number and get his pills, as part of the terms of his release.

On the corner, wind-burned, dull-eyed, they said, Oh, you a union man. There's a pride, Jimmy said. You got it made, they said. All you gotta do is keep tight. Keep it in tight! they laughed. They lived in a shelter off Centre Street and did temporary work unloading trucks for Chinese merchants who owned lighting businesses on Bowery.

When I got out after five years, I would do any job, a Puerto Rican named Cat said. My sentence was for murder. I served my time, I don't care. It happened because I was seeing a woman. She was Dominican. Highly attractive to men. Everybody noticed me with her. This guy, he was a big dude, he liked her and he kept trying to pursue an interest in her. I went to talk to him. He broke my nose, hurt my pride. I came back and knocked on the door. She come out and I said, Get José, and as soon as he come, I had a butcher knife. I jumped on him and kept stabbing him. They gave me murder. When I served my time, I used to jump rope, go for a jog, anything to forget the time. What'd you think of Rikers?

It didn't affect me.

When I passed through there, they had the lawsuit against the city. It would have affected you, homeboy, let me tell you.

All I know is I got used to it.

I got used to it too. That don't mean nothin.

I'm not going to change myself just to do what somebody's tellin me to do.

Neither will I, Cat said. But you can't get the years back.

So be it.

So be it. That don't make it right.

To make it right, he took a loop up to the Bronx on his way out to Nassau and cruised down Webster Avenue. When he got far enough, he saw a woman standing by herself with a black handbag and black boots. She was very fat and pale and had small eyes. After she got the rubber on him, he had some trouble, so he repositioned. She looked at him apologetically and said, I can't do it if you choke me. He just stared at her. Okay, but just like don't choke me or nothing. Then he was fine. Leave it. Don't resist. Just keep at it. His skull ring imprinted her white neck. With her missing teeth and rasping voice, she truly reminded him of his mother, at two hundred instead of three hundred pounds. She had bruises on her skin either from getting smacked around or from Kaposi's sarcoma from AIDS.

The third time he was incarcerated, as an alternative to his full sentence of fifteen months, he was given the option of a five-month intensive rehabilitation program run on a boot-camp model. His common-law wife had just gotten pregnant and there was considerable pressure on him to do the right thing.

He's got to do it and make the most of it, Mrs. Murphy said. I only wish they could have offered this to him the first time this happened, but they didn't have it. The discipline is what he never got from Patrick. Some need more than others. You're not going to get through to him unless you earn his respect, which is why I had high hopes for the union.

In the program, you were required to be awake and in full uniform for count, which was held six times a day. The staff called you

Offender. He was issued bedding, towels, white socks, denim trousers, gray uniform shirts, black oxfords, and a black tie. They did group calisthenics and manual labor, sanded furniture. You could only get so many disciplinary reports, though there was an appeal process. The most common thing to get kicked out for was smoking. In the classroom, a black kid in cornrows raised his hand and told the counselor: I'm in this to win this. Then they mopped their facility and made it smell like cleaning solution, the white winter sun falling in the cell windows, a slice of sky visible.

On a visitation day two months in, Mrs. Murphy told Jimmy that she saw a difference in him. It's paying off already.

They got us running like ten miles every day.

He admitted that he already had two disciplinary reports coming. They're saying I wasn't in uniform at count.

It's a test, Mrs. Murphy said. That's how you have to look at it.

He was agitated that his wife hadn't showed up.

His wife wasn't feeling well, his mother said.

Some of us have to be here whether we feel well or not.

It's not for me to say. You're here, I know. But I'm not gonna add fuel to it.

I'm doing everything in my power in here.

I know. Don't add fuel to it.

He didn't know what he was trying for, he said.

Jim, she begged.

You could have told her to come.

We've got forty-five minutes. Let's keep it together. I can cry on the drive back. I'm all cried-out, she grinned, exposing her missing tooth.

They ended on a hug. Seeya next time.

But towards the end of the five months, when he had already been given a final warning, he and four other offenders rolled a cigarette using an envelope for writing letters home and lit it with a tulip—a twist of toilet paper, which they ignited using a battery and a piece of foil—and smoked it standing on a footlocker and blowing their smoke into the air vent.

After he had been violated and sent to another facility to serve his full sentence, he covered his heartbreak by saying I didn't like it there. They try to make you act like a little square boy.

The new system was different. Fresh off the bus, seven of them crossed the hard yard in orange jumpsuits carrying their blankets, while inmates whistled at them. Someone said, Put your chest down. The staff told you one story, the inmates another. Here it was all about the hustle. They didn't want you to be square. After the urine test, they entered the cell block where inmates in black t-shirts sat at square tables rotated like diamonds. Some wore beads and crosses. One of the smaller new arrivals had the tendency to avoid confrontation, name of Mayfield. He had prominent ears. To Mayfield, they said: You look worried. You know that girl? Brittany? (meaning coward). Nice ears. Smile.

Mayfield let people hit him for fun and was placed in protective custody where you heard banging for hours and it was hard to sleep. He heard the disordered nothingness. Medicated prisoners who walked in circles, tireless walking, saying, I keep going round and round. My Dopaquel was switched to Trazodone. Got me sweating and having chills. Mayfield was going to live like that for the next fifteen years.

Jimmy was tense until he fought. The staff rushed in and broke it up and he kept his head up as he was led away. Twelve hours later, they brought him back and the tension started building again. So did the schemes. The idea was to get ahold of tobacco or coffee or anything for a buzz. He cliqued-up with a couple guys from New York who had in common that they were not black.

One was German-Italian, a young man in whose field-mouse-colored hair you could see the scars in his scalp. What hood you claim? They played cards using sugar packs from the chow hall as chips. That's where I'm from, said Frankie. Bum-rushing Flushing. How come I ain't never heard a you? What level you at?

Prepared to fight again, Jimmy stood up. Frankie hugged him. One love, kid. Frankie from Franklin Street, all my life, since '93. Stay on point. We fight niggers all day in here.

———

He caught another case and this time got sent to Krayville, Indiana, where they admitted him on a summer day. The orientation was brief. The only thing they asked him was, Are you a Nazi or an Aryan?

He named his last prison. I was with the white boys there.

Then they put him on the vast yard with the general population and he could feel something physical immediately, an air pressure, a difficulty breathing.

He saw whites wearing flip-flops and white socks and mustaches and red jumpsuits, being released from the security housing unit, getting patted down, sticking out their tongues, arms out like Christ, white eyes with flat black circles like sharks, getting walked with leashes.

An Aryan told him:

Hey, peckerwood, you hang with us.

After they were done processing him, he rolled it up and moved in with white boys who talked about Mongols.

New York? You can tell us where Jimmy Hoffa's at. Until then, you rent your spot with us.

They went to chow together, the yard together, they moved as a unit, posted sentries when they were working out.

You do laundry. You might have to slam something for the house. We got requirements.

The first thing he learned was that this was a war zone. There were politics and the politics were secret—you're out of bounds asking about it, so don't ask. In the yard, they put their towels out on the ground and did their calisthenics, following cadence called by the mob. He practiced the sequence of squat, step, lunge, squat-thrust, which were to be performed by a column of soldiers in unison while walking forward. Everyone had to be ready. The tension he had felt was constant and real. They jogged together under the Indiana sky, past the sign that said One Person At A Time mounted on the smooth synthetic brick and cement structure, the green glass of the pod windows appearing black in daylight. The facility was constructed like a mathematical puzzle, controlled from a central module by Midwesterners with deep resonant country voices.

The mob taught how to be stabbed under freezing showers, to teach you not to flinch. Their workouts were secret like Shaolin monks. Jimmy held a piece for the whites. It's not about hate, everybody's just cliqued-up, they said, referring to the Nazi signs. It's family. They wore Chinese symbols on their chests, eyelids, meaning strength, stealth, honor. The swastika itself was a Buddhist sign. It represented the pattern of a ghost running in an ancient field. They tattooed their faces, shaved their heads, stole the hardened steel spring from the barber's clippers to carve a dagger out of the metal stock of their bunks, going over and over the same cuts tens of thousands of times, a form of meditation. Don't talk about it, be about it, the powerlifters said, facing 30 years and 52 years, respectively, for burglary and burglary with sexual assault. The mind is a weapon. Tunnel vision comes into play. The guards believe they have power. What they have is the tower, an illusion. Jimmy was given what they called artillery to put in his rectum. He carried it out on the yard and removed it and secreted it in the dirt under the picnic table.

When an incident occurred in the yard, an air-raid buzzer went off that went through the entire prison and out into the fields and trees beyond the walls. Wherever you were, you dropped down on your face and spread your arms out. Five hundred convicts wearing high white sweat socks up to their knees got down on their faces in the dirt. Correctional officers sprinted out across the turf towards two men attacking a third. The frenzy is unbelievable—you watch him getting hit one, two, three, four times—falling and scrambling away, trying to run and falling. Getting hit in the back—the other attacker hits him. The officers are hitting them with batons. The fight tumbles over the picnic tables. The victim is still being stabbed. Another officer sprints around from the other side. One of the men flattens out—you see the knife flip out of his hand. They hit one with gas as he tries to get a last lick in, and he falls on his face. The victim pushes himself away with his sweatshirt in red flaps and his skin showing like someone bitten by a lion.

His mother had gone through the cycle of borrowing money to bail him out when he had argued that he could not properly prepare his defense if he were forced to await trial in jail. Then he had missed his court date. For this, she lost her car.

When asked about her son, she said she had lost hope in him. You don't lose hope, she qualified. But it's easy to do. Why is he in jail? Basically, he's a thief. Drugs and alcohol are a big part of it. I've had my battles too—I don't know anyone who hasn't—but I never got mixed up in drugs. No, I don't feel they should be legal. I don't think that's the answer. We've done the counseling, the rehab thing. It's a heartbreaker. But you don't give up. He's got to find himself.

He popped open the bottom of his deodorant and put his finger in the space where he stashed his ball of foil. The ball of foil had been unrolled and rolled back up again many times. When it was unrolled, you could see it contained a chip of what looked like the wing of a cockroach. His cellie had a needle—a tiny tube like the ink tube from a ballpoint pen with a needle on the end. They dropped the blankets over the bars after lockdown and cooked up and got high.

When he was high, Jimmy sat nodding with his eyes shut, his marked-up white arms extended, folds of fat across his white belly. His cellie, shaved head gray, bulbous and helmet-like above his tan face, sat slumped forward, his state sneakers at odd angles to his legs. Speaking with his eyes closed, his cellie said:

This time a year, we used to slaughter a half dozen hogs and ever-body would come for miles. They come on bikes, trucks, ever which way. We had us a kinda moonshine a man couldn't drink. I had me nigger braids in them days. My teeth was gone be all gold all across here...

Jimmy said, I was the biggest rocker...

What's that?

Rock 'n' roll rocker... I play guitar.

My cousin plays anything you give him.

We used to go out to Nassau... where all the cool people went. There was like twenty girls there. They all used to listen to me rock.

Even high, they did not smile. Jimmy had not smiled for a year. The closest thing to smiling was a kind of short-term tolerance granted to the person talking to you. Then he lay down and covered himself with his sheet and lay like a sack of laundry.

When I get released, he mumbled, I'm gonna learn how to play for real.

When you was trippin, his cellie subsequently remarked (with an air of innocence), you was sayin you was gonna learn how to play guitar.

I know how to play, Jimmy said.

The Aryans were bikers, and choosing his moment, Jimmy let it be known that he had been a biker too. Not a biker, but he had ridden bikes in Bay Shore. He'd done stunts with them, wheelies, putting them up on the front wheel—little-ass rice rockets. One time his bike had flipped over and landed on him and everybody thought he was dead. It hurt like hell, but he'd stood up and walked it off and they were all amazed. Oh yeah, come to think of it, he had been a real biker now that you mention it. He'd ridden a Harley, one of those badass choppers with the long neck in front, him just leaned back like this, shades on, gloves on, cruising down the highway. No, he hadn't been in any chapter or nothing. He'd been a lone wolf. He had gone to, let's see, to Virginia Beach, if he remembered. He'd been out to Vegas, where the chicks went crazy for a guy on a bike. He'd been to this other place—he had a picture of it at home in a drawer—a green field, a barbecue somewhere he couldn't remember, but he could remember the good time he'd had, the freedom and the honor and the good music and what it had all meant to him.

The mob's communications went through the mail in code, on the inside of greeting cards, in ghost writing that showed up under laser light between the words I Love You. Their people on the outside took a piece of cloth and sandwiched black tar heroin into it and ironed it until it was paper-thin. They took two identical greeting cards and split the paper with a razor and reassembled them to form a single card with the contraband inside. The thin translucent brown sliver was worth eight hundred dollars inside the prison.

His birthday came and went in a rainy season, when the staff manned the perimeter of the vast yard wearing camouflage Gortex and the inmates tramped through the mud, doing dips and chin-ups in yellow foul weather gear. He didn't receive the card his mother had sent until three months later, after it had been opened by the prison staff and scanned beneath a laser. It contained nothing but a picture of a cake and candles. There was no money. Money's tight right now – XO Mom.

On their way to chow, they strolled by a cell with wadded bloody towels on the concrete floor. Correctional staff in bloody rubber gloves were lifting up a man who looked like yellow plastic. Crusted and streaked blood on his shaved head, stab holes with rubber tubes such as you would siphon gasoline coming out, like shark bites. He had been murdered with a sword.

A shame about you-know-who, they said when they were eating.

Some days he slept for up to twenty hours, but when he opened his eyes, it was still the same calendar day, the same bus station bathroom light was still flickering in his cell, and he was still hammered by the same sound of the place, the distant slamming and calling, the same disappointed sound of the place.

Another intercepted letter read as follows:

You can't sink my Zen man if you thought cannon stood acclaimed Crusader modus warrior in the great pine cabin broadsword.

After attempting to decode it without success, the prison's gang intelligence unit sent it to the cryptography division at Quantico.

The most notorious convict in the structure was a reader. Jimmy met him while they were being held in adjacent freestanding cages inside an octagonal glassed-in bay. He had tattoos up his neck like a green turtleneck. He read Sun Tzu, Lao Tzu, Machiavelli, Miyamoto Musashi, von Clausewitz. I am a warrior, a knight. I study the bushido code. He had 333 years. You can love the game, but the game loves no one. He described being acquitted of the charge he had believed would send him to prison for life and then convicted for a second murder he had committed in the county jail while awaiting the first trial.

You have to laugh at the way that goes, the legend said—a five-foot-eight man in reading glasses.

I went up behind him, threw a rear naked stranglehold on him, put him to sleep. Snapped his neck. When you snap a neck, you feel the bone pop right here against your chest. Pop, just like that. I pulled out my piece and hit him up. Stuck him in the throat, heart, liver. Ran his gears. Hit him twenty-five times. He started gasping and shaking. I got a pipe and smashed his head until his skull broke. Blood everywhere.

Something else we did, which started the myth you may have heard. Completely untrue. What it was, we were hungry after the work. I made a stove with a piece of a towel rolled up tight. We called that a bomb. I lit the bomb and we cooked grilled cheese sandwiches on his body using him as a stand. The story got around the system. Rumor had it we ate his heart. A complete fabrication.

We had some way-out devils in the structure. All my life, I gave everything I had to be a hitter. Loyalty was my code. When I learned the mob put me in the hat, it shattered me. After the commitment, the work I had put in, the holes I put in enemies? Here I am betrayed. But I ain't no coward, no. Despite my terror, fine, I said, I'll stay on the tier. They were gonna nail me sooner or later anyway. So eventually they did. I got sliced down my face. Ran back to my cell, stuffed it full of coffee, a vasoconstrictor. I didn't run to the infirmary or I would have been placed in protective custody. It took me three weeks and two days, but I finally got the guy who sliced me. Offered him a cigarette, said how about a truce? When he went to take it, I got him in the heart. Laters for him.

I don't have any delusions. I know it's over for me too. My time is coming. This is the life I chose and I accept it.

The code, a version of the Enigma Code from World War II, had been identified and cracked by the Federal cryptographers. The message, which came from an individual in maximum segregation, called for the murder of staff members. The author was under twenty-four-hour surveillance, no human contact. His letter was a triumph of ingenuity.

On the main line, the staff, as always, wore vests and batons, their keys connected to their belts on a long chain that hung down out of the pockets of their green trousers like skaters. Some were female, in green bomber jackets with gold emblems, who evaluated males in animal terms: strong or weak. They had families, no illusions about their safety outside the walls.

I don't go to areas where there's a gang presence outside work. I don't bring my personal life to work with me.

Jimmy lifted his foot up behind him like a horse being shod while they ran a metal detector over the flat sole of his state-issued sneaker. They felt down his clothing, his sweatshirt, the big canvas shorts.

Go, they pointed.

They waved him on and Jimmy joined what they called his family in the yard. He looked like a logger in his wool hat. It was a winter day and the sky was stratospheric blue. Expressionless, he watched the yard, occasionally turning to look over his shoulder, monitoring the other races filing out and going towards their respective camps, the whole time rubbing his hands together in wool work gloves, carrying on a laconic conversation and apparently at ease.

21

SHE WENT TO A store that sold South American soccer jerseys, located next to an abandoned lot and a house with a Pentecostal church on the first floor and the upper floors burned-out. The neighborhood was made up of Guatemalan families. The vans that parked on those streets, like the garage doors, were covered in a certain type of graffiti: just words, no colored pictures—just initials and numbers. MS! MSX3. MS13. GC13. Fuck S42. R2B. Niños malos. Sur 13. The Colombiana, whose sign showed a picture of a woman lying facedown with her hips raised so you could see her jeans, was five blocks away. You were not supposed to see into the soccer store. The window was covered by a flag depicting a hawk and the words Brown Pride.

The back of the store was filled with thrift store clothes in bags. The air smelled heavily of grease. A man she assumed was Mexican was eating fried pork out of a Styrofoam takeout shell. His hair was buzzed down tight all over his head the way they do in the military when they give you white walls, and a darker shadow had been left on the top of his head. He had fat cheeks like Buddha and an exact little mustache. When he lifted his lips, he had a gold tooth.

She gave him a hundred fifty dollars, which he put in the pocket of his red Adidas tracksuit jacket. In return, she got a Nebraska State ID in the name Suzy Lin Hong. Address: 1101 North Burdette Street, Omaha, Nebraska 68101. Hair: Blk. Eyes: Blk. Height: 5'2". DOB: March 3, 1979. You could see cut-off Japanese writing around the edge of her photograph.

The week after she bought the ID, the Sing Tao, El Diario, and the Pakistani Times carried the story of a worksite raid at a meatpacking plant in Greeley, North Carolina, in which ICE had detained over two hundred Hispanic workers suspected of immigration violation, separating them from their families and shipping them to federal detention centers in Pennsylvania and Texas. Zou Lei also read that American senators wanted identities to become electronic. To get a job, you would have to pass something called E-Verify.

Do you think it's any good? Zou Lei asked, showing her ID to a woman who sold tofu cream out of a shopping cart without a license.

Good enough.

The woman, who had an out-of-state ID herself, said she had recently been arrested and sentenced to a half day of cleaning up the subway platform. Rather than being afraid of the police, she was angry with them, complaining that they interfered with her livelihood.

The cop discriminate me. I tell cop, You do your job, let me do mine.

But then a Guyanese Muslim who Zou Lei met north of Kissena Park had a different story to tell. An unshaven young man in a backwards ball cap, he was standing on the dead grass by the parking lot next to Golden City, where he had delivered jasmine rice. His truck was in the parking lot and he was smoking a cigarette.

My aunt's husband who lives in Jersey? Forget some little ID—he had the real thing, a green card. It was in the mail and in the meantime he had the piece of paper they send you first to say that it was coming. The cops busted in on him, saying they were looking for someone else, and when they were there they asked him if he was legal. He was like, fuck yeah I'm legal, and shows them the paper, and the immigration arrested him anyway and put him in the Passaic County jail.

What happens to him? Zou Lei asked.

They fucked him up. The guards went after anyone who was Asian, Muslim, Trini, black, brown, whatever—anything like Arab, because they're so stupid and fucking racist, they think everybody with dark skin is the same. They'd come in with dogs at midnight, tear up the cell, and tear up your legal papers. My uncle has bad health and they left him handcuffed on the floor for eighteen hours before they let him go to the hospital. Then they deported him back to Guyana. It's not like here there. Nobody has anything. They ruined his family. My aunt's kids are in trouble. He can't get back to the States. The lawyer told them she has to try and wait until George Bush is gone.

Zou Lei asked where he thought it was safe.

Canada! he said, throwing his cigarette away and blowing the last of his smoke out. I live in Ozone Park and there's a lot of Hindu, a lot of Trini, but there's no guarantee. I personally don't have to worry, but my family has people who have to worry. I don't know what to tell you.

Do you think I pay too much for the ID?

How much was it?

One hundred fifty.

See, everybody's got these. The cops know they're fake.

On a tip from the Guyanese, Zou Lei went to a two-level urban mini-mall where a crime ring was supposed to be selling counterfeit green cards. There was a nail salon and a Taekwondo school on the second floor. Spanish families took their children there to learn martial arts to protect themselves and hold their heads up. She waited around, leaning on the railing, trying to see what was what, while women got their nails silk-wrapped in the small salon. A half hour went by. A man who was working as a barker for a bar on the first floor kept observing her through his shades.

The NYPD rolled down the street, slowing as they passed. She got a feeling she shouldn't be here. Afraid of being mistaken for a prostitute, she left. As she was coming down the stairs, the barker told her she could drink for free, why not come in? And he gestured at the open doorway of the bar, a black space behind him in which she could see nothing.

She thought she might return another day, but then she read that you could be charged with identity theft for using someone's social, and she decided that it wasn't worth the risk.

Ducking a turnstile could land you in federal detention. Since 9/11, the smallest offense made you deportable, depending on what country you were from. According to the World Journal, there were different classifications of countries and immigrants. Zou Lei didn't know if she would be classified with immigrants from China, a trading partner of the United States, or with those from Jamaica, Guyana, Mexico, Egypt, Pakistan, and Afghanistan.

People said that going to English school was always a safe bet, it could only help you, you could budget thirty dollars a class.

But this was the price of a bus ticket, she thought. The price of a hotel for the night, if you were on the road. Meanwhile, she could practice English to her heart's content with Skinner, a real American, and it wouldn't cost a thing. She shelved the idea of school. For seven dollars, she bought a notebook and a used Chinese-English dictionary called the New Century, and made a half-hearted effort at teaching herself. She opened the notebook and wrote in it, knowing that she was forming her characters wrong, making geometric shapes that the Chinese had never thought of. It looked as if her first language was something else and it was trying to come out of her letters. So she only wrote a few incoherent words on the first page and, after that, stuck the notebook, which had a kitten on the cover, in her woven plastic bag.

Seven dollars would have bought her a pound and a half of lamb, which she now wished she were eating. To get something for her money, she tried reading in the dictionary at random, holding the onionskin pages in her calloused fingers, studying the words and sounding them out, sounding out the definitions, which were strange, quaint, or outmoded—although she may not have known this.

Warrior: One who is martial, a hero. Love: Two scalewings, the giving of the heart. Freedom: Up to the self. The United States is a freedom country.

She had a bad dream about Bridgeport in the night and called him the next day.

She dreamed that ICE agents came to Chinatown in the new white Homeland Security trucks and piled into the mall and closed off all the exits, shut everything down, and started checking all the workers with a biometric scanner. The agents put them all in line, made them raise their arms, and scanned their hands and retinas. Polo and Sassoon were cleared and allowed to go, but the scan caught everyone who wasn't legal: the Mexicans and the illegal women. The agents made them lie down on their stomachs. There was nowhere to run and they were going to get her.

When she called him, he sounded remote, but he agreed to meet her after work.

On her way out of the mall, she stopped in the public restroom on the first floor and cleaned the food off her jeans, combed her hair, put on glitter lipstick from the 99-cent store, put on her New York hat, and turned and looked at herself from the back before she walked out. When she saw him in front of Caldor, she hurried over and took his arm.

He didn't offer to take her anywhere and she didn't want to invite herself to dinner, so she walked with him, looking at pawnshops, sneaker stores.

You are busy today? she asked.

He didn't seem to hear questions about himself.

They reached the markets lit by bare bulbs in wire cages. At the cardboard boxes of produce, she pointed out the persimmons, knotweed, ginseng, a spiked fruit the size of a grenade whose name she could not translate, and the dragon eyes, which looked like olives on a vine.

You know this one? It's call the dragon eye.

She made an OK circle with her thumb and forefinger and clucked her tongue, pointed at her eye, and looked at him.

Longyan. You say it?

A Mexican slashed a box open right behind him and she felt his whole body jump as if he'd been electrocuted.

Skinner?

Yeah. What?

You okay?

He nodded. He looked confused and angry.

The Chinese word is very hard.

Maybe he would like to see a true Asian market. He seemed to agree. She pushed inside and, somewhere in the doorway when they were getting shoved by everyone coming out, he let her arm go. Now she was alone in the store and she didn't know if he was coming. She took a box off a shelf at random. Beijing Royal Jelly. She set it down. She didn't see him.

Munggo, congee, Bullhead. She walked slowly deeper into the smell of refrigerant, root, earth, dry goods, wanting to linger near the front. Honey Flavoured Syrup, Old Fujian Wine, Squid Fish Sauce, Cane Vinegar, Coconut Sport, Sarap-Asim, Chicken Essence Drink. A metal tree with a jerky of shredded squid hanging from hooks. Sweet dried pork cost $7.99. They were selling dried powdery balls of pork in plastic cups and luncheon meat in tins. Spam, Ma Ling, Vitarroz, smoke flavor added. She squatted to see the cans, as if she were fascinated by them. Po-Ku mushrooms, young green jackfruit, loquat, lychee, toddy palms. Everything was the kind of thing you added to something else.

On the middle shelves were the three-in-one instant coffees, Oldtown White Coffee, Milo Fuze, and Glow-San Kentucky. Chiu Cheow Sauce, wheat gluten, peanut gluten, pickled lettuce and Frentel. There was Kewpie mayonnaise, peanut butter, and Kool Aid. The Skippy felt good and heavy. She checked the calories. It cost two dollars and fifty-nine cents.

Maybe, she thought. She didn't know. She put it down.

He came down the aisle when she was in canned fish. Sweet hot sardines were $2.50. The can felt empty, and she put it down.

He picked up a can of smoked bangus.

That's original, he said.

What?

Nothin. Whatever this is.

It's fish. You should eat it, she recommended. She might have been a little angry. It was full of nutrition for the body, she told him. Good for long life.

Cooking oil was stacked in a gold pyramid against a wall, fifty-pound bags of rice on forklift pallets. She decided to take her time in the store to punish him a little. She tried to figure calories per dollar for Plum Rose rice in her head. And then she made him follow her to the back of an aisle to look at the cooking gear: butane gas bottles, rice cookers, kitchen scissors, roach spray. A wok was $8.99. She got down on the floor and dug through what they had on the shelf, trying to see if she'd missed anything. She hadn't. The cheapest rice cooker cost fifteen American dollars and that was too much.

They went past the freezer case of soymilk, the black chickens, and the whole fish on ice. There was so much to eat, she thought. She wasn't all that angry anymore.

You get something? she asked, thinking they could combine ingredients.

I'll pass, he said.

He had seen a tub of wriggling mucus-foaming fish with feelers, the dirty aquarium tanks with heavy things floating in the green water.

They were coming up to the butcher counter and she thought of her father making a fire and butchering a lamb, and she took his arm again.

There were gaunt butchers in pink-stained smocks selling chicken gizzards and feet. Skinner looked through the hanging plastic strips.

A ribcage was being sectioned with a bandsaw. Bone meal sprayed out and Skinner flinched. The butchers yelled what you want? Women with long glossy black hair demanded organs. Small old women called out for the inside of the stomach, the sponge-like stomach lining, the bloodless color of cabbage. Hurry a little faster! The butchers stood on their toes to see them. A kidney in a paper wrapper was handed over the counter.

Zou Lei looked at the price of lamb. She didn't know, she said. She glanced at him, saw him looking away. To her, he appeared tired of being here. Maybe she didn't need.

Some days, she noticed, he would hug her when she came to see him, but he might just as easily open the door and turn his back on her without a word, as he did one evening, and leave her to follow him down the stairs alone to find him lying face-down on his mattress in the dark.

Skinner? You playing hide and seek?

She felt her way to him.

I can put the light?

He said nothing. She sat on his bedside and touched his leg. What has happen to you?

He spoke into the mattress and she couldn't understand him.

What you say?

I said I have a headache.

She rubbed his leg.

You drink too much alcohol. You go to party, it's fine. I'm not jealousy. But too much, it's bad. You are strong man lying in the bed. Look at this strong man. He is lazy man.

She moved closer.

While you go to party, I do some exercise you will like.

She picked up his thick heavy hand and set it on her thigh and flexed her leg.

You feel it?

He took his hand away and rolled over to face the wall. He pulled his Goarmydotcom t-shirt over his face to block the light.

She looked at him more closely and said now she could see how he truly might be sick.

To be near him, she stayed and read his magazines instead of leaving. There was perfect silence except for her flipping the pages until late into the night.

Have I done something to bother you? she asked.

No, he said.

Okay, she said. But I warn you, I'm very tough. Even you aren't nice to me, I don't go away.

Where she was from, a man and woman might live apart for many years, due to economic reasons, only seeing each other once or twice a year when they were given permission by the authorities.

22

HE WENT TO SEE her at her job at eleven in the morning on a weekday. He went inside, but it was the middle of the rush and he couldn't see her, so he left and smoked a cigarette on Main Street in front of Modell's and Burger King.

A cast of characters stood around under the awnings waiting for the bus, smoking, watching the street, going nowhere, not functioning, some of them with canes—the people they called Jerry's kids in the army and razzed each other about being, because so much of the military, including its most outstanding soldiers, came from the lower end of civilian society. A female in pink terry cloth sweatpants was screaming on her phone.

I'll go to jail! she insisted. Yes, I will! I got a baby inside me. At least I'll get fed... Stop talking! Stop talking! What happened to the twenty dollars I gave you?

He finished his cigarette and went back to the mall. The mall was an office building that had been taken over by the Chinese. In its present state, everything had the half-finished, jerry-built appearance of transition from one thing to something else. There were cardboard shipping containers littered around the floor. Some units had bare concrete floors and raw cinder block walls, others had carpets and wall coverings and fluorescent lights. One room was being used to warehouse thousands of dried medicinal herbs, which were stored in a chaos of buckets, tubs, bins, bowls, cups, wooden drawers—containers of every description—anything that could be used to hold something else, even paper envelopes—none of it organized, all of it just lying there, while a twenty-year-old guy with a gold chain chewed wontons with his mouth open and watched a DVD. The sign over his head said Cohen's Fashion Optical. You couldn't tell what was old and what was new. You couldn't tell whether something was coming or going. Things were in the middle of being built and destroyed at the same time. It was an environment he might have recognized.

Senior citizens wearing Red Army hats, people who had lived through thirty years of war and revolution, paced around as if they were on inspection and approved of everything they saw.

He put his shades up on his head and looked for her beyond the customers but could not see her: her counter was still busy in the food court. So he turned around and went back outside again.

This time, he crossed Roosevelt Avenue and went under the train tracks, where two tall Africans were standing, the sun shining on their dull black faces and dusty looking clothes. Ahead was the building where she had first worked, where he had met her, and he saw a knot of men inspecting something, their hands clasped behind their backs. Between their legs he caught a glimpse of flesh. He thought they were staring at someone injured on the street, and he looked around automatically to see if there was more to it: anything burning, relatives crying, calling out for vengeance. But the traffic was flowing normally past the restaurants. He went over and looked over their shoulders and saw that they were looking at a series of blown-up photographs propped up on the sidewalk.

The first one was of an Asian woman in her forties, face in profile, holding up her dress to reveal a blackened buttock, in the center of which was a deep abscess. There was another photo of a woman's torso. Her breasts had been removed. Her chest looked like lasagna. In another image, you saw the white sheet she was lying on. From the attitude of her face, it was clear that she was dead. People had Chinese toe tags. Someone's legs had been photographed to show bruises. In the shot, there was a hand holding a ruler indicating the dimensions. There was a photograph of wadded blood-soaked clothing on a cement floor near a drain.

A woman came towards Skinner as if a magnetic force were pushing her towards him and asked him to sign her clipboard. Her eyes were luminous and although she did not have a forceful voice, she gazed blankly and steadily at him with her eyes and kept talking like a computer that could not be turned off.

The human rights criminal, she said.

I'm not signing anything.

When she persisted, he said:

I don't know you. You can fake those. He shrugged from behind his shades. You've got, what, four bodies? I've got two hundred pictures like that on my camera at home.

A man who was working with her told her in Chinese not to talk to Skinner, and she broke off talking to him immediately.

Skinner looked at the pictures again before he moved on.

No friends of mine, he thought.

At a stand where you could see the models on the magazine covers, Skinner said, Now, that's what I'm talkin about, and a Pakistani turned to watch him.

He smoked a cigarette halfway and snuffed it on his boot sole.

He went across Kissena to a takeout joint and ordered pork fried rice. There was a communication problem with the people who ran the place, but nothing that couldn't be overcome by pointing, or so he thought. A man took the meat off the hook in the window and chopped it with a cleaver right in front of him. They charged him more than he expected. Roast pork. I thought I was getting that one there. See where I'm pointing?

They brought someone else out to explain. You get roast pork. Look, there are two, you get expensive one.

No shit, Skinner said. I bet that was an accident.

He went and sat.

The rice was cold and the grease was larded all throughout the rice and turning thick and white. When corpses burn, he remembered, the fat cooks out and you get wax congealed on everything. His fork was rancid. The smell triggered something inside him and he left his plate and went outside and thought he was going to be okay in the cold, but then two seconds later he bent and gagged and vomited a mouthful of orange stuff in the center of the sidewalk. People went around him and, from a safe distance, looked at him. He went back inside and started pulling napkins out of the dispenser, wiping up his face.

When he was clean, he wiped his eyes and bought a soda somewhere else. He smoked another cigarette. His hands stopped shaking, he wiped his eyes, and he was fine again.

At a newsstand, he made his way to the back and started looking at the magazines, not seeing them, picking them up and dropping them back in the metal slot, one after the other.

The Pakistani's dark face followed him like a radio dish as he was leaving.

You need help?

Not from you.

He went back to her job again and sat at a table in the food court, his face impassive, his body slouched and motionless as if he were stoned—except for his foot jiggling up and down like a motor beneath the table.

When she came out to collect trays, she saw him at once in the teeming crowd.

Hey! I do not see it's you! I'm surprising!

Finally. He lifted up his shades, revealing his bruised-looking eyes. New-pong-yow. Where you been? He blinked at her like somebody waking up and seeing the sun.

You are feeling better today, she said. Yesterday he had been sick. He had gotten better and that was good, she said. And you come to see me. I am so glad. Welcome. Welcome to my job.

She cleaned tables near him so she could talk to him.

Maybe it isn't a good job, she expressed, as she leaned over a table, wiping it with her rag, Skinner watching her moving. It was all immigrants here—had he noticed? But everybody has to work at something, and there shouldn't be any shame attached to a job. When her English was better, she would do something else. It cheered her that he was here, and she went around with a bounce in her step taking trays off the tables, dumping them in the trash, and stacking them on her cart. When she finished the tables near him, she circled out to tables farther away at the edge of the food court, collected their trays and circled back to him.

She asked Skinner what he was doing today.

Chest.

Oh, she said. Your chest?

Yeah. Chest and shoulders.

You go to the gymnasium?

Yeah, he was. He had to go, he said.

I also go to the gymnasium.

You do?

Not now. Will be! I will be soon. For now, I will exercise by my work. You can tell? She squatted up and down fast and picked up a chopstick, winked at him and flipped it into a bucket.

He wanted to know when she was getting off work so he could meet her.

You won't be tired? she asked.

No, no way. That was yesterday, not today.

She didn't want to bother him if he was tired.

It's no bother. He wanted to see her.

She wiped her swollen hands with her rag.

Work is finish at six o'clock.

All right, I'll be here then.

Okay.

You good to go?

Oh, I am exciting. Only five hour more.

We'll go back to the crib.

It was partly a question. He glanced at her to see what she would say. She didn't say she wouldn't.

After she pushed her cart through the restaurant counters to the dishwashing machine in the back and he had watched her go, he picked up his shades and walked out through the crowd and left. His leg had stopped shaking while they were talking, and his hood had fallen off revealing his seamed neck. But it had gotten colder since the morning, the clouds had come in, and he put his hood back up over his head and started walking to keep warm, passing businesses that were boarded-up or being run inside units that had been sealed and broken into, down where they threw the garbage down the stairs, below street level. He saw rolls of carpeting behind a half-shut hinging metal gate.

He came to a bar, one of the few bars in Flushing, and went inside. There were arcade games in the corner. A microwave sat on a counter in an adjoining room that contained folding metal chairs. The power cords had dust on them. There were sofas in front of a supersized TV screen—the old kind with the three colored lights like traffic lights that project onto the screen like a slide projector. The bar itself was just a counter with liquor bottles behind it. There were no taps for draft beers in this bar. If you wanted a beer, they gave you a can out of a cooler, which also held a pack of hotdogs. The lights were off and the space smelled like cleaning solution from the bathroom, which an old man they called Johnny had just cleaned. When Johnny was done, he came out of the bathroom with his mop and asked the bartender what else he should do and the bartender told him, Nothing that I know of. The old man was putting the mop away when Skinner came in and asked for a drink.

The bartender poured him a drink and Skinner sat sipping it watching basketball on TV.

The bartender was a talker, and without an invitation, he started telling him a story. The other night, he said, he'd had to give a guy a ride home. I was pissed too, but he couldn't do anything, he was blind, not a prayer that he could drive, so I said what the hell. We got my car and I dropped him off. It was four in the morning. I come out of his garage, and there's this cop waiting right there after giving someone a DUI.

The bartender had paused in Windexing the bar to tell his story, and he punctuated what he was saying by making faces of astonishment at his own story.

This was a Friday, so you know it would have been a long weekend. Monday or Tuesday before you get in front of the judge at least!

He blew up his cheeks, as if to say, what a thing! Skinner nodded along when he had to. It had turned into a gray day outside. The bartender kept talking. He remarked that he could tell from Skinner's accent that he wasn't local. This led to his asking where Skinner was from and getting out of him that he was a vet. When he heard he was a vet, he took the bottle of Parrot Bay and topped him up.

Skinner already felt the first one and didn't plan on having any more. Thanks, he said.

It's the least I can do, the bartender said and stood there for a minute with his arms propped on the bar and his head half-bowed holding a moment of silence for the armed forces. The old man Johnny had taken his place at the bar while they were talking and was sitting with a can of Budweiser. Now he turned on his seat and worked his mouth, trying to speak.

You was over there?

Skinner didn't hear him.

Johnny's talking to you, the bartender said.

He looked over at the old man moving his mouth.

You was over there in Iraq?

Yeah, Skinner said.

Johnny's a navy man, the bartender told him.

Cool. Hey.

I was in the navy. But what you guys are doing is... is unbelievable.

Skinner threw back his drink and swallowed it. The bartender filled his glass again.

It's on me, chief.

Good looking out, Skinner said, rubbing his face. His knee started bouncing up and down.

This guy's your friend, Johnny said. He'll take care a you.

Wherever you go in the world, look for the Irish bar, the bartender said. They'll help you out. And if they can't help you, they'll know someone who can. He made an expression of taking you into confidence.

Johnny staggered off to the bathroom he had cleaned, to use it, and while he was gone, the bartender took Skinner into his confidence again, telling him that Johnny should have been dead years ago. He shouldn't be alive, he said with his voice lowered.

Skinner took another large swallow of his drink and felt it burn and make him slightly sick and then spread and commence the changes in his brain which felt like shades coming down.

I've been all over the world, the bartender was saying. Brazil, Amsterdam, China.

What were you doing over there?

Fucking whores.

No shit.

I've fucked whores everywhere. I call it touring and whoring.

Skinner didn't understand the man's brogue and made him repeat what he'd said.

Oh, touring. I get it now. You was touring! You never know with people what you're gonna learn.

They toasted each other in formal style.

Another one for my man, Skinner said pointing at Johnny's beer. He shook the bartender's thin freckled hand. Get yourself one, dude.

Don't mind if I do, the bartender said.

Another hour passed this way. The bartender, who wore a black t-shirt, came out from behind the bar, wearing black jeans and long black leather shoes that tapered to a squared-off toe, and went outside, taking a lighter from the black leather holster on his belt, to smoke a cigarette on what was now the street at night, taillights everywhere coming off the freeway, people going home from work, the subway rumbling underneath the bar. Johnny was leaning out of his chair talking to Skinner. The war was the subject of conversation once again.

Women and children, the old man said beseechingly. Women and children. I couldn't understand it.

Skinner looked for the bartender.

Gimme another, dude.

As many as you want, guy.

There was no spout on the bottle and Skinner watched the clear liquor run back on the bartender's knuckles when he poured. Then he drank it and tried to watch the blurry game. The players ran back and forth like herds of deer in a hunting program, like civilians in a hamlet. They fled across the court and then they stopped and smelled the air. They never knew who was going to hit them with the ball.

The commercial came on, the game having ended, and Skinner found himself alone.

Where'd he go?

Who, Johnny?

Yeah, him.

He had to go home, guy.

Skinner tried to stand and fell off his stool and hit his head on the bar. His cell phone and keys fell out of his jeans.

Shit, the bartender said. I thought you guys could hold a lot. I didn't think you really had that much.

He was worried that the owner would see what was going on or, worse still, that they would have a cop come by. Looking over his shoulder, he came around the bar and helped him up.

Hold it. My keys.

I've got your keys. Let's just get you on your way.

As the bartender was supporting him out the door, Skinner's cell phone rang on the floor.

My phone.

The bartender went back and picked it up.

Hello? he said. Just a minute.

He gave the phone to Skinner.

Baby? He brought the phone up to his ear and heard her tiny voice against the sound of traffic. His eyes were closing. Zooey?

She said she hadn't seen him, she had waited, and then had headed home.

Where are you, baby?

At home, she said.

There was silence on the line.

I was waiting for you, he said. That's what I've been doing this whole time.

23

SKINNER THREW BACK A double and did his sarcastic dance. He had been drinking since noon, having taken the subway into the city to drink in the bars over by the Port Authority. Later he couldn't dance. Now it was night and the traffic streamed by down the avenue into the glowing purple black between the buildings.

He went to the strip club on the billboard, not remembering how he navigated there among the theaters and bars, neon rainbows in his eyes. Security let him in, and in the light, the orange light, the waitress who came to get his one drink minimum could not get his attention. She touched his shoulder. Skinner startled. He stared at her narrow-eyed with condemnation. At the next table, he saw a little girl in nunlike habit screaming at her mother's headless body.

What's wrong? she said. I thought you were partying.

The lights went down and the dancer came out and Skinner left. The pill he took was medically not advised with all the alcohol he was consuming. Let me pick you up, he said to a guy with his two friends in the middle of Times Square.

Go fuck your mother, you fucking faggot.

No, not like that. Like this. He held his arms out. Fireman's carry. Come on.

Somebody pushed him and he fell in the street and a cab almost hit him. He got right back up and did not seem to hear that anyone was laughing. This was outside another bar, a Con Ed truck nearby, compressor running.

Finally a teamster let Skinner lift him up, and Skinner ran down the block with him, then did a squat, then ran back, then walked. His breath was rising in the darkness. The teamster ordered Skinner to put him down and Skinner didn't want to do it. The man shifted his weight, which was considerable, and forced Skinner to put him down.

I'm two thirty-eight. You all right.

Skinner tried to pick him up again and the teamster didn't let him. He pushed him down. Be cool. Skinner tried to lift him again. There was a scuffle and other guys got between them. He's strong, the teamster kept saying. A little mofo like that. I don't want to kill him. The fight got broken up. Skinner was gone, they forgot him. The other teamsters started playing fireman's carrying as a game, picking each other up and dropping each other. How much you weigh? How many wings you eat?

Skinner went back to the strip club and, at the door, security told him: Take your hood off. Lose the hood. The camera's gotta see you. They wouldn't let him in. He wandered back and forth in front of the doorway of the club, a black hooded figure, security ignoring him.

There were beginning to be news stories online—interviews with military wives and so on—about returning soldiers, which Skinner watched. And he watched videos uploaded by disaffected soldiers, in which his comrades-in-arms gave testimony about the folly and evil of what they had been a part of.

A National Guardsman who used to be a purchaser for Home Depot had been sent to Iraq as a logistics specialist and his convoy had struck an IED. Now his skull was partly missing. When he turned his head sideways, you couldn't believe he was still alive. His nose and ears were gone. In his interview, he recalled a bad time just after his eighth surgery.

I was suicidal because I thought my daughter would be afraid of me.

Struggling not to cry on camera, he raised his hands to wipe his eyes and you saw his pink charred wrist bones and a finger-like appendage instead of hands.

Sometimes the interviewee was wearing a prison jumpsuit. Skinner watched video after video. He heard:

Scanning. Aware. Symptoms. Whenever I leave for somewhere, I check for guns.

Photograph of self after writing suicide note.

Losing balance. Getting angry. Trouble sleeping. Sleep two hours, stay up 48 hours. Sleep three hours—etcetera.

I took stimulants in Iraq that are illegal in the States, and when I got home the army took them away. There was no logical transition. Drinking took over from there. This is my only friend, I thought. I've had medical problems. Thrown keys through walls. Kicked in windows. Pushed her.

Triggers: door slam, someone yelling. Pins and needles of fear.

Self-isolation. Guilt. I can't get this image of this child out of my head.

Antipsychotics, sleeping meds, tranquilizers.

Tattoos of M16s up and down his arms. Killed child. Killed spouse. At nightclubs. Rapes on base. Said I'm a nice guy with a gun. He put the cabdriver in the trunk of the car and burned him alive in North Carolina.

No one knows what the families get dragged through. An army shrink told my husband that she couldn't treat him for his nightmares. So I called his CO and was told the army doesn't give out hugs to crybabies. And this was after he was already hitting me and had threatened to kill me once.

Traumatic brain injury. They still deployed him. I know I'll never get him back. Our daughter's, like, that's not my father.

I'd say hopeless, lost, depressed. Beheadings. Monster. Laugh at overwhelming violence. Leg blown off.

I pushed her. She jumped away. Fell in the shower. When she stood up she screamed. Her hair was covering her face. It reminded me of things I had seen, of the screams of fear of being attacked, and I reacted. I had my hand over her mouth. This is the mother of my children (voice breaks). She wasn't moving when I got off her (begins crying).

I tried to bring her back, but she was gone.

He came out of a bar and tried to remember where he was. The passenger door of a black sedan parked against the curb popped open and someone called to him.

Hey, guy.

Skinner peered at the vehicle.

We want to ask you something, guy.

What do you want to ask me?

Come here for a minute.

Why can't you ask me from there?

A shadow moved in the front seat and a different voice said, When did you get out, brother?

Oh. Hey. Like, real recently.

Skinner shuffled over to the vehicle.

The passenger wore a bomber jacket. The driver, who wore corrective glasses and a Jets hat, was leaning around him. They were both carrying pistols.

You deployed?

Did I deploy? Yeah, I deployed.

What were you? Not intelligence?

Maybe if I'd been smarter. I was in the infantry.

My man, the driver said. He reached his fist out the door and Skinner bumped it.

Hooah, brother.

Hooah, Skinner said. All the way.

I saw you in there, and I was, like, he's one of my guys.

Definitely, Skinner nodded.

He thought you looked lost, the cop in the bomber jacket said.

No, I'm not.

You from around here?

No. I just came up from base.

You got somewhere to stay?

Oh, yeah. Hell yeah.

Cuz a lot of guys—it's bad. They wind up, you know, like, making thinking errors when they get out.

Yeah.

They have the battle skills, but do they have the civilian skills.

Skinner nodded, his head lowered. Then he covered his eyes.

Both of the men in the car got quiet.

Skinner was having trouble controlling himself. Just a minute, he said. He walked to the back of the sedan, snorted up phlegm and hocked it on the pavement, wiped his eyes, and came back.

The wave had passed. Fuckin stupid, he said and hocked again.

Get in and talk.

I'm good.

You got any family?

Yeah, I mean, I do. I'm good though. I mean, I don't need anyone worrying about me.

You gotta get over that.

I know.

If there's a problem, you fix it, right?

I know.

Do you know who to call?

What, like the VA?

Anybody you can call if you get in trouble—the VA, your family, anyone from your unit, anyone like that. A friend, anyone. As opposed to—as opposed to—for example, drinking twenty-four hours a day.

The driver was staring at him, leaning out at him, neck stretched, mouth a clinched lipless line, glasses reflecting the vapor light.

Okay, Skinner said. Roger that. I appreciate it. I do. I'm good to go.

He's good, the passenger cop said. He's okay.

The driver took his Jets hat off. He was balding with long, dank strings of hair pasted to his dome, and when the hat came off some of them lifted away from his head. He gave a short nod.

Skinner looked across Roosevelt.

I think my bus is here.

His bus is here. Don't miss it, guy, the passenger said.

The driver stuck his fist out the door one more time and Skinner bumped it again.

Be safe, bro.

Hooah, Skinner said, and went around their sedan and across the avenue towards the buses idling in the dark.

24

HE WENT UPSTAIRS TO pay his rent and found the apartment full of people drinking beers and eating subs from Fratelli's pizzeria.

Mrs. Murphy was talking to several different people at once. She snapped her lighter, leaned back and aimed her smoke away from them up at her cupboards. She was wearing the same velvet house-coat that she had worn before and she had a cold cup of coffee sitting next to her on the table, as if she had just come out for breakfast. One of the people she was talking to was a big guy with red hair and the baritone voice of an athlete. He was wearing a Jets jersey in super extra large.

Come in, come in, she told Skinner, who came in. He gave her his rent check and she set her coffee cup on it. Take a beer.

This is Brad from downstairs. The tenant.

I'm John, the big guy said. I'm her stepson.

Yo, Skinner said and shook the guy's hand.

There were about ten other people in the apartment: neighbor-hood women in sweatpants and hoop earrings, young men stopping off from work, their sweatshirts and jeans grimy with black dust from ironwork, faces red from the cold. They all talked with thick New York accents, which made everything they said sound Italian. Not everyone was quick to say hello. The males didn't talk to people they didn't know. It was unclear what the purpose of the gathering was. The big guy was Mrs. Murphy's stepson. He had not grown up with her. He was Patrick's son by another woman, and he was in the NFL.

Skinner popped the cap off a Michelob, hooked the neck of the bottle in his trigger finger, and lifted it to drink, his lips rolled under. His face was covered in stubble and he was in his socks. His heels were standing on his jeans, his boxers showing. He had just taken sertraline half an hour ago and it created a distance between him and the world. He heard the football player's baritone across this distance.

He was talking about his tires. He had left them in the yard behind the house. A guy had done some work, some plumbing, for the family. Through some kind of fast talking, he had gotten the tires from Pat, who hadn't known what they were worth.

Mrs. Murphy said, I know, I saw them. They were here six months. They were covered in mud.

New, they went six hundred dollars apiece.

They weren't new.

Even old, you were talking nineteen hundred, two grand in tires.

Okay. Let's call it that. What did you do about it?

I called the guy. I left messages on the phone. Finally he tells me he doesn't have them.

Well, I doubt he does. He probably sold them.

That doesn't help me much.

I know it doesn't help you. She rolled her eyes. It doesn't help me either.

I know.

If I knew what Patrick was going to do before he did it, I'd be a mind reader. I didn't know what he was doing.

I know that.

I hope you do.

It's just something that happened. Life goes on, the football player said.

Let's hope it does.

How's everything with that situation?

That's what we're gonna find out. At this point, we're hearing April. But the system is so bad.

It'll work out.

Yeah, well, we'll see.

There was a woman with black hair sitting at the kitchen table next to Mrs. Murphy smoking a cigarette. She was sitting folded on the chair with her knees up and her feet pulled in. Sometimes her eyes took a quick measuring look at you and then went back to looking at the ashtray she was sharing with Mrs. Murphy. Her skin was yellowish and rough and she had high cheekbones. Her name was Vicky.

We'll see, she echoed.

And turning to Mrs. Murphy:

Who was the guy he had a problem with?

Some guy named Rick.

Rick from Brooklyn?

From the bar right here.

Yeah. That's Brooklyn Rick. They're the same.

If you say so.

Real skinny? No ass?

That would be him, she said. You know him?

Vicky nodded and let the smoke out of her lungs and blew it upwards.

Oh yeah, she said. He's a thief.

Okay. Figures I let him in my house. Look, he went by the book with me.

He did major time in the pen.

We all have something. Come on. If I was gonna go by that, nobody would be left in this house for a party. You know what I'm saying, Vicky? Let's get real. The guy's a sixty-year-old man with white hair. And him? Mrs. Murphy dropped her voice and looked across the kitchen at her stepson, who was talking to two short wide girls. The size of him?

No doubt. No doubt.

In my younger days, I could have shaken it out of him, thief or no thief.

We know the deal.

There's a whole history, Vicky. I'm not going into it.

Let it lie.

Mm-hm. I'm waiting for the call.

What time is it?

Mrs. Murphy checked her cell phone, which was lying on the table by her coffee cup.

Should be any minute.

Skinner finished his beer and put it in the sink. The bottle fell over when he put it down. He said whoops and, deliberately, set it upright again and watched it to see if it would tip. The woman Vicky had gotten up and was standing with one foot on her chair. I gotta get a bite, she said and she came around the table to the counter and took a half a sub out of the aluminum foil and put it on a paper plate, the shredded lettuce falling out. She cut her eyes sideways at him.

Hey. You Greg's friend?

Who's that?

He's the guy they had before you. I thought he was your friend.

No. Don't know him. I'm not from here.

What are you, in college?

No.

Like LaGuardia? She wants to go there.

Vicky indicated Erin, who was standing with one foot on top of the other foot, her heavy hip leaning against the counter. She was wearing an oversized shirt that came down covering the widest part of her. She had taken the bread off a sandwich and she was picking at the cheese. Her face was angled down. She had an expression of complete equanimity on her face. Since he had arrived, she had ignored him.

No, I'm not in college.

So, what are you, here for work?

No, I'm more like checking it out.

That's cool. Explore your world. So you don't know anyone. You're, like, who is everybody?

I know her and her daughter.

You met Pat, the father?

I don't know.

You'd know. If you shook his hand, you'd know. When he took your arm off.

What's he got, like an Irish voice?

Patrick Murphy? Yeah.

I might of heard him through the floor.

Through the floor? That sounds right, she said. That was him.

He glanced again at Erin, trying to get a look at her face, to see if she had any bruises, any black eyes or fat lips.

So where you from?

I'm from Pittsburgh.

That figures. I hear the twang. You don't sound like you're from the city.

We're rednecks where I'm from.

Someone who overheard them mentioned that John Gambia from the neighborhood had come back from basic training sounding like a redneck.

Come on already. Get the sand out of your shoe, Vicky said.

He took another Michelob. When he opened it, the bottle cap fell and bounced on the linoleum. The star on the back of his neck showed when he bent to pick it up.

Indicating John, she said, You know this guy actually plays for the Jets.

Cool. I'm a Steelers fan.

Uh-oh, John said.

It's all good.

Skinner tried to toast him, but the football player didn't have a bottle. He held up his big fist and Skinner tapped it with his beer.

Everyone wanted to talk to the professional athlete, who, though not much of a talker, had an easy way about him, and spoke to everyone. Generally he didn't stay too long speaking to any one person. Skinner made him stay and talk about strength and conditioning. I played ball in high school, Skinner said. John was polite. He acknowledged having had the clinic run on him in training. The two weeks in the preseason were tough, just as you have surely heard. He began to move away. Skinner kept saying, hold it dude, detaining him.

Squat, bench, chins, sprints.

Okay, said John.

Wait, what about power cleans, dips?

Okay, that's good.

Dips are upper body squats.

Yup.

Burpees, hit-it's, suicides. Six days a week, two times a day.

That's a pretty heavy schedule. What are you doing all this for?

Skinner just shook his head.

I don't know.

How many of those've you had, buddy?

Skinner took a while to answer. Someone else—an older woman with her hair in a scrunchy—came over and said hi to John and gave him a hug. Her voice was gone and half of what she said was whispery air.

It's scary how different I look from one day to the next, isn't it!

She adjusted her scrunchy to hold her pale blond hair up in a stalk above her head. The football player turned to speak with her. In so doing, he presented Skinner with his back.

I've had one.

The football player didn't turn around.

I've had one, Skinner said more loudly. A nineteen-year-old iron-worker with a silver earring and a reflective orange stocking cap began looking at him steadily.

The general conversation turned back to John Gambia and what he was doing in Iraq. It was agreed that he was doing very well.

At this point, the cell phone by Mrs. Murphy's coffee cup rang. It played the chorus from the song: I can't go on, because I love you too much, baby. It was an important call. Everyone went quiet. It's him, she said. He wants to talk to you. And she handed the phone to Vicky who took it into the hallway to talk. The conversation in the kitchen resumed while she was gone. Skinner's eyes were getting heavy. He put his empty on the counter and rubbed his face. He listened to them talking about people he didn't know. Then she came back a few minutes later and gave the phone to Mrs. Murphy. He wants to talk to you now. She turned herself away from the others as much as her size would allow, but anyone who was listening was going to hear her side of the conversation anyway. She said:

What's wrong?... What is it?... Is it the same guard?... Can you do it on a different shift?... Listen to you... I hear you getting fresh with me... Just take it easy... Okay. Just take it easy. We're going to see you soon. Just take it easy, will you?... All right. Goodbye.

The call ended. She set the phone down on the table. She reached for her Slims.

How's he doing? John asked.

He's upset over the phone schedule. That's all the time he had. He's okay though.

He's okay.

Erin asked, Is he still having a problem with the same guard?

Mrs. Murphy eyeballed her daughter.

Vicky, who was folded like a black cat on a kitchen chair, said, Yeah, and tapped her cigarette in the ashtray.

From across the room, Skinner said:

Who're you talkin about?

The question caused a silence in the apartment. People stared at him, then they looked at Mrs. Murphy to see what she would say. From the back of the kitchen, Erin muttered something in a rising singsong voice that you didn't have to hear to understand. The iron-worker with the silver earring exchanged a look with one of his male friends.

My son, Mrs. Murphy answered.

What, is he overseas? Skinner asked. Is he the Army Ranger?

You're getting him confused.

You could say that, someone else said. Not exactly. Haha. Jimmy, no. Not the army. That would be someone else. Can you imagine Jimmy taking orders? No, let's drop it.

But Skinner felt like he was missing something. I'm sayin, is he a brother soldier?

He's not in the army. Put it that way.

He fucked up.

The cops fucked up, if you asked me, Vicky said and nodded at her cigarette.

He's the place you go when you fuck up, John said and laughed. Leave it at that.

Thank you, Mrs. Murphy said. And would you quit the f-word in my kitchen. There was general laughter. And since we're putting it in the street, yes, he's upstate. We get him back in April.

Then you gotta have another one of these, have everybody over.

We'll do something. Do me a favor: next time, get Guinness and you can come. More general laughter. She lit a cigarette and smoked it, talking in a lowered voice to a friend. The episode was forgotten, it seemed. Erin examined the remaining food and asked her mother if she had eaten. No one asked if Skinner wanted something to eat. He had consumed three beers. Mrs. Murphy told her daughter to bring her something. Not the whole thing. Cut it for me.

Skinner's eyes were nearly shut from dopiness.

You wanna see my workout? he asked the ballplayer. You can tell me if it's good.

He was told: That's okay, hoss. Another time.

25

HE TOOK A DRINK from a flask of Bacardi Scorched Cherry and watched an execution on his laptop. A man's body tensed while his killer sawed at his neck. Two men kneeled on him. The audio was bad, and Skinner turned the volume up. That sound was him protesting. The clock was running. The film advanced. The man had become inanimate in the last thirty seconds. Now they lifted up the head, separating it from the corpse.

Skinner took another drink from his bottle. The audio was bad because there was sand in his laptop. His hearing was sixty percent in his strong-side ear, the side he held his weapon on. Battlefield dirt got in your body through the lungs and through wounds.

He watched IEDs detonating, the explosion blotting out the vehicle, the men, the road, then the brown cloud rolling down and spreading out, and you could see the vehicle at an angle. He watched guys who got hit by a sniper, getting punched down. He watched a wounded fighter lying in the dirt. The ground was smeared with a wide red swath of blood. The fighter lifted his AK-47 and the good guys shot him. The sparks went through his body at angles: through his shoulder, chest. Now he lay unmoving. He watched his guys shooting from a rooftop, ten minutes of jumping footage showing three or four guys, the M60 shaking in bursts, the guys talking, pointing over there, the M60 being turned, the casings falling out like dry feces, set to death metal.

He listened to cock rock, thrash metal, big rock ballads, country and western—the numbers they used to play in battle. He turned the decibels all the way up, and it still felt as if he couldn't hear it. And it wasn't because he was deaf, it was because nothing sounded like anything after battle.

In his mind, he knew that she was special. He could picture her lying on his bed with the poncholiner winding between her legs and across her bare hip like a green snake and her phoenix eyes on him, a combat fantasy. She was what he had ached for when he had been over there. When he had believed he was going to die, the idea of never having a woman to love him had summed up all his pain. Now, as he sat there with the flask empty on the linoleum at his feet, he checked himself and found his ache was missing. The world was dull or annoying to him, and she was just like any other female, he felt: she had certain functions. And he had seen those functions turned inside out by high explosives, he knew what was inside people, and there was nothing there. It was gross. It was boring. It was sickening and that was all.

The loss of this feeling horrified him. It was yet another thing that didn't work on him.

When I was younger, I always wanted to be in love with somebody someday. The thought that that was over, that I couldn't feel that anymore, this really hit me hard. It took my hope away.

She set up the steam table, dialed up the flame, mopped the kitchen, threw the breaker for the counter lights. The other women came and the noise began and she went back to the hallway behind the kitchen and dumped her tub of slop from yesterday into the garbage.

In midmorning, she checked her phone. No message. She shoved her cart down the hallway, accelerating past doorways that gave onto the insides of the kitchens, the cutaway inner works of the counter, the rodent dead beneath the steam table, the mass of customers on the other side, then the wall again. A skinny old man in a white apron splotched with yellow grease leaned out into the tunnel and dropped an armful of empty boxes in her way and she almost ran him over.

She blasted her trays with the sprayer before jamming them in the conveyor belt, which went into the dishwasher, a two-foot-square stainless aluminum box connected by a tube to a wall-mounted soap bladder. She threw the lever and let it run.

On the floor she stood over kids with North Face parkas and perm-up hair and sunglasses who were playing with their food, and waited for their trays. A Hong Kong boy was talking about banana boat people and laughing huhuhu.

You gotta let people eat, he told her.

Incorrect, she said and took his tray.

He followed along behind a young man in a Frontrunners jacket and baggy jeans with his drawers showing, who took him around the corner and said, Lemme see twenty. What you got? They traded what they were respectively holding, hand to hand. Then he went into the newsstand on Roosevelt and bought a pack of Dutch Masters. Dismissively, with an air of infinite superiority and languor, the Pakistani put his change on the counter, as if he were untouchable. Skinner raked the dimes and pennies into his hand and left without a word.

Under the expressway, he made a little staging area to get his baggy out and split one of the cigars open. He brushed the tobacco away, and blew it away, and the grains fell on the cardboard of a campsite, the used-up aerosol cans rusting in multicolored plastic bags.

Then Skinner climbed the ramp and smoked his blunt alone in the middle of everything, hiking back and forth over the overpass above the expressway. In the middle of the arch, he stuck his fingers through the fence and held himself. The traffic poured by underneath him. If you looked one way, among those fire escapes, Zou Lei was over there. Three klicks to the east, that was where he lived. Looking this way, past Manhattan in the smoky distance, if you went far enough, was his unit in the barracks, the guys in Warrior Transition, in the group rooms where their wheelchairs were placed in formation and they did modified PT.

And behind him—he turned to face the other way—out there, if you kept going and going, eventually, was the war.

Imagine if this was Iraq right now, he thought. You'd be lighting up all these cars. He gazed at the sliding chains of traffic. These people have no idea. He took a hit, squatting now, holding in the smoke. I'm high as fuck. If I was there, if this was the Box, I'd have a buddy to pass this to.

In his narcotic state, he saw the sand going on and on across the continent. The broken palm trees and mud buildings and corrugated steel lean-tos and dead trucks and the domes and spires of the mosques. He could hear the loudspeakers wired by a man who weighed twenty pounds less and looked twenty years older and who was the same age as he was, a goat herder with missing fingers. He heard the static and the ram's horn and the voices as they spoke together, wearing robes the same color as the landscape, kneeling together, rising together, chanting together. He could see them as if he were watching them through binoculars and the Arabian dusk was coming down. He saw the dim blue sky and smelled the sunbaked human waste and saw the dark forms of his many friends, their gear, their white eyes and very occasional smiles. He tasted the smell of burning tires, hashish, gun oil, animals, coal fire, chicken and rice and Tabasco sauce. The weight of the gear. The tearing down of the body. All the things you complained about. And the thing that was greater—the war itself. It was the one thing. You went outside the wire, and each time, either you died or you did not.

He did sit-ups on the floor of his room, the dirt sticking to his back. He knew the grit was there from how it stuck to his scar tissue. He put his jeans on, his boots on, his hoodie and the camouflage. No laundry, no shopping. Sitting on the bus, then the train, not reading or thinking or even looking at anything. Just feeling the train rocking around the curve and going into the tunnel. The gray soot day smudged over everything, the tracks, the footprints all over the floor of the car. The decorative blue tiles said Hunter's Point as the subway coasted by the platform underground. Like the antique tilework that he had seen holes blown through, shards you crunched through, scraping and popping under their boots. Finding blood on the tiles. Building materials collapsed and torn open and out, the twisted rebar. When the walls were holed or sheared clean away, the cross-section looked like fish gills from the cavities in the cinder blocks. Sand in mounds that felt weird to step on because of something under it that slipped or rolled that wasn't sand. The surface was oxidized black and when you kicked it up, the inside was yellow inside its cut edges like you had cut into an organ. Footprints left these yellow cuts in the sand. The smell of something foul came out. Shit or garbage or dead people with sand over it. He thought of that.

He went to the city and did nothing. Went back home and lay on the poncholiner, not doing anything except lying there with the small lamp on next to the bed, his magazines on the pressed-wood night table, the pornography right there if he turned his head to look, but he did not. His earphones and his cell phone were mixed in with his possessions on the floor somewhere, the twisted jeans and socks and camouflage. Behind his head, the thing propping his head up was the pistol in a towel. He heard the thump of people or furniture upstairs. The window was a black square. What day is it, what month is it, what hour of the night? The one animate thing in the room was the boiler in the closet. There was nothing to eat or drink.

Eventually, he sat up. Then he pushed himself up to standing. Stood looking down at the mess on the floor, hunting for a final MRE. He gave up and felt the pockets of his jacket. A wrapper crinkled in his hand. He took it out, finding only the Indian's head and the desiccant. A tiny chip of jerky. Skinner crushed the wrapper and let it go and it floated to the floor. Fuck it. There was no room inspection here. There was no point in going out to check inside the fridge, but he went anyway, jacked the door open—it was that old-fashioned pump-action kind of door—and the cold hissed out at him like the Arab voices, offering him hashish, calling him a dog.

He went back into the bedroom, now seeing the pornography and his bottles of medication. He shook out pills into his hand, blue diamond, white hexagon, pink oval. Slapped them into his mouth and went out to the kitchen with his lower jaw stuck out like a bird to hold them and bent and sucked water from the kitchen tap.

Where was his phone? It took effort to charge it up, especially when all he wants to do now is pitch himself down on the poncholiner. But if you don't do A, then B doesn't happen, and C, you die. So he made himself do it. Then he threw himself down in the bed— the feet scraped an inch on the floor. The poncholiner sticking to his skin where it remembered him, your body always losing water in the desert, the shadow of himself imprinted on the nylon. His head had a rock in it from the medication. Brad's-eye-view of the world was just the slick green of the poncholiner, one of his hands—the other he felt trapped under him—the yellow spill of the lamplight, the table with his skyline of pill bottles. In the shine on the glossy cover, he could make out the trace of a beautiful woman's leg and a spike heel.

The army had given him anti-anxiety medication, antipsychotic medication, and something to help him sleep. Whatever else these chemicals did to him, they did not stop him from having nightmares.

He was sleeping, but his head was running like an engine. The mortar was coming down at a thousand feet per second. He reexperienced the detonation, his mouth open, a red light behind his eyes, which was neurological, not physical, and his ears bursting inward, and the difficulty breathing. He was confused, but he knew something.

In his bed, he bucked and started struggling.

He was trying to do something—he could feel it hurting his hands—but he didn't know what it was yet, because he was disoriented. He knew it mattered more than anything else, and he knew he was going to fail at it. He had a feeling of love and anguish in his heart. He was clawing in the sand. He heard himself screaming for Jake.

He felt him, the chest was canvas over steel, the head was bare. He could not find his face, just sand. He had to get him up. He grabbed him by his harness, climbed to his feet and tried to lift him up.

They were carrying ninety pounds of gear per man, give or take, and Skinner could barely stand up on his own he was so fatigued. He strained with everything he had, and for a second he raised him up, but there was no way to hold him up. His back gave out, he got pulled down, and fell on him.

He fell face first in the sand, breathed it in, and coughed it up and spat it out. His own gear weight threatened to suffocate him. He pushed himself up. Big bench press. Their hands reached for each other. Skinner was trying to get his balance and took his hand away. He got his knees under him. Something metal bit his knee and sand was hanging in the shorts he wore, as if he had shit his pants, swaying between his legs, heavy, pulling them off. Sconyers was dying and he was reaching with his hand. They gripped hands. The feeling of the rough sand and the rough unmistakable live feeling of the man's hand was what shocked Skinner awake—feeling as if his friend had literally reached out from the other side and grabbed his hand. Do it now or else. They gripped like two guys saying hey, and he felt the other's weight and the great immovable weight of their combined battle rattle and pulled, and he woke up physically straining, clutching the edge of the mattress, as if he was going to put his arms around it and bend it in half against the steel springs and fold it around himself. Lift his entire bed into the air. The house out of its foundations.

He had a wild, drugged, unslept, disoriented feeling. He talked to the room. He checked his phone, looked out the window, listened to the house. It was five-thirty and he hadn't slept. I can't do anything, he thought, even sleep. His urine striking the water in the toilet in the small bright bathroom. Turning away from the sight of his own face in the mirror. He snapped the light off. Stunned and stupid in the dark. His head ached.

The floor creaked up in the apartment overhead and Mrs. Murphy's door opened and then somebody came out and down the three steps to the landing above the basement stairs, opened the side door of the house, and left. The door slammed. Boots on the ground—the weight of a big man leaving for the day. Skinner tracking the whole thing, frozen as if hidden waiting in a listening post or an ambush, until whoever it was (and it must have been Mr. Murphy with his brogue) got into the pickup and drove away.

If he could have slept, he would have, but he could not. He got dressed on automatic, in the same unwashed clothes as yesterday and the day before and the day before, as if he were living in the field. The pistol was in plain view on the bed. He put the Berretta in his assault pack and wore it out.

Halfway down the block, he stopped. Was he going to the gym? His fatigue was a massive heavy thing and he didn't want to carry anything at all. He went back around the side of the house, head lowered in case anyone was watching him, and closed himself in. Clicked the lock. Went down into his room and took the assault pack off. He took the pistol out and laid it down in the open where he placed his head. I'm not going anywhere. You're not going anywhere, he told himself. You had your chance. He fell down on the bed with his arm over his eyes. Lay there just taking shallow breaths. Not sleeping. Hearing his heart like it belonged to someone else. Eventually working his boots off. They dropped on the floor. He pulled the pillow over his head and the nine slipped and fell between the mattress and the wall.

Later, he rolled over and touched what the weapon had done, a white divot in the plaster. He ran his fingers over it and the tiny white grains snowed down. The chittering out there belonged to birds. A background noise combined with the drawn-out sound of a mile-long roll of tape being peeled up of tires going by between the buildings and the trees.

He thought about executing himself. Just being very quiet and still within his own mind. No grief at the moment. Should I do it now? The thought actually calmed him once he faced it. It was something he could finally understand. Shortly it took a back burner to his just needing to eat.

The second time he left the house, he made it to the bus stop. The late winter sun was up and shining on us all, the unamused females who did medical billing, the guys in do-rags and sideways hats, either truants or going to some kind of gig in a stockroom. Strong-jawed Central American men who worked construction, a Timberland backpack over one shoulder, covered in dust. Skinner made it to the Dunkin Donuts by the subway and got a coffee. The nice Indian lady with the gold stud in her nose said, Regular, darling? Milk and sugar? Skinner said, Yeah, why not? She said, Why not, darling? You want special, one bagel cream cheese more for ninety-nine cent? Yeah, okay. Okay, darling, you got it. And he took his hot sweet coffee and his bagel and sat on the last high chair at the window with the bums and watched the crowd stream by in the sun. The Indian voice saying darling. Skinner warming up inside. The periodic roar from underground.

26

AFTER FOUR DAYS OF him not calling her, her anger turned into something else, into something like a weight that was too heavy for her to carry, and she stopped running.

She went to work, where she forgot what she was doing. She watched her hands cleaning trays and wiping tables and wondered why she was working. On her break, she stood on the loading dock and stared out into space beyond the fire escapes.

Sunnie said, You didn't eat. You will be unable to work well.

You're right, Zou Lei said. Her mind felt hollow like her stomach, and she got a strange smile on her face.

She called up the bootlegger from Wenzhou again, who met her and gave her the latest American movies, which he had videotaped at theaters on 42nd Street. He gave her some more martial arts and some pornography with titles like Virgin Blossom Grows Up. He gave her a different cell phone number and then he drove away to safety. She carried her backpack full of movies down into the Flushing Main Street subway station, where the NYPD had been checking bags all month, and, as if sleepwalking, she walked right in front of the cops' table and went through the turnstile. She felt them look at her, and her brief fear felt better than her loneliness.

She boarded the train and rode with her head pressed to the window, watching the rooftops going by, the buildings becoming houses, the treetops coming up, disappearing again, the great splashes of graffiti.

The track made her think of a highway down which a truck will come towards a girl on the roadside and he will not be on it.

Then Skinner came back from wherever he had been and she thought, God was with us.

The delivery man backed inside pulling his hand truck over the threshold, braced his Timberland against the rung at the base of the hand truck, gripped the top box, and set his stack down. The weight levered his other foot off the ground. He wore a turtleneck sweater, gloves and a wool-lined Red Army hat with ear flaps. He went down the stack of boxes, slapping them as he went: Superior King, ocean scallop, eel fish, mushroom ears, lotus, oyster, sesame oil, chilies, brill fish, cornstarch. He pinned the invoice against the Superior King box, took a ballpoint pen out from under his earflap, ripped away the pink copy after they had signed it. He tipped the stack, hooked the rung with his boot, pulled the blade out from under the load, spun the hand truck around and wheeled out.

He wheeled down the loading dock ramp, threw his cart in the back of his graffitied-up Isuzu. His door slammed, the engine roared. She could hear it from the hallway. The cab would smell like take-out noodles. She saw him driving out beneath the fire escapes, turning by the Sheraton. She saw the sun through his windshield as he bounced in his seat, shifting the gear stick, the engine rattling him. On the dash, he had a book of invoices and a road atlas to navigate by. Every day he went somewhere different, navigating the alleys that fed out onto Northern Boulevard, the Silk Road.

27

ON DAYS WHEN HE could function, he worked out in a one-room gym above a furniture store on a side street. It was in the area, but it was hard to find. He went there in his boots. It was just a room with a rotted floor with weights in it. It had an old-fashioned sheet metal ceiling embossed with flowers and leaves and painted over white, and he took her there.

They went past Kissena Park, mist hanging above the ground, the baseball diamond obscured. He led her past the high school. A man in construction boots was stretched out sleeping beneath the underhang. She heard birds in the mist in the high oaks.

They went up a back street across from the cemetery. The street had a guardrail below which a highway travelled east to Long Island, shaking when trucks passed. Residential houses lined the street, yellowed newspapers and dead leaves piled against the curb. There was a graffiti drawing of a face with vampire teeth on a wall. His gym was in a cinder block building that looked like a small factory with a roll-down metal gate instead of a door and when you looked inside, you expected to smell fluorocarbons and see workmen in respirators painting autobodies.

They went in the cement doorway and climbed up the rubber tread stairs, each of them in turn stepping over the spit on the stairs. Skinner stepped over it first in his boots and Zou Lei coming after him stepped over it next in her Closeout City sneakers when she came to it. From the stairs, you could hear the weights banging and the hip-hop playing.

They went inside and checked in at the wooden counter, which displayed a sign saying Dues Must Be Paid. There was a blender behind the counter, and they sold American Bodybuilder Nitro Speed Stack, Cellmass, Animal Pack, Creaforce, Isopure, and Rage. An autographed picture of Bernie Cole advertising Valeo elastic wrist wraps hung above the pay phone next to where the rates were posted.

This was her first time in an American gymnasium, she said. She insisted on paying the five dollars herself.

On the gym floor, a short guy with a stud earring took three quick breaths as if he were about to jump into icy water and heaved a pair of dumbbells over his chest. He lifted them five and a half times while his friends stood around him, ready to spot him. Come on! they said. He straightened his arms. Six! they said. That's the one! He dropped the weights and they hit the rubber floor with a huge thud—she turned at the sound—that rattled the entire gym, from the plaster walls up to the sheet metal ceiling. When he jumped up after, his friends congratulated him. He pointed at someone the way athletes point at fans in the stands, and winked. He wore jeans and a gold chain bracelet.

Skinner asked her if she wanted him to help her, but she said not to worry about her, she knew what to do: she had brought her magazine pages. At her insistence, Skinner went off on his own, and she maneuvered around the lifters in boots, gold chains, sweatpants, and do-rags to hunt for a pair of dumbbells that were light enough for her to use. The rusted dumbbell rack ran the length of the plaster wall like one of those knee-high bars for locking up bicycles. She found a pair of ten-pound weights and started doing lunges.

Guys wandered in front of her, getting in her way, their broad backs in her way, chests inflated, their arms held out from their sides. When they noticed her, they reacted like cattle who don't know how to move for a truck as it crawls along behind them, honking in the road.

She moved to a far corner between an old BodyMasters universal and a window painted shut around an air conditioner.

She had started over doing her lunges when Skinner came to check on her, having seen her in the corner. Was she good?

I'm good.

Are you okay here?

I'm okay. I like it. I must get used to it.

He asked to see her magazine article.

She unfolded the pages for him, the creases soft as linen from being folded and unfolded so many times. He reviewed the pictures of Ms. Fitness' routine.

Is this what you want to do?

It's crowded, I think.

No, we can do this, he said. You're gonna get your workout. Come on.

First he took her to the squat rack, which was free because all the guys were working on their upper bodies. He set up the bar for her and showed her how to stand and how to lift it off the rack on her shoulders. Together they figured out how much weight was right for her. When she was ready, he had her back out and he stood behind her with his arms under her arms to spot her.

Okay, he said, and she squatted and he squatted with her. She squatted very fast in a robotic military way that yielded nothing to the barbell or the pressures on her joints.

It's okay to slow it down. Two seconds down, one second up. Feet through the floor when you're going up. Eyes on the ceiling. One-two.

The next time she squatted, she did it slowly, which made it harder, and she laughed. You're doing good, he said. She started getting hot, her navy tracksuit whispering between them. She felt him behind her, his arms brushing her ribcage as if he were about to cup her breasts. The exercise became very demanding on her legs and heart. The only thing that mattered was if she could make her legs stand up. When she was afraid to squat again because she thought if she did she wouldn't be able to stand back up, she made a desperate sound that meant I quit.

They walked in together like two people in leg irons taking steps at the same time and racked the bar. Then she moaned aaiiii and wanted to collapse.

He changed the weight on the bar, putting the big plates on, and lifted the bar off the rack and backed out and squatted. The big plates rattled like dishes in a cupboard when a train goes by as he went up and down. There was no point in spotting him. It was more weight than she could ever lift. Halfway through his set, he started resting, sucking up air, before he squatted. When he squatted, he started straining at the bottom, exactly as if he were constipated and trying to force himself to shit. Then he would manage to stand again. She watched him. His face turned red, he was gasping.

She didn't think he could do another. He squatted again and when he tried to stand, his back rounded forward. Thinking he was in trouble, she ran to help him. The barbell had 225 pounds on it. She felt his heart pounding through his back and his body shaking as she struggled to help him. He groaned aaaghh and he stood up. She had no idea if she had helped him. He walked the barbell in and reracked it and immediately turned away from it as if it made him sick.

Thanks, he said, his chest heaving and his face covered in sweat.

He took his sweatshirt off soaked in sweat, threw it on the ground, and limped around to the side of the rack to take the plates off for her. Underneath, his Jack Daniels No. 7 Whiskey t-shirt was soaked through. His thick tattooed forearms were wet. The sight of him filled her with determination.

She took the bar off onto her back and got in position and began to squat, already expecting the pain before it began. She went to the last rep where she couldn't hold herself anymore and he had to pick her up under her arms. She screamed out loud.

The pain made her angry and she stalked off. Then she returned, serious and ready to spot him. He loaded the bar deliberately, and she helped him do it.

They worked through her entire program, Skinner leading the way. He did everything that she did, set for set, even though it was a woman's program. When they needed to know what was next, they would check the magazine pages, their noses sweating on it, the pages coming apart in her hands, and with his head down he would lead her to the next piece of equipment. She followed him, stepping around the men, a V of sweat down her front as if she had been digging sand all day.

Guys noticed them and said, That's how you do it. Go hard or go home. They bumped Skinner's fist, holding in their own fists the sponge or friction paper or other homemade device with which they gripped the weights.

The last exercise they did was flutter kicks. He and Zou Lei lay down on the floor and moved their legs like goose-stepping soldiers. They got to fifty and her feet fell on the ground. One hundred, he said. No, she said. But she pulled her feet up again. They continued kicking and counting together, chanting the way everyone does in group calisthenics. At one hundred, both of their sets of feet fell on the ground. She groaned and held her stomach. When they stood, they left behind sweat patterns in the shapes of themselves. She stared down at their spirit-patterns on the ground. The intensity of the exercise made her think strange things.

Now, they were resting on the back stairs, where the gym stored its ladders and junk. Plaster buckets, cardboard boxes, paint rollers blocked the fire exit below. He had bought them MuscleTech protein drinks in French Vanilla. Sucking the heavy liquid up the straw was another form of weightlifting for her neck. She patted his damp solid shoulder through his sweatshirt.

You give me a good working out today.

He reached over and pinched her behind.

That's gonna be tired after today.

Aaii, she cried but leaned forward so he could feel it better.

Someone came down the back stairs looking for the exit, and he stopped gripping her until the guy figured out you couldn't leave from here and went away.

Can't get out here, dude, Skinner said.

When they were alone again:

You let your hair grow, she said and touched his damp head. His dark hair stood up stiff with no direction to it, just radiating out of his head. She made a fist in his hair, and he let her rock his head from side to side. Too much hair.

You like it short?

Yes. She rubbed his cheek with the whiskers on it. You are such good teacher today. You don't want to be like soldier no more?

Nah, he said. He rubbed his whiskery face. I'm sick of the army. I'm gonna grow my hair down to my ass. I'm gonna get a beard down to here. What do you think? He held his hand down at his waist.

She said, Maybe it should be longer.

What do you think about here, to the knees?

That's better.

And I'm gonna get a robe too.

A robe?

Yeah, like one of them long dresses. And a turban.

Oh! she said. You should get a turban.

I know, he said. I should. Gonna start praying five times a day. You know what that's about.

Oh, yes, she said.

I'm gonna pray—and he brought his hands up to his face as if he were washing his face with God's word or God's water—and said: Allahu akbar.

Good, she said. Very good. What else you will do?

Well, I'm definitely going to blow myself up. I'm going to go into the Dunkin Donuts and blow myself up and kill, like, a good ten people. All the traffic is gonna get fucked-up for like 45 minutes. People will be late for work. And then of course I'll go to heaven for my reward of 77 virgins. Only I won't want virgins. I'm gonna ask for some hoochie mamas.

You will be very busy in heaven, she said. I can visit you or you are too busy in this hoochie mama?

It'd be nice to stay in touch, he said. Do you mind waiting in line?

I wait in line. I think it is worth it. Because I am better than those 77. I think when you see me, you will pick me.

I'd pick you, he said.

You do?

Yeah, I would.

She sucked on her straw and finished her protein drink, which popped and rattled in the straw. She swung her foot, staring straight ahead, her tracksuit and her clothes beneath it wet and cooling. He laid his hand on her leg, which felt smooth and shapely and solid and naked under the thin polyester. He felt the muscles flexing in independent groups as her knee moved.

Their palms were brown with rust from the bars. Even though her hands were calloused, she had torn her palm doing deadlifts. He held her sweaty palm and she squeezed her hand open and shut around him. He felt the metal, dirt, and sweat on her hand, which created a glue between them.

In the afternoon, they went down to Jackson Heights where the whorehouses were. The whole street was meseras bars with Central American men sitting stone drunk at the tables, their hoods over their heads, sleeping on their arms, holding forties, using the bottle to climb up like a banister. Skinner told her at night the trestles in front of the fruit markets would move all by themselves—a sight to make you jump at two in the morning—and this seeming paranormal activity was because a body was sleeping under it.

The men who slept out in the Park of the Americas had purple blackened faces. Their skin was puckered and quilted. They slept directly on the concrete, no shoes on, and urine running downhill from them, leaves and twigs in their hair.

A Mazda with silver rims spun around the corner and drove away under the long shadow of the elevated tracks. All down the block,

Guatemalans were cooking a hash of gray brains, black sausage and corn on the cob at their generator-powered trucks, the women in aprons and ball caps holding tongs, arranging a ring of pig's heads turned to leather masks by roasting, black holes where the eyes were or had been before they were cooked out. An inside-the-animal-smell.

They told her they had goat and she bought a taco and ate it, dripping hot grease over her fingers and licking up chips of onion and flakes of cilantro off her fingers, still tasting the rust on her hands.

While she waited in the park, he went to a barbershop that had a hundred photographs of Latin heads with fades in the window and got his hair cut in a military high and tight. You could get a cesa, mohawk, or skinfade for ten dollars. The barbershop was located on 85th Street next to Nathaly's Bridal. The barber was a Hispanic youth, younger than Skinner, with a fat white face. He had a small spiked stud in his chin. Males in white snap-back hats lounged all around the shop, texting on their cell phones. The Spanish music was turned all the way up, so that the drumbeats popped your eardrums. Skinner tilted his head forward under the pressure of the clippers, and the kid pushed the clippers up the back of his head. When he was done, he flashed a hand mirror behind his head.

You want some alcohol on it, so you don't catch no bumps?

Skinner said go ahead, and the kid sprayed his scalp with cold alcohol, which he slapped and rubbed into Skinner's skin.

That shit's gotta be mad burning.

I got my ears back. My girl'll like it.

The barber asked if his girl was Mexican.

No.

You're white though, right?

Yeah.

What's your girl? She white too?

She's Chinese.

Word? How come you ain't goin out with a black girl? Don't wanna jump in the mud?

The barber made one of his boys laugh and they slapped hands.

He turned back to Skinner. Ten, yo, he said. Skinner checked that his hair was even, then took his wallet out and paid him.

When she saw him, she called him shuaige! handsome boy! and rubbed the back of his scalp in the same place the barber had done.

They were so tired it was hard to climb the stairs up to the train. The seven came and they got on, and newspapers and dirt were all over the floor. She sat down and he sat sideways and put his boots up on the seat and lay back with his head in her lap and closed his eyes. She held his head and stroked his forehead. They spoke to each other under the roar of the train. What? she asked. She bent down to hear him and breathed the rubbing alcohol on his scalp.

Come home with me.

She stroked his now-cropped hair.

Will you?

She nodded, gazing down at him.

People got on all around them as the train went down the line. They got on carrying their food, a bundle of parchment cornhusks like dried rattlesnake skins. Through their bags you could read the words Aztec Maize. Everyone sat all together around them, pressed against her side, wedged in at the end of Skinner's feet. He moved his feet for them, to not step on them. Zou Lei rubbed his ears between her fingers. They rocked with the train. Both of them dozed, people's legs bumping against their legs. Other people dozed as well, tattoos of crosses on their knuckles, the word Serena in italic script on the inside of a pregnant woman's wrist.

They went back to his room, he was very nice, and she fell asleep on him while he smoked a Marlboro and when the night came she didn't want to leave.

She was lying half on him with her leg on top of his leg. His arm was around her and her face was fitted like a jigsaw piece into the crook of his neck. When he tightened his arm around her, her back yielded supply and she arched against him and her breasts pressed his chest. When he looked down, he could see the solid muscle of her rear divided by the triangle of her pink boy shorts.

She asked him if it was okay if she stayed the night and, stubbing out his cigarette, he told her of course. He even joked about it, saying he wondered if this meant he was a pimp.

She thanked him.

You liked the gym?

I love it. We had a good day today. You are so good today.

Today was the way it should be.

She agreed it was.

We're going to do that every day from now on.

I want it to be. Imagine, she thought, how great it would be if they did.

He had taken his pills and she could feel him going into a different state of consciousness beneath her.

Every single day, he said.

The house was quiet, the bedside lamp was on, it was a night in late winter.

She felt the whole earth traveling across the cosmos. The cosmos was something like the Siberian steppe and the earth was a rider traveling across it. It came south out of the larch forest where the dead of her ancestors lived and hunted reindeer. The rider continued south on horseback to the endless grassland. She was riding behind him, and as they rode she saw little flowers coming out in bloom in the oatmeal-colored land. He wore a wooden mask with a heavy beak, so he could become a hawk and find the way. They were on the verge of descending into a valley. They would have ripe green pastures, apple trees to which birds flocked, singing.

Something woke her in the night. She opened her eyes. She was looking at the speckled acoustic ceiling. The house was silent, but she believed that a sound had waked her. She moved her eyes. The yellow bedside lamp was dim through the parchment-colored lampshade. The far wall looked grainy in the shadow. She looked to see if the door was closed, the lock button pushed in. The closet door was open and the boiler visible.

Something made her turn her head and look at Skinner. She put her hand out to touch him and his whole back was wet. The cotton stuck to him. Wherever she touched him, he was cold and wet. The poncholiner under them was wet too.

A sense of strangeness came from his body, as if he did not know her. When she spoke, he answered her, but she could hear he was not there. She asked: Skinner, do you know where you are? and he said, Yeah, I'm fine. But the way he said it, she knew he was not awake and she was afraid to say anything else.

He began making choking sounds in his sleep. She realized he was sobbing. She watched him with astonishment.

What happened? he begged. Oh, what happened? Oh my God, why did this happen?

She wanted to comfort him, but she had a premonition that he would spin around and strike her if she touched him.

It's okay, nothing's happen, she told him.

He nodded with his eyes shut, and she believed he was conscious and had heard her. She got him to release the poncholiner from his fists and put it over him again. She curled up behind him, her own heart beating, and stared at his back. Gradually she calmed down because she felt him calming down and she fell asleep again.

She woke up again and the room looked the same as it had looked all night. The light was still on, but when she looked up at the window, she could see blue-gray dawn coming in.

She crawled over him and got out of bed, making an effort not to wake him, and looked back at him. His cropped brown hair, the white walls above his ears, pimples in his scalp. The faded green tattoo on his seamed neck. Bad skin on his forehead. Stubbled face. His mouth open against the pillow. He had taken another pill, and now he looked like someone drugged and dumped on the roadside, lying on a hill outside the mosque in Kashgar.

She opened his door, listened to the strange house and, hearing nothing, went across the shadowed basement to the bathroom and she switched the light on. The royal blue walls sprang up. She locked herself in and put her clothes in a little pile on top of her sneakers and used his shower. It was a pristine bathroom and there was no sign that anyone used it except for his crushed tube of Aquafresh in the sink. When she was done, she put everything back the way she found it, straightening the bath mat, wiping up her wet footprints, and hanging his towel on the bar on the frosted glass door of the shower compartment. She straightened his towel, matching up the corners, smoothing out the wrinkles. It said Camp Manhattan, Kuwait, in all capital black letters. She put on her tracksuit, snapped her bra in place, opened the door to let the steam out, combed her wet hair. Her legs were so sore it was hard to kneel to tie her sneakers. She said, Goodbye, boy, when she left for work but he didn't answer; he was still riding in the steppe.

She called him in the afternoon. He did not answer. She left a message thanking him again. She was so sore, she could barely walk. I cannot hurry at my job. She said that she would see him.

She called again that night, but he was very depressed and all of his responses were wooden. Still, she persisted. I am in your bed last night, she told him. Something is wrong.

He said nothing.

You are crying very bad at night.

If you say so.

I am next to you and I hear it. I am there, so I know.

Okay. So?

So, I'm telling you, I know it's bad. I want to do somethings about it. What's going on?

I don't know.

What is it?

He would not answer.

I want to help this thing, whatever's happening.

You can't help it.

It's the war?

Yeah.

You need someone to help you, she said.

She rinsed the dried drips of Coca-Cola out of his Subway cup and filled it up with tap water and brought it to him so he could take his pills. There were four bottles of pills, but she had seen a fifth one. She saw the fifth bottle lying on the floor between the wheel on the foot of the bed and the wall and picked it up. He thanked her.

That's the one I sleep with.

He took his blue hexagonal pill while she watched him. She was wearing her jeans and Hollister sweatshirt. The lacy black underwear she had stuffed in her back pocket. He swallowed and she took the cup out of his hand and set it in the kitchen.

Move over your body, she told him, so she could sit. He moved over and watched her examining each of his pill bottles under the bedside lamp, studying the chemical names—Zoloft, Ambien, Sero-quel. She tried to read the dosages in English. Blue, pink, yellow, white, red, she repeated, memorizing.

That's what they gave me. You know anything about that stuff?

We should keep it well. Not messy.

So I don't take the wrong one by accident.

We keep it all in one place from now on. If you take one, put it back.

I will.

If he wanted to lie down, first he had to arrange his boots next to his bed and put his assault pack where he could reach it. Then she was allowed to climb over him to the inboard side of the bed and hug him from there, so he would know where she was.

She stroked his ear. You can tell me your dream, she said.

At her urging, he began to reveal his symptoms, if not his dreams.

Have you seen how I get distracted, how my eye goes like this? He had her watch his eyes. Look at the right one. See how it's shaking?

She could not tell.

How I can't stop looking over there?

That she saw. He kept looking over her head, weak side-strong side, to the entrance of the room, which led out into the world where cars were always coming, always getting closer, approaching him and his brother soldiers at sandbagged roadblocks.

Chronic anxiety was something she understood.

Headlights coming at me, crowds, whenever I hear the intercom radio on the subway, he said. Potholes in the street. Car doors. You know what a bullet sounds like? Have you ever had a wasp flying really close to your ear?

They entered the search words Sick + Soldier on his laptop. From the screen, a man in a v-neck sweater talked to them from in front of a bookcase in a well-lit office. Skinner lit a Marlboro and listened with her. The video ran out, it froze. Their feed was bad. He reached over and hit a key on the machine and his ashes fell on the keypad to join the sand. This fucking busted thing, he said. The video was loading, they had to wait. It restarted and she watched it. He got up and finished his cigarette in the other room.

Have you seen the way I get mad even when I'm trying to be nice?

Something has shook your mind. It could be some bruise inside the head.

28

WHENEVER SUNNIE NEEDED A break, Zou Lei had an arrangement with her that she would take her place on the line. Frequently, she simply told Sunnie, You need a break, sister. Sunnie would laugh uncertainly and say, I don't really.

Yes, you do. You shouldn't work too hard. Here's a cup of soup.

Oh, my. But I'm full already. You want to practice the menu, don't you?

Yes, I have to practice.

Well, okay. Are you sure you understand the order?

If I practice, I'll get it. The turkey is separate.

Okay, I guess there's no harm then, as long as Sassoon won't mind.

She's not here, Zou Lei said, taking the big spoon from her. I got it from here. If you want, you can just hang out right there by the tea pot and have your soup, and if there's any emergency, I can ask you what to do, so nothing'll go wrong. Very tranquil.

Well, okay.

You're the coach, I'm the trainee. Strictly criticize my mistakes.

I'm nobody's teacher, Sunnie smiled shyly, taking her place by the hot water cistern.

You're helping me, Zou Lei said.

You're industrious, Sunnie would say.

Angela, in front of whom all this was taking place, said, Does anybody know what you're doing?

Sunnie stared at her in great anxiety. She had second thoughts, but Zou Lei held onto the dipper.

You manage your register, Zou Lei told Angela, We'll manage this.

He called her at four in the morning and started talking, his voice like a loud ant coming out of the cell phone, and her neighbor sighed through the boards. Just minute, she whispered. She took her sweatshirt and found her sandals and went out on the stoop. The sky was a lighter shade of black than the park behind the gas station across the boulevard, the streetlights casting their peculiar glow on the pavement. He was saying he couldn't sleep. She agreed to meet him at McDonald's.

On her way to McDonald's, the shuttered gates of businesses were covered in graffiti you never saw in daytime and she thought they resembled a thousand tattooed eyelids. The chairs were upside down on the tables so they could mop.

Skinner arrived ten minutes later, nearly invisible in his black hood. He behaved with an almost formal politeness, thanking her for coming, his eyes hidden.

I need a soda, if you don't mind waiting a second.

It's okay, she said.

He bought her a bacon egg and cheese biscuit, then started telling her about something and it became him telling her about Iraq and she stopped eating. He sat with his elbows on his knees, holding the drink cup under the table, talking in a low voice while she listened leaning towards him, twisted sidesaddle in her chair, her jacket riding up, showing her bare back. Every ten seconds his eyes scanned left and right and came back and rested on her face. He took a drink of his soda.

It was hard to fix his dry mouth, his headache, his memory of his friend exploding and the pieces of his body raining on his helmet.

We were about as far apart as there to here, he said, pointing at the trash can against the wall, which was gray and green with black trim. There was an ice cream cup on the floor that hadn't made it into the trash can. The swinging lid was unable to shut and the trash was bulging out. He told her what a mortar was. It goes like this. He made an arc with his finger. So he was there. Boom, it hits him. I went to get him. We wound up back in the hospital here.

He went into a long digression about the hospital, then said:

I don't know why I couldn't lift him.

She watched him try and speak.

I feel like I know I could have tried harder.

She handed him her napkin and he blew his nose.

Like I let him die.

He wiped his eyes and they filled again.

They talked until the day shift employees began coming in. A white girl in a hairnet came out and started turning over the chairs, and a Central American man old enough to be her father took a dust-pan and swept up the ice cream cup and changed the trash. People could be seen walking in the darkness past the window. A black man in padded Delta Airlines coveralls and corrective glasses came in and bought an orange juice before heading to LaGuardia. The sky was getting lighter. They moved to a booth and he put his arm around her and she lay on him. The restaurant got busy and loud. Chinese mothers came in yelling in Teochow dialect to their children, carrying them on their backs the way mothers do in the third world.

She wanted a Shamrock Shake, and he bought one for her. He asked her how her job was going.

Anbu jiuban. It means you do the job like this: She imitated making a step with her foot, then another.

By the steps, she said. The tape she used to fix her shoes was coming out the heels.

He asked her if she wanted anything else, and she said no, she had more than enough already. She took a suck of her mint green shake and her cheeks hollowed and she smiled.

They were sitting under the No Loitering sign on the second floor where people came with their plastic bags to sit for hours and it smelled like BO. A young black junkie was sleeping with his mouth open in the corner, his yellow teeth showing. Pop music was playing softly. The bathroom door was token-operated, but the mechanism was broken, so you could use it.

Shangmian you zhengce, xiamian you duice. The leader has the policy, but the ones down below has another policy. The leader thinks he is in charge, but he only has two eyes. Two eye cannot watch twenty people.

If my boss yell at me, like this: and she demonstrated what she would do if she were yelled at: she put up a hand and deflected the force of the yell.

It make her very angry when I use this power so she can't do nothing.

He couldn't understand what anyone could be yelling at her about.

Any small thing. A sesame seed small thing. The small thread. Pull this thread, soon it's the whole carpet come unwind.

There were many different ethnic groups in China and it was just a fact of life that they didn't always get along. In my last job, the one where you met me, the boss was from Malaysia. In this job, Guangzhou, Hong Kong. The workers are from Zhangzhou, Quanzhou, Wenzhou, Fuzhou, Guangdong, Guangxi, many place. Mexico, Sinaloa. The men call me chiquita. Guatemalans. Those people that come on a long journey. Everyone needs this job so they will come here. Even the Arab. Even the terrorist.

A dark Indian-blooded Mexican man in slacks, a motorcycle jacket, dress shoes, and a red Yankees hat, sat with his daughters and wife at the next table. Outside across the street you could see the Footlocker sign next to Barone Pizzeria. Skinner sat with his boots planted on the gray tile floor, watching her dutifully.

Something bad had happened to her not long ago, she said. I believe my life is over, but somethings save me. Did he know? It is the end, I think. Instead it is the beginning.

You must keep on to your hope, for both of us, she told him, because maybe some good thing will happen.

29

JIMMY'S MOTHER DID NOT pick him up. He took the Greyhound bus from Krayville to the Manhattan Port Authority terminal with multiple stops on the way, a twenty-hour journey. There was some concern that he wouldn't make it, that he would stop off somewhere and get sidetracked.

He showed up after eleven o'clock at night. Mrs. Murphy was still up in the kitchen, checking her cell phone for the time. Erin was reading the calorie information on a can of soup. The kitchen smelled like liver and onions that the father, Patrick, had cooked earlier. He had left the pan with water in it and the pan was in the sink. Gray things floated in the water. The father was not here.

Then Erin heard a sound and said, That's him! and went to let him in. Jimmy, her brother, her mother's son, entered the house: a stranger, smelling strange, smelling dirty, extremely weird and quiet, as if there were some great terrible thing contracting his vocal cords. He came in in clothes that he had last worn in the 90s. You heard Erin talking to him in the vestibule. The apartment door opened, Jimmy came in. Here he came—a large man walking behind Erin, carrying a cardboard box, like some kind of additional penance.

She's gonna flip, Erin was saying. Look who's here.

Mrs. Murphy held out her arms and said, Get over here. Jimmy put down his box on the floor and went over and bent down and hugged her. Hey, ma.

At the door, he didn't presume that he would be allowed in. Apparently he thought it was possible that he might be turned away.

He took a seat at the kitchen table, and because he didn't talk, his mother and half-sister debated what he could have, whether Fratelli's was still open this late, and why they hadn't ordered.

He's not saying anything.

Please. The man just got here, Erin. He doesn't have to say a thing.

I'll take a cigarette.

Mrs. Murphy pushed her pack across the tabletop. There! she said, and he took one of the long women's cigarettes and lit it. He smoked it by taking a quick hit and holding the cigarette cupped and hidden in his big hand.

That's the most macho way any man has ever smoked a Slim, Erin remarked.

Gradually, he started talking, his voice so rough and hoarse, it sounded as if his vocal cords were dragging on concrete. Whatever he had to say had nothing to do with ordinary life. It was about the way the rules on the Greyhound to the city were poorly thought out and unfairly applied. He had seen the authorities being made fools of in their bus stations by people selling sex and drugs.

Eventually, Erin left them, climbed upstairs softly on her big white legs.

He said yes to a beer with a trace of amusement, as if he found it quaint to be offered anything for free, even by his mother. He drank his beer with self-satisfaction as if he had won a prize while his mother carried on a conversation with him.

She thought he had smelled like alcohol when he had come in. He admitted he had snuck one on the bus. The guy next to me was an alcoholic. They put me next to him and he offered me my first beer in ten years. What was I gonna do?

An old look of recognition passed between mother and son.

Very late at night, he confessed to his mother, I feel like I'm not ready to be on the outside. She heard his confession and told him it would be all right. She told him what some old acquaintance had said about restarting life on the outside after a long time behind bars, that the fear passes.

The way everybody's got cell phones now, he said. I never had that. The only people who had cell phones used to be drug dealers when I went away. So I guess that's what I should of done. I might of done a few drugs, but I never sold them. If I'd of sold them like they said I done, I would a been better off. Fifteen-year-old niggers don't have nothing to make them feel special no more.

All right, she said finally. They were going to bed, and she heaved herself up to standing, the table tilting and jolting under the pressure of her hand.

She told him he could go up to his old room.

Jimmy said he was thinking he could take the basement. His mother told him the basement was being rented to a tenant.

That's an easy hustle. I wish I could get somebody to give me money like that.

He picked up his box and went up the narrow stairs to the disorderly interior of the upper house where his room had been. It was still there, with the blinds broken and the night showing through the window. They had left laundry hampers on his floor. He went into his closet, which had a sliding hollow wood door with a metal cup inlaid in the wood as a handle. It had been knocked off the track and hung sideways. He found photographs of old friends, himself as a skinny teenager making a weird gesture with his arm, a gang sign, in 1992. His hard hat was back there with stickers on it. American flag. Irish clover. Zofo. He found an electric guitar with broken strings.

The posters were rolling off the walls. He shut the door and a poster rolled down, the back of the paper white and empty. Before hiding it, he opened up his prison box and looked inside: letters, cards, a copy of Outlaw Biker, a Lipton's Cup-a-Soup, Psalms, a shaving mirror, a pair of prison-issue white boxer shorts issued by CCA, the Corrections Corporation of America, a Capri Sun juice pack, an old Heavy Metal magazine, a red cowboy bandana.

Unable to sleep, he went downstairs and turned on the TV in the front room.

In the basement, Skinner heard the television and the sound of a heavy, unfamiliar individual moving over the floor.

He took a shower with all the shampoo bottles that belonged to each member of the household except for him. As a matter of habit, he spent very little time in the shower, barely getting wet—got in and got out and went back to his room and dressed immediately. He combed his hair carefully, looking at himself from all angles in the aluminum shaving mirror.

A shout from below:

Jimmy! Mom wants to know if you can come down here.

He went downstairs and let them make him eggs. While he was waiting for them to cook, his mother, instead of asking him what his plans were, asked him to take a look at the kitchen cabinet door, the hinge. Jimmy moved himself, he stood up from the table and moved his weight—of his body, the somber weight of his eyes, his wet beard from the shower, the weight of his damp white skin under his plaid shirt—across the room and looked at the hinge.

There's nothing wrong with it.

Can you fix it?

He did not automatically say yes.

It's just a screw, he said.

He would quote back to people all the responsibilities he had undertaken for them, including things they had never asked him to do, but nevertheless things he was doing or was soon to do for them—or things that he had to do for other members of the household or for someone else entirely, some other entity, such as the government—simply things that he would have to do—suggesting that he was trying to help everyone as fast as he could—not that he wouldn't be happy to oblige—but if you could just wait your turn, because you weren't just imposing on him, you were infringing on someone else's rights. Jimmy had commitments to many people, you had to understand. He was just trying to be fair to everybody. Patrick's truck: Jimmy alone would be perceptive enough to hear that there was a problem with the front wheel bearing. Bathroom tiles were another thing. No offense, but their house had not been that well-maintained in his absence. He wasn't saying anything, but, his room, if he was supposed to live there, had turned into their laundry hamper. He had a small responsibility to himself to make it livable. The cupboard he would deal with when he had time.

He gave an understanding smile, because he got what was going on. No one was planning to compensate him for all the work he was planning to do. That was the way it was. That was fine. But there were some basic things he had to do for himself, and the State hadn't given him money for clothes or toiletries. The State had kicked him out. And it was a little too soon for him to start thinking about hustles unless the idea was for him to get violated right away. So he needed twenty bucks to go to the store. He knew she had it. He would get his mother whatever she wanted while he was out there.

When he was gone, Mrs. Murphy said, He's got to get back in the union. They'd take him back. They have their own rules that they go by. They don't base it on the conviction. What he did did not go that far to the point that he's out for good. He has a shot, if he wants it. He's got two options: either the union or he works with Patrick. Patrick, I don't really see. The way things are, he don't have enough work for the two of them, not every day. With Patrick, it's now you see it, now you don't. I see a problem there, with the up and down. Jim needs the routine every day that they gave him in the union. The other men were good for him when they were on the dig. He made every shift on that. You know, he told me, ma, I was there every shift. My whole life I would disappear. I know, I says, I remember. He used to hide when Patrick called him. He used to pretend he was out of the house when he was here the whole time. He cut school, which would be nothing new in this family. The middle of the day, I'd hear a sound—he was in the basement. Didn't you hear us calling? I says. He says, Yeah, but ma, I don't want to go with him, with Patrick.

I says, you know he's gonna beat the shit out of you. No, he won't this time. So, now I'm gonna get a prize fight in my kitchen. Patrick beat the shit out of him.

On the dig, he made every shift. Once he went in the trailer and put his belt on, that was it, that was what it took for him. He never violated that. He went to work, back here to Feeney's, then right back here. They had their fun, but there was a limit. He always knew what it was, he said. He knew he had to be ready for the next shift, so he used to stop himself. He's got to find that limit again.

In the evening, Jimmy came back and there was no mention of the money or what he had done. He sat in the front room on one of the couches watching the TV. I'm gonna get cable for you, he told his mother. In prison, they had watched cooking shows, celebrity reality TV, reality TV in which a house was built and you saw the craft and skill, the whole thing coming together like a puzzle. He had loved those.

Oh here. He set a carton of Slims on the kitchen table—an entire carton—which cost far more than the twenty dollars she had given him.

You trying to kill me? she said, chuckling. I need to hide these from myself. She turned herself around in her chair in stages and sought a drawer to hide the cigarettes in.

30

I WENT IN JAIL, she whispered.

You? What for?

I'm illegal alien in this country. She watched him. You don't know?

No. You never told me.

I am. No visa. No paper.

And you got arrested for that?

Yes.

How'd you get here?

I smuggle across the border.

The border of what?

Mexico. First I come to Mexico from Southeast Asia and then I take a truck.

She told him her journey had led to Archer, down south, and then the other east coast cities. In Connecticut, the police had arrested her coming out of a store to buy some things for dinner, some soda.

How long did they give you?

Three months.

Shit.

Yes. But that's the problem, they don't tell me. I don't know it's going to be three month. Nobody tells me when I can get out, so I don't know nothing. Some people says I can be a year there, some says it can be longer.

They didn't tell you?

No, I just sit in jail waiting, and I don't know anything.

Now he was appalled. You got fucking stop-lossed! That's the most fucked-up thing to do to someone...

She agreed. And she had a hard time with being closed-in. I think it make me lose my mind, so I am afraid of these police. Really that's why I come to Queens, because so many foreign people is here, I think the cops can't look for us.

What would happen if you got stopped by the cops? You'd go back?

I don't know. Maybe something bad for me.

What's the worst they could do?

I go to jail or deport back to China.

Can you do anything about it?

I don't know. Maybe I can go to a lawyer, apply asylum. I think before 9/11 it's easier than now.

Do they know you're Muslim? Do the cops know?

No. I don't think they know. Not too many people know what's Uighur people. I just think no matter any kind of people, to stay in the U.S. it's not easy right now.

So what's that mean, you just gotta live not knowing what's gonna happen to you?

I think so. She sighed. She raised her hands palm up and slapped them down on her thighs. Nothing I can do.

Skinner looked distraught. At her suggestion, they went outside in the lovely white-gold spring sunshine and wandered among the houses on 40th Road, where it seemed to both of them that it was an ordinary day and that their fears were exaggerated. But when they went back to his basement later and the golden light was cut by shadows, Skinner got very upset and wouldn't speak. After she coaxed him repeatedly to tell her what was wrong, he said, I've got to stop fucking up. I can't let you get deported.

He recalled a checkpoint on the road to Syria. Refugees from Baghdad were coming north in an attempt to flee the civil war. By political arrangement, Iraqi policemen controlled the checkpoint with American soldiers in a supporting role. In practice, this meant that the Iraqi police, who had been infiltrated by various mafias, could do whatever they wanted. Some GIs complained the policemen were levying exorbitant tolls on anyone not in the Zafir tribe. Others said they were turning Shiite Muslims back, mockingly telling them to go back to their villages where they would be killed by Sunni death squads.

Skinner witnessed an Iraqi policeman pull a girl over to the roadside and interrogate her, going through her bag, demanding to know why she was traveling alone. She was very young, maybe twelve years old. Her family had been killed in Baghdad. A GI told the man to give her a break. The Iraqi insisted that she wasn't allowed to travel without a husband.

The Iraqi took her by the hand and led her away from the road where the land dipped down into a hidden wadi. Down in the maze of brown hills were a series of abandoned open-roofed buildings that were sometimes used as a latrine.

I saw she was scared.

We went to our First Sergeant, who ordered us to not do anything. We never saw the girl again. The next time I saw the Iraqi was two days later, and I asked him where she was. He asked me if I worried about dogs. She was a bad girl, a Ba'athist, an enemy of America, so he had found a husband for her.

The obvious solution was for Zou Lei and Skinner to work together, she said. They should combine forces and help each other with their respective problems.

She brought him around to talking constructively about the things that they should do. Above all, they should not dwell on sad things from the past. It would be the first of many similar talks that they would have in which they planned for the future. The bright side, she said, was that she had met him and they could form an army of their own, a two-person unit, to fight these difficult battles involving his mental recovery and her immigration status.

31

Jim. If you're coming, then come on.

It was five and the house was completely dark except downstairs where the kitchen light was on and Patrick, with small eyes and his hair combed back damp and flat, was wearing a plaid shirt and a diamond-stitched down vest and Dickies or something like Dickies—janitor's pants—but without the brand name, all of his clothes faded and flattened, the puff taken out of the down, as if crushed out by the man who wore them. He was more impressive than his clothing. He spoke at a normal volume despite the hour. The effect was preemptory.

In his room, Jim knocked over his lamp looking for what he wanted to wear, cursed, and set the lamp upright and it fell again.

Mrs. Murphy appeared at the bottom of the stairs, her hair in curlers.

He's coming. He'll be right down. Do you men want coffee?

Patrick said something Irish.

Give him a minute.

Jimmy came down, not hurrying, no longer outweighed by his stepfather. There were four plaster buckets waiting in the kitchen to be carried out to the truck and a yellow four-foot level. The house creaked as the two large males carried everything outside. Mrs. Murphy went back to bed.

In the basement, Skinner heard the pickup cough to life and drive away.

There was no discussion between Mr. Murphy and Jimmy of what it was like to be freed after a long period of incarceration. They drove beneath the streetlights, which were still on, on 40th Road. Patrick remarked he didn't want to hear jungle music. You didn't pick it up in there, did you? No, said Jimmy, mildly. Then turn the radio on. The radio was tuned to a call-in program in which the host was defending American torture.

Ladies and gentlemen, that's not torture. Stress positions, that's not torture. That is nowhere near as bad as what these people have done for thousands of years. The beheading, stoning, burning, burying alive, flogging, flaying the skin, and so on. The cruelties inflicted on the members of their own religion. Maybe these liberals would feel differently if they had lost someone on September Eleventh: a beloved father, husband, wife, a son or daughter. Let's open the phone lines. Hello, Ed, you're on the air.

Hey, I just want to say I appreciate your show.

Thank you, my man.

My brother served in Operation Enduring Freedom, so he's seen these lies we're seeing now up close, how the media will take what they're doing, which is, they might have built a school, and they don't show that. They only want to know about the bad stuff. That's what we're seeing. And you get these people, for whatever reason, they want to believe the baby-killer hype. You give fresh water to Iraqi kids and you're a baby killer.

Both the caller and the host laughed with exasperation.

I know, Ed. We're at a time when it's out-of-fashion to love this country apparently. And I want to extend my thanks to you and your brother. God bless him for his service. We are so grateful to our brave men and women in uniform. And the irony, Ed, is brave men and women like your brother go to this godforsaken country, they volunteered to go, while meanwhile people back here have the, the—they are complaining about them. When they don't have to do it. They're not the ones. The military goes and gets the job done and the armchair liberals complain. It's just upside-down to me.

It is.

Thank you, Ed. We've got John in Maspeth.

They drove to a construction supply outlet on College Point Boulevard, next door to a Dunkin Donuts.

You've got time to get yourself something, Patrick said as he got out. His thirty-two-year-old stepson declined, stayed in the passenger seat. Jimmy was putting up with something. He was not happy, this was clear. But he would not complain. You would have to beg him to know how you had offended him. You would have to draw him out. Patrick would not do this. Patrick went into Dunkin Donuts and waited in line, bigger and taller than anyone else in line, than the young muscular Puerto Rican repairmen with tattooed forearms and a stud in the earlobe. He was the primary figure you would notice through the window. But Jimmy had banished him. Jimmy was derisively going through the contents of the glove box. Parking tickets, receipts, the registration bearing Patrick's full, three-word Irish name. It was expired. Wasn't it? He smirked. He checked the date. What was the date? He turned the key in the ignition and the radio came on. Like a technician, a craftsman, a musician, Jimmy concentrated on the radio dial, turning it, tuning it. The stations were different than they used to be. If there was no Deep Purple, then at least there should be Elvis. When Patrick came back, Frankie Valli was playing and Jimmy was fine-tuning the dial. He was distracted now. He did not look up. Patrick put their coffees on the dash, smalls. There was a deal for two donuts in a crinkling wax bag. Jimmy received what he was given. He would be tolerant through the entire exercise, the shabbiness of the truck, his stepfather's unwillingness to put two dollars in his hand directly out of fear that it would be spent on something other than coffee. Now it was time to assert himself.

Where we going today? he demanded.

Enormous crabs with long spider arms bent and hooked in in the tanks in the window of the Favor Taste Restaurant. At a lot where they did recycling called Andy Metal, a man in a dust mask threw a piece of aluminum up in the air and it landed on top of a mountain of other scrap and stayed.

Perma Base cement board, Super-Tek one-step thin-set mortar, Vision-Pro vinyl siding, Lehigh Portland cement, angle iron, hubless pipe UPC. All of it untended, Jimmy noticed.

Dark 5'3" kids with earrings went by. One wore yellow high-tops with a swoosh.

Golden Fields vegetables. North Shore laundry bags with black grease on the bottoms of the bags piled outside the side entrance of a restaurant where the kitchen boys were sitting on the concrete.

Women walked on high heels across the boulevard, walking as if they were sick, as if they had been sold into geisha slavery.

Jimmy watched.

The onrush of the Chinese. Their scuffing, heedless, lobotomized walking, as if retarded, as if forced to ingest pesticide as children. Women with wicked slant eyes, the faces of evil stepmothers. A pinched, insane or troubled face, the brow pinched, struggling with a constant problem, unable to think, blocked by something lodged in the brain above the eyes. They were pregnant. They pushed a baby carriage, held a child's hand, pulling a chain of children holding hands across the sidewalk.

A sign outside a filthy doorway said Slimming Hot Wrap, Diamond Peel Facial, Acne Facial, Sensitive Facial, Bodywork.

He carried a sink into someone's house and held it while Patrick spun the fasteners underneath. They put a bead of silicon between the porcelain and the wall. Patrick turned the faucet and the water came out, hit the sink, and went down the drain.

On the ride back, Jimmy said he was aware that they somehow had found the cash to renovate the basement while his room had holes in the walls. He understood—wink, wink. It was the same thing he would have done. It was a chance to make a buck.

Jimmy did not tell Patrick this—he watched who he said this to—but once when Erin and a few of her friends were hanging around the house and the subject of the war came up, Jimmy said that it was a scam.

Like how?

Like anything. For money.

Like you think they're profiting?

Jimmy, eyes narrowed, drinking a beer, made a face, a face that said of course, it was so obvious how could you be such a fool that you would think otherwise. His disgust was not with the profit motive but with the naivety of the question.

One of them said he knew someone who, because he had been in Vietnam, knew what happened when planes hit buildings and this was not what had happened on 9/11, the planes had not been vaporized completely, which would have happened. Rather, pieces of the fuselage had been found. This proved that it was not what we were all told it had been! Do you think 9/11 was an inside job?

Obviously.

That's so fucked-up, they said with awe and delight.

Skinner met Jimmy in the following way:

Skinner had become aware of someone new in the house. He had been hearing an unfamiliar voice through his ceiling, that of a man without a brogue. The man was just a set of footsteps to him, a weight on the floor. He didn't know who he was.

He went to the bodega on the corner where the train tracks came in. The bodega sold waterpipes lined up in the window like rifles in an armory. Skinner paid for a pack of Camels. A trace of blue curled down the box like smoke to indicate the mentholated flavor. He put the pack in his pocket and smoked one cigarette, staring at Northern Boulevard. A broken parking meter had a jacket tied around it. After his cigarette, he began walking back to his basement. He went past the Dutch houses and down the line of still-bare trees under the rain-heavy sky.

He neared the Irish bar, where a guy in black urban combat gear— loose-fit denim, Timberlands, vest, and SWAT-style ball cap—had a chain wrapped around his knuckles, holding a tiger-striped pit bull on a leash.

A big guy came striding around the corner with the energy of a man about to chop down an entire forest singlehandedly. He bounced up and down as if on springs, his long hair swinging back and forth, the plane of his face lifted displaying the short lines of his mouth and eyes. He was over six feet tall, weighed two-twenty. The beard on his face made him look like a 70s biker. Skinner was struck by an unusual detail: he was wearing a red bandana tied around his thigh. He entered the bar, handing off his lit cigarette to the pit bull's owner, who took it without a word, presumably to hold for him until he returned.

The same evening when Skinner went outside to watch for Zou Lei coming up Sanford Avenue, a figure caught his eye. It was a man walking far away down the avenue, passing in and out of trees—probably half a mile away in the dusk—nearly out of M16 range—but the way he walked was unmistakable. It was the man from the bar, and Skinner had seen him twice in one day.

Then on a weeknight towards the end of the first week in April, Skinner saw him a third time as he was coming home. This time, the Long Island Railroad had just roared by through the just-beginning-to-bloom trees. The noise had made Skinner flinch and when he looked up, the man appeared, passing in front of a white house. He was slightly ahead of Skinner, who recognized him and watched him indirectly. They crossed 158th Street together and their paths started converging on the Murphy's driveway. It became obvious that they were both going into the Murphy's house. Neither spoke. The man went first, and Skinner followed behind him.

Once they had gone in, Skinner would hear him talking to Erin, would hear his footsteps go into the upstairs apartment where they would become the footsteps with which he was growing familiar overhead, and he would realize who he was in the family: he was Mrs. Murphy's son, and he was living here, he was the weight on the floor.

Before this, in the moments while they were negotiating the door and their sudden proximity to one another, Skinner would perceive him for the first time from close range. It was an indirect seeing, an impression of a stranger in the gloom of the entryway, a tall presence elevated above him by the landing.

The guy had left the door open for him but hadn't held it.

Good looking out, Skinner said, and the man looked down at him as if the slightest pleasantry was unheard-of where he was from.

32

ZOU LEI TOLD SASSOON that she would cover Zhang Zhuojin's shift on Sunday, as long as she would get paid for the extra hours. She made a specific point of asking Sassoon whether the extra hours would be recorded. Sassoon irritably dismissed her concerns, but on Sunday Zhang Zhuojin arrived anyway, which led Zou Lei to wonder which of them was getting paid. She urged Zhuojin to go home, but she refused and suggested that Zou Lei was attempting to con her in some way.

Zou Lei wrote both their names in the same square on the schedule and wrote We Are Both Here and drew an arrow to their names.

She asked Zhuojin if she minded letting her run the steam table.

I don't control you, Zhuojin said.

Business was slow that afternoon and the bosses were not there, but despite this, an unaccountable stress prevailed. As Zou Lei stood at the line, she could hear Zhuojin in the back smashing steel pots around beneath the slow drip of the Taiwanese pop music coming out of the speakers in the ceiling. She claimed she had to make ten gallons of soup, a product that Zou Lei had never known them to sell. Only one customer came between two and four p.m. and he asked for yuk haam or mincemeat. Zhuojin understood his meaning and insisted that they make it for him. Towards quitting time, she came running from the back carrying a smoking steel pot, the veins in her throat standing out above her tendons, and dumped its liquid contents in a pickle bucket. A tongue of heat rose up on the stainless refrigerator door. Zou Lei told her she needn't have carried that heavy thing alone. She could have burned herself. Looking in the bucket, she saw the liquid still turning over on itself, pieces of black material that she identified as fish skin churning up from the bottom.

The red-haired bartender acted reserved when Skinner came in. After Skinner drank in front of him, he loosened-up, almost as if he were the one drinking. On Skinner's second tumbler of Parrot Bay, the bartender came over and, suddenly lively, began telling him about his trouble with women.

I made the mistake of telling her my real name. Check the phone-book. There're a lot of Chins and Kims, but there ain't too many McIntyres in Flushing anymore. You know how many there are? One. That's right, me. So there you have it, she calls me up. Is this the residence of John McIntyre, the dirty so-and-such and so forth?!

He pretended to hold a receiver away from his ear, bugging his eyes.

Never use your real name. Number one rule with women.

My girlfriend's Chinese too, Skinner said.

Well then you better tell her your last name's Kim or God help you.

She's gonna get deported.

Well then you don't have to worry, assuming you're having trouble with her.

There's no trouble. I want her to stay. It's the government trying to take her away.

Have they started proceedings?

I don't know what all they're doing.

There's a thing called detention and removal. I'm an immigrant myself, so I know all about it. They'll detain somebody and then they'll start the removal proceedings. First she'll be arrested by Immigration or, now, it's Homeland that'll get her.

If they do that shit, Skinner muttered, I'll burn the fucking flag of this fucking country and wipe my ass with the ashes.

So you like her and you want her to stay? Do you like her enough to marry her?

Skinner looked in his glass and said, Yeah.

Well then why don't you marry her? You're an American citizen, aren't you? Because, you never know, there are some guys in the army who aren't even citizens, but you are, right? If a citizen marries some-one from another country, you can bring her over and she can stay here. Haven't you ever heard of mail-order brides from Russia? Just ask her, if you want to do it. Of course, I'm not saying you do want to get married. I could never get married myself. I like to go from one to the next. I get tired of them and I can't stay still. But if you want to keep yours here and you don't mind it, just marry her. Though Homeland will make you jump through hoops, I imagine. But it'll slow them down from getting rid of her.

The door to the back alley was open and the old navy man who should have been dead was half-visible in the doorway, putting the trash out. Along with the sound of garbage cans scraping concrete, his voice could be heard talking unintelligibly. John McIntyre, who could somehow tell what he was saying, replied to him.

Meanwhile, Skinner went over to the Flushing Mall, his phone to his ear, and called Zou Lei.

When she came outside in the purple dusk at quitting time, he was waiting. They ate pizza slices while the streetlights came on, went down past the gas station and walked along the river.

She was so moved she didn't talk for nearly a mile.

What are you thinking?

You have a great heart, Skinner!

He liked it that she was happy.

Just you say you will marry to me, it's incredible.

They were headed north in the direction of College Point and the river was getting wider and the buildings were getting smaller and sparser. Ahead, there was an elevated highway standing by itself above a wasteground. The wind picked up.

Today I know what is a real American, she said.

She breathed deep, took in the space, the distant lights across the black water. She could not believe her fortune. How life surprised her. She looked at him with new recognition in the dark.

I'm gonna quit smoking, he told her.

In the front of the house, the windows were covered by white shutters and lace curtains. In the back, there was lumber decaying in the yard next to a rusted can of flashing cement. The house had several stories, maybe three. There were too many windows to see them all. The ones on the upstairs floors were open gray squares reflecting the gray of the sky and the asphalt. The roofs rolled out like tongues, missing squares, tar showing. Rained-on yellow insulation and silver sheathing bulged out of an attic window.

When she went around the side of the house, there were windows above her. Her angle to them was oblique, so she couldn't see anything through them. At night, sometimes they would one or two be lit. The window immediately to her right when she stood at the door was an aperture into their kitchen. She would hear low voices coming from this window, and sometimes when she knocked on the door the voices would stop, resuming when Skinner's footsteps would come up from the basement to let her in. Often, rather than knocking, she would call him on her phone to alert him that she was outside. She had never rung the bell. She had to assume that they heard him answering the door and leading a visitor downstairs.

All through the winter, she had avoided being seen. She had not once come face to face with anyone who lived there. Visiting him had become routine; she took for granted that she could come and go.

The whole house gradually took on only one meaning for her, the meaning of him. To lay eyes on it was to see him directly, and she would react to the sight of it based on how things were going between them: if they were getting along, she felt happy, and if they were fighting, she got depressed. While she avoided the Americans, she had never been afraid to enter their house.

One afternoon that spring, when she was standing at the door after knocking, she thought she heard someone come to the kitchen window and look at her and then say something about her to whoever else was in the kitchen.

Who's outside?

I'll look. Some dink. Did you order Chinese?

Not us. Must be the tenant.

33

GETTING MARRIED WAS A wonderful idea, she said, but it would not be simple or easy. There might be costs, from seeing a lawyer to buying a ring. And marrying him might not be enough in itself to allow her to stay in the country legally. They might face many more legal and practical obstacles. That was why she urged him to think twice before he did this. In addition, she said, he was a young man and he might regret this later. She didn't want to take advantage of him…

I don't see why it can't work out, he said.

She was just afraid it would be a lot of struggle for him and he already had a struggle on his own. What if I add my burdens to yours? Maybe we should wait.

Waiting didn't make any sense, he said. If there was something you wanted to do, you better do it today, because you didn't know what was going to happen tomorrow.

On a Sunday morning, she and Skinner walked up Main Street in the direction of Franklin Avenue, passing produce markets. When they were almost to the top of the hill, the produce line ended and Zou Lei's eye was caught by a set of tubs. The tubs were in front of a store whose sign was invisible. She told Skinner she wanted to see something and she went closer and saw the tubs contained dried prune-like things. On the cardboard, in Chinese, had been written: Six kinds of dates. Temporary shelves laid across cinder blocks held lily flower, lotus seeds, boiled peanuts, bars of Darlie Double Action Two Mint Powers, and Fan Medicated Soap.

What are you looking at? he asked, coming over. She was visoring her eyes and looking through the glass.

I think it's the Chinese medicine.

Chinese medicine?

Yes. That's what it is.

She turned to him. Skinner, I think we can go inside. We can look for something that can help you. It can cure many things that the Western medicine feels helpless.

She reached for his elbow.

Oh, he said. Okay.

You can come inside?

All right.

You don't mind?

No.

They went inside and it smelled like ginger. There was an island full of dried things in the center of the floor: animals that looked like plants, plants that looked like animals, sheets of horn, cartilage, treelike sprouts of bone, wood, or root. The walls were covered in medication boxes just like Duane Reade, except the medications were different. They sold Goupi Medicated Plaster. There were rows of apothecary jars behind the counter containing abalone. In the back of the store, there was a giant wall of labeled drawers like the card catalog at a library or safety deposit boxes in a bank.

Three men in suit jackets manned the counter, negotiating with a group of customers speaking Chinese. The men had cell phones and keys on their belts. One of them—a balding man in glasses—said, Ten percent off—Ten—and made a cross with his index fingers to indicate the Chinese character for ten.

Another man who had been watching the negotiation turned and looked at Skinner and Zou Lei. His eyes passed over Skinner and he asked Zou Lei, What do you want?

I've brought my friend to get medicine. He's suffered shock. The shock was severe.

But the man put up a finger right away to stop her. He didn't know what she was talking about, so she would have to talk to Mr. Jia. He indicated him by lifting his chin at him and then turned away with his hands behind his back and walked away to another part of the counter.

She made a loop around the store, passing the male performance enhancers in the case at the back: Hard Ten Days, Hard Black Ant, Street Overlord, German Bullwhip. To her, they weren't remarkable, and Skinner didn't see them.

Skinner picked up a handful of gold foil-wrapped candy out of a tray in the center island.

Think these are good?

Maybe, she said.

He smelled the candy through the wrapper. Smell that, he said. What's that smell?

She hunted for the word. A strip of cardboard, which had been sliced out of a cardboard box, stuck out of the tray, saying Gold Tree Ginger Candy. The characters had been written deftly with a pointed laundry marker.

It's the ginger.

Should I get them?

I think we need to find something that can help you, not just taste good.

True. He dropped the candy back in the tray. I just don't know what any of this stuff does.

I don't know either, but we can look.

She began going through the products on the shelves one after the other, looking at them, turning them over, putting them back: Dacon Pain Patch, Foot Patch, Organic Sorghum Groats, Motherwort Tea, Vita-Kidney, Vita-Hero (Male Enhancement), hawthorn berry, Banlangen Isatis Root Supplement, Chickenbonegrass Abri Tea, Tibet Guava Tea, Fried Semen Coicis (Job's Tears).

There was a poster on the wall catty-corner to the apothecary jars, showing a very white-skinned woman holding up the OK sign with her long-fingered porcelain hand. She was looking at you through the O of the OK sign. In Chinese, it said: When your monthly is OK, everything's OK. With her other eye, she was winking.

The other customers went out and Zou Lei went back to the counter to talk to Mr. Jia, who was now free.

What does she want? Mr. Jia asked his associate over his glasses.

She wants to tell you herself.

I'll tell you.

Good. You tell me! Mr. Jia told Zou Lei over his glasses. He kept his chin lowered and stared at her with a droll expression as if this were a comic situation and he could barely suppress his laughter.

I've brought my friend to get medicine, she said, and began to explain what was going on with Skinner. I don't know what to call it. He served in the army in Iraq. There was too much shock there. There were many bombs that went off constantly. The bombs went off in his ear in an unbroken chain. He suffered shock. Himself, he is very brave, but he has anxiety. He drinks more than amount.

He was wounded?

Yes, he was wounded. His back was wounded. But also he suffered some concussion in his head.

Mr. Jia gestured to Skinner to come over. Let me see your arm. You can push the sleeve up. But Skinner found it easier to take his hoodie off entirely. Mr. Jia looked at the other men and said, The American boy's muscles are so big, he can't push his sleeve up. And they all smiled. In English, he told Skinner:

You are big man. Good!

He took Skinner's arm and felt his wrist pulse for fifteen seconds. Then he told Skinner to open his mouth and stick his tongue out. He moved his hands towards Skinner's face as if he were going to touch his tongue and Skinner flinched.

Look at that! A soldier is that easy to scare! he said to the other men.

And, in English: Don't worry. Not touch. Only look.

Mr. Jia squinted through his spectacles at Skinner's tongue.

I already see it. I already tell. You have disease. The internal body not working right. He called his associates over and told Zou Lei to look as well. You see? He reached out towards Skinner's face again, and Skinner blinked. You see that reaction? It's the disorder. A normal soldier is not afraid of the single hand. He would block my hand. Instead he flinches. His pulse is throbbing-surging, a sign of shock.

Oh, yes. We see it, the associates said. It's very clear. His reactions are disordered.

You see it too? Mr. Jia demanded of Zou Lei.

You get a hit! he shouted at Skinner. Almost the same like punch. Piiyaa! He slapped his hands together. Skinner blinked. Affect body, affect mind. No balance. Right? Now, one day happy, one day sad.

The pharmacist pretended to be sad like a little child, boohooing and rubbing his eyes with his fists.

Right?

Skinner just stared, but Zou Lei agreed that that was it and Mr. Jia burst into a smile.

He told his associate to bring him the Primary Wuzhihuang, an orange box the size of a fifth of vodka. He showed them the gold seal on the box, making sure that Zou Lei read it: National Brand of China.

Return the balance, he said. Look. You read. He pointed at the ingredients: Pure polygonatum, coronarium, angelica sinensis, scutellaria barbata. Pure, he underlined—the one word he tried to say.

The fact that the ingredients were pure was what justified the price of $59.99, he explained.

She hesitated, and asked him if he understood what was wrong with Skinner. She wanted to describe his symptoms again to make sure there was no confusion.

The symptoms come from the cause, don't they? Then we must treat the cause, not the symptom. That's what makes Chinese medicine superior to Western medicine. Putting a Band-Aid on a disease doesn't fix it. The disease is still present. We must treat the inside. His imbalance was caused on the inside. This medicine works on the inside. You have heard of cells, haven't you? The cells in the body, yes? This medicine powerfully goes into the cells. It cures the cells. Then what do you think happens? Naturally, it cures the body. Fix the cell, fix the entire body.

What about his drinking?

This one. He pointed at the Scutellaria in the ingredients. Toxins out, he said.

He has psychological pain.

He's schizophrenic?

No. He has sadness.

If his body feels better, his mind will feel better. For his glorious service, I'll give you ten percent off.

She was going to ask him another question, but the door opened and other customers came in and Mr. Jia went out from behind the counter to greet them. They were Chinese and were already telling him what they wanted.

What'd he say?

He say he will give a discount.

Together they contemplated the orange box stamped with gold writing.

How are you supposed to take this? Is it like MetRx where you just mix it in juice?

She read the bilingual directions on the box.

You make the tea.

Tea?

You would have to buy a pot finally to boil the water.

I could get one next door. Do you think I should?

She was thinking of the old expression, What kind of medicine are you selling me in your gourd? She didn't say that she didn't trust the pharmacist, but she did remark that the medicine cost a lot.

It's only money.

He wanted to try something to see if it would work.

Then maybe yes, she said. After all so did she.

One of the associates came over and took Skinner's bank card. Zou Lei said the pharmacist had agreed to give them ten percent off. But he told her that they only got the discount if they were paying cash. He rang up the sale with tax, and it was sixty-five dollars. He put the box in a plastic bag and left it on the counter and walked away from them with the receipt.

At midday it rained and they hid out under the scaffold where they had eaten shaokao. The rain passed over and the sun returned and they went over the hill and down the other side where the street spread out. They crossed Elder Avenue and went into the park. The street was wet and drying in the sun after the rain. In the immediate distance, she saw a group of buildings: Booth Memorial Hospital. Beneath a tree, a middle-aged woman was performing Chinese opera. They walked through the weed-grown field where Zou Lei had run all winter, the ground rutted by construction equipment. The woman pressed her fingers together and rotated her wrists in a way that would always look like Uighur dance to her. When they were closer, they heard her off-key song. They went up to the handball courts where there was no one else. A tennis ball was lying in a puddle and Zou Lei picked it up. She looked back at him and he was watching her, the plastic bag that contained his medicine hanging from his hand. The skyline was behind him.

What's wrong?

Nothing.

Do you want to play?

No, he said.

She gave him the ball and he threw it. It hit the cement and left a wet mark.

34

Jimmy was at Feeney's, where they were playing Keno, playing Boardwalk. If you held a piece of metal, you'd be more likely to get hit by lightning, Rick shouted. This machine don't pay. Bad luck? No luck. They sang along with Dust in the Wind. It smelled like pot from somewhere, someone was blazing out.

Represent. You look like Mick Jagger stoned on heroin, Gladys said to Rick.

Bumpers stickers next to the jukebox said: I Heart the Red Lights. I'm Union and Proud of It. Steamfitters Local 683. Drinkingwithbob.com—The guy's out of his freaking mind!!! Derrickmen. Elevator Constructors. New York and vicinity. My Goodness, My Guinness.

Ray, in jean shorts and white sneakers, was going to pick something on the jukebox, when a man with wiry matted hair shuffled up behind him.

Can you play some rock 'n' roll?

Don't worry about it. Go sit down.

Yesterday someone tried to cut my hair, he mumbled.

What? Go sit down.

The man shuffled back to the bar and tried to climb back on his seat and got distracted by the women. He shuffled over to them and mumbled.

I can't understand this guy. You know what? Go sit back down until you can talk.

The jukebox went on and Gladys, who had a gaunt masculine face, and Rosy and a third woman with white hair and a purse on the bar started singing: Heartbeat! Hot Stuff! A little louder, baby! They talked along with the talking part of the song: The lips that used to touch yours so tenderly.

The drunk lurched away from Jimmy, who had an empty stool on either side of him, who sat oversized and mountainous and unspeaking.

Ray went back behind the bar and met Jimmy's eyes. Another? Jimmy's response was an acquiescence with the eyes.

Absolut, was it? Absolut Blue. He served him and put the bottle back under the mirror and the photographs, stuck in the frame of the mirror, of people drinking in the bar.

A guy with shades on his head, a little mustache, and a short-sleeved shirt, came in grinning, dancing in through the doorway. He danced up to the bar high-fiving everyone and said, Hey, can I have a pint? He saw Jimmy and said, Jim. What's up?

They conferred in low voices, Jimmy silent, unmoving, and for-ward-facing, the other talking eagerly in his ear.

You see all the counterfeit twenties out there? They're beautiful and they move like water.

Rosy was yelling, The whole foundation of a relationship is loy-alty! If you don't got loyalty, you don't got shit!

Would you stop hitting the bar? Gladys said.

They exploded with braying laughter.

Who's the dumbest guy in this bar?

You are, Rick.

You're fuckin right.

What's the difference between White Castles and filet mignon?

Hey, I eat steak every night. If I can't buy it, I steal it.

Jimmy went to the airshaft in the back, where they smoked drugs, and while he was gone, the house painter whispered to Ray:

Did you see him? He's changed.

Not easy to come back after that, I expect.

Ten years.

Ray changed the subject, turned the lights off over the pool table. The house painter danced over to Gladys and Rosy and the third woman.

My good girls.

Give me a break, man, Rick was saying to the machine, sitting on his flat ass in dark blue jeans on the stool with his spine curved and his white Nikes on the rungs. I'll pick this fuckin machine up and drag it out of this bar. I'll piss on this machine. You couldn't get a hit on this fuckin machine if you hit it with a fuckin stick. This machine don't fuckin pay. Rick hit the button, kept hitting the button. That ain't a hit. That ain't nothin. I'd like to beat this with a stick. He jabbed the button. Aaagh. I swear I'll never play this again. That's a nice hand. I seen alotta shit in my life, but this is the biggest piece a shit I've seen. The machine don't flip you a bone. I put sixty-five dollars in it. They're supposed to flip you a little bone to pacify you. I'm gonna cash this thing out. I'm gonna get out a this fuckin rat race. Oh, please, man. He hit the button. He hit the button. You give me nothin! Crooked bastards. I'm gonna have a heartattack. I'm gonna drop on the floor.

Jimmy went out to smoke on the street next to John Foley in his gold watch and sleeveless sweater. Bending over, sloppy, gyrating, broad-shouldered Emmett said, If you came to my house, I'd hide the valuables! and Jimmy looked at him, but he was talking to someone else, to Stan, a tall frame of man with a flat top and square black-framed glasses and a tie and a gray shirt untucked, as if he had just come from a telemarketing job.

It's Section 8, Stan said. He was living with Haitians in Bensonhurst. In Flatbush. I don't do nothin in Brooklyn if I can help it. I'm careful what I buy in Brooklyn.

Inside the bar, Rick was circling the pool table. Turn on the light. I wanna get a tan. I used to have a beautiful chain, he told the house painter who was showing him several pieces of jewelry, spreading them out on the pool table. Forty-two pennyweight. I had it in hock. I got the notice it's in the pawnshop, they're about to pawn it. I forgot all about it. A year later, my mother asks me, Where's my chain? You lost my chain. It cost a hundred seventy-five dollars. I says, What are you, crazy? The price of gold is up now.

Emmett came inside and felt the chains, pouring them from one hand to another and draping them over his fingers, to see them in the light that Ray had turned back on.

Manhattan was bought from the Indians for less than that.

Where'd you get these? Emmett asked and laughed his queasy laugh.

What'd you say your name was? You from the DA's office? Detective what?

Rick pulled out a roll of cash, all hundreds. Here: Take five hundred dollars. He threw money on the pool table. The house painter folded his jewelry up in a bandana, looked over his shoulder, folded it up and put it away.

Who's the toughest guy in this bar?

You are, Rick.

On the street, Stan, from Alaska by way of North Carolina, was telling Jimmy about the automatic ninety days they gave you in Orlando. I was lying on a bench and there was a bottle nearby—it wasn't mine. The biggest building in Orlando is the jail. Jail has gone corporate in this country.

The neighborhood has changed, Jimmy said.

The Chinese, they're taking advantage of our religious freedoms. Why do you need thirteen churches on one block?

He had drunk boilermakers with Pat Murphy back in the day. That was his drink, your dad. A boilermaker man. Hey, Gladys, Gladdie. When was the last time you saw Pat?

Pat? Patrick Murphy? I saw him at St. Andrews. That's his kid right there. Wait, he was right there.

He's right here. I'm talkin to him.

Oh, my mistake. Hey. I thought you were there. What's up, how you doin? Jimmy! Aw, c'mere!

She hugged him with her ropey arms, wearing a black tank top, with her large nose and ghoul's face. Ya gotta light? So, she said, blowing out her smoke, When I heard you was back, I said it's about fuckin time.

Jimmy blew out his smoke, nodded down to her, glanced at the street.

This is a good area, but we're getting bought out.

Skinner was asleep in his room when he was awakened by a sound. It was eleven in the morning and the house was otherwise quiet. A diffuse gray light devoid of shadows came in the grating. He had fallen asleep four hours ago and his last memory was of birds trilling in the dawn. He heard the sound again, got up and opened his door and saw Jimmy looking under his sink.

You again, he thought.

He went behind him to the refrigerator, took a beer out. Neither man spoke in the fifteen-by-ten-foot kitchen. The other's hunched shoulders and long hair moved beneath the sink. Skinner went back into his room and put his headphones on. He would forget everything staring at the wall. He would be like that for hours, dealing with his depression.

There was nothing ever wrong with the sink, he said later. Why mess with it?

And he crushed his empty beer can and dropped it on the floor.

As time went by, he would notice that sometimes during the quiet part of the day when no one was around, he would hear soft sounds coming from somewhere overhead, possibly the landing. They were very faint and subtle, so he didn't pay any attention to them, but they would continue, their location seeming to shift, and he would think that they were coming from the basement. But this could have been his imagination. He was usually too depressed to get up and look. By the time he did, he never saw anything or anyone. He thought he was hearing things because of mefloquine. The whole thing was so vague, it didn't mean anything until later.

35

SHE WAS LEARNING CANTONESE because she had to. Gwat was bone and river rice meant slippery noodles, tuber stem of water lily, fatty meat and offcuts of the pork. She greeted Rambo in Cantonese and he ignored her, told her to mop the floor. She learned to say, Hou-geng, which meant wonderful. Hougeng! she said as she fetched the mop. She said it whenever they made her do something. She found herself saying it all the time.

She took a place on line without asking and started serving in the middle of the rush. She felt Sassoon watching her dipping Thousand Island dressing on a customer's chunks of iceberg lettuce. She piled rice next to the meat in its jellied brown sauce and handed the dinner plate across the counter.

In her heart, she believed she was more Chinese than they were because the army was the marrow of the nation and she stood at parade rest behind the line while they slouched and texted on their phones, but China was a big nation.

Satay, made with onions, garlic, krill, and soy sauce, was pro-nounced sa-de in their dialect.

She overheard Angela telling her friend he ought to come to work at the restaurant as a summer job. The friend was a tall young man from Hong Kong who had been in her sister's class in high school in Jamaica, Queens. The boss would hire him on her say-so, Angela said. We've got lots of room here. Daifong meant room. Zou Lei understood this.

She had spent years surviving around people she didn't like and couldn't understand. Her coworkers believed that blacks had large but nonworking penises, like dragons in southern superstition. She learned they called them jiekwan.

She couldn't understand what a customer was telling her—whatever he was saying sounded very strange, the f's and h's were switched—and she leaned over the counter and asked him as quietly as she could if he spoke the common language.

Midway through the rush, Sunnie bustled in and Sassoon told Zou Lei, You can go now.

Hahaha, Angela said. You should see your face.

When she left the mall in the evening, the streets were awash with people coming off the buses, coming out of the subway station with every roar of the train coming in, welling up onto the street in waves. After a long shift, she had a great feeling of disorientation and had to get reacquainted with everything. The markets stood tilted by the weight of the produce trucked in from Sinaloa in the dusk. There was the money she had saved in her pocket against her hip—the point of her sixty-hour weeks down in the kitchen. She could feel the folded bills through her worn-thin pocket liner, touching her underwear, her skin. The faint outline of her progress.

She went to see him, prepared to talk about their plans, and as soon as she saw him, misgiving filled her. His room was heavy with the smell of sweat and smoke. He had been sitting for hours doing absolutely nothing.

I don't think it's good, she said.

I do, he said, staring sideways, his jaw working.

She was sitting on the corner of his bed—the only place to sit—wearing her jeans and torn t-shirt. She could feel her face getting older in his presence, the lines deepening by her mouth. For a moment, she observed him, wondering what to say.

Summer will be here. The sun will be shining bright, she said and grabbed his hard clammy white bare foot with her discolored calloused hand.

He did not answer.

Take a walk with me.

Skinner took his Marlboros off the bedside table, shook the pack, and caught a cigarette on his lip.

I don't think so.

He was muscled and tattooed, but his shirt was off and there was a fold in the fat across his stomach, and even the permanently tanned parts of his body were turning the color of cigarette smoke.

Skinner.

What?

Did you take the meds?

Yes. I even drank the Chinese crap, I had two cups of it and it doesn't do anything. Nothing does anything.

They sat with that statement for a while.

I won't give up, she finally said. Will you? She touched his foot again. I think you promise to me. Do you remember?

What if—here was a thought that just came to her—he simply drove ahead, in military style, as if there were nothing wrong with him?

I think you can get the job.

He was sitting with one leg out, one leg bent, his thick Gothic-lettered forearm resting on his knee, the cigarette now burning in his fingers. The leg of his boxers hung open and she could see his genitals. He did not respond to her. He dragged on the cigarette, his brow knitted, and blew the smoke out, watched it spread, held the cigarette sideways while it burned and blew on it, made it glow, as if he intended to use it to start a larger fire, which would be instrumental in their survival in a manner she did not yet understand.

I think you get a job, Skinner, she repeated. I think it's good. She gave him reasons, that it was healthy for the body to get out, to move, and healthy for the heart too, though what she was really trying to say was, it was healthy for the mind, for his mind.

When he didn't respond to her, she wondered if as a man his pride had been offended by what she had said. She apologized if that was so. Shuwozhiyan. I sorry. But I tell you straight. Sometimes even the man listen to the woman.

When he didn't speak, she stared at him, waiting for him to say anything.

Nishengqima? You mad? Skinner?

She tried to make contact with his bruised-looking eyes, but he just kept staring sideways.

She began humming a song to herself.

He told her to shut up.

This pulled the power cord right out of her. She got up and left his room and went into the kitchen and held herself on the sink. He heard the water run in the sink. Then he heard some movement and then a door closed and then he realized that she had gone and left the basement entirely.

When he wanted another drink, Jimmy went around the bar and served himself. He described himself as a silent partner in the bar, ordering drinks for friends and saying that they were on the house. I only fuck with good people, he said.

A guy rode up on his bike and came inside and took off his shades and said, Turner, right? I was locked down with you, wasn't I?

They shook hands Viking-style, gripping each other's forearms.

This dude was good people, he told the bar after a couple of drinks. Is this where you hang out? I'm gonna bring all the boys.

You wanna talk some business?

They went into the airshaft and he gave Jimmy some red pills in his big hand and laughed with his pale blue eyes after they had both taken them, his sunglasses up on his sunburned forehead. He had fringe on his leather jacket sleeves and keys and a rabbit's foot hanging from his belt. In the most ingratiating way he said, I'm sorry man, I'm gonna have to get some money for them later. He even apologized for that.

But that was no problem, Jimmy said. Business is business. They left the airshaft, acting secretive—the biker put his shades on—and Jimmy told Ray if anyone's looking for me, I'm not here. They went out front and spoke in confidence in front of the man's bike. He smoked a cigarillo and got on the bike and straddled it and demonstrated how he rode. Then Jimmy got on and kickstarted it and revved it. They came back inside, slapping each other on the shoulders, and Jimmy gestured for Ray to pour his friend a drink.

On you? Ray asked.

Jimmy pretended not to hear him.

On you, the biker told Ray.

It's not on me.

He told me it was.

Hey, Jimmy's good for business, Gladys said. Ain't he Ray?

As long as it's on somebody, Ray said and poured liquor in the glass.

Gladys put her arm around Jimmy's neck. Jimmy's shoulders tightened uneasily.

Hey, yo, Ray, don't we make a cute couple? Hey, Ray, howbout a refill, baby?

She released Jimmy and sat on a stool around the angle of the bar.

What's new with Vicky?

My kid's in good hands. That's the only thing I look at.

But Jimmy hinted that he was displeased with Vicky about something that had occurred while he'd been away. She tried to hide it from him, but he had found out, as was to be expected. He knew a lot of people, he had a lot of sources. She didn't know he knew. How foolish of her. He didn't care about the thing she had done in itself. It was her thinking that she could get away with lying to him that bothered him.

Totally, Vickie said.

She'll learn.

You're word's gotta be bond.

She knows her place as far as motherhood. That's all I look at.

Besides, he said, he was getting a TV from Rick—if Rick ever got off the Keno machine and fulfilled his obligations. He was going to get cable down in the basement of his mother's house.

The reds were kicking in. He would, he said, have the walls covered in his artwork, dragons nine feet tall. It would be his new headquarters. Hit the remote and there'd be music throbbing through the floor. He could jam down there on his guitar and his artistry would provide a cover for his capers. He would be very selective about who he allowed into his abode.

In other words, your kid's mother's not invited.

No cops, no unreliable people, no snitches. No baseheads. No two-born bitches.

You're smart, Gladys said.

———

When they fought, she was nearly incapacitated by sadness, but that was inside. On the outside, her limbs still moved: she pressed on, she went to work. She cinched her apron, centered the visor's logo between her eyes as if it mattered. Inside, she was thinking, I'm alone. I've been alone since I was a child. Her face twisted at the thought. I will die, she said and she was angry. Her head did not feel right. The place she thought from felt deformed by a pressure. She was so lonely.

Once he turned on her in his basement and told her she had no right to be his friend so don't try, she hadn't earned it, who the fuck did she think she was, etcetera.

She left and broke down sobbing in a basketball court where boys were playing ball. In Uighur she cried, I know I'm not going to make it! I am so sad!—and the rending sound of her weeping echoed off the concrete surfaces.

She told herself that when she couldn't take it anymore she was simply going to start walking, she was going to go and never stop until she crossed the continent or something happened to her and she became a ghost.

It took him calling her for several days to make it up with her. She would not meet with him and remained cold. She would say things like, I know I shouldn't take my time with you. You are too young.

Please. Just please, he said.

He met her in the parking lot outside her job, his jaw scraped red from shaving, his hair still wet, throat smelling like sport gel deodorant. It was dusk and they hadn't been near each other in a week. She went with him back to his basement. When she undressed, under her work clothes, she was wearing black lace lingerie that she had bought for him at a Spanish store on Junction Boulevard.

Love is hard, she said. You have to train the boy. Just like dog. The bigger the dog, the more you have to hit him.

Feel free, he said. I ought to hit myself.

He had held a gun to his head in the bathroom mirror, but he didn't tell her this.

He swore he wouldn't fight with her again and then he did. Instead of getting better, his anger started getting worse, spilling out into the street, involving cab drivers and other strangers. They started talking about it as the biggest thing he had to change.

When they made up, she experienced powerful well-being. Immortality flowed back into her like the juice in a plant stem. She immediately began to taste her life again and the two of them would plan for the future. This took the form of fantasy. He would forget the war. He would stop fucking up. She would get her green card. He would bench press three hundred pounds by August. They would have a few hours of this when things were pleasant and then the feeling between them would turn wrong again.

She began to watch for the signs of his mood changing. She began to expect her happiness to be taken away from her. The worse life got, the more she needed her happiness with him.

36

THE TWO MEN WENT down the stairs into the basement, the basement of their own house, and woke the tenant up at 7:30 in the morning. We're having a look at the boiler, Patrick said. The door was opened by Skinner in boxer shorts and combat boots. He barely looked at them, made a yeah whatever motion with his arm, and the men came in. Skinner went back over to the bed and surfed the Internet. They opened his closet and spoke to each other. Jimmy took the bucket from underneath the cock of the boiler and carried it to the bathroom and poured the rusty water in the toilet, which made it flush, while Patrick checked the risers. The bucket was replaced where it had been. They let out the boiling water for a minute until Patrick said that was enough to take the pressure off, and then left without speaking to Skinner, who lay not moving on his side. His cigarettes and beer cans were all over the room. There was a porn magazine in plain view with a big pink animated exclamation point, a star, covering the spot between a woman's legs. Candy Spreads! He was trashing the room. You could smell the marijuana.

Her pay was less than it had been last time even though she had worked more hours. She took her envelope to the office in the back.

Look, Little Zou is here. What does Little Zou want? Your pay is wrong? You let me see.

He held his long hand out. She gave him her envelope and he looked inside it.

Why do you say your pay is not correct?

It's not enough, it can't be. What about the added hours? To make more, that's why I came here. You know—she tried to say—there had to be something she could do. Working hard was not the problem.

He let her talk.

May I have Little Zou's permission to speak? Have you learn the menu? You do not know it. Sassoon say you have not learn the menu.

Why not? So that is one. There is two. Two is, the next step is serving on the line. In society, we are one step, another step, another step, another—very orderly. The gentle motion of his large, smooth, long-nailed hand. It is not chaos. He laughed, How can you not understand? I am here, he showed her, making a claw. I am one jump to top of mountain—one jump to sky—to heaven! You think it is real? No. No such thing. One at a time is real. We make small money today, big money tomorrow.

She disagreed, saying that she had been working on the line but that Sassoon kept sending her to the back.

What was the date?

The date when I worked on the line?

Yes. Date, hour. I check with Sassoon.

She was at a loss to give him the exact dates when she had worked on the line. I mean, there was a Sunday. Zhuojin was here.

Zhuojin is not a manager, he said.

What are you trying to do to me? Are you trying to rip me off?

I discover that Little Zou doesn't really have military attitude. The military attitude: Yes, Sir! No matter what, follow the orders. Right? Not question them. Question, question, I have question—more like Angela. Not the traditional girl.

I do have military training.

Oh, I see. What military training was that? Maybe I don't understand.

Mrs. Murphy's door opened and she called down the stairs.

Skinner? Could you come up here a minute?

He went up to her kitchen where she was sitting behind her table reviewing him, her cigarette going in her hand.

I've got some mail for you.

There was a letter from the Department of Defense. He took it off her table.

I hear that things are a mess down there. Is that true?

No. Only in my area.

What do you mean your area?

Like my room.

The room's a mess?

It's not a mess. It's messy. It would be fine if I put everything away.

Well, I'm hearing it's more than that.

What are you hearing?

I'm hearing that the room is getting damaged. There are beer cans all over the floor and it smells like pot. You wanna tell me about that?

Tell you what about it?

That you're doing drugs in this house.

Not me.

Not you?

No, he said. No. No way. Clean and sober.

I've heard that before.

No, really. He pulled his shirt off and turned around, ignoring her instruction to keep his shirt on. Take a look, he said. An evenly spaced line of large red boils formed a train track through the keloid scar on his ribcage and tapered off into purple marks higher up on his shoulders half-camouflaged within his tattoo, left there by surgical staples. You see that? I'm taking painkillers for that.

She put her hand up. Do me a favor, put the shirt back on.

He continued pleading his case as he struggled to pull the shirt back on.

We're not going to get anywhere talking about it. You've been told.

He nodded vigorously.

You've been given a warning.

I got it.

She told Erin later, he's lucky the warning came from me. He's got smut magazines down there, from what I hear. Patrick would have thrown him out, as in thrown him out.

Smut magazines?

Nude smut opened up right on the floor. And he's got pills, don't forget pills. I can't get down there myself to see this, thank God. Jimmy was the one who brought it to my attention about the pot smoke. So heavy he got a high from walking in the room. He goes, ma, it gave me a contact high from going in.

The women looked at each other.

Yeah. My thought exactly. If it gets his attention, it's gotta be good. So that's what's downstairs.

If you think about it, she added, there is a good side though.

What?

The fact of who I heard it from.

Like as far as?

That it's coming from Jim. Instead of Jim keeping it to himself so he could have a buddy down there to get high with. Which is what would have happened ten years ago.

He was wearing a brown nonmilitary t-shirt with the sleeves ripped off and he was sweeping his floor. She could see where his army tan ended at mid-bicep. He was sweeping the lightweight plastic broom into the dustpan, trying to get the dust, which was sticking to his bristles, up off the linoleum. His clothes had been picked up, his bags were packed, and the sun was coming down through the grate.

He dumped his dustpan in a Hefty bag he had in the corner. He replaced his broom and dustpan against the wall. Almost everything that used to be scattered around the room was packed away in his two bags—the camouflage duffle and the assault pack. She also noted that the window was open. Was he spring cleaning?

Field day.

I think you are going somewhere.

No. Just neatening up.

It's very neat.

Did I do good?

You are good, she said. But I think you go somewhere.

I'm not going anywhere.

I know I have to go somewhere. Somewhere far. I always know.

You mean China?

I don't know. Maybe I go more far. Maybe go to America. Meet a man. A man his arm has the tattoo, tattoo of American flag. A man who sweep his room.

They lay down on his poncholiner together to rest, not have sex.

I was picking up my bags, he told her.

He showed her what he meant, getting up and slinging the bags on his shoulders while she watched from the bed. The sun was going dark and it was getting chilly in the room. He stood awkwardly burdened in this way for several minutes. She got up and joined him. She put her arm around his neck and stepped into his arms and he picked her up and held her. He held all his belongings and her as well for as long as he could while the sun went down.

There was no proof that anything had happened to his magazine except the fact that he couldn't find it. The last he had seen it, it had either been on his night table or in the john. He was bad about locking his room door even when he left the Berretta at home and it would have been easy to take. On the other hand, it was just as possible he had misplaced it. The only thing he knew was he didn't have it anymore. It was, or had been, hardcore pornography, before it disappeared.

He unpacked his gear looking for it, wondering if he was crazy. As he pulled his clothes out of his duffel bag, they smelled like pot. He looked at his pills and tried to figure out if he had taken too many and done something to his head, had a blackout. He found another prescription bag of medications with three full pill bottles in it, which he had not known he even had, and set them on his bedside.

He found the letter from the Defense Department that Mrs. Murphy had given him and for the first time he opened it and read it. An army med board had determined that his psychological trauma had not been caused by the war and he wouldn't be getting any money for it.

Fuck you, army doctor motherfuckers.

He went around the basement motherfuckering them for a long time, talking aloud and steadily, picking things up and putting them down. He was looking for something but he had forgotten what it was.

You didn't come to work.
 I know. I was busy.
 Like hell.
 You don't wanna believe me, don't.
 I don't believe you.

Jimmy shrugged. Patrick's eyes got smaller. He took a drink.

What business are you in?

What are you talking about?

You're busy, I'm asking what business you're in if you're a fookin businessman.

Ends.

What? What the fook are they?

Ends. Making ends.

Is that what you're doing here at one-thirty in the afternoon, making your ends?

Could be. Is that why you're here?

Never mind me.

It's one-thirty in the afternoon. Why're you here?

I fixed a lady's toilet while you were sleeping, that's why I'm here.

I wasn't sleeping.

You were fookin sleeping.

Get your facts straight.

You were sleeping or doing your fookin junk.

I wasn't doing that either. Get your facts straight.

You tell me to straighten my facts again.

You're the boss.

You're goddamn right I'm the boss. And you better learn to live with it or you'll get trown the fook out.

Thrown out of what?

You better wipe that cocky fookin smile off. You're gonna get trown the fook out. Out of my house.

It's not your house.

The fook it isn't.

It's not your name on the deed.

You'll get trown the fook out.

So throw me out.

I will, so help me.

Have another first. Get your strength up.

I'll shove it up your ass another. When I was your age, I could go through ten men like you! Twenty men like you! You little sonofabitch.

By now the bartender and several other men had come between Patrick and his stepson. Hey! Hey! they were yelling, and Patrick swore he'd kick to death the next man who touched him. Jimmy smiled at him.

Watch your ticker. You're turning red.

You're a fookin nigger. You're a fookin waste and you've always been the same. All the time in there was wasted on you. You're still nothing but a nigger.

Jimmy stood up and stopped smiling and the men in the bar finally convinced him to leave.

You're the bigger man, they said.

Skinner had a dream and this was what he saw:

The house, the purple basement. The carpeted stairs going down into the basement. Someone is outside Skinner's door, someone is in the basement. He sees this big guy moving around his kitchen. The guy doesn't say anything to him.

Way up into the house: the front room, the sheets on things like a morgue. The parts of the house you do not see.

The back of the house: things are piled high. There are curios and yard equipment. You might open a door and it would hit a bed—a mattress on cinder blocks, there is laundry piled all over the room, a hamper, there is no floor space. There is a broken alarm clock. The screen is falling out of the window. It is ripped and it is in the room.

You go upstairs. First: The hallway. The hallway leads away from the mustard-colored kitchen. All the appliances: the stove, the refrigerator are mustard colored. They are old, from the eighties. The cupboards are from the seventies. There is a cuckoo clock, there are wooden things that are on the walls, there are sheets over the couches and chairs. Is someone lying under a sheet? No one has left by the front door of the house: we do not use it. There are things hanging from the eaves in front. The wind chimes hung by the six-foot daughter.

The hallway appears to have pictures on the walls, old pictures. Maybe it doesn't. Maybe the walls are bare. It is blue.

37

THE HEAT WAS COMING. She believed she knew what to expect. The summer would be celebrated by people of every nation in the city. People marauding after work, discontented. Thugs surfing on the sides of cars, flagging. Going into the garbage cans and throwing bottles in the street. Immigrants working, forever working, watching people going by who have days off, time off, while they don't. Trying to stay cool. Families with five young children going to Dunkin Donuts for a night out together in the air conditioning. The littered floors, the strange lone males reading the newspaper. Cabdrivers and dysfunctional individuals sitting in the window of the all-night Tropical. Messed-up guys with Puerto Rican flag hats talking to waitresses, high-fiving them, saying when do you get off? Spanish girls with Indian blood, slave blood, mopping floors at three a.m. Caribbeans saying we were brought here as slaves from India. We got together with the blacks and threw the British out. Now we listen to dub step. Let me tell you where it's hot like fire burning. Where the party's at. Where you can get robbed, stuck, shook, bucked and maybe fucked down on one hundred and ninth going towards Far Rockaway. Where no one's gonna feel bad for you if you have problems.

The Wenzhounese will sit outside in folding chairs in their pajamas on Cromellin Street, talking on the steps, fanning themselves in the gleaming night. The women will be pregnant and still they will be taking out the garbage, collecting bags of recycling, saving little fistfuls of money, little investments that, like children, will turn into something later.

But for now, we'll all have to deal with the heat first—all of us no matter where we're from.

A seventeen-year-old holding a pit bull on a leash will have a wing of hair over her forehead, tight short shorts, bare legs, mascara, and she will regard Zou Lei with hatred when the males turn their heads to watch Zou Lei as she goes by beneath the tracks. Because Zou Lei will have found that you can literally buy a pair of shorts on 103rd Street for a dollar ninety-nine and all the girls of every flag will wear shorts, including her.

People will try to sell her anything they can. They will need the money, but so will she. A South American in a soccer jersey with blue eyes who speaks no English will try to sell her a watch on Corona Avenue, but she will not buy it. At the end of the season, it will be in her nature to move on. Six to nine months in a place, no more. The graffiti on the rocks where the LIRR roars by Skinner's house says GLCS. Pocos Pero Locos. There's a spraypainted heart and the words: Brazalhax y Soldado. She sees herself and Skinner leaving come fall.

They hired a new boy, a friend of Angela's, who went to Cardozo, and Polo marveled how he understood everything right away, he knew computers too, he was a talent at the age of seventeen. The young man went by the name of Monroe. Sassoon put him in the front even though he was surly and openly rude to her. He had a loud voice and you could always hear him. He complained about everything, saying, This job suck dick. People liked him very much for his good looks.

On the schedule, Monroe's name appeared where Zou Lei's name used to. They had given him one of her afternoons. She asked Sassoon how this was going to affect her pay. Sassoon told her she wasn't in charge of pay, just hours. The issue of pay was between her and Polo and Polo wasn't available to speak with her. Zou Lei said that that was very convenient. Several other employees who were afraid that Sassoon would lose her temper interceded. They told Zou Lei not to worry about her money, the boss wasn't about to steal from her. They told her that she was getting jealous of the talented young man.

There, there. It doesn't do to be jealous.

Released from work early, Zou Lei went outside and found it raining on the street, the rain coming down so hard it turned white when it hit the asphalt. She ran four blocks with her jacket over her head and took shelter under the scaffold in front of Footlocker, the aluminum drumming overhead, and stared at the sneakers on Lucite pedestals. Water squished out of the holes in her sneakers when she went into the air-conditioned store. Hip-hop was playing. The back of her denim jacket was soaked through. She took it off and folded it over her arm and picked up a Nike women's running shoe so light she could hardly feel it. When she tried to put it on, she found it anchored to the wall by an antitheft cable in a plastic sheath. She looked at another Nike and an Asics and then she checked the prices.

Under her jacket, she was just wearing her uniform shirt and you could tell she was cold in the air conditioning through the orange fabric of her shirt. She threw her wet hair back and picked up a Reebok Mountaineer, which was fifty percent off, and inspected the hard new well-defined treads.

Next paycheck or the one after next. Something like that. She bounced her hip to the stereo beat. The rain was going to end and the sun was going to come out and shine on her while she sweated, running for the horizon like a camel.

The downpour ended and she put the Reebok down and headed back uphill. As she passed the open drains, she heard the sewer rushing like a waterfall.

When she got home, the immigrant apartment smelled like a wet rag and she found all their shoes had been piled in front of her accordion door. The TV was playing out of another tenant's shed and the tenant, a stocky woman, was in the hall working the plastic-handled mop inside the kitchenette, pushing the black stuff on the floor around. The kitchen window was open and you could see the rain beginning again.

Going to her room, their hips collided. She parried the mop handle. The woman wasn't looking. They did not speak, only the television did—in the common language of Mandarin. The woman had mopped the hall until it smelled like the latrines in China.

The pile of shoes fell over when Zou Lei opened the accordion door and she used her foot to shove them out of her way.

Kicking them just makes everything disorderly, the woman said.

Where do they go? Zou Lei asked.

It doesn't matter. Just line them up.

They lined the shoes up in pairs. Zou Lei went to wash her hands afterwards with the liquid soap she had always thought belonged to all of them.

Everyone has their own products, the woman said. That's civilization.

38

A GUY WAS PUTTING baby oil on his chest in front of the library, in front of the Falungong table with the photographs of atrocities. He had fresh pink scars on his chest from stab marks.

Yo, what's up, Jimmy Irish.

Jimmy responded to his greeting affably, and you would think it was because of the sunshine on this first of the hot days of summer, when you could smell the concrete and the grass growing out of the cracks in the sidewalk, as well as the baby oil and the coconut butter and Davidoff's Cool Water and African oil in the subway crowd and Diorissimo coming from women's blouses. You would not think that Jimmy had just received the news that his common-law wife Vicky had taken his kid and moved to Bayonne. He wanted to take his mother's car and go look for them. His mother warned him that he would wind up back in prison if he did this.

The guy slapped himself with baby oil: arms, stomach, chest. They watched the Chinese schoolgirls going by with teddy bears attached to their knapsacks on key rings.

Yo, what's up. How old are you?

He turned on his phone, which played on speaker, playing a Motown love song. I need you, a man whispered, so badly.

Two other males were there: Frankie and a fourth guy, who was screaming about immigrants with his arms spread wide, screaming and screaming, backing up to the curb and running back in, winding up, and punching the air, showing what had happened in his fight at the gas station.

There's too many of them! he screamed, holding his can of Bud Light.

Frankie, with his hair combed back wet, wearing a red tank top over his gut and gray sweatpants said, This nigga woke me up at five-thirty, beloved.

It was early and the gates were down on some of the stores, except for the bodega that a Pakistani ran, which specialized in lotto. The casino bus waited by the bodega and the Chinese with their hands clasped behind their backs like Deng Xiaoping touring the brigade fields of the south waited to board it. The fourth guy stood in the middle of the sidewalk facing the procession of Chinese coming up the block towards the bus, carrying boxes, going to work.

Here they come, he said. He took a fast swig of the beer, throwing his head back, throwing it at his own face, and stared at them again, wiping foam off his mouth.

A woman from China in a lacy blouse and black skirt came up the street in heels with little bows on them.

What's up, sexy? Goin to work? Look, she's dressed up, lookin nice.

Gonna go whack guys off all day.

Her husband's a jerk.

No more Similac. No more pampers. No more water. Somebody's gotta tell'em.

Tell'em what, beloved?

Tell'em there's too many of them.

The guy who was oiled up tried to bum a cigarette off Jimmy, who said, It's my last one.

The fourth guy had tons of cigarettes. He had two packs—both of them Chinese brands in red boxes with gold—Jinlongmingpai Xiangyan—that he kept taking out of his pockets, opening and closing them, taking out cigarettes and putting them behind his ears, in his mouth, offering them to other guys.

Take one. Take one. Take one, brother, he said. We're all white men. Go ahead. Go on, the fourth guy said, handing him more loose cigarettes, which the sunbather took in his mineral oil-covered hands and laid next to him on the stained granite.

Look at all he gave me!

Give me one, Jimmy commanded him. Give Frank one too.

Don't take them all.

Gimme a light. Hook me up with fire.

They blew their smoke out, and the sunbather, holding his cigarette in his mouth, made the end bob up and down like an erection as he watched the women.

Bravo! he called to one and clapped.

The fourth guy picked his Bud Light up off the sidewalk and took another swig of it. We're all white, American. I don't play that shit.

What's mine is yours, brother. What's mine is yours. Look at me. What's mine is yours.

Well, what's mine ain't yours, Jimmy told the fourth guy, who took this in stride, seeming not to hear. Because he was already screaming about the gas station again. He started really screaming, his neck turning red, really screaming, saying he couldn't fight them all. He was wearing a number 25 brown jersey over a white shirt, khaki shorts with no belt that keep falling off, and he constantly had to roll the waistband over to make them tighter. There were slices all over his forearms. His hands were filthy. He was saying how he had kept slipping during the fight, which had been a punching, kicking, grappling fight, when they pushed him down, which he demonstrated, throwing himself down and jumping up again, momentarily knock-kneed like a little kid, and jumping up and kicking, his sneaker flashing within an inch of their faces. Jimmy yawned.

They had been smoking crack all night, Frankie said. With blunts, beloved.

Jimmy scratched the shamrock on his hand.

But I kept slippin down! The floor, it's too slippery for me to fight them.

From the Armor-All, right? Frankie said. From the Armor-All on the floor.

Yeah. I needed to get out here, the fourth guy said, backing up across the sidewalk to the curb where the planter was and the Chinese bus was waiting. I needed to get out here to have room. Once I got room, I don't care if there're ten of them. I don't care. I don't care, I'll kill them. That's when I'll kill them.

He poured beer in his mouth and bent over, still drinking out of the blue can, pouring it past his mouth, watering the planter with beer, letting the can drop, stamping on it with his sneaker, walking away from it, spreading his arms and yelling, I'll fuckin kill'em.

Chinese people turned their heads.

They met people that they knew and people that they knew met them. A passenger hailed them from the cab of a graffiti-covered delivery truck with a gash in the peak, which had been inflicted by a low clearance, now taped up with garbage bags.

Guado! they yelled across the intersection. The fourth guy ran out to him and climbed up on the step and talked to him through the window until the light changed and then ran back through the cars.

Frankie had been out a while. He had been in and out. This nigga got me locked up. Thirty days on the Island! He had been saved after his mother had died. Oh-nine oh-nine ninety-nine. Colon cancer, beloved. Dearly beloved. But he still lived down here, around the corner from the Punjabis in the low-rise projects on Blossom. His tattoos were 777. John 3:15. A tattoo of his skin being ripped by claws underneath as if a tiger were inside him. His hands were pink from scabs as if he had psoriasis, but it was from fighting. He had a black plastic bag on the ground by his foot, which he was stepping on. He bent down and took out a bottle of Arizona Iced Tea from it, spit on the cap, rubbed it. Took the cap off and drank from it. Offered it. It's clean.

So you been out all this time, Jimmy said as if that were a nice thing.

I went down to the World Trade Center the day after 9/11 when it was still smoking, nigga. Ain't nothin changing but the weather.

The fourth guy started talking about the fight at the carwash again. Here's what we do. We go over there. Over on Kissena by my house. Fuckin immigrants. You got papers? You legal? Okay, fine. Only this time I'll have somethin on me. He demonstrated what had happened, what would happen next time, obviously a natural athlete despite what he had done to himself. Because these Mexicans were going to stick him. He darted in and pressed his fist to Jimmy's belly. A real fast city guy. But that's when I go for eyes, throats. I'll kill somebody without a knife. With an elbow. He backed up and ran in swinging his fist and stopping short. Frankie and Jimmy barely noticed, laughed. He got into your face, head-to-head, insisting that you listen, saying look at me, look at me, look at me. This is what I'll do. I'll get me a pipe. A nice pipe. A tire iron! Frankie interjected. Yeah, one a them. You hit somebody in the head with a pipe, you know it. I'll get up early in the morning and go down there and do it.

Frankie called him Charlie. What's your middle name? James, right? C-J! Your last name's French, right? C-Rock! he laughed and winked at Jimmy, who was ignoring them both, inspecting the cigarette burning down to the shamrock between his battered knuckles.

Charlie took out his two packs of Chinese cigarettes again. He would give you the shirt off his back. He put another cigarette behind his ear. When he demonstrated how he had been fighting, in the course of gesticulating, he dropped the cigarette he was smoking on the wet sidewalk at his feet, picked it up and kept puffing.

I need to get outside. It was too small. I needed to get outside where I had room. My father would have whipped a can of chew at them and hit them right in the face. A can a Copenhagen. I wanna go back there today. I should ask for the owner of the carwash and just go up and hit him right in the face. With my fist. With a Belgian brick. That would be the logical thing to do. That would take care of it, wouldn't it? Or maybe it wouldn't. I don't know.

But you kicked one of their's food, Frankie said.

No. Yeah, I was mad. I kicked his food. Not him. A different one. This big one with gold all across his fuckin teeth. If I had a gun, I would of killed him. I would have killed seven of them. If I go back there, there'll be seven dead guys. Fourteen of them. Then maybe I've got a chance. Self-defense is a right. But a white guy, a citizen? He beat the palms of his hands together for emphasis. What are the cops gonna do? Are they gonna listen to me, a white guy? A army vet?

He had slightly crooked teeth. Red neck. Hair in a graying high-and-tight.

You mean over an immigrant?

C'mon! Exactly. He put his hands together as if they were being handcuffed. He marched away from them and back. I'm gonna go to jail for a long time. A long time this time. The MS-13, the Mexicans'll be there. The Chinese. I trust the blacks before I trust them. Maybe not so much. Not necessarily. I'm gonna go straight to the Aryans. Sieg heil. I stand with them. Born and raised. Aryans. White power. I'll be in jail with the fuckin MS-13—he imitated them making their devil horns, praying with their hands upside down to Jesus, Jesus save me—he imitated this with disgust. Get the fuck outta here... They don't talk about this thing over here that happened, what they did to a girl, they shoved a pipe up her pussy, up her ass. They killed her, a poor Chinese girl. The Mexicans don't talk about that. Oh no. Some people don't deserve to live.

Someone coming by on the street, coming out of the bodega, scratching a lotto card, caught his attention, because he thought he was Mexican. But he corrected himself and said, Oh no, he's Turkish. Charlie got right up in Jimmy's face and said, Let me tell you about a Turkish guy. A Turkish guy, if he fixes your car, you'll be back again a day later. He'll do something to it. An Indian'll just rob you...

Frankie said, The only cars I ever owned was a minivan and a 91 Nissan Maxima. I still got it.

I'm outnumbered! There's too many of them. Here they come.

Falungong ladies in white and red tracksuits were coming up the street from the park where they turned the dharmic wheel, a practice for which they would have been persecuted in China. Charlie blocked the path of a shrunken Buddhist grandmother in her early seventies. When she moved, he moved. He started dancing and danced up on her, wiggling his pelvis. She was laughing. All right, he said and let her by.

Look at this nigga.

Jimmy spat on the sidewalk.

He's fuckin whacked. The sunbather with the stabbed-up chest turned up his music player.

Dance, nigga! Frankie called.

Charlie danced up behind a Chinese guy coming out of the bodega, a hollow-chested slump-shouldered man in glasses who, sensing what was going on behind him, turned around and, laughing, exposing terrible teeth, pointed up and away with a doughy white arm, as if telling Charlie where to go. As if telling him to take the bus. They had a grinning stand-off and Charlie high-fived him. People were smiling. When this was over, the slumped man scuffed over to the other Chinese, who carried money satchels, collecting fees for the bus, and began conversing with them.

Charlie came back to the guys and asked when the liquor store was opening. Frankie told him it was opening in five minutes. Charlie said, That's what you said twenty minutes ago. He helped a Chinese guy carry a box down the block, asking him, Is that heavy? then picking it up and saying, That's not too bad. Then running away with it, calling back, See ya! Then bringing it back to him and saying, I wouldn't of done that.

He's got ADHD disorder, Frankie said. He's got too much energy in his brain or somethin. He was in the army in Afghanistan. That's how he wound up in jail. His wife was fuckin around. He fucked them both up, threw them through a glass window. He did two years.

I did eight years in the army. No, two years eight months and fifteen days. I did three years in jail.

You did two years, nigga.

That's right, two years. I been stabbed. Been shot. Been there, done that. But then I got locked up again.

You got me locked up last time, nigga.

Frankie shook his large skull from side to side hitting his shoulders with his skull on either side like a boxer loosening up his neck before sparring.

Charlie pulled up the sleeve of his jersey and flexed his white arm, showing his army tattoo to Jimmy. He had been a combat medic in Iraq. Frankie said, Show him your thing, nigga. Charlie pulled up his shirt in front and pushed down his khaki shorts down off his hipbone exposing his pubic hair, showing the scar that was on his hipbone.

You got a magnet? All I want is to get this metal out of me.

Watch this, Frankie said. Hey, Charlie, what's that from? You get shot or what?

I need a magnet to get this out.

What's it from, nigga?

An IED.

In Iraq, right?

When Iraq was mentioned, Charlie jumped away. He wouldn't let anyone touch him. Frankie put a hand on his shoulder and Charlie looked at his shoulder where you touched him as if he felt defiled by your sympathy.

What's wrong? C-Rock?

He turned around and marched away, hurrying down the block, as if something awful had happened.

Frankie winked at Jimmy, who smirked.

The liquor store was opening and they went down to it, leaving the sunbather, who nodded at them, nodding to his music, which sounded as if it had a scratchy connection. He had an unfilled-in tattoo, just an outline of an animal drawn during a period of institutionalization on his shining oiled white arm.

Charlie was coming back up the street walking with the young attractive short-haired Chinese-American woman who ran the liquor store. He was offering to help her open the gate and she was saying, That's okay. He started yanking on the handle before she had the lock off. Wait, she said. After they got the gate up, he made a sound of dismay and showed her his hands, which were black with dirt now. You can wash them in there, she said, pointing back at the bodega.

A black guy with his hand in a brace came over to the liquor store and bumped fists, using his good fist, with Frankie. He had a scar over his left eye, through the eyelid, wore a blue horizontally striped shirt, was over two hundred pounds, about 45 – 50 something. Charley went over to him to clasp hands with him and the guy said, Ow, not my bad hand, motherfucker.

They were drinking a clear plastic flask of Georgi vodka now, and Charlie started talking about the gas station fight again.

Am I gonna hear about this all goddamn day? asked Frankie. The two of them had never been locked up together, thank God. Charlie had been in jail in Long Island. His wife was a cunt. Renee. You threw that bitch through a glass window, didn't you?

Where were you? Charlie asked. He appealed to Jimmy. This guy was nowhere to be found. I was outnumbered and he wasn't there.

Sometimes you take a loss, Jimmy said.

Frankie covered his mouth laughing.

Yeah, I just took one, Charlie said, and began on another story. I fought in the World's Fair. I was fifteen! I was fifteen. I fought Ramirez. You know who that is? I never lost. I had one hundred-twenty, two hundred fights. The first round I knocked him down. The second round there was a standing eight count. The third round, he got knocked down. His name was Ramirez. You know what the judge's name was? Ramirez. They called it a draw.

And you're still talking about it?

I can't get a break. My father didn't come to any of my fights—

Oh, my father! Frankie mocked.

—Now look at me, Charlie said. I'm a loser. He hit himself in the head with the plastic Georgi bottle.

Tell him he's a loser for hitting himself with a bottle.

For a few minutes, Charlie went and stood by a mailbox on the corner.

Look at him. He's runnin outta steam. Up all night smoking... You runnin outta steam, nigga?

It was getting hotter, the sun was shining. Charlie shook his head at them, apparently tired, or simply unable to speak. He took his jersey off, wearing his white t-shirt underneath, and looked as if he was resting. A few minutes later, he came back, drinking from the flask and getting revved up again. They looked at each other and examined each other, finding things to talk about. Frankie had a scar on his face.

My father had HIV. I went to see him in the hospital and these niggers said don't touch him, you'll get AIDS. I said, You ignorant fuckin niggers. I fought them. One of them had a razor and I got sliced.

Frankie snatched the vodka away from Charlie and drank the rest and threw the plastic bottle bouncing on the ground. He shook his head between his shoulders as if he were going to spar again.

You don't wanna gas me up, nigga! he bellowed. Howbout my man Kenny the Flushing Flash who's my neighbor down the block?

It's about respect, Charlie insisted.

Whatever, Jimmy said.

Charlie insisted, Look at me. He got head-to-head with Jimmy, who pushed him away. He staggered back and came back in. It's about simple respect, he said. He stank of vodka and cigarettes through his mouth, face, skin, his red throat. He described how the cops had come into his house and asked to hear his wife play the violin. She was known throughout the neighborhood. They followed me all the way through that park to those two buildings there, you see them two? and as soon as I stepped across the line, they arrested me. Can you believe that? Fourteen cops came into my house, and before they left, they asked to hear her play the piano. The cop was putting his hand on her back and going like this: It's gonna be okay. There, there. Charlie stared in Jimmy's eyes, waiting for a response. The piano, he said. After they all had coffee in my house. My wife was wearing a nightgown. They're not supposed to do that.

He was in my house! My house! Charlie screamed. His throat expanded.

That's interesting, Jimmy said.

Your wife's nice, the cop told me. How does her pussy smell? I was handcuffed. I headbutted him. Right there. They beat me down outside. I was in a wheelchair.

They fucked you up bad, bro, Frankie said.

My mother was crying. I couldn't see.

He hit his head on a wall, while the other two observed.

Harder, Frankie told him. Charlie knocked his forehead against the granite again, making a coconut sound. You got any meth? Any shrooms? Any mescaline? Any angel dust? so I can put my head right through this fuckin wall?

I got weed.

Na, weed's no good.

They went across the avenue and sat by the Punjabi grocery, near the rail fence in the sun.

We're just three white men. You're white, right? We're dinosaurs, son. They don't make'em like they used to, beloved.

What do you think I am? Jimmy asked. Frankie avoided his eyes. Jimmy ground out his cigarette on the asphalt making a gritty sound under his boot.

Charlie was talking about the casino bus, saying it went to Foxwoods, reporting what they gave you. They gave you a coupon for the beef flambé and thirty dollars you could gamble. That ain't bad. Whaddya say, let's go. C'mon. I got you guys.

You don't got me, Jimmy told him.

Yes, I do. C'mon.

He had left his jersey on the fence, and Frankie shouted: I'm always babysittin him. Pick your shit up. He lost a 250-dollar phone.

I got you, Charlie insisted.

Put your money away. You got rent, nigga!

Casting a glance at Jim, Frank said he was going home to roll a blunt. He stood up in the sun, his sweatpants pushed up above his fat calves. You need to go on a diet, motherfucker, Jimmy said, not getting up to go with him. I know I do, nigga. Frankie lingered for a minute. Jimmy pretended to find Charlie interesting. Charlie was still talking about common respect.

Frankie went around the corner, as if to leave, and seconds later ducked back, snatched the jersey off the fence and ran with it.

Charlie sprinted after him and Frankie stopped and they pushed their chests into each other as if they were guarding each other in basketball, threatening each other, whispering in each other's faces: Do something. Do something. Do something. I'm not afraid of you, Charlie insisted, standing on his toes to be taller than him.

The jersey got thrown on the ground and Frankie spit on it. You won't give me your shirt, but you'll leave it there for some nigger.

Charlie picked his jersey up.

Let's go in the backyard. I wanna fight you now.

I'm not afraid of you.

The stand-off went on for three or four minutes. They went back and forth. Jimmy eyed the street for cops.

Fuck you, I'm not afraid of you, Charlie said walking away, outweighed. He went over to a tree and kicked it and went away, swinging his jersey, turning back to flip Frank off, calling out: Fuck you! and then coming back, because he had thought of something else:

Hey, enjoy those cigarettes I bought you.

I will.

Thanks for having my back. Thanks for that, after I bought you cigarettes. Thanks for your help.

Hey, Frankie smiled. Help you never.

Enjoy those cigarettes.

I'm gonna smoke them.

Fuck you.

Loser! You're a loser. Sieg heil.

Go preach your fuckin bible! Go home and whack off! I'll never talk to you again, Charlie said and walked away. Then Frankie followed him, yelling, Yo! and Charlie went back to him and on the street where Indian women were pushing past with shopping carts they kept arguing.

Then Charlie went to Jimmy, who was leaning on the weathered fence, his eyes closed, face lifted up to the morning sun, a foot propped up behind him, his arms out holding the fence, posed like Jesus in the crucifixion, the bandana around his head like the crown.

It's the drugs with him, Charlie said. He's a druggie. The drugs come before everything.

Then do somethin about it, Jimmy sneered.

Frankie heard this.

Do something about what? he asked.

Ask your boy.

I'm askin you, nigga.

And I'm tellin you ask your boy.

And I'm askin you.

Jimmy made a derisive sound. He handled the situation that was developing a bit differently from either of them. I'm not getting excited like you tough guys, he said in his hoarse voice. He and Frankie went towards each other, but there was no chest-to-chest shoving. At one point, Frankie squared off with him and Jimmy dared him, Go ahead. Touch me. I'll bury you right here. He spoke with his flat delivery, while Frankie argued with him at length. Jimmy cut him off.

Nobody cares about your shit. I'll leave youse out here with your fuckin gooks and your fuckin stories, the both a youse.

You're trippin.

You're talkin. Jimmy made a talking puppet mouth with his four-leaf clover hand.

Frankie debated with him, saying Jimmy wasn't the only mother-fucker who'd been to jail. I met you in there, kid. He suggested that Jimmy was unfairly coming between him and his friend Charlie. All he had wanted was to go to the beach today. They could have gone to Rockaway. He appealed to Charlie James, holding out his arms with his numerical tattoos and his dirty hands. Not to mention that he wasn't backing down, beloved.

You're gettin off the subject.

What?

You gotta problem, do somethin.

Frankie wanted understanding.

I got nothing for you. Do it or don't, Jimmy said. Yeah, ten years he had done. It was the same as life to him. So go ahead. Nobody cares. I don't.

39

SHE TOOK THE SUBWAY to East Broadway in Manhattan, where it seemed that there were more immigration lawyers than in Flushing, as well as more job- and housing-referral services. The explanation for this was that East Broadway's Chinese community had been created, in large part, through illegal immigration from Fuzhou. She went up a stairway next to a woman boiling peanuts in an electric cauldron on the sidewalk and wandered into a maze of second-floor offices being used for an assortment of businesses. The sign over one doorway said Li the Accountant; down the hall there was the Black Dragon Blue Body Tattoo Studio. Behind a crystal clear pane of plate glass, a tattoo artist in his thirties was engraving an outline drawing on the chunky arm of a shirtless young man. The steady buzzing of the stylus came through the glass.

Other businesses didn't give their names, just bullet-point lists of services performed: Insurance, Register Marriage, Divorce, Government Housing, Apply For Benefit, Passport Without Needing Birth Certificate, H1 Visa, Send Baby To China. A clerk who sat alone at a computer in one of these offices, unattended by her employers, told Zou Lei that they weren't real lawyers and that they couldn't do everything the bullet points said they could do; Zou Lei should go to one of the many bona-fide lawyers in the area.

Taking her advice, Zou Lei returned to the street. The buildings were all shoved in next to each other like books in an overpacked library shelf. A sign for a law office stuck out like an index tab. It was attached to a modern building tucked between two tenements. She went into a mirrored-glass vestibule under CCTV surveillance. An emerald green ring lit up around the elevator call button when she hit it. The elevator opened and she saw the inside was paneled in dark wood like a lounge where Hong Kong tycoons drank cognac in the movies, another security camera running in the ceiling. She rode it to the attorney's office on the second floor, a vertical distance of ten feet, which she could have climbed faster than the elevator moved, had there been stairs. The elevator moved slowly because of the expensive heavy inlaid wood. She got off in a polygonal marble-floored reception area.

They've squeezed a palace into this narrow building, she thought.

There was no one behind the reception counter. Through a section of glass wall, she saw women working at a row of heavy metal desks. In addition to their computers and phones, their desks were weighed down with stacks of manila folders. It was a busy office; the women were all working continuously, entering data, answering phones, handing files to other women who came from other rooms. The level of tension was equal to that of a fast food restaurant at the rush. Unlike the restaurant business, silence predominated. The exception to this was an extended discussion one clerk was holding with a client seeking legal advice, a slump-shouldered woman in an Izod shirt.

Zou Lei leaned around the glass wall partition and waited for several seconds looking in. When no one acknowledged her, she walked in and started down the line of desks, looking for anyone who was free. A young female wearing many-pocketed jeans asked, What do you want?

I want to do immigration.

Do you have a case open?

Zou Lei wasn't sure how to answer.

So you want to file an application?

I don't know. I think I can talk to a lawyer.

The lawyer can't see you now.

Zou Lei asked when the lawyer could see her.

The woman hung up her phone and got up and walked Zou Lei out of the office and back to the reception area and had her sit in one of three curvy rosewood chairs and knocked on the lawyer's door and asked him in a tiny murmur when he'd be free. The man's voice told her fifteen minutes. She closed the door and told Zou Lei fifteen minutes and marched back into the secretaries' office.

Zou Lei sat there looking at the diplomas on the walls. The lawyer had been recognized by the mayor's office and by the Amoy Freemason Society of New York City. A framed piece of calligraphy spoke of leaping horses as a metaphor for the lawyer's ability and spring rain for the author's gratitude. On the reception desk, he had a little display of business cards on heavy paper stock listing all the languages he spoke. His voice continued talking on the other side of his door in English.

After a minute, she went back to the young woman to ask how much it would cost to talk to the lawyer.

Without a word, the girl put down what she was doing and marched back to the lawyer's door and whispered to him again. Zou Lei could hear the Cantonese word for hundred. She came back and reported to Zou Lei it would be a hundred dollars.

Zou Lei was concerned by this, because it was a lot of money. How much time would he give her for a hundred dollars? Could she talk to the lawyer for a shorter time for less money?

The young woman turned on her heel and went back to the lawyer's door and murmured with him again.

The lawyer stood up and came out of his office. He was an exceptionally tall man, wearing a white Brooks Brothers dress shirt, red and navy striped tie, and long black oxfords that clicked on the marble floor. He had a gold ring with a diamond in it on his little finger. He looked as if his feet could be rotated through 180 degrees—in other words that his knees were loose, like shopping cart wheels that spin around. He hurried out and stopped in the middle of the marble floor and said, Yeah, hi. So you can't spend a hundred? He asked her what she needed help with.

Before she could answer, the girl came back and interrupted them. Zou Lei waited while he went with her and told her how to do something related to filing a real estate case. He came back and spoke to Zou Lei again. She didn't know where to begin describing her problem. He cut her short. How much do you want to spend?

She tried to guess what to say.

Thirty dollars.

Fine. She'll make you out a bill. I'll talk to you when I'm done.

He hurried back into his office and shut the door and started talking in English again. There were no windows, but there was a clock to watch the time. Another door opened and an American came out wearing a yarmulke and said goodbye to all the women in the office, who ignored him.

Tell Alvin I'm going, he said.

He hit the button on the elevator and waited, and when it came, two Chinese men who looked like deliverymen got off and sat themselves in the other two rosewood chairs and put their plastic bags between their feet and read the Sing Tao. The elbow of the one closer to her pushed into her arm. She leaned sideways and felt her wallet under her hip.

She got up and went back into the clerk's office and got the attention of a different, older clerk, a prim straight-haired woman with glasses and painful-looking acne. Zou Lei could tell she was from Mainland China and addressed her in Mandarin.

I'm supposed to talk to the lawyer, but that girl never told him what I'm here to talk about, so how do I know if it will have any significance, and then thirty dollars will be gone for nothing.

What do you want to see him about?

I want to do immigration. I don't want to get caught.

By Immigration?

Yes, by Immigration. I was caught once already and it's fearful.

The woman let her sit in the seat at the side of her desk. They spoke Mandarin.

Do you have a case?

No. This is the first time to see a lawyer.

How did you come to this country? Did you have a visa?

No, no visa.

How did you come here? You...

Snuck in.

Snuck in from Mexico? In a truck?

Yes, a truck.

When they arrested you and let you go, they would have given you a piece of paper. Do you have it?

I think so.

Let me see it.

No, on my body I don't have it. I have it at home.

Bring it next time, because that will make a difference when filing a petition. You want to file a petition?

Okay. Yes. I think, whatever is possible. I don't know what is possible right now. I want to stay in this country if it's possible. An American says he can marry me. That's the real thing I want to know. Can I get married with him even if I have no identity?

The lawyer came out of his office to put a folder in a wire basket, saw Zou Lei and said, So you're not going to talk to me after all?

Okay. He asked a secretary for the 285 Broadway case and went back into his office.

You should get married right away to help your petition, the woman told Zou Lei.

Can I do it with no identity?

Is he American?

Yes, a soldier.

And he's an American citizen?

Yes. Citizen.

You go to the marriage office and check. They will give you the requirements. But you should do that as fast as possible and then come back when you've gotten married. Then you can open a case.

She told Zou Lei that she would have to leave the country and go back to China for a visa interview. It was possible that her application might take an unspecified length of time and might not be approved, leaving her stranded in China.

Zou Lei questioned whether she'd even be able to fly back without her passport. The woman told her that you could apply for a passport at the Chinese consulate, but that doing so was risky, because, she said, I think they check, and it could make it easier to be deported.

She echoed Zou Lei's fear that it was very easy to get arrested, and that that was something she had to avoid at all cost, because since 9/11, there was no telling what immigration arrest could entail.

Then she seemed to contradict what she had said earlier, now implying that at no point would Zou Lei have to go back to China. She mentioned that the laws had become very broad and that the government was unpredictable at this time. Things might become easier in the future.

They talked for no more than three minutes—the woman spoke rapidly and expressionlessly, her eyes invisible behind her glasses—and then, as if a clock had run out, she stopped talking to Zou Lei and returned her attention to her computer. The phone bleeped, she picked it up, said, Yes, I'm doing that, and hung up.

Thank you for your help, Zou Lei said. Do you have a card?

The woman gave her a card, but when she looked at it, she saw it was the same business card they had up front: it was simply the lawyer's card.

As she was leaving, the lawyer came out and spoke to her while he put another folder in the wire basket. I overheard you. If you're getting married, it better be a real marriage or you'll be in big trouble. That I'll tell you for free. Free advice.

She didn't understand what he meant. What do you mean? Maybe we're ordinary people, but the feeling between us is real.

40

AFTER LEAVING THE LAWYER'S office, she went directly back to Flushing to see Skinner. While they were talking, he got up and opened his refrigerator. He stood for a full half a minute staring into it, not saying a word.

What is it?

Look.

There was six-pack sitting in the fridge on the cruddy wire rack.

It's beer.

Yup.

She didn't understand what the problem was. He made a circuit of the basement looking in the trash, kicking over his shirts, looking under them, checking under the bed while she gazed after him, puzzled by his behavior. He circled back to the kitchen, flipping the cupboard doors open and shut. He finally came to rest by the counter with an expression on his face that said he knew something and wasn't happy about it.

She asked him what was going on. He shook his head.

Nothing. Some bullshit.

Had he lost something?

I had two six-packs in there.

So?

Now there's one.

You drink it?

Nope.

You sure?

Yup. He pointed at the trash. No empties.

Someone take it?

Roger that.

Who?

I know who.

Who?

He lit a cigarette.

Dude who lives upstairs.

She didn't know who he was talking about and assumed he meant the man they heard yelling at his daughter.

Any indication of a problem with his landlord sent a vibration back up the network of her plans. She and Skinner had just been talking about her visit to the lawyer, which ultimately connected to everything, including where to live. She had speculated that she might move in with him here.

What you are going to do?

He shook his head as if it wasn't worth mentioning. He took one of the six beers that remained out of the icebox and set it on the table and for a minute watched the water run down the outside of the cold can. Wasn't he going to close the icebox door? Oh, yeah. He drew on his cigarette and closed the door and changed the subject back to the lawyer.

Skinner saw Jimmy in the crowd on the 7 train platform at the 42nd Street stop. At the time, he didn't care about the theft of the beer, or imagined he didn't. He would have simply said hello. Great numbers of people going home from work stood between them. He lost him on the packed train and, getting off at the end of the line, he didn't see him. When he got back to the house, he listened to the Murphys through their walls. A sense of familiar fear developed inside him, possibly set off by the act of listening. He thought of knocking on their door and explaining how his mind worked to Jimmy's mother.

He went to 162nd Street and looked at the bar's green door, which seemed too small for the man as he pictured him. He went into Leiser's Liquors, under its yellow awning, and selected a bottle of rum. They sold Asian wines and spirits, a sign of a changing neighborhood. He paid with his card. The guy behind the counter swiped it through the reader and Skinner felt the friction, the tug between the plastic and the magnet as it pulled money out of the bank a mile away. Zou Lei passed his branch location every day on her way to work. He hadn't checked his balance in weeks. Would he have anything left for her?

Or would she share whatever he had, the cigarette, the hot canteen water, the sentence all of them had faced lying in the sand and garbage, keeping their heads below cover?

He drank in the basement until ten at night and traveled out again. Jake had shared it with him, he thought. His intoxication took away the Mexicans in front of their houses. When he almost blundered into them, they called him cabrón. The alcohol had taken away a great deal of his consciousness and still that was not nearly enough.

He vaguely perceived a group of large young males exiting the smoke shop. A Puerto Rican in a vest popped the cellophane off a cigar and tucked it above his ear. On Skinner's way back with a Gatorade, Skinner saw them drinking out of paper bags outside the China Garden. Even in his stupor, he recognized the tall one as Jimmy from across the street.

Guado nudged Jimmy on the arm. You see this fool?

Skinner spat on the ground the way they had spit at him when calling him a shitbird.

The next day, he woke to find a piece of wadded up trash on his stairs. It was a chewing gum wrapper and it wasn't his. The bit of litter had a piece of chewed gum in it.

Throw shit on my stairs, asshole.

He picked it up and tossed it up on the Murphys' landing.

On more than one occasion during the ensuing weeks, when returning to the house after being away, he would find a kitchen chair had been moved or a cabinet door opened.

Around the same time, he was walking down 40th Road when youths in front of a corner store began shouting, Hey! Where you going?

He recognized one of the youths from around the neighborhood. He thought he had seen him take a cigarette from Jimmy. As he continued down the block, one of them yelled:

I thought you was hard! Come back here, etcetera. I thought you wanna head up with my boy!

At his landlady's apartment, he had no contact with Jimmy; the two of them acted as if nothing was going on. He saw him on the street in Flushing. Nothing happened in the crowd. But the sidewalk next to the ocher buildings on Sanford Avenue was narrow. One night, Skinner saw Jimmy coming at him and knew he wasn't going to move. He was carrying the Berretta nine millimeter in his army backpack. He had plans with Zou Lei, so he crossed the street.

———

As she drew near, the side of Skinner's house opened and a man came out on long legs. He had a bandana tied around his head, and the bandana ends hung down with his hair as if they were a part of his hair and his beard and his hair was made of strips of cloth.

Without thinking, she stopped in mid-stride and put her head down, covering her face with her hat brim, and altered course, pretending to be going somewhere else, taking tiny time-marking steps, marching in place to keep away from him until he left. She felt him watching her, and she felt it when his stare was lifted from her.

Then he walked away and she looked after him while he was going, seeing him cross the street and lope around the corner and disappear. She wondered if he could see her even though he wasn't looking at her, with eyes behind his head. He seemed to know that she would backtrack and go to the house that he had come out of. He pretended to be looking somewhere else, but they were the only two people on the street.

If a girl is traveling in the steppe and she sees nothing but a single moving dot in the great distance, the dot sees her. Stag, man, wolf.

———

At three in the morning, the avenue was dark except for a single house in which one window gave off a low frequency radiation, a glowing ambiguous rose-violet light emanating from white lace curtains, a nightlight left on in a woman's bedroom.

The avenue was empty, wide, its vacancy inviting you to travel not merely two ways along the road but any way you wanted, into the sideways darkness. A penetrable wall of houses and stores, whose copings and parapets cut shadows against the sky. A giant supermarket by the freeway. At the other end, a railroad bridge and the projects. The dark spaces behind the tracks. Black ferns grew between the houses to eat the hot exhaust from the expressway.

Inconspicuous among other dark silent vehicles lining the curbs, there was a pickup truck parked near the softly glowing house.

A black sedan glided off the Van Wyck, paused at the flashing red traffic signal by the supermarket and turned down the avenue. It passed the high-walled lot and the dumpsters outside the diner whose sign said Steaks – Chops – Seafood, cruised past the construction supply outlets with Chinese signs and stopped mid-block.

An Asian woman got out of the sedan: big purse, short skirt, high heels, a large animal tattoo on her upper thigh. Snapping her lighter, she lit a cigarette. The car with its large radio antenna she'd come in drove away. Balanced on her high heels, she walked across the empty avenue, heading for the house whose window pulsed with the same violet wavelength as her halter top.

As she walked around in front of the pickup, she was suddenly startled, her heels striking the asphalt in a series of quick steps. She had seen the man in the driver's seat, his bearded mouth, his ringed fist on the steering wheel, where he had been sitting watching the house and now watching her. She threw away her cigarette and, before marching into the house, stared back at him with loathing.

41

THEY TOOK THE SUBWAY from Queens down to Canal Street in Manhattan. It was full of African, Bangladeshi, and Chinese vendors, selling I Love New York shirts and counterfeit Rolexes. From here they walked down to the city buildings. The big gray granite buildings took up block after block. At the criminal and family courts, the doorways were four stories high and there were crowds outside waiting to get in through the metal detectors. They crossed the street and walked parallel to a plaza with modern sculpture in it, and they passed the Supreme Court building. Down the side, they saw concrete barricades and fortifications and sentry posts. Those streets were not passable. They were empty canyons of concrete. They passed tourists and a different class of attorney, wearing a seersucker suit or a large hat with a round flat brim and a silk ribbon or some other stylish touch. They looked as if they were wearing costumes with their gold spectacles and straw hats. There was a coffee and organic muffin vendor on the corner. They saw paramilitary policemen in hats and jackets with the names of their units, in jump boots and bloused trousers, drinking coffee and talking with other security men in blazers and crewcuts. Then came the next city building with columns. They walked under the columns, which were stories high, and they saw flagstone courtyards and brass doors and pigeons and old stone bollards with anchor chains hung between them, from the days when the city was a maritime port.

When they tried to go inside, the security man at the doorway said, Can I help you?

Both he and his partner were wearing bulletproof vests and Police windbreakers. The second cop was Hispanic and stood with his jump boots planted wide apart.

Skinner said, We're looking for the place where you get married.

That's not here. He advised him of the correct address, but in a manner that was too rapid to be understood.

Where's that?

Two blocks back that way. Give you five minutes to think about it.

I've thought about it.

That's good.

Have a nice day, sir.

I've thought about it. I don't need to think about it.

Both cops turned their attention on Skinner in a particular way, suggesting a potentially higher level of interest in him. With their guns and gear, they outweighed him by at least three hundred pounds.

Have a nice day, they told him.

Skinner rejoined Zou Lei, who was waiting for him at the end of the courtyard, out of sight.

You don't have to fight with them.

She kept walking and he followed her. They went back through the plaza with the modern art and the colonnaded higher court buildings. The tourists joked in Dutch and Italian, and underneath their voices, the silence of the plaza was huge, ringed by empty streets and sentries drinking coffee.

They found they had been sent to the same building the criminal courts were in. There was a hot dog vendor on the corner where guys in suits—grooms and defendants—were eating pretzels. The marriage office was on the side facing south. The brass door was pushed open and an interracial couple came running out: a young woman holding up her wedding dress and a black guy wearing a pinstripe suit that was tight around his thighs. She had a white flower in her blond hair. Skinner moved in and grabbed the heavy door before it closed and opened it for Zou Lei, who entered in her jeans.

The granite floor in the lobby was the color of red earth and the shaded lamps gave the space a candlelit appearance. There was a velvet rope, as at a club. They got in line behind a large party of Spanish people who had come with a bride in a pink wedding dress who was taller than her mother. Someone was carrying a camera with a professional flash. The vaulted ceiling sent down the echoes of their footsteps and laughter. The brother and father were wearing black formal suits and cowboy boots. Zou Lei and Skinner didn't speak. She looked past the information desk. Deeper inside the room, wedding parties were standing at touch screen terminals, applying for marriage licenses. The information desk was manned by a young Asian American man, a college graduate, who spoke accent-free English.

When it was their turn, Zou Lei and Skinner went up to the counter and Zou Lei asked how you got married. The young man placed an information card on the countertop and turned it so she could see it. You bring me your passport, driver's license, then you go to the kiosk, apply for your license, and pay the fee. When the application prints out, you can come back and see the judge in 24 hours, unless you're active duty military, then you can do it sooner.

Zou Lei leaned on the counter, holding her head, studying the requirements on the card. The young man looked at the line behind her.

If you need to think about it, you can wait over there.

Give her a second, Skinner said. We might have a question.

Are you the groom?

Yeah.

What if it's some problem with the ID? Zou Lei asked.

Do you have a passport?

Maybe I have, but I want to use some ID from out-of-state.

That's fine.

I think it over.

The clerk took the information card back from her.

She needs that, Skinner said.

He gave her the card back.

Sorry about that. Anything else I can help you with?

Zou Lei said no and she and Skinner left the office. Around back of the Metropolitan Detention Center there was a park and through the spiked iron fence you could see the signs for Bail Bonds and diseased old saloons with blackened windows. She took her ID out and rubbed it with her thumb and looked at it. Skinner sat on a green bench and smoked a Marlboro and watched Chinese people of an older generation playing mahjong among the pigeons.

If she registered her marriage using a fake ID and an alias, would the marriage be legally legitimate? She went to the law office to ask the Mandarin-speaking clerk with whom she had spoken earlier. The woman told her to get married using her real name. But how was she supposed to do that? The woman told her she could go to the DMV to apply for a New York State ID card. She had forgotten the details of Zou Lei's situation. Zou Lei reminded her that she didn't have papers. The woman said she remembered now. The office was busy. She told Zou Lei she should come back later.

Zou Lei went to the City Clerk's Office again, intending to ask about the requirements for applying for an ID card, and waited to speak to the assistant. He must have misunderstood her. He wrote an address on a scrap of white paper and gave it to her. She hurried outside and realized she didn't know what it was for.

Skinner, medicated, depressed, and nihilistic, sat slumped in the basement watching IEDs exploding on his laptop, Iraqis getting shot and flopping down, the world ending one person at a time. The line shortening, getting closer to him, his turn approaching.

At work they cut her hours again. When there wasn't enough for her to do, a frequent occurrence, she loitered in the back hallway that connected the kitchens, talking with the Mexicans, Tomas and Miguel. She wiped her hands, went over to the chopping table, spent the afternoon making dumplings and shelling snow peas or washing dishes. Her time up front was over.

If they cut her hours any more, she was going to have to go back to collecting cans, just as she had done to survive in the brigade fields of central China.

She took a bathroom break to read the classifieds.

Class A license, $Opportunity$, Mac Operator, see Ms. Chen, must speak a mouth of fluent English. Garment, Bayshine, ladies missy fashion, patternmaker, Cantonese preferred. Earnestly seeking Junior CAD. Brooklyn nanny, Heaven Pest Control, housekeeper, egg donor, masseuse.

The next morning, she went to the park late, sometime after nine, and started running, thinking about what to do. When she got to the basketball courts, she didn't have a reason to stop. She crossed the fence line that demarcated the end of the field and kept running in the bright sun, her pace picking up. She didn't have work today. The grass and trees and the exhaust-filled atmosphere trapped the heat. She crossed a road where the cab of a tractor-trailer was parked alone. It looked like a mutant part, a head on wheels, whose weirdness could be seen now that it had broken off and escaped from the trailer. The parkland continued on the other side of the road, turned into a golf course, seen through trees to her right. The sun rose higher. She ran over a highway and through a factory lot, oil rags dried to the asphalt. She was headed for the buildings that she thought of as her mountains. She had stopped thinking about him. Sweat poured out of her, sweating her t-shirt across her breasts. She got a saddle-shaped patch of wet on the seat of her jean shorts as if she were riding a wet horse. It was approaching noon. The towers had been very far away after all. Where the grass ended, she gazed around her in the dazzling sun. She stopped. Her socks were soaked. She peeled her shirt away from her chest and flapped it. The garbage lay on the ground becoming part of it. The tall buildings that resembled mountains were simply government projects, silent in the ticking heat. That was all they were.

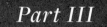

Part III

42

JIMMY WAS OUT ON Roosevelt Avenue, striding under the shadow of the elevated train, its trestles and piers, rivets and graffiti, trucks selling pigs' heads and brains and intestines, with the Mexican voices and the sound of the generators. There were alleys going in from the street where immigrants could get their hair done or buy their kind of music. They sold jeans and lingerie and cell phones and high heels and glass pipes and Spanish romances in the street, a man with a mustache seizing a raven-haired woman by the hips, thrusting his hand down into the open neck of her peasant blouse. The mannequins had arched asses and torpedo breasts and stood on their toes and wore big black wigs and supersonic glasses. The bars came every doorway and they were dark. Loud music was playing inside, as if the world's biggest fiesta were taking place. But if you looked into the music, you saw a room with the lights off and three or four disheveled men with their heads down on a table covered in an Olympic number of big beer bottles, and it was a scene of migrants getting plastered in a bus station.

It smelled like fried chicken and french fries and grilled corn. There was construction too—the city drilling in the street. The horns were honking, and a cheap ugly car gunned around the others. The occupants all wore the same red and black Bulls hats, black braids, white sleeveless undershirts, the males with zits and thick white biceps and tattoos. The big girls were dressed up the same as the boys, yelling, Yo, make a left, nigga, and the acne-covered driver bent over the wheel, gesturing, yelling, Move, nigga, to another car. Boxing gloves with the Puerto Rican flag hung from the rearview mirror, and the car, filled with the big bodies of these large young people, sped away on its cheap toy-like rims.

And a woman with the spirit was holding up the bible and preaching with a microphone in the middle of an island under the tracks, speaking an unceasing, uninterrupted litany that grew faster and louder and became climactic and deafening and violent coming from her loudspeakers.

He crossed 85th Street in the crowd. A Chinese man in gray trousers and a gold chain and a v-neck was leaning on a parking meter. As Jimmy approached, the man caught his eye and asked, Massage? He pointed out a pair of Asian women standing halfway down the block. Jimmy approached them. One looked like a farmer with a spotted weather-beaten face and a purse worn across her shoulder and a soft hat in the shape of a lampshade to keep the sun off. The other was wearing makeup and a t-shirt and had pineapple-sized breasts. She had heavy glossy black hair done up in a twist and pinned to the back of her head.

You, Jimmy specified. The t-shirt-wearer put on a smile and said, Oh yeah, and led him in a doorway. She was in her upper forties and acted intoxicated. He followed her up a low-ceilinged stairway, which led up to a single destination, an apartment where the lights were off and the door was always open. She had a wide flat rear end and the seat of her jeans had sequins. On the stairs she looked back over her shoulder to make sure he was still coming. She gave him a secret smile. Then they went into the apartment.

The apartment was hot: hotter than all the collected heat of the summer day. It was as if they had a space heater on as well: frightening hot, like you might not come out of it breathing. And there was no fresh air. It was air that had been used and breathed, like the atmosphere in a jail. He made the connection to jail immediately. The smell and texture of the air came from food and people's bodies and other things which were never aired out and blown away but were re-breathed. The air had a weight and pressure that was different from outside air as a result. There was a strong smell of boiled ramen noodles and skin lotion. If there were windows, they were sealed and painted over. The apartment was a narrow pitch-black maze that got darker as you went in. She went down a tunnel towards a red glow, and Jimmy walked behind her. The glow came from a curtain, which she moved aside. He was twice her height. She looked at him and smiled. Dipping his head, he stepped into a red-lit compartment. There was barely room for both him and the massage table. The table had a hole for your face to breathe when you were face-down.

How much?

She told him. He took out his money and she watched the money in his hands until he handed it to her. She folded the money and disappeared.

He took his t-shirt off, an xxxl t-shirt with a faded logo for a tool brand across the mottled fabric, and exposed himself. He looked like a white meaty insect whose exoskeleton has been peeled away exposing the mechanical workings of muscles and white sacks of flesh, which had never been in the open air before. He took his jeans off, baring his long legs.

And he stood in the red glow, unclothed except for the bandana around his head, watching the curtain. He put his shades on and positioned himself facing the doorway with his legs spread and his chin back as if he were sunning himself in the red light.

Like a pitcher on the mound, he licked three fingers, then reached down and fiddled with the end of his uncircumcised penis.

She came back inside, wearing fuzzy pink slippers and carrying towels and sheets in her arms.

No, no, no, she tutted. You lie down.

His fist, the one with the rings on it, hit her in the mouth.

She went back into the wall and hit her head. The towels and sheets dropped out of her hands. The whites of her eyes showed and she tumbled to the floor. Her knees drew in and she covered her face and let out a grief-stricken sound.

Jimmy went around to where she was and hit her again.

Oh! she screamed. No! She crawled into the corner. The clip that held her hair in place had popped open and hung caught in her loose hair.

She was trying to hide from him. He wrenched her arm behind her back and almost broke it. She let out a scream. The sounds had nowhere to go. He punched the back of her head. He hooked his fist around in front and got her face. Oh! she screamed and started crying. He shoved her around to make her face him and got her back against the wall and wrenched her hands away from her face and hit her again.

Show me your face.

She flinched and he twisted her hands away again.

I'll break the arm.

Okay. Okay. Okay. I do nothing.

Show me the face.

No, she pleaded.

It was impossible for her to overcome the reflex to cover up. She was too scared, but he improved her. He worked on her until he was getting where he wanted.

Why? Why? she said. It was a calm question. But she asked it blind, because her eyes were swollen in bulging hard blue hematomas.

She performed fellatio on him. She removed her clothing and underwear and got up on the table. He sodomized her and at his insistence she performed fellatio on him again. The way he did it, she was severely injured. He made an engine-revving noise when he was driving into her. She screamed into a towel. What he was doing sounded like a boxer hitting a heavy bag with wet gloves. He arched his back. When he rested, he blew air and got his wind back, his sides sweating in the hot room. He looked like a man on a child. The child's head was mummified. Then he went into another frenzy when he had his wind back. She gagged and threw up in the towel he wrapped her head in. There were ramen noodles in her stomach.

You got the virus now, he told her as he was pulling up his jeans.

She was standing there half-bowing, her face unrecognizable as human. She appeared to be wearing a slick shiny bumpy thick eyeless mask, wetness around the eye slits.

HIV, he said. Better get checked.

You stink, he added.

Something was not finished in him. There was evil and crazy in the room. Possibly he was going to go all the way.

He took the money out of her jeans, her cell phone, and ID. He patted her on the head. Smile, he said. She did not react.

You no call police, he told her in pidgin English, so she would understand. Some mechanical cam had flipped inside his brain, he realized: he wasn't going to go any farther this time. He left the red room and his footsteps moved away down the black hallway.

The woman remained tottering where she was. Five minutes passed. She had heard him leave. She tried out her voice, making a sound, and it was a croak. In the hot room, she was shaking like someone naked in the snowy wilderness. She went through the curtain and began walking down the hall, stepping on broken linoleum in the darkness, groping her way.

On the street, in the afternoon sun, Jimmy bought a hotdog at a busy intersection under the tracks, among Spanish and Bangladeshi

vendors selling spiritual guides, anatomical charts, novellas, tapes-
tries of Aztec maidens and warriors, eagles, the words Brown and
Proud. He kept his shades on. He was about ten blocks down from
the scene and he felt secure. Expressionless, he watched the street as
he ate by the hotdog cart. The intersection smelled like cotton candy.
It was awash in a sea of people coming off the train, the Spanish
mothers arguing with their daughters about what they could afford.

He noticed stains on his fingers and he thought it was ketchup,
but he sniffed it and it was from fingering her.

Napkin, he said.

He went into a bar, a black hole in the street, and bought a beer
using her money and went into the bathroom and took down his
jeans and looked at the crusted red around his groin. He took out
her ID and read the name. Li, Chiao-Yee, Vickie. The hologram was
wrong, and her supposed address in Elmhurst was spelled without
the r: Elmhust. The picture was of someone else, a younger woman
with shorter hair and a serious expression. He stuck it in the garbage.

After another beer, he got in a Lincoln cab and rode back the way
he had come, looking out for any kind of commotion. And, in fact,
there was something: at a spot on the avenue, people were gathered
watching something going on, but he could not see what. They were
looking towards a building with graffiti on the roof and a massage
sign in the window. He believed that this was the scene. He caught a
flash of a uniformed cop holding his radio sideways and talking into
it urgently. The cop, a young man, was looking over peoples' heads.
The attitude of someone focused on a task. The Lincoln accelerated
and beat the light, leaving the other traffic behind. The knot of tension was back there. The car seemed to fly along more freely now,
the tracks laddering overhead. They swooped up and down over the
bridge into Flushing Chinatown. They broke out the other side into
East Flushing, the ghetto buildings tagged in Spanish, the decaying
houses of the Irish.

Jimmy got out of the Lincoln and went into his three-story house.
His mother was on the phone. She put her hand over the mouth-
piece. I'm doing subs, she said. You want one?

I wish, he said.

Then get something.

I would, but.

It'll be on me, Jim, she said.

Jimmy hung out on the hot street, bought skewers from the Chinese, stood out by the Falungong tables, letting them proselytize to him while he looked at their medical photographs. He met guys he knew and they passed a bottle with him. One said, If I knew a job, I'd do it right now. Jimmy bit the meat off with his teeth, with his dog-muzzle jaw.

I know a job.

What job?

I can't tell you that.

The Buddhist human rights protestors were handing out flyers that showed a genderless being holding a glowing circle in its abdomen: the dharmic wheel. They wore long-billed visors and large sunglasses. A poster showed people and bicycles all knocked over in a pile. Their white shirts were soaked in blood and there was blood splashed and splattered all over the ground. One of them who had not been killed yet was still trying to stand up—the photograph caught him as he was climbing to his feet. It had been taken in the grainy dark. There was a blurred violet city sky and streaks of light over the soviet city square. The headline asked, Why does the People's Liberation Army only attack Chinese people?

Jimmy turned his head to hear music that was playing somewhere in the street, his wild long hair swung around his head, and he pretended to play guitar.

His friend was looking at photos of a woman on a steel table. She appeared to be resting calmly on a white sheet with her eyes swollen shut like eggs. The other pictures were close-ups of her injuries. They went down the length of her and ended with her toe, which had a tag on it.

Another photograph, taken earlier, showed her posing against a backdrop of parasol trees, wearing a summer dress and making V-signs with both hands. The caption in Chinese said: Wen Fengyu as an undergraduate studying forestry at Hebei Polytechnic College on school vacation to the Beijing Summer Palace in 1994 just after being introduced into the Falungong Great Way.

What is this shit? his friend said.

Remarkably, Jimmy was able to explain it to him. This is how she died. He indicated the Falungong members in their glasses. They told me what they did to kill her. They've got their politics, their different cliques. Chinese, Japanese, it's all a different hustle depending on which one you deal with. They got organization. These guys with the tables right here, they got an organization. They're out here collecting donations so they can start another crime wave. Gimme a drink a that.

The metal on his fingers struck the bottle when he took it and swigged from it.

Every time one of their people gets taken out, they put their picture up. Like take this one here in the picture. I knew her. She used to work around the corner.

Where?

Right over there.

Doing what?

Whaddayou think? In the massage joint over here on 41st Road. That's where they all go. They run their whole game outta there. Smack, guns, girls, whatever you can name, Jimmy said. They was watching her. You better believe they knew everything she did.

He elaborated on how she had been completely unaware of any danger until the last minute. She would never have fallen for anything that was not professionally done, he asserted. He took another drink of the bottle. And then another. He said:

She thought she was smart. When she got caught, she said, All right, you're good. But she had a nice ass. She had to give it up. I guess you caught me, so I have to go by the rules. So, they said okay, if that's how you feel. So they fucked her. So far, so good. That's legit. You got me fair and square. As a woman in her position she understood her duties. But she was spiteful. Oh no, she says, I ain't gonna call the cops. Just let me go. She went to get her purse and it wasn't there. Why's there no clothes? Because there's nowhere to go. They're all the way underground. All right, now she gets her guard up. That's when she knows she's fallen for something, and now she wants to talk her way out of it like she's talked her way out of everything before. Only now it's not working. This guy don't buy any of her crap about her hard life. He says, here's what I'll do. For every time you lied, you're gonna get it. He beats her down like no man ever. She screams and cries for, oh, about two days. By the end, he gives her a mirror and she's totally destroyed. She ain't never gonna walk again. Ain't never gonna have a kid. She's begging for her mother. Mommy mommy mommy please don't kill me. He told her the good news. You ain't never getting out of here. And her eyes were just like this big. She begged to suck his dick. Nope. Want this? Nope. Want that? Nope. You ain't leaving. You're gonna die and it ain't gonna be fun. Cry all you want. Jimmy raised his fingers adorned again with skull rings and pressed the corners of his eyes where the tears would go. Nobody cares about your sad brown eyes. That was the end of her and she could not believe it.

43

When she got to work, she found out she wasn't on the schedule—the high school kid Monroe was there instead of her—and so in the middle of the morning she left the mall and went to 158th Street. Before she arrived, she called Skinner but couldn't reach him.

She knocked on the basement window. Skinner! she whispered. It was about eleven in the morning.

The door was opened by the man she had seen before, who she understood to be the landlord's son. She had just jogged up a hot street and she was flushed. Her t-shirt, which came from a used-clothing rack on Junction Boulevard, had the words Hand Full across her breasts. The man looked down at her and told her:

He ain't here.

But she hadn't said who she was looking for.

The man asked her if she wanted to come in anyway.

She turned around and walked several blocks away, and when she couldn't get Skinner on the phone, she went back to Main Street, eventually wandering down to the park by Elder Avenue.

On East Broadway, she went to the Fuzhou Fan-Meaning Work Introduction Corp.—the name was a play on the word Benevolent—and waited to speak to someone behind the old-fashioned railway ticket window. Men in white socks and waiters' pants stood all around talking on their phones, discussing monthly salaries. A man shouted into his cell phone: Two thousand four hundred. But the cook is dishonest! A sign said No Spitting On Floor. You received a free map of Fuzhou down to the sea. A job introduction cost thirty-five dollars. The options were tail cook, main cook, takeout, delivery, cashier, miscellaneous, and wet nurse. You could also get a social security card without a birth certificate. It said this right on the wall in Chinese next to the minimum wage law printed in English.

When it was her turn, the woman who spoke to her through the cutout in the Plexiglas told her she had work available in a number of different states.

I can't go out-of-state, Zou Lei said. I'll think about it.

She went outside and bought the Chinese newspaper and called a number from the classifieds but couldn't make sense of what they were saying on the other end. Every call cost minutes on her phone. She hung up and made another call and then another. It was late afternoon and she'd burned off everything in her stomach. She bought a seventy-five-cent roll containing meat floss. Give me two of those, she said. She took them in their wax paper sleeves and ate them on the steps by the stands selling cured squid and yellow croaker, the antique flower shops with dark red doors, and the basement rooms for playing mahjong.

Not far beyond the projects at the end of the park, nearby her towers, she found Muslim kids playing in the street. They were playing in the hydrant spray, sharing a bicycle, having water fights. She put her hand in the water and put water on her face. A group of men in coveralls was working on a car. She stepped over the compressed air hose as she passed their garage, which smelled like oil rags, her leg muscles tight from running. The asphalt shone and she saw rainbows in the street. Little girls in headscarves, tiny nuns, stood on a fire escape, pretending they were in jail. They threw a cup of water down on a boy who dodged away, ran back screaming. She passed forklifts parked in front of warehouses, which were scrap yards. A rusted sign above a storefront showed a green flag and crescent moon for Islam. The sign was covered in spores of dirt. Three Central American men wearing string backpacks came rolling a shopping cart down the sidewalk carrying a long piece of aluminum from a street lamp. They went into a warehouse to have it weighed.

Ahead she saw a gas station whose roof was covered in hundreds of small American flags, the kind for waving at parades. The space on the roof had run out and then whoever ran the gas station had put more flags on the next roof up, making two decks of flags, thereby creating a great two-tiered raft of red white and blue, the result of a thousand trips up and down a ladder to fetch more flags.

She came to a window filled with photographs of Pashtun nomads. In the photographs, women sat on chairs strapped to a camel's back. Another photograph showed men running horses on a brown field playing polo, the field unbounded except for mountains, true mountains, in the geographic distance, allowing you to see the seams and sections of the land. The men, who looked Mongolian, in turquoise, red, and black costumes, were playing polo with the carcass of a calf, ringed by a massed fringe of spectators. The nomads were like something not of this world. They appeared both African and Caucasian in their stiff kabuki-like robes and blankets. They wore blankets on their heads. Three of them were women and a girl who appeared as tall and forbidding as the turbaned men. Behind them were their tents made of camel skins.

The grocer had a business license in the window in the name of Tesha Noor, Ramzy Grocery and Meat, and a poster giving the ninety-nine names of Allah, including the Preserver, the Delayer, the Last, and the Reckoner. And in the bottom of the window, pressed to the glass by a stack of Cortas chickpeas, he had a crumpled leaflet from the NYPD, which said, If You Suspect Terrorism, and the number to call.

She went in the open door and down the aisle of sultan oil, stacks of bread, sacks of rice, and barrels of pistachios and almonds. In the back of the store, she found the owner cutting meat behind the meat case, which held sheep's ribs, legs, head, and gray intestines. He wore a white doppa like a little cake on his head and an embroidered vest and a shirt with no collar. He was a short stocky man. His fleshy Caucasian face was round like a bread. When he saw her, he put his knife down and wiped his hands on his apron.

I help you something?

Yahshimusiz, she said.

Oh, he smiled, wiping his wet muscular hands again. Yahshimusiz. You talk a little bit different from me.

I'm Uighur people.

I'm Uzbek.

He was an Uzbek tribesman from Afghanistan, from Aqcha. Twenty years of war, going on thirty. Picture the green pasture and the small trees like little puffs from far away with a little snake of mist sneaking out of the hills, a single isolated flat-roofed mud-brick dwelling like a mountain pueblo. His family lived across the river on the other side of the heavily fortified border with its concrete barriers and electrified fences. They were from Bukhara, a place he had never been and yet was proud of. In the air, he drew the outline of the great mosaic tile mosque.

We play the buzkashi. Riding a horse—beautiful animal. When it's loud, it's like thunder. He mimed riding. Pointing out in the distance, he said, In the east, it's mountains like nothing you never seen.

What do you think you're talking about? That's my home! Zou Lei told him. Yes! When I was little girl, my mother told me stories and I am looking at those mountain. Maybe 150 miles away. I think I can go to them, always. The sky in there is the most blue, most blue I ever seen.

And the people is good too, he said. Believe it. The people has a heart. The butcher spoke of their hospitality and the treatment of guests.

Even he has nothing, he is generous.

Yeah, because if you are my guest, I will protect you. You are in my house. You are safe.

You give your word.

Because I am a man, I care for my honor.

How long had he been in America? she asked. How had he gotten to this point, where he had a store that belonged to him?

Fifteen years, Tesha said. Look at that, he said, holding up a cut of meat. Beautiful, fresh one hundred percent.

Together they admired it.

Did he ever think of going back to Afghanistan? she asked.

I cannot go.

Because the war?

Because war. Nobody can go. I have my wife. I cannot go. Even if I go alone, I cannot go. It's very bad. You can't believe what's going on. If I tell you, you can't believe. I don't want to tell you what I know, what I see myself. Make you want to never see, to take out your own eyes. I can't talk about it.

It's a beautiful mountains.

It's a beautiful country, my friend, but you cannot go. Maybe you know. Where you from? China? So maybe you don't know. You know George Bush? He want to kill everyone. The Americans kill everyone. He kills more than the other one, bin Laden. That's what he do to us. All my life, I love America, why you think I come here.

Now Bush take it and he—the butcher flung his arms out—he do like that, throw in garbage, make it garbage. He don't have to do it. Bin Laden is shit in my country, but now America is going down.

Let me tell you what happen, he continued. You see this one, the gas station when you come in? The one has all the flags. He was good people, nice guy. Muslim guy, right? Been here like me long time. After 9/11, one day, he disappear. Vanish. Gone. I used to see them all the time. Now I see his kid, nice kid. Why I don't see your dad? My dad's gone. What you mean gone? Gone, he says. I think they take him. Some people say he get in a car. For two years, disappeared.

Don't tell me that.

It's Homeland Security. Happen right here. The family put up pictures and everything. It kill them. All their face are falling down. You know where he is? The whole time he is right here in Queens. Nobody can see him and he is right there, right there in Queensboro Plaza. They got a building it looks like the post office. By the time, they know about it, they put him in another jail in Texas. Five years. When the family say, okay, let's go to court—you think he's done something—No. We going to keep him. No, we will send him to the Middle East.

Five years, she said. I don't know if I can survive. When I was in jail, it was very hard for me.

They catch you for what?

For immigration.

By the greatness of God they let you out.

Yes, thank God. Now I am trying to fix my identity.

You don't have the…

No. I have to fix this problem, she said. And she began to let her worries out for him to hear, since he was willing to listen. I cannot make money. I have to pay the lawyer. The lawyer is more money. It's bad for me.

What's your work?

Restaurant.

Chinese restaurant?

Yes. She cried a little talking about it, and wiped her eyes. My boss take the money.

Tesha sighed as he listened to her and felt helpless. I wish my wife was here. Sarah! The problem was that his wife would not understand her, because his wife spoke Tarjeek. His wife was at the Friday prayers.

Who's your boss, what is he? Muslim? Chinese? No offense, but Chinese people—a lot of my customer Chinese, so I got to be careful—but Chinese people are cold.

I know, she said. Everything is business to them.

He gave her bread, insisting that she take it even after she refused, and he repeated his wish that his wife were here. Also, he had yogurt, if she wanted it, and he directed her attention to where he kept it in the small dark refrigerated case. For bread, he had the huge one like Afghanistan, and the little one too, like this, like Turkish pita. Whatever you need.

And another thing—this was important: A lot of people came to his store, he said. Here in the doorway, he had a bulletin board where they put up messages if they needed help. You could find exchange, he said. You can leave a note to ask for help.

He had a cardboard shelf, the kind that folds up like a box and sits on the floor, that held business cards and free newspapers. He told her to take an immigration attorney's card. Rahmat, she said, taking a card and holding it with her bread. And he had these—and he pointed out a pile of small folded newspapers in Urdu and Chinese.

My wife makes samsa. She cut it up the ingredients very fine like this—and he sawed his hand across his palm. Beautiful. Almost like home. You gotta try it. If you have time, come back.

His wife came in through the back door and Tesha spoke to her in Tarjeek. The woman came around the counter in her black polyester robe, bringing Zou Lei a cup of water. At the same time, another customer was coming in and the butcher had to speak with him, so that was how Zou Lei finished talking with him. He put his hand on his heart and told her to come back.

Rahmat, she said.

His wife Sarah had an idea and took her by the hand out onto the hot street and led her to a house next door to a boarded-up building with weeds coming through the boards. She pulled Zou Lei towards the door through which you could see a rectangular carpeted room, empty shoes and sandals just inside the door. The entrance was propped open with a trash can. Men in robes and slacks were converging on this place from all over the street. Zou Lei saw their beards and realized it was a mosque. A man stepped inside and took his sandals off and went in to join the others kneeling in front of the black flag and the dais.

The butcher's wife gave her to a man and wished her well. The man guided her down to the women's entrance, a separate doorway in what appeared to be a residential house, and told her to go downstairs. Zou Lei went inside, seeing a staircase and another pile of shoes and smelling a heavy smell of air freshener. Through a doorway she could see the men entering the mosque on the first floor. She removed her sneakers and went down the stairs and into the basement.

The basement was a closed rectangular room draped with strings of plastic flowers and enormous black flags emblazoned in golden script. One end of the room was rigged with a shower curtain rod and wires. There were spotlights bolted to the ceiling, as if the room was used to make videos, but they were off. Women sat on the carpeted floor, their legs folded like deer, and faced a television resting on a sequined dais. The television was broadcasting a live video image of what was happening in the men's prayer room upstairs.

They told her to go into the bathroom and purify herself. She was observed from the doorway as she washed her hands with gooey liquid soap. A woman muffled in black indicated, Your feet too. Zou Lei, who was thirsty from running, drank from the tap. Your feet, the woman insisted, her veil edged in silver thread. Zou Lei put her foot in the sink and washed it.

When she was done, she was told she could take her place with the others, so she went out and sat on the carpet at the back of the room behind them all. She sat one knee bent, her tanned face and bare calves burnished and dark, the sweat on her forehead gleaming and the crotch of her tight denim leggings wet, and waited.

The carpet was divided into rectangles and you sat within your rectangle. Overhead, the first floor was filling up with men, who could be heard through the ceiling as they came in and lined up in rows. They handed out plastic prayer beads and round flat stones and you placed the stone in front of you in the rectangle in which you sat. The women watched what was happening on the television, which was trained on the figure of a man in a black turban beneath a spotlight. He stood up and the TV showed the men standing up. The women stood up and Zou Lei stood up with them. Someone began to sing upstairs and she watched the back of his head on the monitor as he sang towards the black banners.

Allahu akbar! everyone cried out on both floors of the building. Allahu akbar, Zou Lei said.

The singing stopped and the mullah turned around. He was a man of medium height in his sixties with a gremlin-like face surrounded by a white beard that made it look as if you were seeing the head of a brown figurine in white wrapping paper. A microphone scratched and thumped. He spoke for several minutes, moving his hands, flexing his fingers, sometimes raising an index finger as he lectured. On each hand, he wore a ring with a large oval stone in it.

In His Name, the Name of the Prophet, and the clan of the Prophet, that which is open, that which is hidden, praise be to God. For surely, there is Good versus Evil. Therefore, command what is Right and forbid Evil (praise be to God). Science in the mouth of the Unfaithful One (created by fire, the Uncreated One) is deceiving. He who uses false names, by their numbers will he be exposed. True numerology is proof unto me, as I am proof unto Him (the Supreme). Ibn Al-Nawawi, third ayat. Therefore, the Science of Righteousness is used to learn real Truth (all praise). But when the sawat is subtracted from daily life, zero minus one computes to negative infinity and all existence is banished. A believer who is faithful (blessings be upon you) and who keeps the day will live three hundred seventy-five years on earth and ten thousand eight hundred years in Heaven. (Praise God, in the words of the Faithful One) his reward will I make for him out of gold. With the birth of Knowledge, Life is born. With the birth of Ignorance, Death is born, affecting every living thing, even things that are inanimate (cannot live hereafter). Fifth verse, ayat 37. Thus Life is given or taken according to Number Theory (Number Science, all blessings be unto the Imam of Time) discovered over seven hundred years in the past before modern computers. The Ninety-nine Names of Him Who is the Most Highest were computed before modern methods. Relief will be granted at a future time, whose number has been computed as three million.

When he finished speaking, the mullah turned around and the singing began again, the singer rapidly enunciating verses that went on and on for many minutes, his voice quavering at difficult notes, pronouncing hundreds upon hundreds of words deftly and rapidly without tripping up. Then the mullah took control again and called the cadence as they prayed. God is great! a woman wailed, as if she had been hypnotized. They raised their hands up to their faces, seemed to read them like a book, flung them down and bowed. The entire building dropped to its knees and the women put their foreheads on the carpet in front of the television. They pressed their foreheads on their prayer stones. Zou Lei did this to.

When she raised her head between bows, she noticed a giant silver statue of a hand high up on the wall. It was garlanded with plastic flowers and it had an eye in the center of the palm.

When the praying was over, the women turned to each other and touched each other's hands. A woman took Zou Lei's hand and trapped it like a fish between her hands and slid her hands off. Then they touched their hearts. They gestured at their mouths with their dark fingers, inviting her to eat with them.

They unrolled a strip of green wood-patterned vinyl on the floor and someone passed out plastic plates and Dixie cups of water, no cutlery. The vinyl strip represented their table. Sit, they told Zou Lei. She sat cross-legged, her jeans still damp from sweating. There was an aluminum baking pan full of dal curry. They tore their flatbread into pieces and used it to pinch up the lentils.

While they were eating, a man in a shalwar kameez entered the basement carrying another aluminum baking pan and the women started putting money into it, filling it with dollars.

I don't have money, Zou Lei lied.

It's okay, the women told her. More food?

One of them tore up a piece of bread for her and put the pieces on her plate. They watched her guzzling water. Zou Lei wiped the curry off her plate and ate it off her fingers. Good, she said. They refilled her water cup.

Thank you.

No, she was told. Bimsallah.

Bimsallah, she repeated.

Good, they said.

They wanted to know what she was. What are you, Nepal woman?

After she had eaten, she went upstairs with the others to find her shoes again. The mullah had been told about her. She saw him through the doorway, regarding her and nodding as a man pointed her out. The man wore spectacles and a dress shirt through which the white shadow of his undershirt was visible. When she was outside the man approached her, carrying a Koran.

May I ask you something? Why did you come here with your arms and legs uncovered?

Someone tell me to come here.

I see. You want to learn about our faith. Do you know Islam? It is the true faith. The true one. We teach one God, that's Allah. Maybe you feel much better now after the prayers. Maybe you feel you have refreshment. Don't you feel that way? And he let out a laugh like a hotelier greeting wealthy guests.

So! It's new for you, but it's very important for you. But, something you should know, in our faith, you must cover your arms, legs, and the head. Then you can learn with us. I make some book for you and you will study. Then I will convert you. Do you have a cell phone? You can give me your number.

I don't understand nothing the imam said, Zou Lei told him.

It's different language for you, it's very hard, I know, but it's not a problem. I will make book for you in English. I will personally help you to guide you to God.

Okay, okay, she said, but she didn't give him her number. Her dried sweat had left licks of salt on her temples, down her bare thighs. Her hair was stiff and she pushed it back with her hand, and took another bite of the flatbread Tesha the butcher had given her.

My mother was Muslim people, she said, chewing. I know about God, but it's too many rules.

No, no, no. You are wrong, he said. No, no, no. You make a big mistake to say that. Let me tell you something about God. He is like the shade of a tree on a hot day. How can I say? It is like you are burning in the sun and you feel very uncomfortable. You are thirsty and you would like some good things to drink. All you have to do is open this door and go in where it is cool and refreshing. That is God.

But, he said, you cannot have these beautiful things if you lead a bad life, if you are sinning, doing what you want. Of course you must live properly and obey the law. He pointed at the bilingual Arabic and English sign over the mosque's doorway, which he read aloud for her. It said Preparation For The Next Life.

He studied her reaction. She squinted at him, creasing the fine white lines by her eyes that came from working in the sun starting when she was perhaps six years old.

I have a long way home, she said and started leaving.

Of course, you must go, he said and patted his Koran. Don't be late for your husband.

As she left, he told her to come that Sunday, if she could, at two o'clock, because there would be another meal, and he would be here.

The kids on the block were still playing in wet t-shirts, running through a fire hydrant gushing in the street. A car went by and the sun spot in the windshield left a direct impression on her eye, a shape when she blinked. She had finished her bread and her stomach felt heavy and her legs had stiffened up. She did not want to run anymore, but it was a long way back and there was no bus she knew of.

A kid with a big voice tried to get her in a game with his friends.

I have to go home long way.

How far you go? the boy asked, attempting to run along with her.

Twenty mile.

He fell back behind her, gave up running.

You go that far every day? he called.

Goodbye, she waved.

He was about eleven, she had made a great impression on him, and he couldn't stop following her with his big eyes.

Fight the power! he raised his high voice and yelled down the block after her.

44

It was two-something in the morning and Skinner was on the 7 train. When the train braked, his legs slid sideways on the seat. His jeans were hanging off his hips and the cuffs were under the heels of his boots. His empty drink can rolled out of his hands and across the floor of the car. It came to rest beneath the sneaker of a Mexican who trapped it like a soccer ball and kicked it away again. People were sleeping and reading the bible. The train rocked on, the doors banged open, and the heat came in from the outdoor platforms, the station names slashed with graffiti. Skinner woke up having to vomit. He got off the train, fell through the turnstile, and threw up on the landing of the tall staircase. Then he used the handrail to climb down to the street.

At the bottom, he stuck his finger in his throat and vomited again. He stepped over his throw-up and staggered on, past a trash can tipped over in the street. The awnings were all in Spanish. He must have thought he recognized the cinder block building beneath the tracks, must have thought it was the lounge where he and Zou Lei had gone to drink together their first night. It was a locked warehouse. He put his hand on the building as if to keep it where it was, or to keep himself from leaving it.

Apparently, however, he wandered away from the tracks, down into the backstreets that cut the blocks into triangles. The fire escapes hung against the dirty buildings like lightning bolts. He passed vegetable markets with the shutters down and the produce put away, the wooden trestles chained to the wall with nothing on them. Behind them, men were sleeping, comatose from drinking, wrapped in blankets, lying on cardboard. Someone groaned. In the Park of the Americas, Skinner may have seen a man drifting like a zombie in the dark.

A rhythmic, low-frequency sound was coming from somewhere. There was music, which from a distance, sounded Romanian.

He held himself on the fence around the park and began urinating. There was yelling and a man came sprinting down the empty street, his leather shoes slapping, and ran around the corner of a dilapidated house. Several seconds later, another man came chasing after him, running very fast for a man his size, and followed him around the corner. Skinner, still urinating, stared after them. The second man had been carrying a ten-inch butcher knife. Nothing came back out of the darkness between the houses into which they had disappeared.

The low-frequency sound was coming from a truck idling. It was parked in front of a club with a blacked-out window. He went inside. A bath of blue light. There were people in the corners dressed in cowboy hats and boots. A fat man wearing an enormous LA Dodgers shirt stared at Skinner with drugged eyes. Skinner stared back at him and was acknowledged with a nod. It was so formal, it might have been mockery. A mirrored ball turned above their heads. A woman climbed up from her table by the door and tried to speak to him in Spanish. Skinner said, I don't know. He fell into a table. She went to the bar and came back with an opened Coronita. He gave her what he had and it was four dollars. She took his dollars to the bar and showed them to the woman there who had the face of a troll and big maternal breasts and, yes, it would be okay.

At the next table from Skinner, there were no women, only men. They had their backs to him. One man, who had an elongated body like a panther in mid-leap, was leaning in, talking to the others, talking in a self-punctuating way, gesturing with his long-fingered tattooed hand. A neatly folded and ironed bandana hung from his waist. All the men had neat short hair. Some were razor bald and their skulls were tattooed. Skinner saw a scorpion on someone's cheek. They wore clean clothing and clean plain sneakers with rounded toes. The same ironed and folded bandana hung from all of their pockets.

When the speaker finished speaking, he tilted back in his chair and rested his arm on Skinner's table. Skinner looked at the arm on his table. The smell of a different deodorant or laundry detergent brand was noticeable. The man seemed to be aware of Skinner. He seemed to be holding his head in profile to look behind him. He turned his head all the way back to look at Skinner directly. When he did, his entire face was black with tattoo ink except his eyes. There was a cross on his forehead, a skull with horns and Gothic letters, scorpions, webs and leaves and thorns and spiral lines, like tornadoes around his eyes. He acted handsome and confident.

Just doing something different, huh?

Gettin drunk.

Same as everybody. Everybody drunking. But it's different, right?

What?

You is. You is different from everybody. Where you from?

Pennsylvania.

What you say?

Pennsylvania.

So, what you doin here instead of Pennsylvania?

Gettin wasted.

Qué? one of the others at the young man's table asked. Skinner's response was translated into Spanish. In the blue light, someone else, someone with his lip and the bridge of his nose tattooed, glared at Skinner.

What else?

That's it.

The speaker in his white sweater let his chair tilt forward again and for several minutes they didn't talk, while Skinner was left staring at the man's elongated back.

Dude. Hey, dude.

Skinner nudged the man's shoulder with his Coronita. The tattooed face turned back around.

Where the fuck are you from?

Why the fuck you wanna know?

Later, the man held his hand out and beckoned over one of the short women and talked to her commandingly—you could hear the cadence of how he talked and see the way he didn't look at her when he talked. She took the neatly folded bills, folded like their bandanas, from between his long tattooed fingers and later returned from the bar with another round of beers and limes.

Hey, dude. Hey. Hey, motherfucker. You wanna know where I'm from.

I know where you from.

The fuck you do. I'm from Iraq.

What happen to Pennsylvania?

You tell me. What happened to your face?

What? Qué? the others asked.

All this shit. What's that for?

It's like religion. For him—the speaker pointed upwards in the dark. And that one too—he pointed down at the floor.

Who's down there?

You know who is down there. Everybody knows.

Skinner swayed and the man pushed him off with his elbow.

Careful, carnal.

Hey. Hey, dude.

Skinner held out his hand until the guy shook it and threw it away. Skinner tried to get the others at the table to shake his hand. He was stared at and ignored. Someone told him to sit the fuck down before he got hurt. This wedo wants attention.

Are you a CI? the speaker smiled. Confidential informant?

I'm a trigger-puller, Skinner said.

The man's eyes moved: the whites, which looked blue in the blue light, turned in his decorated face. And the last exchange that Skinner would recall having with him before Skinner found himself wandering through Flushing Meadow Park went something like this:

You kill people?

A few.

Which one?

The enemy. The Iraqis.

Anyones is fun?

A couple. We used to play chicken with them. Like one time, these two idiots were in a house. Our translator tells them to come out, it was okay. Then as soon as they came out, we'd light them up and they'd run back in. Then the translator would fuck with them. He'd say what did you do wrong? You must have showed a weapon. They were swearing on Allah, no, they didn't have no weapons. So the translator tells them, okay, I'll talk to the Americans for you. So then he goes, I've talked to the Americans and you can come out now. But this time, he tells them, you've got to sing a song. He teaches them a song right there on the battlefield. They're hiding behind this piece of wall singing it. He's like, no, you're off-key. The United States didn't come here to this fucked-up country to hear you motherfuckers singing off-key. He made them rehearse. So they come out. The translator was telling them to do their best, making like this was American Idol. He's yellin at them: you're being judged. Everything is cool. They're coming out, so far so good, they're singing. Everything is cool. Then, boom, we engage his friend. Now, one guy's left. The translator tells the guy, your friend was making you sound bad. Now sing it by yourself. This one's for all the marbles. How bad you want it? He sang the whole fucking thing, and we applauded.

We picked up a head on the battlefield and made somebody carry it. My sergeant put it between a body's legs. He made it wink. We took corpses and made them do nasty shit. Like sit them up, like Weekend at Bernie's, wearing shades. Or have them fuck and make a movie. Whatever you can think of. Dress them up. Play WWF. Body-slamming body bags. We shot their fuckin camels every chance we got. We shot their donkeys. I probably laughed at shit that no one would believe.

You get in trouble? the tattooed man asked.

No. Whenever somebody got killed who wasn't supposed to, we just dropped a weapon on them, or some wire, if we had to.

So you're slick.

Not so much slick as experienced. As far as that, maybe.

But tell me, how did the song go?

I'm not singing it.

We have a song like that too, I think, in my country. It's called a wedding song, the way we sing it. You tell a woman, she got two choices: you can love me for tonight, or you can marry my gun and he will love you forever.

Pulling up his clean white sweater, he showed Skinner the tattoo on his forearm.

What's that supposed to be?

She getting fucked. Real good. With a plastic bag over her head.

Skinner laughed. You're a fuckin idiot.

The handsome man laughed too. You see? You laughing. May as well enjoy it.

Who's that behind her?

There was a skeleton with a pistol aimed at the asphyxiating woman's head.

That's the best man she ever gonna know.

45

You ARE HERE FOR me at all? she asked Skinner.

What more do you want?

I feel like everything it's just my problem.

He heard this with a disturbing lack of surprise, failing to remonstrate.

I don't know what to do, if I can get married with you, if it put me in trouble, I don't know. I try to figure it out, it's okay, but it's no one I can ask. Everything cost money—

You mean, this is about money?

No, it's not about the money—

After all the times I took you out?

No, it's not money! Money, it makes me worry, but it's the small thing compared with somethings else.

In mid-sentence, she started crying, wiped her face and kept trying to talk.

Something else is more important, I know. I don't want to ask nothing out of you, out of no one, I rather to be alone than take advantage from you. I'm worry for you all this time. I see you stay inside this room and I feel scared. What happens to you, I don't know. So I try to bring you some things too. I can't do much because of money. If I have a way, I would take you to the hospital, Skinner. I would give anything I have, because if I lose you, I feel like I'm losing everything.

She kept wiping the tears off her face so she could keep talking to him.

And you hurt me, Skinner. You hurt me so much. You throw me away, leave me in the street, you run away. And you don't call me, not for two or three day. You don't think about that! You never even say sorry to me. Why not? Because you don't have to, because I'm Muslim people, immigrant? So you don't respect? If it was your mother, you would leave her like that? I give myself to you. To you maybe it's just nothing, some girl like this dirty book you read, some garbage person. Is it true?

No! he said, That's not true. I never thought of you like that. I never treated you like garbage.

You say, to get married, fine, it doesn't matter whether we do or not, like you don't care.

Treat you like garbage? he repeated, squinting at the basement wall. I never once treated you like garbage. Don't go saying I did. You want to talk about garbage, I know a little something about that, and you haven't been getting treated like garbage, not from me. I've seen a few people getting treated like garbage and it doesn't look like this. It's a little bit different from this. I'd say this is pretty good. There's a long way down from here. And I'm sorry if I'm not perfect. I'm really sorry if I ruined your plans on Saturday when I took you out, yet again, for lunch. I've done a lot of things wrong. I guess that's just another one. Have to add that in to all my other mistakes. Sorry you had to meet a fuckup. Sorry I'm not your idea of a perfect whatever. Yeah, I'm real sorry. As you sit there and tell me what you want from me. As you order me to marry you the proper way.

She rubbed her face in the crook of her elbow, muttered, I don't talk to you.

Man, he said, whew. He bit his lip, shaking his head. I don't know... No, you're gonna talk to me. You're not gonna call me a shitbag to my face. In my room. In my country. That I fought for. While you did what? Sneaked over the border? Yeah. I owe you. Here. Let me see what I got.

He took his wallet off the bedside table and threw it across the room. It hit her chest and fell on the floor. She stood up immediately to leave him.

Wait! he said, jumped up, and tried to stop her. She went crazy fighting him, kicking. He held her around the waist, pulling her back to the bed. No! she cried. They fell. Wait, wait, wait, I'm sorry—he repeated, saying it in her ear, driving his weight into her on the mattress. She headbutted him sideways, twisted under him and punched him in the head. He got on top of her, tried to pin her arms. She kneed him in the back. He winced. She stared up at him through her hair all wild around her panicked desperate face, covered in sweat and tears. They looked at each other. She kneed him in the back again where she had hurt him the first time.

Go ahead. Get it out of your system.

She kneed him again.

He frowned.

I hope it hurt, you fucking asshole. You call me NAMES? she screamed. NAMES? Sini sikey kot ghuy. She bucked and swiped at his face again. You don't know how scared you will be. I take your eye. I'm sorry, he said. She laughed at him and went wild trying to hit him.

Please don't fight, he said.

I hate you.

That's fine. I just don't want anyone getting hurt.

I hate you. You had me but now you don't. Now you will be alone. Get off me.

He got off her.

She got up off the bed and straightened up her shirt and pants, fixed her hair. He asked her what she was doing. She told him, it was finished—meaning they were.

Zooey, please don't go.

She looked right through him to the door through which she would be leaving and told him to get out of her way. His begging didn't move her. This was really it.

Skinner said, I can't believe this. I didn't know this would happen today. His voice had gotten quiet and shaky.

You get what you wanted.

It's not what I wanted.

Since he couldn't change her mind about leaving, there was one thing she should know before she left. He moved from the door. I'm not stopping you—you can go any time you want—I'm just showing you something.

She watched while he fetched his assault pack, sat down, unzipped the pouch, reached in and pulled his hand out holding a heavy military-issue handgun. It took her brain an extra second to see this.

Don't be scared, he said, pointing the weapon at his head.

Skinner, don't!

It's okay. Don't move. You're fine right there. Just listen. I want you to know something. I'm—his face cringed and tears rivered over his cheeks. He paused. I'm no good. I'm no good. I'm no fucking good. I'm no fucking good. I want to die. No one knows. I'm sorry. I'm really. He paused again. I'm sorrier than I can tell you. You deserve better. But never doubt you meant the world to me. You can go now. He closed his eyes and breathed.

Skinner, I'm coming toward you. Don't do anything. Just take calm. I touch your arm. This my hand. I am friend.

With the lightest touch, as if she were holding a nightingale in one of her mother's stories, she placed her hands on his arm and gently guided the weapon down from his head. She had to take his fingers off the handle one by one, lifted the firearm out of his grasp and set it as far away as she could in the corner.

They lay holding each other on his bed for a long time.

I say a prayer to God for us.

Thank you. Tell him I said hi.

Later he asked if she still wanted to leave him, and she shook her head.

There must be a God.

I don't know you have a gun.

I know.

Maybe we can take the bullets out.

He got up and unloaded it and put it away.

Maybe we ought to eat something.

I don't want you to buy the dinner for me again. It's not fair to you.

I didn't mean that, Zooey. Would you please share my dinner with me?

Maybe we should do something else.

Oh. Okay. You sure?

Yes. She extended her arms to him. But when they tried to make love, he had difficulty; he kept falling out of her.

It's okay. It's okay.

No it isn't.

Yes it's okay. I help you.

Finally, he was able. When he was done, they were both hot and sweaty and dirt from the mattress was embedded in their knees. He was relieved that it had worked in the end, but it had taken him a long time. He asked if she was okay, and she said that she was fine. She was going to take a shower. Night had come down on them while they had been working on the bed. The room felt filled with smoke. It was just his eyes, a loneliness. A place on earth without a power grid. A wilderness of rubble. He turned the bedside lamp on as an orange campfire against the wild. The harem-purple walls came up and he was back in Queens where the colors had been chosen by the people from whom he rented.

One thing, you better wear your clothes out there. There could be someone out there.

Someone's in the basement?

This dude comes down. You never know.

Okay.

Used to treating everything outside the immediate confines of the sleeping area as a public space, she thought nothing of this and acted accordingly, exiting the room fully dressed, taking along his Camp Manhattan towel.

After she had showered, dressed, and brushed her wet hair, he took her to Fratelli's for pizza. While they ate, he reached across the orange table, trying to reach for something of hers. It felt like a particularly dark night. He settled for her elbow. She was using both hands to hold up the triangular pizza slice, which kept buckling in the middle, like a corpse being carried to a helicopter. He held her elbow, watched her chest move as she performed the functions of life—breathing, eating.

It's just the pills.

I know. You are a young strong man.

Today everything was weird.

The sweet sharp pain that foreshadows weeping visited him again in the throat and eyes. He put his head down, glanced sideways at his reflection in the vertical mirrored strips that covered the wall of the pizza parlor. His eyes looked like someone had sprayed roach spray in them, an allergic response. He thought of chafed, reddened mucous membranes after the friction of sex.

Did you notice anything when we were... ?

Just you are tired.

No, I mean, did you notice anything? Did you hear anything?

Just I hear the sound we making.

Nothing else?

What else?

Like something outside the room.

She looked up at the ceiling, at the ceiling fan, remembering.

I heard some sound. I think like somethings falling on the ground. You think someone is there?

Apparently he did think so. She asked who he thought could have done such a thing. Skinner asked if she remembered how he had been having things disappear—a magazine, some medication, his six-pack of beer? He thought the guy who was stealing from him was spying on them as well. Skinner knew he came down in the basement because he had seen him under the sink.

He's been in my room to fix the boiler. Right after that, Mrs. Murphy complains about my room to me. Remember how I cleaned it up? That was him. So I know he's down there, he's seen everything. When I go out, when I come back, there's always something moved like he was down there. And none of this ever happened before him. This all started happening after he showed up. The other day, I saw him out here and it's like there's something on between us. Like something's gonna happen.

Why he does this things to you?

I don't know what his problem is. You ever see this guy? He's like this pretty big dude, real tall, walks up and down like he's going boing-boing on springs, like he wants to kill somebody. He's got a little beard right here.

Yes, she said. I know him.

You do?

One day I come to find you and you aren't here. He open the door. I think it's him.

Really? You serious? You know it was him?

She said she thought so.

What'd he say to you?

He try to invite me inside.

What'd you do?

I say no. I go away. But he try to convince me.

He came onto you?

Maybe, yes, I think so. Skinner's face contorted. But, she told Skinner, it didn't mean anything to her. It wasn't the only time a man had tried to talk to her in Flushing. A lot of man try to trick the woman.

Like who?

This one boy, he call me Ma. It's very funny. I think, You call to your mother?

What was he, a black dude?

He is black. Hey, Ma! he say.

What'd you say?

I have to go.

What was that, on Main Street?

Yes, in Chinatown. Nothing happen. I think he just look at me as I walk away. Say some things, Ma! like he call his mother.

I mean, I can understand that. That's normal cause of how you look and everything.

She asked him if he felt all right, and he said he just felt tired.

When they got home, they were teetering on the edge of sadness again. He asked her if they could lie down on the bed together and hug each other until she had to go. They held each other for quite a while, keeping the bedside light on for comfort. Do you love me? he asked. She said she wouldn't be lying in his bed with him if she didn't love him. His jaw flexed, his eyes squeezed and a pulse of tears ran down his nose, a thin stream that dried sixty seconds later. She held his head, rubbing the back of his neck where his haircut ended.

I love you, he said.

She did not respond and he wondered if the words sounded as empty to her as they had to him. He stroked her back and hip. There was nothing he could say that was equal to the curve of her hip.

No man can touch me except you.

That's right, he said.

At eleven o'clock, he sat up suddenly and said, Wait a minute. Went and grabbed his boots, told her not to move. Stay right here, I want to see something. Before he left, he got the gun and then he ran upstairs, leaving her distressed and confused.

He ran around the house and came up the alley on the other side to the grating above their window. She stood on the bed and whispered, What you doing?

I'm looking at our privacy. Can you see me up here?

No. I barely see you.

All right. Just a minute. I'm coming back.

He came back around the house. She heard him locking the house door after he came back in, then thumping down the stairs in his boots and checking everywhere: the bathroom, the kitchen, the closet, all the corners.

What happened?

I heard something.

She asked him please to put the gun away. She was really upset again.

I know I heard something outside. With the bedside light on, it isn't good. You can see everything from up there.

46

IT WAS A LONG ride and she had to transfer twice to get to the Bronx. The white people got off and the blacks and Spanish got on and stayed on. The train filled, got dark with dark people, and smelled like coconut skin-sweat and cherry incense. From Westchester Avenue, she took a bus east to Soundview. The bus traveled down an eight-lane avenue overlooked by project housing on a human-dwarfing scale. She rang the bell and got off. Each tower looked like a battleship planted in the ground and sticking up in the sky, rusting, and she counted twenty of them. She asked directions of a Haitian woman wearing church shoes. Go on down pass, she said. The woman had a deeply seamed face. A concrete staircase led down a dusty hill to where there were low, flat-roofed buildings, forklifts in the street. At the bottom, she found the address she was looking for, a factory.

There were bars over the windows and ripped dresses over the bars, so you couldn't see inside. Strips of ripped fabric were tied everywhere, to the grates and wire mesh, the handle of the door covered in Spanish graffiti. The walls inside were written up in magic marker. Looking for a way in, she went inside a hallway like a cattle chute that ended in a steel mesh door. On the drop ceiling, she saw the writing: Viva Ei. There was no way in—the door was locked. Through the holes in the steel mesh, she heard the fans blowing and the machines running and saw the boxes, the piles of fabric in different colors, and the women at the tables. Going back outside, she passed a flex gate through which the interior was visible, but it was padlocked. A starved man with the cancerous sun-beaten skin of a farmworker was taping up boxes, cutting the packing tape with a tape-handled razor. He didn't look at her when she asked the way in.

Around the corner, she found another barred entrance that had been left ajar. Chinese was written in magic marker all over the plaster. It said: This factory's phone number is—and the numbers were crossed out, and there were more numbers and more names and messages in Chinese. Outside an alcove, beneath the pipes, someone had written: You cannot have a bowel movement in the toilet or you will be responsible for cleaning.

She stepped over cardboard boxes piled next to the breaker boxes, a copy of the minimum wage law taped to the bricks, and the whirring became louder and she saw the rows and rows of tables, the women back to front, working barefoot, pressing the pedals, operating the lever with a knee. Someone's radio was playing and you could barely hear it in the pervasive hushing of the fans. The sewing machines clicked like telegraph machines. At the far back of the room, under the rafters, next to the padded ironing boards used to flatten the garments before they were boxed, there were piles of empty cardboard boxes and other junk, old sewing machines and metal chairs with strips of rotted fabric tied to them like sodden headscarves, and more garments piled in canvas bins, property of the postal service.

The factory smelled like old wood and cardboard. There was cardboard under the machines down with their bare feet to catch the oil from the Juki sewers furred in dust, strips of lucky red fabric tied to the spindle bobbins.

There were about seventeen women working, a few in their twenties or thirties, most appearing older. A large number of them wore glasses. They did not look at her, keeping their eyes on their work, backs hunched, the impression of a brassiere strap visible across their hunched backs. It was hot and they favored sleeveless rayon blouses or t-shirts. She saw them going gray.

One who was still young got up to go to the filthy refrigerator, apparently to look at her lunch in its red plastic bag, and her t-shirt showed a cartoon of someone sleeping next to the caption: Wake At Your Own Risk. She wore knee-length shorts like Zou Lei, was very thin, almost red-skinned, and had a jutting jaw and short wild hair, tripping along when she walked in her plastic sandals. She went into the bathroom you couldn't use for a bowel movement and came out with a wet paper towel, which she rubbed over her skinny arms to cool off in front of a fan. She glanced at Zou Lei and gestured, spoke, gestured, barely able to be heard over the fan, saying:

Behind you, the man. See him.

Zou Lei turned and saw a man leaning back in an office chair with his feet up on a desk with an unplugged rice cooker on it. The wall above him had Ms. Asia Swimsuit Beauty contestants cut out from the paper taped to the bricks. The white-skinned women posed in one-piece bikinis, one hand to their 1960s hairdos, one hand to the hip. The man was wearing distressed jeans that were nearly iridescent.

He looked at her sideways and took a call on his cell phone. When he was done talking, he stood and felt his pockets for a lighter, picked up a pack of White Cotton cigarettes off the desk, put one in his mouth, felt his hips again for a lighter, and took the unlit cigarette out of his mouth and scuffed his way to the office, his long arms hanging from his spine like wet laundry, as if everything was too much for him in this heat.

She followed him into the office, which was a small shed, and it was ice cold. There was an air conditioner set at sixty degrees blowing frigid air into the closet-sized space. He sighed and rotated his lighter in his hand, tapping it on the desk and rotating it with his fingers. His pinkie finger had a long sharp nail. He never looked at her directly. They were surrounded by boxes of main labels to be stitched into garments and tubs of machine attachments, needles, Pegasus bobbins and screws, fan belts, a jug of 80-weight gear oil, rolls of thread in black, white, blue, and glint, a fax machine with its green light winking, and a mini fridge. He spoke Toisan Cantonese; Mandarin annoyed him. She agreed with everything, even the things she couldn't understand. She kept the military training to herself.

He asked: You a seamstress?

Naturally, she said.

He didn't seem to care. He ran the different departments down for her: Lak gwat. He switched to English, annoyed she didn't understand. Marrow. Baby hem. Binding. Pearl. Fifty cent a piece. Maybe ten cent. It depend. The different department grab the bundle. Sometime work overnight if they have to push the order out.

There were no days off. If you didn't show up, you didn't earn, that was all.

Any question?

She had no questions that she could ask him. There was no final statement made as to whether she was hired or not, or whether she would report to work tomorrow. This was neither asked nor answered. The conversation ended when she realized that he wasn't going to say anything else to her.

One last thing happened. As she was trying to leave the building, she saw a man pulling the gate shut and putting a bike chain through it, locking them in, and she started yelling involuntarily: Hey! What're you doing? I'm leaving!

He was an older guy, a bachelor type in an undershirt, the kind who knew the way things worked and didn't have a problem with it. He gave her a look of crafty amusement.

Relax. The other door is open there, he said.

———

I wanted to speak to you about something, Skinner.

What's that?

A prostitute from Flushing came here looking for you.

What do you mean? When?

I'm not sure of the day.

Wait a minute. I'm kind of confused. I don't know any prostitutes from Flushing. I'm trying to figure out who it could have been. Was she Asian-looking?

I don't know. My son said he spoke with her.

And he knows her how?

My son said he recognized her from Flushing.

You say he recognized her?

That's correct. He recognized her. Coming to this house, looking for you.

Skinner had no reply to this.

I just thought you should know.

When he was lying in bed, he had a dream that someone was outside his window grating wearing MOP gear, releasing sarin down into the basement, that the gas was dripping all over him in his bed and he was breathing it in, and that by the time he woke up, it was already too late to save him. He gave himself both atropine shots to no avail. The green camouflaged figure came down into the basement in hood and gas mask and took Zou Lei away into the other room where Skinner couldn't see what was happening. He was dying, paralyzed. He could hear her screaming and the table banging. Then she was brought back in with her head hanging. The figure straddled her like a goat on her hands and knees and began to strangle her with a hose.

This went on for an extended period of time, punctuated by rests, during which one of the things she said was No. Then her air was cut off and her face went purple and her legs straightened out behind her. Skinner began weeping in his sleep. Stop, he sobbed. Don't do that to her.

He watched the man apply pressure until she stopped shaking, and then continue it far past that point, jamming a broom handle in the garrote to torque it. The man jammed it in and left it tight for several minutes. Her personality, her personhood were long lost. The garrote made the head bloated. A distorted face that was not the way she had ever looked before when it was her.

———

When Jimmy was with his crew, they saw Skinner coming and they waited until he got close. Guado was prepared to say something or do something. The point was to keep him guessing. What they said might be friendly. Have a good day, guy. Or they said something you could barely hear and half a block later you knew it was an insult. Sometimes just a word. Your brain would unfold it while you were walking. Or, depending, they would let you know you were being sized-up, and when you showed the slightest reaction, tensing up your shoulders or the way you walked, somebody would yell, Don't fuck with me! all crazy.

Skinner got closer and Guado murmured, He ain't shit. Then louder: What's up, big boy!

Nothing, Skinner said.

Jimmy: A little fuckee suckee. And then Jimmy watched Skinner's face as he kept walking.

It was perfectly true that Jimmy had a few things that did not belong to him and that one of them was a Hustler that had been purchased at a PX on a military base, the PX being next to the pharmacy where you received your Zoloft, Ambien, Valium, Risperidone, your psychotics and your anti-psychotics.

One of the girls bore a rough resemblance to her in that she had brown hair, the same small build, though she was perhaps a little airbrushed. Either way, she had not heard his footsteps on the basement stairs when she was getting done. Based on how she sounded, he thought she was uneducated and lower class. A beautiful feminine lady of an exotic arousal. The vet, her boyfriend, was a punk.

Once, the kid had tried to confront him, so to speak. Jimmy was prowling around the basement and the knothead came out of his room and started whining about how I know you took my shit.

But there was no nothing behind it, which is what Jimmy expected, so he did more little things as little tests, just as games, feeling all along, if you can't take it, you shouldn't be living here. You can't even show your woman a good time.

On his stairs, Skinner found a business card for an escort service. It said Outcalls Only, there was a phone number, Flushing, New York, and the picture was a tan Asian woman in a thong, black-and-white palm trees. For Perfect Ass, it said.

Skinner kept it as evidence, storing it in his assault pack thinking, After I waste this motherfucker, I'll show them.

47

For a series of days on and around July 4th, when Monroe was at family picnics having roast pork with relatives he disdained, they let her work the front. By sometime in the afternoon, her feet would hurt from standing up all day and she would check the time, hipshot and bored in her tight jeans and the always-dirty food-encrusted uniform shirt. She dug the ladle into the rice, folded the rice over and glanced out over the counter, barely hearing the monotonous roar of the customers ordering in Chinese, the trays clattering, the kitchen racket, the syrupy pop songs. Only her predicament existed to her. She went round the elements of her life again: Skinner, papers, cops, marriage, lawyer, money, job, housing, Skinner, his illness, money. Every planet in the orbit was another unknown. At night, she turned the fan on in the hot plywood shed and couldn't sleep until the room cooled off toward morning. Her head hurt. Periodically, day or night, she suffered a jab of panic: What if someone locked her up again just because he thought it was his job? And then she saw the cell. She tried to breathe and think of what to do. You will at least try to do something, she told herself. You will go with Skinner and get married. But should I get an ID in my legal name first? A good one? This reintroduced the problem of arrest. Or getting robbed or ripped-off. And money. Money. She was running out of money. If I can't pay rent, then what? She lifted her foot and held the instep of her sneaker to stretch her thigh and a tremor such as you might see on a horse's flank shot down her leg.

Above all, she wanted to do something she could control. She wanted to reject every solution that involved going through a government office. It wasn't realistic, but she wished she could reduce everything to the simple physical test of running away.

That evening she went to see Skinner and he met her in a state of paranoia, pacing back and forth in the sunset shadows on the corner. The buildings across from the train tracks cast walls of gloom over the avenue. He greeted her by looking around her at the empty street, the train tracks, the sniper positions in the windows, the roofs, hitching up his beltless jeans and saying come on, let's get inside. Then he went around the basement checking their perimeter, looking in the bathroom, peeking around the corner into the kitchen area, opening his closet and gazing at the boiler.

To her horror, she saw he had the gun in his hand, and she told him to put it away or she would leave.

He had taken something that made him manic, she thought.

We have to try to take it easy, she said, to make the right decision. She told him she had decided that, if he was still willing, getting married was probably the best thing they could do to ensure that she wouldn't be deported and that they shouldn't delay any longer. What did he think?

He was all for it. Good to go. Let's go now. You never knew what might happen tomorrow.

She pointed out they couldn't go now, the office would be closed.

Then we'll go tomorrow. You never knew what was gonna happen the day after tomorrow. Or the day after that. Or the day after that. They had to do it soon. He had a plan too. You wanna hear? I've decided I'm going back!

Back to where?

Where else? The Sand Box. I'm done here. Making all these thinking errors. All the problems. I used to be a highly locked-on soldier. I need to get back in there. And I know when I do, it's going to be the best thing for everyone, instead of stewing over it from three thousand miles away.

He told her that in his first firefight he had been more excited than at any point in his life, before or since.

He told her he wanted to go back as a contractor. He would make one hundred forty thousand dollars in one year. Their problems would be over, he said.

Then the next day, Sassoon was back at work and Zou Lei was consigned to dishwashing duty again. As ever, she was reviewing her situation. Today was Friday. She would take action and go to the marriage office with Skinner first thing on Monday even if she had to miss a day of work. That was the first priority. The marriage registration fee was forty dollars. Her rent, a hundred dollars for the week, was due every Monday; so she needed one hundred forty dollars on Monday, plus another twenty dollars to eat. Payday was the following Friday. She didn't know what they would be paying her exactly—she expected to be shortchanged—but as long as she had enough to live on with enough left over to pay the lawyer to open her case, she could then work on getting another job. Other jobs might be out-of-state—you had to go where the work was. Could she travel back and forth to see her lawyer and for court? No, she thought. She had to stay here. She'd look for another restaurant job in the city. Money wouldn't be a problem if Skinner made one hundred forty thousand dollars, but that wasn't going to happen. He had been on cocaine or amphetamines, she thought. Maybe she could get him to invest in a vendor cart and they could work together selling shaokao right here in Flushing. The investment for a cart was ten thousand dollars. They could get the license in his name. She saw them working together at the top of the hill, living in their own apartment with a refrigerator and TV. How clean she'd keep it! Together they would go to the gym.

Zhang Zhuojin came over to Zou Lei at eleven-thirty and said: You better talk to someone. That boy is squeezing you out.

She went to check the schedule. All her days were gone.

At lunch, the illegal women talked about it.

Better ask for justice from the boss.

Speak a sentence of justice to him.

Speak to him. She should, shouldn't she?

She still has hope. The boss likes her.

The boss likes her and Sassoon likes the boy.

An old leopard ensnaring a young lynx.

Talk to Polo. Shake your flowers and branches at him.

Zou Lei went up front to talk to Sassoon. The high school kid was standing right there laughing with Angela. What you want? Sassoon said, and the others turned to listen. Zou Lei said, Nothing. I forget.

She stole a piece of steak and ate it surreptitiously in the back corridor where the deliveries came in and the Mexicans were cutting vegetables.

Chinita! Cuál es tu comida preferida?

Adiós, she told them, and went to shake their hands after she was done eating and had wiped her hands off with the napkin she had held the steak in.

Welbe put down his knife and held her hand. Where are you going? he asked in Spanish. In English: Where? He smiled off at possible places beyond the walls—an engraved cross on his front tooth. She noticed she was a hair taller than he was.

I find out, she said.

He was in his basement dreaming. He was aware of the presence of life even though it was not directly audible through the structures of buildings. His mind was aware. On the other side of the shingles, tiles and sheathing, the reinforced block, gypsum, Douglas fir and paper, there were people breathing, watching TV, wanting to live. They had vital signs, blood pressure, pulse. Shine a light in their eyes and their pupils would contract unless they had a brain injury or were in shock.

They were locked up tight right now, but if a firefight exploded on this street right now—and Skinner could see the tracers leaping overhead, that furious popping, popping up like burning golf balls, stapling through autobodies, glass exploding—you would hear them screaming for it to stop. In the morning you would see the blood on the splintered walls. You would see them come outside blinking, coming together, picking through the sharp things, wood and metal, talking about what to do. Standing in groups, they haven't slept.

His dream evolved. The firing had stopped. He was walking through the wreckage of a street, glass crunching beneath his boots. Blood was mixed in the glass, sometimes bright and shining red, almost orange in the air. He saw the inside of a car splashed and splattered with flesh. There was nothing human left. What had been done to the bodies was not possible to reconstruct. They had been wrenched by giant hands, smashed, severed, filled with gas, perforated, burned, flung across space. A limb lay on a seat—arm or leg, no telling. He saw clothing. A pile of organs, a liver in the red clothes. A vertebra in the driver's seat. Everything had been blasted free of its identity—shirt, pants, or robe—male or female—you couldn't tell from clumped wet hair.

The vehicles were transformed as well, the heat having created rainbows in the body paint. Past the cars, he saw holes in the buildings, in the storefronts, tunnels leading in, glass blown out, brand-new sneakers in the street.

He was not alone. There was a crater in the sidewalk. He lay down and put his arm inside and clasped hands with the occupant of the pit and pulled him out. His body lifted easily—Skinner had the necessary strength. It was his friend at last. They shared a cigarette.

The next store was a Dunkin Donuts. They went inside, cleared away the glass with their boots, picked their way around the dead woman who was stuffed behind the counter and started taking donuts out of the tray.

They were starved and hungry.

Careful, dog.

Sconyers picked glass off Skinner's donut before he bit it.

Is there coffee?

They found chocolate milk in the drink case. They found a booth to sit in at the back and lay their weapons on the table.

Goddamn this is a score.

Hell yeah, doggie.

Skinner put his boots up and crossed his ankles. His boot toes were brown with dried gore. He tapped them together.

I'm glad you didn't die, man. Everything's good in my world now, he said.

Skinner's friend had changed since he had seen him last. In the dream, the colorful tattoos that had always decorated Sconyers' arms had apparently spread, now flowing up his throat and covering his face in black spirals, scorpions, and thorns.

———

After she left the mall, she went to Footlocker and asked for a pair of Asics. The sales associate who helped her was so silent and unspeaking that she almost thought he didn't speak English, or that he spoke a different dialect. It turned out he only talked to a narrow group of people—other blacks with whom he was friends. He looked right through her when she asked if they had a smaller size. Then his face came alive when someone came out of the stockroom and whooped.

He hollered back, laughing and joking and full of comprehension. He told her to hold on, and went away.

She tried the shoes on and bounced on her toes. They made her feet feel spring-loaded. She stomped lightly on the carpeted floor.

The sales associate came back. Whenever she said anything, he pretended to be confused. What happened? he asked, meaning, What did you say?

How much the discount?

He wasn't sure.

She tried to ask if you needed to have a social to work here.

Yeah, he said, and took the sneaker box up to the register.

She paid in cash, giving the young woman at the register a one hundred dollar bill. Zou Lei's pay was issued in cash, usually in hundreds and fifties. The young woman, who had very dark skin, bumps on her cheeks, and a weave made of glossy black Chinese hair, took the bill. Then she seemed to forget what she was doing. She didn't know how to ring the sale. She called out, How much do you take off on these? No one answered her. She made a snapping noise with her mouth. Her white eyes rolling at the boys, she murmured, They stupid.

A less-shy girl yelled, Yo! Malik!

What?

She asking you something. Tell her.

Malik said, No idea.

This whole time, the hundred dollar bill was in the woman's hand and Zou Lei was watching it.

A manager came—a bigger man than all of them—an overweight unshaven man with a sloping head and sloping shoulders as if his entire body had melted down to his waist, and even his features had been affected, his eyes angling down, the sides of his mouth angling down like a picture of glumness—and then he spoke with this mouth in a businesslike and professionally courteous, corporate way. He told the woman what to do. The hundred dollars went into the drawer. The woman put the change on the counter. Zou Lei counted it. The woman said, Next.

Zou Lei wore the sneakers outside. They felt wonderful, comfortable and weightless, and as soon as she walked out of the store, she wanted to go back and ask for her money back.

You are stupid. You are so stupid.

48

SHE THOUGHT HE WAS taking her for something to eat and at that moment she believed she had never been so relieved to see him. They passed the Sheraton LaGuardia, the parking lot, a nightclub called the Ends of the Earth KTV, a play on words in Chinese, a pun on: the earth is wide.

She wanted to know where they were going, but he didn't say.

They came to a block of three-story buildings and black iron fire escapes. There was an escort service on the top floor. One of the units had been sealed by the city marshal. In the basement, immigrants met to play mahjong for friendship and association, for business planning. They put spirit money in a brazier. They burned a car—a purple BMW the size of a shoebox that they bought from a Taoist temple. The temple specialized in helping you get what you wanted in the next life. They poked the ashes of the BMW with a metal rod to read the future.

Skinner opened a dark-stained wooden door.

Go on.

She went into the social club with her arms crossed.

Have a drink.

I don't drink.

Why not?

I don't need it. I think I have to make some decision.

You can have a drink. Since when does that interfere with a decision?

She was sitting on the stool like a statue. A bad feeling had developed between them. She got down from the bar stool and left.

Skinner caught up with her on Main Street, catching her by the elbow and turning her around.

What are you doing?

He was making an effort to contain his anger.

I am leaving.

What for?

You don't need me.

What do you mean I don't need you?

She crossed her arms and stared away from him and wouldn't talk. Night was falling. He asked her what he did wrong. She didn't say anything. He was left looking at the side of her face. Her jaw was set. He had been angry to begin with. Her silence had an effect on him and he started goading her, insulting her on the street. Tell me what your problem is. He started breathing, waiting for her to speak. He had become enraged. You're so goddamn perfect. Tell me one reason why your opinion matters.

His voice rose.

Tell me what you've done. Why I should care.

Zou Lei blinked but didn't speak.

A Chinese man noticed them fighting and watched.

You too good to talk to me now?

Skinner took a step back to protect her. He was afraid to be near her when he lost it. He waited for her to say something—stop me, he thought—but she didn't and he ignited.

Hey! he bellowed. Hey! You motherfucking look at me! He had his face an inch from her face. I treated you like a human being!

She flinched. All over the street, people started looking.

He wheeled and walked into a turbaned construction worker dead-on, shoulder-butting him. The man fell back a step.

Hey, buddy!

Is there a problem? Is there? Is there?

The Sikh swore and threw his Sawzall in his truck.

Black kids pointed out the scene to their friends, smiling silently.

Skinner on his way to nowhere, sailing down Roosevelt, kicked a sheet of plywood that leaned against the parking lot fence and it made a deep reverberating echo in the street.

He would probably have broken a window and got himself arrested.

A force flew by—Zou Lei—she stopped and blocked his path. The sight of her gaze hurt his eyes. She was nearly choking. The words came spitting and wrenching out of her. He understood nothing, and he realized she was speaking in another language.

I don't know what you're saying.

Don't know what you're saying, she mocked.

Then he blinked and she was halfway across the street.

Wait a minute, Skinner said, and took off after her.

She broke into a run.

Skinner ran after her, thinking he would catch her inside ten yards.

But instead of letting him catch her, she started accelerating, and within seconds, they were in a dead heat with her in the lead. She was leading them towards the projects, the derricks, and the water. There were a scattering of people coming the other way, and they moved aside from the force of the two runners, Zou Lei light and spring-loaded and Skinner on her tail, his desert boots whopping the pavement.

She made the corner and took them between the projects on the left and the unseen water on the right. She took them under a high stone bridge that crossed the avenue and led them uphill, the projects left behind, and the blackness of the canal no longer visible. To their right, across the wide boulevard, there was now a line of two-story houses and then, spotlit in snow-white sodium lights, were warehouses in sheet-metal buildings the size of airplane hangars. The cash and carry. On the left, they were running by store windows, some of them lit, some of them dark. Zou Lei fled through squares of light and dark and Skinner followed.

The pace of the run was now starting to tell on him. All the symptoms started. His breathing was coming hard, his legs were getting heavy, his blood was thickening, caramelizing like sugar in a hot pan and turning to acid. The feeling of slow-drowning beset him, the knowing you're not going to catch her. He could hear his boots hitting the sidewalk as he hung on.

He looked ahead at Zou Lei to see if she was fatiguing. Through his sweat-burning eyes, his viewfinder bouncing up and down, he could see her running light and whiplike.

The warehouses were back there somewhere. The terrain was changing. She took him across a parking lot in front of a diner. He caught a blurred glimpse of Steaks – Chops – Seafood and the words stayed with him in a dumb chant until he forgot them in his battle to keep pace. Beyond the diner, there were areas of a greater, bluer darkness that he could not interpret and he tried to guess where she was taking him, but he couldn't think and he stopped trying.

She's fucking fast, he thought.

They were crossing an area where the asphalt had been stripped off the boulevard and he was thinking: be careful not to step in a hole—but not acting on the thought, unable to do anything but keep going, balanced on the edge of pain he could barely make himself tolerate, and just lucky he didn't step wrong and pop his ankle.

Now they were running under a scaffolding framed out of two-by-fours and plywood. She cleared the end of the wooden tunnel before he did and he lost sight of her for several seconds and then cleared the tunnel himself and picked her up again, perceiving the running woman as a shadow on the greater field of darkness.

They were far from the lights of stores. They were in a concrete expanse of road, a highway rising from the darkness, headlights shooting up the ramp in bursts like tracer rounds. She tromped over the caved-in sidewalk and veered out into the deserted roadway. Skinner made out trees, the small pale flags of littered paper blown against a fence, a field. A board rattled underfoot, then he had crossed the roadway, and he felt his boots thudding on dirt.

Now there was the chance of losing her because the field was blackness all around. As he ran, he panned his eyes for silhouette or movement and, seeing nothing, kept running blind. He felt his legs slowing because he could not see her and he was lost. But he kept milling onward, now hoping not to catch her but just not to lose her—to stay with her and follow her and meet up with her at the end, wherever that would be.

His night vision began accumulating enough to see the ever-shifting patch of ground in front of him where his boot was landing, dry grass over dirt. He sank into the mindless drone of dropping one boot in front of the other and striving for nothing more than staying with his team. When his legs slowed, he sped them up again. Still he couldn't see her.

From time to time, he raised his head. Saturated with dark energy, the sky glowed like a television screen after the power gets turned off. On either wing, he saw distant lights and buildings. He was running in an endless field. He tripped but didn't fall. It cost too much to swear. Even to think what he would say. His horrendous breathing was disconnected from him. The next time he raised his head, he saw amber vapor lights coming through the trees. He now caught sight of a silhouette the size of a front sight post migrating laterally against the amber glow and knew it was her. He huffed the sweat off his lip. The front sight post disappeared and emerged again, separating from the ink blot of a tree, light shimmering like mercury around the branches.

Houses came in view between the trees, a street bathed in the spectrum of the lights. He could not see a fence but learned that there was one when he saw her figure rise and hang above the dark earth. Then he blinked and she was in the street among the houses. Not wanting to lose her, he pounded after her until the fence appeared like something being brought to the surface of water. He hit the fence and was climbing over it, the wire clashing and rattling.

He dropped on the pavement without breaking an ankle, his heart rate soaring from going over the fence. Another street met this one in a T. He went the way she had gone, the sweat raining off his face, elbows, wrists, chin, nose—every ledge of himself.

Nearly out of balance, he careened onto a long ribbon of road rolling downhill and uphill through pools of shadow and peach-violet light. A pair of dots bouncing up and down: the heels of her running shoes. His brain deciphered the rest of the figure from the heels. A figure traveling steadily down the ribbon of road ahead of him.

He chased her into hypnosis. The road kept rolling through quiet houses with nothing to jerk him out of his run-dream. The scenery evolved in phases. The ghetto went away. The lawns got bigger. For a time, maybe a mile, maybe two, he saw high shaped dark hedges and mini mansions. There was no sidewalk. You weren't supposed to come here from somewhere else. Later, the hedges went away and the lawns shrank back down to postage stamps. The graffiti came back—on the side of a groceria. Impressions bounced off him as if he were drunk. A pickup idling. A dude in a sleeveless shirt coming out of the groceria with a six-pack, noticing Skinner, connecting him to the girl who had just run by a second before, and wondering if he was some nut who was trying to hurt her.

Losing the will to keep running, Skinner was bargaining with himself. Twenty minutes since the park. Three miles. He put the pain away. The pain came back. Five more minutes. Five more minutes and come see me again. The pain came back every five steps. He put it away. Come on, he said. The pain was rising. She must be fuckin going faster. I'll hang for another five minutes. He heard himself wheezing harder beneath the flogging rhythm of the run.

Just from here to there, he thought, picking a house in his view-finder. Then forgetting which one. He was down to bargaining sec-ond-by-second, his pride slipping. Everything on him was slamming, every organ. Couldn't keep track of anything. His shoulder whacked the side mirror of a parked van. If there had been an IED in front of him, he would have stepped on it. It would have hurt too much to change course. His legs were quitting. All he could do was run in a straight line and now he was losing even that.

At the end of the street, she turned the corner and this defeated him. He couldn't run anymore, he had to limp. Try and keep mov-ing. Stay with her. He tried to shuffle. He made himself jog to the corner.

There she was, hands on hips, face dripping, walking in a circle in the roadway.

Skinner walked towards her, and even this distance seemed like a long one to traverse and gave him time to wonder if she would be a stranger to him now because during the run she had been a distant figure without a face.

Hey, he said.

He hobbled towards her. Hey. Hey, he said. Can I talk to you? Twisted his shirt and a pint of water splattered on the pavement. I didn't mean any of that.

Not any of it, he said.

I'm so stupid.

Baby?

She paused in her circling and bent to touch her toes. Tight jeans from behind, anatomical view. When she raised up, she flipped her wet hair back. It slapped like a rope. He couldn't for the life of him remember what he had been angry about. He was alive, heart still beating.

Steam rising from them in the vapor light.

49

He kept apologizing to her. She didn't say much of anything to him except that she was tired and needed water. They stopped at a bodega on 41st Road and she waited outside while he went in. Numb after her marathon, she wondered if she should leave him there, but she couldn't.

He came out with a water, spilling it in his hurry to open it for her as if she were a casualty he was tending, and she took the bottle from him and drank the entire liter down, finding she wanted it more desperately the more she drank.

Will you come back with me?

Lead the way, she indicated.

They went back to his house, their slick sweat congealing, turning into a grit-sweat syrup, hamstrings stiffening, chaffed skin beginning to burn in their sogging clothes, which exuded a sharp ketone rankness. The adrenaline faded out of her. She asked him if she could use the shower when they were inside and he said of course.

From the shower, she heard him talking to the pizza man.

When she got out, Skinner gave her one of his t-shirts to wear and she sat on the edge of his mattress, her wet hair smelling like shampoo and her bare legs crossed, wearing his t-shirt like a woman in a short dress at a party, noncommittally observing her surroundings. The pizza came and Skinner opened the box for her and held it on his knees.

She told him to eat as well.

You ran my dick in the dirt.

Yeah?

I'm not gonna lie. You kicked my ass. I haven't been running like I should. The smoking's catching up with me.

You said many times you should quit.

Yeah, I did say that.

Yes. You said many things.

I meant them.

Of course, you meant them.

I stayed with you on the run no matter how bad it was, didn't I?

Because you feel guilty maybe, because you yell at me.

Yeah, that's exactly why. I do feel guilty. I didn't want to do anything I did.

Maybe I didn't want to go in jail, but I did it anyway. It's many things I didn't want to do. It's life. I think number one thing for me, I get the job. It could be out-of-state. I get a job include the room, include the meal.

He put the pizza box aside and kneeled in front of her.

Wait a minute.

No, Skinner, I don't hate you, but I have to make my life.

Zooey, listen.

She didn't want to listen. He said she didn't have to go. She didn't understand: he would give her everything. When she said she wouldn't take whatever this everything was that he was offering, he made her listen again, urging her to stop making refusals. He would not relent; he finally got her to listen. He gripped her hips and shook her slightly until she finally gazed down at him.

I'll explain what everything means. I've got some money in the bank, Zooey. He put his wallet on the floor at her feet. It's the rest of what they paid me. I'm giving it to you. These are my keys to this room. I can sleep in the field. I don't give a fuck, but you can't be out there. I'm giving this to you. That's what I mean by everything. I mean everything. He put his keys next to his wallet on the floor at her feet. I mean all the pizza, the fridge, whatever's in it, everything. My cigarettes, he said. My laptop. I want you to have everything I can give you. I have no other plans. I'll get married tomorrow. We'll go to the lawyer. That's what I mean by everything. Look— He looked around the room for her Asics. He held them up in one hand like a shoe salesman. Lawyer. He set them by the wallet and keys. He picked up his desert boots. Marriage. He set them with the sneakers and told her to look down at this diagram of objects he was presenting her with.

There are things I can't do, so let me at least do what I can.

Money, keys to a room, a legal arrangement of uncertain efficacy: a significant but short list. She didn't know whether it was more right to refuse or to accept this everything that he was so ready to part with. And what was he keeping for himself? His drugs, the gun that was hidden somewhere among the camouflage gear in the corner? There was still a lot of unfilled space on the black tiled floor between her feet.

He touched the wallet again.

I've got several thousand dollars. I started with ten. I wish I had it all for you.

I can't accept.

Yeah you can.

He took his bank card and started pushing it into her hand, repeating the PIN to her. She told him to stop, reaching down and touching his stubble on which his sweat had dried leaving behind salt.

All right, he said, but remember it.

She teared-up suddenly and looked away.

I'll remember, she said.

Then she told him: Put the card away properly or it will get lost.

I will, but tell me you don't hate me.

He tucked the bank card in her shoe.

I don't hate anyone.

Do you hate me?

No.

He crawled up into the bed with her.

Wait.

She moved the pizza box.

They lay down together in his bed and one more time before he fell asleep, he asked her if everything was okay. I feel your heart beating like you're worried. You're not worried are you?

No.

This isn't that bad of a situation.

I know.

Goodnight kiss, he said.

She kissed him.

They slept together on his bed.

As dawn began to cast its light into the basement, they became visible. They were lying facing each other, their heads together, knees almost touching, like two apostrophes.

The light strengthened gradually and silently, changing from gray to rose to gold. The soft gold sunlight and the fluttering leafy shadows stretched across the bed and the bodies of the sleepers and the walls, making the bedroom into a forest glade, beautiful and hushed. She must have seen this vision. She dreamed that they were running in the forest.

50

AT SEVEN O'CLOCK THAT morning, a Saturday morning, he woke up, and the first thing he knew was that he was the same as yesterday. He checked himself: The body that lay curled against him was an insufferable weight that inspired no feeling. Except that she was a burden. Except irritability. He did not want to be awake. The faint sound of a neighbor talking on the quiet street enraged him. The mixture of sun and leafy shadows on the walls of his room, which another observer would have found calm and lovely, made him think of rubble, of a broken stressful world that could not be kept away by something as flimsy as a wall and that he was incompetent to handle and from which no one could ever be safe. He was exhausted and had a headache and couldn't think clearly enough to figure out what he should medicate himself with to get through the morning.

It became clear to him that he was in trouble: he could not let her see his state of mind. If she lost faith in him, if he sensed her condemnation, if they fought—his self-preservation instinct told him to avoid any of these outcomes at all cost.

He lay there thinking strategically for an hour as if he were in a lying-up position and the enemy was close by. His awareness of what could happen if things went wrong with her made it possible for him to exercise the necessary discipline.

He averted his face from her before he moved. She opened her eyes and asked if he was getting up.

He placed his large hand over her eyes so she wouldn't see him.

Keep sleeping.

Okay.

I just want to PT.

You're not tired? You are great.

I told you, I'm changing for the better.

He pressed his hand to her face again and told her to rest.

Close your eyes.

Thank you, she said.

He was tying his boots, and then he picked up his wallet and keys, all the elements of last night's little scene, which he now felt had been coerced from him under false pretenses, because in the light of day, he didn't think he owed anything to anyone who hadn't shared his war.

I'll be back in a couple hours.

She leaned up on her elbow in the bed.

I wait here for you, Skinner, she told him.

Once he was outside on the street, the image of her alone in that basement looking back at him would strike him with its loneliness. But for the moment, he was struggling with his irritation. He almost told her, Hey, the gun's in the corner. If anybody comes in, shoot them.

It would have destroyed everything for them if he had said this, he knew, and yet he barely stopped himself. To break contact with her eyes, instead, he busied himself setting the lock on the bedroom door so that she would be somewhat safe while he was gone.

In the heavy heat, he went to the park on Elder Avenue. On the way down Bowne, there were Central American women shouldering sacks of laundry as big as they were, lugging them down the line of storefronts, each one a square hole, the door wedged open for air, a pegboard on the wall with hooks for 99-cent products, a fogged-up drink case with Olde English forty-ounces standing in the water at the bottom, a fan blowing, the lights off to save energy. The bodegas handled lotto, accepted WIC. In the laundromat, you saw the vinyl peeling off the walls, the washing machines going round and round, and a Chinese woman in pajamas with a plastic broom shoving chairs around. Next door, a white-haired man sat alone in a dark space that was a bar, the back door open to let the air through. You saw him in silhouette against the rectangular view of the back alley where garbage was. He wasn't moving, as if facing the liquor had taken the power of movement right out of him.

A cluster of women with long brown feet stood arguing on the sidewalk in front of the grocery store, which was fronted by a row of cylindrical cement-filled stanchions so you couldn't steal the carts. They were arguing over a bag of rice and their food stamp benefit, in

Urdu. Skinner slipped around them, sliding between them and the stanchions, and went up a ramp that led into the buildings. There were wire mesh fences and vines coming over the concrete walls with more rusted fencing on top and dumpsters below. The courts in the center were surrounded by brown brick buildings, full of corners and alleys, shoebox-shaped cameras aimed at the paths.

A group of males was playing an unspeaking game of half-court basketball, the only sound that of the ball and their running feet pounding off the bricks and asphalt. Other guys were drifting around inside the fenced enclosure of the handball courts, and they were talking and smoking. Somebody had a bottle in a paper bag. The smell of pot hung over the courts.

I'm high as fuck, somebody said.

Stay high, said someone else.

It was in the upper nineties already and getting hotter. Skinner pulled his elbow behind his head, stretching the Chinese writing on his tricep. He reached up and grasped the exercise bar and let himself hang, feeling his entire body weight all the way down to his boots, took a quick breath and started doing chin-ups.

The backboard banged and rattled from a shot hitting it. Skinner, still hanging, his arms used-up, looked up at the bar, gulped air and chinned himself again.

Between sets, Skinner paced around under the bars, wiping his face with his black shirt. His forearms looked bigger than his calves. The basketball players were taking a break. You want in? they asked when they wanted to be replaced. Skinner saw them going into the handball court where a man in tinted yellow glasses was selling them drinks out of a picnic cooler on a four-wheel dolly. Then they sat against the wall and watched the game go on that they had left, the graffiti above their heads saying In Memory of P. Gupta Celt One St.

Skinner limped down the sideline, his hands swollen and curled from the bar, his short dark hair flattened to his skull as if he had dipped his head in a river, and went into the handball court. As soon as he stepped through the hole in the rusted fence, the guy in yellow shades got up and challenged him. You chillin? The man was over forty, the same height as Skinner, wearing big madras shorts and Closeout City sneakers. He had tattoos around his eyes, visible through his glasses. What you need? He popped up the lid of his cooler, showing the Gatorade bottles floating in the melted ice. I got blue and red.

Skinner saw his last Red Bull and said he'd take it.

You got it, guy.

Skinner cracked it and drank it, an upside-down flame of sweat on his chest.

Cool you off, the vendor said. Hot day and shit. He put Skinner's money in the pocket of his knee-length shorts. Skinner belched and walked away.

The vendor and the youths, some of them on bicycles, went back to talking. Some had come from other neighborhoods and this became the subject of their discussion.

You couldn't do what I'm doing now. Not where I was from, the vendor said. East New York. Pinkerton Avenue. Niggas would run up on you and rob you for what little you got. He grabbed at the leg of his plaid shorts to show the way they ripped your pockets for the money. We were the lowest of the low, the ghettoist of the ghetto.

A black man wearing thick round prescription glasses and a sleeveless undershirt said, We had to stay on point with that shit. The bottle in brown paper rested on the asphalt at his feet in church shoes. His trousers were unfastened at the top and his hipbone kept them up. He's my cousin. Me and him been out here twelve years.

This is Disneyland, the vendor said.

Disneyland. My man. Let me get some on that.

The black man leaned like an alien, reaching out with a long bent arm. The vendor clasped his hand and threw the hand away without looking at him.

My life was nothing but violence, the vendor said. Shot wounds, stab wounds. He gestured at his arms, torso. Of course he had served time, though he didn't want to talk about it. The tattoos said it all. He removed his tinted glasses and had the young guys look at his face. It said Fuck Ya on his eyelids. That's how I felt. BK on his face for Brooklyn. Another Brooklyn in script on his neck. A star between his eyes. Black tear drops on his cheek. Now, I'm just out here staying humble. I found religion. I'm just keeping humble every day, trying to make a dollar.

His alleged cousin took a drink and said, You don't see that every day. Staying humble. Let me get some on that. His hand floated out like a manta ray on the end of his vein-wrapped arm until someone shook it. But look, look, he said. Lemme tellya. Money and family don't mix. He held up a pack of Dunhills so everyone could see. You see the kind a cigarettes I'm smoking, so you know I don't tell nothing but the truth.

Skinner was doing pushups with his boots up on a ledge. When he was done, he had trouble standing up. He sat down and did nothing for quite a while, just sat at the bottom of a slide, his chin dripping, looking down at the sweat drips falling between his fingers.

When he looked up, he saw a pit bull, a beautiful powerful animal with tight glossy skin over striated muscles, towing its owner across the court. The owner walked leaning back, holding the thick leather leash wrapped around his fist. The animal turned its obscene head towards Skinner, who watched it curiously as it panted at him with its jaws open and pink things hanging out.

Time had gotten away from him in the heat. Skinner checked his phone, which had condensation under the screen, and frowned, confused. He hobbled down the ramp, squinting at the relentless cars going by, the low rooftops. The sun lit up everything and the concrete hurt your eyes.

You there? he said into the phone. Her voicemail had picked up. Hit me back, he told the recording.

He started walking up Sanford Avenue, passing graffiti that mentioned the streets he was passing and the people who lived there. Dek 142 St Love Trouble CSNR. In some of the yards, there were plastic toys and swings and rubbish, road cones, construction equipment parked, because the people ran their own landscaping company and this was where they lived. He thought he would hear from her within ten blocks. He heard hammers and a Skillsaw. A car went by playing R&B, coming from Nassau County. You could feel Saturday night starting in the afternoon.

Down a back street, he saw males crawling in and out of a dead house, doing a gut-out, throwing rotted wood in a van.

When she hadn't called him back by the time he reached his street, he thought, She must be in the shower. The house looked the same as always, the three layers of roofs rolled out like dirty tongues separating each floor. From here, he saw the shed in back, the attic window stuffed with yellow-gray insulation. He went around the yard's faded Jesus and let himself in. Jogging down the stairs, he called out her name, Zou Lei.

Something made him stop and listen. No one answered. Zooey, he said again. But he could hear he was alone.

He went down the stairs and snapped the light on in the bathroom and looked inside and found it empty. Striding to the kitchen, he stuck his head around the corner and looked up-down-left-right. There was no one there, just the cabinets and sink and the refrigerator. The bedroom door was locked. Zooey? he said. He used his key and opened it. His room was empty—she was not there. He stood there staring at the bed, the last place he had seen her.

What the fuck? he thought. The room looked wrong to him. The bed was at an angle to the wall and the poncholiner was lying on the floor.

He went back up on the street and looked both ways, seeing nothing but the rows of houses and cars going off for miles. There could be a million reasons she was not here, he thought. It'll be the thing you never thought of. He went back downstairs and dialed her on his phone, waiting leaning on the wall, his forehead pressed into his sweating bicep, waiting for it to ring.

The satellite connected and, a second later, he heard a cell phone ringing. It was in the basement with him. He followed the sound into his bedroom and looked around for it. It was coming from somewhere around his bedside table. He kneeled and looked under the table and saw her belly bag. The ringing was coming out of it. He snatched the bag and tore the zipper open and found her cell phone, his name flashing on her screen.

The bag contained all her things—her wallet, money, house key. He took them out and searched through them, something he had never done before, but they were hers. His hands were fluttery, but that was just his body acting up. He put them away again in the bag and tried to zip it shut. He could hear his fingers fumbling, the fine motor control gone. He could not shut the zipper. When he left the bag on the table, none of the things in it fit the way they should. They bulged out like bad conclusions.

She's fine, he said. Control yourself. Ten seconds from now, she's going to walk in that door.

He went back and started searching through the basement again, this time more thoroughly, prepared to pull everything apart, to rip apart the bedding and dump the drawers out.

He went back over the carpeting on the stairs, checking for anything that might have been dropped. He zipped his hand over the million machine-made stitches. There was nothing he could see. There were no notes or messages. Nothing cut his fingers, no broken glass. He went back into the bathroom and opened the frosted glass shower door and looked inside the shower compartment, even though he could tell there was no shadow of a folded body through the frosted glass. The toilet had not been used. He opened all the cupboards in the kitchen and checked inside the refrigerator pointlessly. He looked between the refrigerator and the wall, in that gap where dust balls gathered due to the electricity. In the bedroom, he pulled the closet door open and looked at the copper lines and the boiler dripping rust.

He turned around and looked at the bed again and the sight of it affected him in a way that no other part of the basement did. It looked like someone had kicked the bed. He pictured someone having a violent tantrum—not her, but someone else. But no one else had been here with her. His mind was prone to freakish thoughts, but he felt sick and weak.

Going closer, he clearly saw that the bed frame had been shifted at an angle to the wall.

He moved it back, realigning it. It was a single-sized mattress on a metal frame, the kind where the two halves slide together so you can adjust the size, and it was not hard to move. The wheels fell back into the dents in the linoleum where they had always been.

He got down and glanced under the bed. There was a balled-up sock and an old condom wrapper. The pizza box had been moved under the bed for some reason. When he pulled it out and examined it, it looked to him as if it had been stepped on in the center, a detail that troubled him because it didn't seem like something she would do.

He picked up the poncholiner and felt it. Brought it to his face and smelled it. Shook it. Nothing fell out of it. He felt through every inch of it. His heart was beating and he did not know why. He stared at the mattress. Touched it with his hand. She had been lying here.

He kneeled there waiting for the next thing he would do. More than anything, he was perplexed.

He put the poncholiner back on the bed, an unconscious cleaning-up gesture preparatory to getting to his feet, and this was how he discovered her shoes. When he moved the green military blanket, it was like moving a curtain, and underneath it was a surprise. His brain had been expecting bare linoleum. He found himself looking at a brand-new pair of women's Asics in phosphorescent peach trim. They were hers and, for a fraction of a second, it was like finding an Easter egg. He had a flash of success. Then the implications started spreading.

Why am I looking at someone's shoes and the person who belongs in them is gone?

There was no one here to say, It's just war, that's what happens.

He took a long struggling breath in through his nose, lifting his chest like an asthmatic trying to prevent an attack.

Immigration? Jimmy? Either way, that motherfucker.

He had started dialing 9-1-1 while storming around the room, throwing things around, getting out his gear, his sheath knife, his lips white—throwing glances at the ceiling. Afraid of what the cops might make him say, he never made the call. He wanted to call Jake and say, I'm sitting in my basement with my gun in my hand and I'm going to go upstairs and do the guy above me. Tell me what to do.

I do not know. I do not know. This cannot be.

His hands were wet. He told himself to chill. He started hiding his weapons from himself. He did not trust himself to make the right decision, so he left his room and actually locked his door, locking himself away from the firearm. And then he climbed the stairs to the Murphy's apartment and knocked.

There were voices on the other side and they stopped talking. He waited in the shadowed alcove for someone to answer him. His landlady spoke.

Who is it? Is that you, Skinner? Come in, it's open.

She was sitting where she always sat, wearing her same housedress, an unlit Slim in one fist and a Bic lighter in the other. She was in the middle of saying:

From day one, I told her they'll never give you the entire place. The men have it all week and they're not gonna give it up. I says do it at your place.

On the other side of the kitchen, all in black, Erin did not acknowledge Skinner. To her mother, she said:

Her house isn't big enough.

Yes, it is with the yard. It better be. Because I'll tell you now, she ain't getting the hall. Hello, Skinner.

Until she spoke, he had not known what he was going to say. His voice cracked, his throat making a strange music: Is your son at home?

Is my son at home? Jimmy?

Is he here?

He might be, Mrs. Murphy said. Concerning what do you need him?

I need to talk to him.

What do you need to talk to him about?

I just need to talk to him.

You need to talk to him.

Yeah. I need to talk to him. I need to talk to him now.

Erin made a scoffing sound.

You want to tell me what this is about, pray tell?

I don't know. I was gonna ask you the same thing, Mrs. Murphy. I don't know if he's got something to tell me or if you've got something to tell me. Did anything happen here today while I was gone?

Did what happen?

I don't know. I want someone to tell me.

They stared at each other. She was about to tell him to get out of her house.

Jim-my! Erin yelled.

Don't, Mrs. Murphy said.

Let him handle it. He wants to talk to him so badly, let him talk to him, Erin said.

Jimmy, don't come down here! Mrs. Murphy yelled.

What's the problem? Erin said. Let him. He wants him. You want to talk to him, right? Here he is.

Jimmy entered the kitchen coming out of the bluish hallway lined with old framed pictures. He walked in lackadaisically, swinging his arm. At the end of his arm were the rings on his fingers and they appeared to be heavy. He was sizing up the room.

What? Jimmy asked with his bearded chin raised.

Skinner looked at him with abhorrence.

What'd you do to her?

What? Jimmy demanded.

One of them—maybe both of them—took a step forward, and the next instant they were fighting.

Jimmy! Mrs. Murphy barked.

There was no sense of being hit. Skinner fell on the floor and scrambled up. It was mayhem and he heard silverware. He was in terror. They pitched over together. They were fighting on the floor and the family was screaming and he was being crushed and couldn't breathe. A hand got free and he got punched in the head. His head hit the floor and silverware jumped. He got punched again. Jimmy was grinding him with a forearm trying to break his nose. The man's skin in his face. They slid across the floor leaving his nose blood on the floor and wiping it with their legs. His shirt was being used to choke him. He sat up, got punched and blinked. He freed his legs and started kicking. His shirt ripped. They stood and something fell and broke. He was gasping, no strength in him for anything, and tried to swing his fist. Got hit in the face. Goddamn prick, Jimmy snarled, hitting him, Skinner bending over. They careened backward and Skinner stepped on a broken wooden drawer and slipped and a fork shot across the floor from under his foot.

Kick his stupid ass! the daughter screamed in her high voice.

Do not destroy my goddamn kitchen! Take him outside!

They fell and clutched on the floor, clawing at faces, Skinner pushing Jimmy's chin away. Against his cheek, he felt Jimmy's heart pounding under his fat heated chest. Headlocking each other, they breathed, ribcages flexing up and down, resting. Skinner taking long ragged hill-running breaths, trying to get to his feet again. His shorts had come halfway down and his jockstrap was visible.

Mrs. Murphy was on the phone, waiting to be connected. That's it! she said. They're taking this little fucking shithead to jail.

Yes, I need the cops here, she said. There's a man trying to attack my son.

The fight went on and then it broke apart with Skinner not eager to continue. He had been shoved outside and now he was pacing back and forth in the driveway, his Army Strong shirt ripped down and red marks around his neck and blood welling out of his nose and smeared on his wrist where he had been wiping it. His eyes were on the ground. Jimmy turned his back on him and went back inside the house. Skinner pulled his shorts up.

Erin had come to the doorway to watch him. I got him, she said into the house. If he tries anything my brother'll put him in the hospital.

She had been taunting him.

We'll see what the cops say when they get here, she told Skinner. And you got your ass kicked.

Skinner spit blood.

Fuck you, bitch.

His voice was high and shaky.

Why are you still here? Why don't you just go?

What, and leave my property?

After you destroyed our property? You know, my brother isn't done with you, she said. You better leave town.

Skinner used his torn shirt to wipe his face.

The police walked up the driveway behind him.

Hey, howyadoin this afternoon, sir? Is this your house? Step over here for me. You got any ID for me? You have a fight with somebody? A kid who lives here? Where do you live? Why'd you fight?

The police radio was making noise. Skinner pointed at the house and tried to talk, and a river of fuck words came out his mouth. Take it easy, they said. Don't get excited. The daughter observed him from the doorway. He's crazy. He scares everybody.

A cop who looked like a high school football coach with fuzzy hair on his arms said, Whaddya say let's go inside, and urged Erin inside. Lifting up his shades, he stepped slowly and carefully through the Murphy's doorway and followed her into the house. Where's the other guy? Is he in here?

The police were feeling through the pockets of Skinner's basketball shorts in the driveway.

They keep sayin I'm crazy. They don't know shit about crazy.

Four cops stood in a semicircle around him.

Last chance, one said.

Skinner gritted his teeth.

They knocked him down and kneeled on his spine, where the shrapnel damage had been done, and handcuffed him.

You gonna calm it down now?

They put a nightstick between his forearm and his shoulder blade and made him walk down to the street. Someone opened a car door.

I got him. Quit fighting.

I'm not!

They put him in the backseat and closed him in.

Kid's strong.

Take him in?

See what's what inside first.

Now he was sitting in the caged area in the backseat of a patrol car, twisting his head, looking around, his dark pained eyes staring out like a panicked horse, trying to see what was going on. He leaned forward without his hands and wiped his nose on his knee, squeezing a bubble of blood out of his nose and smearing it on his leg.

About ten minutes later, the cops came out and got in and talked up front without including Skinner. He asked them if he was going to jail. One of them looked in the rearview.

You're going.

What about the other guy?

What about him?

Skinner hit his head on the window. They told him what would happen if he broke it.

Fine, he said staring at his lap.

51

THEY DROVE HIM TO Chinatown. His head was down the entire way. He listened to the police radio. He felt the world going by outside the windows and he didn't want to see. Saturday evening was gearing up on the street. He could hear the cars gunning their engines and the music. The handcuffs were digging into the bone of his right wrist. At the traffic lights, he felt people looking at him. One member of a group of guys in white undershirts and afros observed him cynically while smoking a cigarette. The police car turned onto a crowded street that led past markets selling fruit. Skinner could hear Chinese being spoken. He could feel the sunset without looking up to see it.

They pulled over and parked on a block he didn't recognize. The smell of Chinese food was so good, he asked the cops if they could let him eat something. One of the officers said that they would work something out, but it was just to get Skinner to come along. Neither of the policemen looked at him. One of them held his elbow with a black leather glove, the other—a pale, slightly overweight blond-haired man with soft arms—went ahead carrying a clear plastic iced-coffee drink cup from Dunkin Donuts that he was throwing out. The garbage can in front of the precinct was too full to throw the cup out and he had to set it carefully on top of other trash and hope it didn't fall. Then he went ahead and held the door for them and the other cop walked Skinner inside and pushed him through the turnstile.

A phone was ringing, being answered by a woman who sounded like his landlady. He saw the elevated desk and the six-foot men in dark blue uniforms standing behind it watching him come in. There was a gold-fringed American flag in the corner.

The cops who had arrested him lifted up their shades onto their foreheads and exchanged their paperwork with an officer behind the desk—a young guy no different from a lot of six-foot guys who served in uniform. And he was chewing a sandwich. He put his sandwich down and brushed the rye seeds off his hands and talked over Skinner's head.

What's this?

This is the assault.

Skinner stood there with his hands behind his back while they called him the prisoner and handled him with gloves. Heavily sunburned men came in carrying gym bags to start a shift, and someone said, Mikey, how was the shore? A short guy with a gray crewcut and raccoon eyes without his sunglasses, said, I'll tell you later, and trudged up the stairs, past the child abduction bulletins. The arresting officers checked if Skinner had warrants. Skinner shook his head.

I told you I didn't. I told you I shouldn't be here.

Open your mouth and let me see inside, the senior arresting officer demanded—a big man with a brush mustache and a roll of fat on the back of his neck. Pretend you're at the doctor.

His wallet went in a manila envelope, and the guy behind the counter dropped it in a drawer. They took his bootlaces. He looked down, sucking in his waist, while they cut the drawstring out of his basketball shorts with a Spyderco. The big cop's partner, the pale slightly overweight blond guy with soft arms, snapped the lock blade shut and said, We're going over here. Skinner followed him across the tile floor, his boots flopping under his feet. He saw the stairs, a dented steel door, a sign saying No Firearms Beyond This Point. The cop held the door for him and Skinner entered the arrest room. He saw the yellow-ocher benches inside the mesh cage of the holding pen, the paint blistered off the lock. His cuffs were removed. Skinner's wrist had a double red line in the skin. The cop unlocked the cage door with a set of flat gold keys and told him to take a seat. Do not lie down. Skinner stepped inside and the door clashed shut on him, and the entire metal webwork thrummed.

From inside the cage, he saw everything outside the cage through the black lines of the wire mesh. The convex mirror on the ceiling showed a warped scene of stillness—fluorescent light and tile the color of an olive in a jar. Even when he moved, when he doubled over and rested his head on his knee, his movement was nowhere reflected in it. Nor when he raised his head and sighed Fuck at the yellow ceiling. Nothing moved except the clock. A poster on the wall said No Hope In Dope.

An hour later, the door opened and the blond cop came back and let him out. He told Skinner where to stand and what to look at and took his mugshot from across the room with the click of a mouse on a computer just like the DMV. They went through the fingerprinting process together. The cop held Skinner's finger on the platen glass of a copy machine-type scanner, and Skinner's fingerprint appeared on the computer screen next to the image of his sweating face.

How long am I gonna be here?

Could be a couple hours depending on what else is going on. We do the paperwork, do what we gotta do, the DA does their thing. It varies.

I mean how much time am I gonna get?

That depends. You got priors?

I had a disorderly conduct.

When was that?

Before the army. Way back when.

You were in the army?

Yeah.

You a vet?

Yeah.

Iraq?

Yeah. Three tours. This is my shirt. I thought you could see what it says. This is my shrapnel.

Oh, shit.

Ten-thousand feet per second, dude. Collapsed lung. Listen, that fucking motherfucking shitbag fuckhead I was fighting with. You gotta listen to me. That motherfucker's bad news. He's the one who oughta fuckin be here. He's a fuckin convict.

What's his name?

Jimmy. Jimmy fucking Murphy.

You know what he was in prison for? Was it narcotics?

For fucking his mother, for all I know. He's a shitbag.

Okay, got it. Step in for me again. Watch the door.

The cop locked him in again.

I'm Brad, dude. What's your name?

What it says on my uniform. O'Donnell.

The cop told him to sit tight and left, shutting the arrest room door. Three hours later, Skinner was still staring at the door through the wire X's, waiting for him to come back. Skinner was propped up on the cage, his arms wrapped around his waist, holding his stomach, suffering with his hunger. Not moving, like an animal conserving energy, partly camouflaged by the steel mesh. Listening to the precinct outside the door, a cell phone ringtone playing a few bars of Billy Joel.

Plainclothes cops brought in an arrestee, a short young male with the creased face of a forty-year-old sharecropper, in his boxers, tripping with his pants around his ankles. They opened the holding pen and put him in in handcuffs. Y'all play hard, he said, in a voice both high and deep at once, as if there were a clarinet reed in his chest. He sat in the middle of the bench with his knees spread and raised his cuffed hands together and gave the cops the finger. Y'all see what I'm holding? The cage filled up with black males between the ages of thirteen and eighteen, making hand signs at the police and shouting out. The smallest had an afro that looked like the points of a star. One said, Hey, yo, cop, can I axe a question. He had his penis out. Skinner muttered, Shit, and looked away. They tried to get his attention by kicking his boot toe with their unlaced Jordans. He could smell them. One wedged his knee against Skinner's knee and pretended not to notice he was there. Skinner moved away and cradled his head in his hand, waiting for time to pass until the cops would feed them, his eyes shut, hearing:

Glenmore niggas. Nigga runnin toward us pullin up. Started dumpin at us. Beek! Beek! Beek! That's 8 block. Started throwin at him. They killt him. You know where the Pioneer be at. I know what you talkin bout. They used to call it 8 block. Almost caught my son in the stomach if I hadn't duck. By Howard. My grandparents live over there. He run a blood gang. Nigga on the island. He ran up on one nigga and smoked that nigga. I was shook. Them niggas stay doin that. He got shot in the leg, both legs. His face, his face was like this, bleekin. He kicked me with his boot. Ain't nothin I could do the way that nigga hit me so hard. My uncle came down. My shit was swollen. Buddha came down. I was shook, son. Almost two days later in the summertime. I know where he went. He went around the block again. We broke the bat in two pieces. I was kickin him in the face. Buddha like, That's enough. You gotta go home. Niggas jumped me. I whaled on that sucka. Shorty tight with Buddha. She tried to take my ring off, nigga. Second time she wanna pop it off.

We broke the coffee table, nigga. We threw this nigga into the coffee table and nigga stuck him. Beek. To the chess.

A plainclothes cop who looked like a short muscular white rapper in a baseball jersey, denim shorts, and a baseball hat worn low over his eyes, came in and called Skinner's name.

Right here, Skinner said.

Step out for me. He opened the cage. Just you. Sit down, he told a youth.

But my mother waiting for me.

Skinner walked out.

White faggot.

You're getting a get out of jail free card. The guy you had a fight with has some problems, so that's in your favor.

Thank you! he shouted. His voice sounded aggressive.

Thank your arresting officer.

The cop gave Skinner a form to sign and then tore off the white and the yellow copies and gave them to him.

This is when your court date is.

That's it?

Unless you wanna stay.

Skinner got his property back at the front desk. He took his envelope without a word and walked out through the turnstile and shoved out through the front door into the warm night air, the sudden noise lifting off the streets into the purple sky.

He sat down on the curb and laced his desert boots back up. He was very stiff and sore and to stand again, he had to get up on his hands and knees like somebody with muscular dystrophy.

Now what the fuck do I do? he begged.

The traffic flew by him leaving taillights in his retinas. The desk appearance ticket, which he had folded, dropped out of his pocket and he picked it up. When he stood up, he was facing the parking lot. Chinatown was on the other side of it. Come on, he told himself, and started hiking. By the time he thought of looking back at the police station, he was already blocks away from it, having turned downhill into the neon lights on Roosevelt Avenue. She'll be there, he told himself. He had rolled the desk appearance ticket up and was twisting it into a hard stick in his hands, his palm prints on the paper.

On the way, he stopped at McDonald's and ate his food standing up, mashing his sandwich into his face. The Coke made him groan and whisper, Goddamn. He took it with him, hurrying on, and side-armed it at a garbage can outside a furniture store when he was down to the ice. He weaved through the crowd, taking his shirt off as he went, wiping his face, wiping ketchup off his hands, exposing his tattooed white body in the headlights.

The block out to the freeway seemed to go on for miles. He would have run, but the most his legs could do was fast-walk. He scanned the laundry-hung windows of the identical brickface houses, identifying what he thought was her apartment, looking for a light. She was going to be there and she was going to fling her arms around him when she saw him.

He jogged the last ten yards to her door and started knocking.

Zou Lei! he called. He backed up in the street and looked up at the windows. He shouted her name again. No one answered. He heard a Chinese voice inside the walls. It wasn't her. He banged on the door some more. Hello! he yelled.

Finally, he got someone to come to the window on the second floor. From in the street, he could only see a shadow of a head.

Zou Lei! Can you get her?

What?

Can you get my girlfriend? Let me describe her. She's five foot three. Chinese. She lives right in there.

Nobody here.

You didn't check. I'm asking you to check.

No here.

Just check for me. Knock.

The shadow went away, Skinner believed, at first, to check, but then, as the minutes went by, he knew no one was coming back.

Hey! he called.

There was no answer.

Can you talk to me?

He was yelling to himself on the street, amid the garbage cans, the wrought iron security grills, the shirts and pants and bras on the clotheslines, the general silence.

52

WHEN HIS BODY MOVED next to her, she woke immediately. She went from running in her dream-forest to watching him climbing over her and putting on his jockstrap. She watched him dressing in basketball shorts, tying up his boots, moving around and collecting up his things as if he had somewhere to be.

She tried to make sense of what he was doing.

Did he have a previous appointment? she wondered, something he had forgotten to mention when he had kneeled at her feet last night and told her of his renewed commitment?

Perhaps she sensed an inconsistency between the idea of his giving her everything and his leaving now, his face hidden from her.

She wanted to tell him about her dream, that she had just been dreaming of them running together. But she was afraid he wouldn't want to hear it, so she kept silent. She told him to have a good workout.

He pulled the door shut taking the keys—the keys he had symbolically promised her last night—leaving her stranded in his room.

The room was set below ground level. The bed she lay on was under the sidewalk. The sunlight fell through a barred grating overhead. The basement housed the silent boiler, copper lines and the pipes for kitchen and bathroom, all of which were buried below ground. The water from the entire house ran down and drained into a sewer pipe beneath her in the rock. The floor tiles had been laid over ten years ago and the glue that bonded them to the concrete slab had chemically degraded. Tiles would slip sideways when they were stepped on, revealing the concrete slab, which drew up dampness from the earth. It was a strange shitty room, she thought, and it bothered her to be here alone. She wondered why anyone would have painted it this garish whorehouse purple unless they were using it as a set for pornographic filming.

She tried to sleep again, but instead ended up worrying about every particular and contingency of her situation. In an effort to control her anxiety, she got up and put on her bra and found the clothes she had run in.

As she was putting on her shorts, she was aware of noises from the people upstairs. It was the ordinary commotion of people gathering and going out together. She heard women talking, briefly loud as the apartment door opened and closed, their muted voices on the street.

It annoyed her that she was stuck here waiting for Skinner. Thinking of calling him, she checked the time and saw it was ten o'clock. She was getting hungry and considered going to look in the refrigerator.

From outside, the sound of cars reached her faintly. The insulation of the room was troubling, the degree to which it swallowed sound.

It distressed her that it was already ten o'clock and he hadn't called her. She sat down on the bed again and dozed or tranced sitting up. She abandoned the thought of eating. She was getting very sad.

He had left her without making love to her.

I'm alone, she kept thinking. I'm alone. I'm alone. I'm alone. Alone. Alone. Death. Death. Alone.

You've been here before, she said.

She frightened herself, imagining what if the door was locked from the other side? What if the man she loved was a stranger? What if this was an isolation cell and you were never going to leave it?

She stood up in the sun-filled room and started getting organized. To stop herself from thinking about Skinner, to contain the thought of him, she zipped her cell phone in her belly pouch and set it on the nightstand. She straightened her hair and tied it back and looked around for her socks.

At this point, she heard a sound in the outer basement but thought it was coming from outside.

It occurred to her that she was missing something that belonged to her, and she realized it was her sneakers. Her hair was still tangled and she took a comb to it while looking around the floor. She heard something again and paused with her comb in her hand.

For a minute she wondered if it was Skinner coming back.

Skinner? she asked.

There was no answer.

She lowered the comb.

As she stood there, she felt a presence approach the other side of the bedroom door. It was such a strong impression, she almost thought she could see a man-shaped shadow through the wood. The hair rose on the back of her neck. She did not move. She thought it could have been her imagination.

A male voice spoke through the door.

She stood frozen and momentarily scared.

The doorknob was jiggled.

Open it, he said.

From the preemptory character of the voice, her first thought was that it was the police.

She glanced down at her belly bag on the bedside table, which contained her money, key, and now her cell phone—the things she couldn't lose. She couldn't see her Asics, which were hidden under the pizza box, and in her panic she couldn't recall where they were.

The man said something else, uttering it as if his mouth was full, as if his tongue was thick, engorged.

She called out: My boyfriend sleeping, come back later!

Then she heard keys.

The lock clicked. When the door began opening, she yelled No! and ran to push it shut.

As soon as she saw his face, she knew what was going to happen and her heart sickened. He shoved her in the chest with both hands. The force threw her straight back across the room and onto the bed.

The instant her back hit the bed, she bounced up and dodged right past him. By the time Jimmy had reacted with his long loping body, she was already up the basement stairs, had ripped the door open, and was running barefoot in the street.

The next thing she knew, she was out on the avenue and she didn't know how far she had run. The sun was in her eyes, cars were driving by, and she didn't feel the pain of her heels hitting the cement, just impact.

Her momentum spun down from running to jogging to frantic walking. She was gasping for air. She turned and walked backwards, looking behind her, ready to run again. Something in her wanted to laugh. She stopped and stared back up the avenue looking for anyone following her and saw no one.

My heaven. My heaven, she thought.

Oh, my heaven.

She had trouble seeing the street signs. She recognized Kissena when she was already on it, the soles of her feet burned from the pavement, trying to avoid stepping on broken glass.

What now? Everything of hers had been left back there.

My heaven, what had happened?

At a ninety-nine cent store, she stopped and begged a woman in an umbrella visor to let her have a pair of shower shoes. A passerby overheard Zou Lei and gave her a dollar. She was a slender woman in her forties with luminous eyes, the kind of woman that wound up in detention in China. I am a Buddhist, she smiled. Zou Lei thanked her and popped the plastic thread that held the rubber sandals together and put her blackened feet in them.

She looked around for some idea of what to do. The Buddhist had disappeared in the crowd of heads with black hair, the short-sleeved rayon blouses, and the plastic toys and gadgets making sounds, the strains of swelling music, saccharin recorded women's voices saying buy one get one free. A skinny man was cutting sugarcane with a knife, the long green peelings falling about his ankles.

She crossed Main Street and went downhill towards the freeway. At her house, she tried the door and it was locked. For a time, she paced with her arms crossed. It wasn't that she even wanted to get inside. She wanted Skinner here. She whirled around in a circle, sighed and bit her lip. What on earth do I do? She held her head. She would make herself wait. When he found her gone, he would necessarily come here.

After she got tired of pacing, she squatted down in that deep Asian squat, monitoring the approach to the house from between parked cars, her work-stained hand holding the top of her head and her blackened feet pressed against the hot sidewalk, toes gripping her sandals. A wisp of hair hung across her face. Her mouth was half-open and her brown eyes rested on the trees at the end of the block, watching them for movement.

The sun moved. In the late afternoon, people who worked Saturdays too appeared out of the trees and began coming down the block and going into their houses. Another hour went by. She made herself wait. One of a thousand bachelor immigrants in a t-shirt and jeans came tripping down the hill with his shadow behind him, his head hung. His clothes and hands were covered in paint and plaster. They knew each other by sight, she had drunk his Sunkist. She watched him see her. He must have seen her distress. She watched him decide it did not involve him and go into his house.

When she couldn't keep still any longer, she stood and lifted one foot and then the other, as if she had to urinate. Arms crossed, she hurried up a concrete path through a sea of ferns and weeds, which had grown deep in the hot weather, and stood at the boulevard's edge to squint at the horizon. There was no more than an inch of evening sky between the gas station's roof and the orange sun.

She made a rule: if you thought he wasn't coming and you were going to give up, then, if you waited a little more, you would be rewarded and he would come.

53

IT WAS NIGHT. THE trucks gunned down the freeway and the sound reverberated over her, the air blast whoofing between the houses. She had started walking after sundown, when the sky changed colors above the fragmented clouds, after she had given up and held out a little more and not been rewarded, and this had happened twice. All she knew was that she had been abandoned. She was desperate and could not bear to think. She didn't know what she was doing. She was going to go away, just go and keep going until the world ended or she ended.

Somehow she had gotten on the train without paying, and now she was riding in the hypnotic noise. They went underground in Manhattan, the white people got off, and the subway headed into Brooklyn. The air conditioning was raining on the gray seats, on the West Indians and Africans. A policeman put his head out on the platform at every stop.

At the last stop, the track ended and another train was parked there on the other track. The crowd got off and she got off. The cops switched trains. There was beige marine paint on the walls. It smelled like a toilet. Jamaicans bounded up the cement steps as she was going down. Little thin children followed them in thrift clothes. There was water on the sidewalk, and she could smell the sewer. She saw in people's second-floor windows above restaurants and discount stores. The fried-food smell hit her. Cars drove through the intersection, a channel of soft green and violet neon lights, playing music. A starved shaved-headed cholo was driving a gold car. They were coming in from somewhere else, looking for a good time. You saw their serious faces, playing different music in each car, their friends in the back seats in baseball hats, being driven. Someone honked in celebration. A Cadillac jalopy driven by a single male stopped at the light. His music was exuberant, and he was calling out: We can get it bumping like champagne bubbles! He had no headlights. She crossed in front of him and headed down Liberty Avenue.

She passed the Good Hope Restaurant, the Sparkles Bar and Lounge, a young male standing up on a bike, slaloming in the street, his black hat sideways and a cigarette behind his ear. His shirt said Hustle Trees. She passed homeless scrap hunters with dank iron-gray hair and gloves and sweatpants, digging in the garbage. They were Indian, they knew each other. They stopped and consulted with each other where the better hunting was, and one went off, towing his shopping cart behind him. A women walked by her like a zombie with scar tissue from a burn on her cheek and jaw. She passed the Dabar Halal Restaurant, a green awning and white light and cab drivers eating off of trays.

As she left the intersection behind, the street got darker. Looking back, she saw a red police light strobing in the traffic, glowing on the low houses from which reggae played. Ahead, she saw an unlit mosque behind a car lot festooned with triangular flags strung up in the shadow. Above the telephone lines, there was a dime-sized moon. She was heading east to Freeport. The cars came by in bursts in the half-mile stretches between markets selling fruit. The other stores were closed. Taped to the side of a building, she saw a poster for a healer. The words, which she did not stop to try and read, said Remove Black Magic. In the picture, the healer's uplifted face was painted red and yellow. She passed by boarded-up storefront churches with massive trees rising up behind them and spreading over them in the dark. A faded sign on a board above her head said the Seven Crowns of Glory. A man came along in a hood, beard, shorts, socks like puttees, having harnessed himself with two clotheslines, pulling a shopping cart after him, loaded like a caravan with garbage bags. A black car cruised by booming: One nation... under God... real niggas... getting money. Women getting ready for a party in a parked van traded makeup from their purses. The streets became irregular, cut in triangles. She came to buses parked along the median, cars left on the sidewalk. Her path was blocked by a wrecked Crown Victoria with the doors torn off, the back seat in the front seat, the roof compressed like a sandwich, and the windshield glass blown out on the pavement, and she went around it and kept walking in the street. She cheated over for the oncoming traffic. There began to be auto repairs. She saw a Domino's. The driver in his blue and red shirt got out of his car and went inside dragging the insulated bag for the pizzas.

For a quarter mile there would be nothing, and then she would encounter a person. She would see two guys in janitor's trousers sitting on a porch half hidden by a hedge, opening a bottle. Then she would come to the valley of light around a gas station where a young male, his skin the same color as his black t-shirt, was putting gas in a dented Elantra. There was barbed wire on top of a beverage distributor. She crossed a freeway, and it felt like the rest of America, the vast concrete speedway echoing and echoing. Back in the streets again, she passed cars parked on the side of the road, two women in the front texting, perhaps Hispanic. One wore glasses, had a long nose. She passed the club JouVay next to a masonry supply, music reverberating up through the roof.

Late as it was on a Saturday night, you still saw people here and there struggling with laundry bags, garbage bags full of clothes, perhaps moving somewhere else to stay or engaged in some kind of labor. She saw four women sitting around on cars in the hot night apparently doing nothing except talking. A drunken Central American man was headed towards them, taking long staggering runs back and forth down the sidewalk. They had short hair like lesbians. One of the big women stood up where she had been sitting in a doorway with her girlfriends. He stared speechlessly at her, then staggered on as if he had decided that it was all no use. Hey, papito, come back! the woman called. Let him go, her girlfriends said. The woman said, No. I need that money. Afuera, she called loudly in a pleasant voice. Papi, ven aquí!

Zou Lei walked through them, pressing on against the cars flying by, against the pavement and the time of night, against the understanding that she should have stopped miles ago, that what she was doing did not make sense. She could not stop. Twenty minutes later, she had a bad spell when everything caught up with her at once. She suddenly got hit by hunger, as if something had gotten switched-off inside her, and she didn't know what to do. She was standing on a corner in the dark, having gotten beyond the lounges and BBQ ribs and the wines and liquors, to a barren terrain of salvage yards. The avenue itself had become a highway, cars speeding by, raising dust from the gravel in the road, and the gutters were filled with trash and water. The only thing between her feet and the pavement was her shower shoes. There was nothing to go back to if she turned back.

She had nothing in her stomach. She looked like a prostitute out here. There was nothing in her pockets and she was scared.

A wide car with little fins above the taillights separated from the wave of traffic and came slowing down to the curb and stopped. The people in the car were a black couple. An NYPD van stopped behind it. She was afraid to stay where she was, and she kept moving. The light was on in the police van and she saw one of the officers, his hair gelled up, take a quick glance at her as he entered information in a keyboard mounted on the dash. In her mind, she practiced saying, My friend live up the street. I come out for bread. I get lost. I so sorry.

What would happen if she told him what had happened to her today? If I weren't lucky, maybe I would not be here. She had escaped, but she had lost her money, her ID, her phone, even her shoes.

The officer would say, That could very possibly be true, but the situation he was dealing with now was that she was somebody without ID, and until we can make sure you are who you say you are, we're gonna hold onto you.

And then he would handcuff her and put her in the van. Whaddya think? his partner would ask, opening the log book. They'd book her for prostitution, because this was a known track, and put her in the pen in East New York.

This near encounter switched her hunger off and energized her out of fear, and she walked several more miles through the middle of the night before she again remembered that she was tired.

The police van's white, red, and orange flashers disappeared behind her as the road bent and she passed silos for sand and gravel, a diagonal conveyor belt against the sky, cement trucks nose to tail like elephants behind a fence. An alley full of smashed-up cars and glass. East Coast Auto Salvage. There was a black field with powerful lights behind it, blinding if you stared at them even from a half-mile away. A compressor was running. Every now and then a car full of young men coming from Long Island came by, not gangbanging, just poor. Women drove by alone, texting, headed to a party. Cars came by, just-sold, with white writing still on the windows, saying 4/S, how many miles. High weeds were growing from the median. The houses looked like country shacks. She saw ferns. It looked like where you would park a truck off the highway going south. The trees in the lots were wild.

She passed a burned-out laundromat, the Deeper Life Bible Church, and saw a single tall black woman with a kind of physical correctness, careful posture, in slacks, turning down a side street, headed in the direction of thudding music, appearing dignified and fatalistic.

The burned-out buildings came more frequently, until everything had a dead deserted feeling. A mural had been painted on a roll-down gate, showing the pyramids and pharaohs of Egypt looming like mountainous thunderclouds above the New York skyline, in which the Towers were still standing. It said Civilization Began In Africa. Step In At Your Own Risk. But the store it was for was ripped-out and ransacked from within. You could see through the holes in the bricks. Further on, the sounds of deep music came from behind the houses, from what sounded like a well hidden behind abandoned and burned-out squats, mattresses and sofas in piles of trash next to dark porches you were afraid to look upon. There were no more city blocks, it just went on and on. As she cleared the corners of buildings, she saw scenes in the trees behind them, distant silent figures in white shirts milling around a car with all the doors open. Everyone wore an article of red, whether it was their shorts or hat. There was the sense of strangers who lived among each other, robbing each other, predicting who would be robbed next. The road ran by a park area that was dead gray in the dull light, and the houses behind it were utterly silent. She heard a string of pistol reports. A bearded man ambling in the street lifting his shirt and touching his flat belly noticed her the way you notice money lying on the sidewalk. He looked around, as if to see if anyone had claimed her. The Freeport bus flew by her and she would have tried to board it, but it didn't stop.

Fearing to go on, she turned north, and the road took her past trellises and crickets and white iron fences, like something from a bayou. It was still a ghetto. She passed one-story bars with blue lights and a tall Jamaican guarding the door in a pastel jacket and gator shoes. She crossed Mexico Street and Murdoch Avenue. Cars tricked out for Saturday night with unusual light configurations, double headlights, went zipping by, pulled sudden turns, still hunting that party, gunning into the back streets. One gave a sudden blatting roar, dodged around a jeep, and drag-raced away, sounding like a motorcycle droning off into the distance. She passed posters outside churches waging spiritual warfare. People came out of clubs dressed like sweet sixteens. The night had turned from hot to temperate. There were mosquitoes. Things started getting quiet. There were long spaces between the cars. She saw a house with the porch door open and the TV so big it seemed to invite her inside, but no one was visible. She heard an air conditioner running. Crossing under the train tracks, she heard crickets in the brush. On the other side, a billboard in the weeds showed women in strapless dresses toasting her with vodka, eyes shut, laughing.

In someone's yard, a clutter of handmade signs on boards and bedsheets caught her eye: Don't Smoke Anything. Drinking = Damage, Disease, Devil. The same letter D was used as the beginning for all the words. Smoking = Sin, Suffer, Satan. People Going Places Ride When They Wear Adidas. A Texas State flag hung on the porch. It said Ministry on the roof.

The sight of it all distracted her. She stepped into the street without looking, and a car sped out of nowhere and almost hit her. When she went back to pick her shoe up, the streetlights started reeling and she had to catch her balance. Fatigue had made her dizzy drunk. She felt strange, but the feeling went away when she was moving. She went back to walking and she was all right. But she could not think. The moon looked like a streetlight, and she had trouble remembering that it was in the sky instead of down here with her.

She walked north on Woodhill through spider webs and hearing crickets. The silent dark houses and power lines. Thunder from a jet in the sky. The largest tree she had yet seen was looming up above her. The leaves rustled, a sound of onset, of something coming to boil and seething. Then a bus—a new, clean air-conditioned hydrogen bus—lit like an airport shuttle—zipped by and blocked out the leafy rustling with the smooth firm sound of its engine.

Then she crossed an avenue without street signs, revelers pulling u-turns. The Cambria Heights Academy. Again, the distant gunshots.

Down a dark street, she saw one light: a dull blue interior through an open window and, in its isolation, it looked like somewhere a crime would take place. Someone said hi from a car. A mailbox said Khan. South Asian flags had been stuck in the ground like quills.

She made it to Hillside Avenue and beheld an apartment building with a headband of blue neon wrapped around it. A homeless man, bearded like a prophet in surgical gloves, came along pulling a shopping cart and picked a plastic bottle out of the gutter. She passed brick apartment buildings, two-tone walls. A cool breeze blew. The avenue went for miles in both directions. She was depressed with hunger and seeing spots. She continued east. An ambulance or cop car drove toward her and passed in silence, no sirens, just lights flickering and flashing like burning sparklers.

She thought, All I have to do is stay awake until morning and then somewhere I can eat something. Then she remembered she didn't have any money.

A car pulled up at the light with the stereo bumping and she ignored whatever the young men in ball caps yelled at her.

She passed a brick building housing an Islamic community center in salmon-colored brick. The avenue widened, smoothed, acquired a median ahead. A bus went by and it was orange and had an N for Nassau instead of a Q for Queens. She passed a big bright gas station covered in flags as if still celebrating a grand opening. The roof was lower than the gas stations in the desert in the west, where the Chinese build them so high they look like they are spiders on telescoping legs. Over the top of this one she saw big trees.

Now Zou Lei was in a gas station looking at all the cookies and milk and potato chips in a trance, having lost track of how she had gotten here. Droop-lipped men in dress shirts and slacks were coming in and out, paying for coffee and the Punjabi Times and going back out to their taxis. The wall clock said three a.m. She felt as if time had jumped ahead.

A curly haired young man with an earnest, devoted, sacrificial manner stood very erect behind the counter serving the cabdrivers. He had a slender neck and hair on his throat and large brown eyes. After each of the drivers paid, he said a sincere bimsallah. She asked him if she could have a cup of water.

Take it, please, he said. I will show you.

He came out from the glass enclosed area and opened the cupboards for her, gave her a paper cup. Here is the hot one—he pointed out the red lever on the coffee maker. She was so tired her fatigue was overrunning her in waves. She thought she was dreaming. I don't have money, she said out loud. It seemed he didn't hear her. When he went back to the register, she shielded what she was doing from him with her body and poured herself a milk and coffee. She tore sugars in it, drank it down to the brown silt of sugar at the bottom, and filled her cup again. She kept her back to him as she drank. Behind her, she heard him ring a sale. She examined a pack of Twinkies, looked up at the mirror, and put them down. Another cab driver came in. She went back and picked the Twinkies up and began to leave. The young man watched her leaving.

I will get money, she said. It's okay?

Okay, he said, lowering his eyelids.

She took the food outside and ate it right outside and fell asleep sitting slumped on the curb for several minutes.

Immediately, she dreamed. She had sensations of color, turmoil, voice, but saw none of the usual scenes or human beings who exist in ordinary waking life. Her mind felt drenched in wet images and thrashing. She thought her head was tumbling in a sack that had been pitched off a mountain and she was hitting fir trees.

She lay there, half-slumped over on the curb under the amber lights on the edge of the eight-lane avenue with her feet extended out in front of her. Her feet and ankles were black from dirt. The soles of her feet were stuck to her shower shoes. The calluses on her feet were yellow and black. She was forming blisters underneath the skin. Her mouth hung open. She began to fall sideways and she jerked awake.

She couldn't focus her eyes or remember where she was. When she looked around, all she saw was fields of black and purple streaked with lights, and she heard the oceanic sounds of traffic in the distance. She fell asleep again and jerked her head awake again, scared she was going to see a cop coming up to her. This time she forced herself to keep her eyes open. She could not think. All she knew was that she had to keep moving until daytime. She made herself stand up, and it was hard. As soon as her weight came on her feet, she winced. She stood there tottering, sweaty and dirty, looking down at her feet. Her heels were bruised from walking without padding. Grit beneath her heel made her suck her breath in in pain when she stepped on it. She hobbled over to a curb by the compressed air machine and sat back down and looked at herself. She took her sandal off and brushed the sand off her foot. The sole of her foot felt sticky like glue, as if the rubber of the shoes had been melted by friction. The straps had sawed into her skin, she discovered. Between her toes, there was a red raw circle where she'd been cut by the toe piece. Touching her foot made her hands feel dirty. The shoes themselves were coming apart.

The treads were completely flat. She did one foot, then the other, placed her feet gingerly back in the sandals, and stood up again.

She adjusted herself, pulled her shorts down. Getting her bearings, she figured out which way she had been going before she stopped and then she turned herself that way and slowly, stiffly, started moving on.

For some time thereafter, she walked in a state of half-awakeness past things she half-perceived. Francis Lewis Boulevard. The Belle Aire playground. A black woman thin as an African with dyed blond hair prowling on a traffic island. A sprinkler was whisking in the grass. The public restroom door was open and you could see the sink and stall. Two cars drove by booming rap. She passed the on-ramp for the Grand Central Parkway. She passed the Satya Sanatan Dharma Mandir, a place of worship. A spiked iron fence. The Creedmoor Psychiatric Facility—the buildings set at random angles, an iron gate left open. She could see weeds in the asphalt like rice paddy squares. It looked abandoned. Ambulances parked in a fleet. A section of the fence hit by a car. Beneath the mercury lights, she saw a shadow that didn't belong to her and looked around to see who was following her, but there was no one there.

For what seemed like miles, she journeyed past old apartment houses with lawns and rusted placards for Fallout Shelters. Girish Bulsara, MD. Bala Ji Grocery. Apna Baza Cash & Carry. Patel Halal Meat. Great long stretches between anything. A Mexican taco truck serving two laborers. Graffiti on a traffic light box: NW$. The Cross Island Parkway.

The landscape changed. The road divided and angled north. She passed a clean suburban high school. They had a black field of neatly mowed grass and football goal posts. She saw pine cones on the asphalt. The road was wide and flat and clean and there was nearly absolute stillness. It was cool and pleasant. She heard crickets.

She had been walking for a long time now, and somewhere along the way, she had completely waked up. Thinking it was dawn, she looked at the sky, but there was no sign of it: It was still night, the sky was indigo-black and she could see the clouds. Whatever time it was, her mind felt fresh and clear and the rest of her was comfortable. Her legs were warmed up and she didn't feel them. Her feet had stopped hurting her. She just felt pressure when she put them down, no pain, and the rhythm of walking. Passing someone's house with a stake bed truck parked in front of it, she looked to her left and saw a wall of forest. She could go for miles like this, which meant she knew she was going to make it through to morning.

She would hear cars coming before she could see them. The sound would build and build and then the car would break past her and she'd see the taillights going away. She started wondering what if someone was coming to find her. Each time a car came, the rising pitch of the sound created a feeling of suspense, which lingered in the silence after it was gone, during which she waited to hear the next one coming.

What if the next one you hear is Skinner coming?

A white Malibu sped by her without stopping and went on in a pool of light moving up the black road between the houses towards the night sky.

No, no, of course that wasn't him. He's not out here, she said to herself. He doesn't have a car. She would meet him further on. She would have to last the entire night. In the morning, when the sun comes up—that was when she would see him. She would have to walk a very long way, but if she did everything correctly and didn't give in, then she would be rewarded. But for this to work, she would really have to push herself. She would have to keep going a long, long way. You'll have to really move your legs this time, she said. It won't be easy. He won't just appear. She would have to go all the way to the mountains. That, finally, would make him appear.

She started to form a plan of what she would do to make the distance long enough. She would keep pushing east until the time was right, and then she would go north when it was possible and then go back. She would go on foot all the way to his house, and when the door opened, Skinner would be standing there. He would open the door with his eyes worried and when he saw her, his eyes would relax in that instant and the weight would fall off his heart. She imagined the relief and joy of embracing him in his doorway. This made her long to be with him right now. It will happen soon, she said. And she had to keep her heart down as if it had wings in it and was going to fly out of her chest.

She slapped a mosquito on her leg as she passed a white colonnaded funeral home surrounded by shaped hedges with a light box sign like a motel saying Have A Blessed Day and a name in flowery script. She passed a refrigerated shed for ice cubes outside a service station backed by trees. Voices reached her from someone filling up. She could smell the gasoline but couldn't see who it was.

After what could have been another mile, she passed a CVS, brilliantly lit and silent, and then came to a stadium parking lot for a Super Stop & Shop, the asphalt buckled, carts left out at random.

A digital sign in front of the Valley National Bank said 4:59, 70°. She decided that this was the sign she had been looking for. Now I'll turn, she said.

At the next street, she made a left, crossing behind a strip mall, hearing the hum of refrigeration out back of the loading dock and dumpsters, and started heading north.

She was on a smaller road and it was very dark and quiet and felt like the country. The road was lined with hedgerows higher than her head, so she was walking along a dark wall. There could have been country houses behind the hedges. Sometimes she glimpsed them. And there were trees yet higher than the hedges and homes. The sidewalk was narrow and hard to walk on and sometimes you couldn't walk on it and she walked in the street, looking above the treetops to see if dawn was coming. The moon was over her left eye. She passed a hospital. A lighted bus kiosk. Dark soft greensward, hedges, flag poles. A chapel in white. The hospital's campus numbered like an airport parking lot with light box signs: 1A, 2C, and so on. There were beds of flowers, the hum of ventilation. Sprinklers clicked on and started whisking on the grass. They wet her legs.

The eastern sky had shapes of light in it behind the puzzle pieces of clouds. A panel truck tore by and blew air over her. She crossed over a stone bridge above a parkway and saw her shadow on a Do Not Enter sign, posted at the onramp, meant for cars. She saw the morning star. The Lakeville Jewish Center. Countryside Montessori School. She got the sidewalk back—a thin ribbon between grass and fence. The sky had changed. Dawn was breaking. The blue gray light of dawn fell on everything—on her. The trees and leaves were silhouetted in sprays of leaves against the sky. She was passing through a vine-shrouded forest, willows, falling plants, beards of leaves, the giant faces of old bearded men rendered in leaves. She broke another spider web, actually saw the spider in the streetlight. It was very big: as big as two thumbs. They strung up nets from the telephone poles. She smelled the soil.

Because the shoulder was uneven, she walked in sand and gravel between the uncut grass and the white line. The odor of trees and grass was very strong. Pine also. She had to run up on the grassy shoulder when the cars sped past, and her sandals slipped. Her foot slipped and she broke a sandal. The toe piece popped out. She put it back together, birds calling around her.

Everywhere were trees. An oak had clouds of leaves. There were ivy cascades and split-rail fences. The moon looked like a tiny sun in the mist. In the east, she saw very pale pink on the clouds and pale blue where there was open sky. The pink was intensifying. All the light was different. She could see the road and herself in dim blue daylight.

At a highway, the asphalt smelled like oil and vulcanized tires. A sign said West 495 New York. In the bushes, the other sign said East 495 Riverhead. She had a great vivid panorama of the sunrise sky. The clouds grew in vaporous streaks, some ribbed like the glossy belly of a fish, as if they contained linear bones. These clouds caught the sun, which was as yet unseen. They looked like x-ray images—gauzy, overlapping, transparent.

She went under the highway and the air temperature in the underpass was warmer, like a dwelling. When she came out the other side, the new day was even brighter.

The road was dangerous; she couldn't see who was coming and had to cross to the other side owing to the curve. She walked by a golf course, breaking through spider web after spider web and wiping them out of her hair. It seemed no one had walked here except for her. Four well-nourished older males in spandex and cleated shoes and protective helmets raced by on feather-light bicycles that whirred. The road began to go uphill and she was climbing now. She saw a gargantuan water tower on steel legs up ahead. A squirrel on the power lines. Leonardo's La Dolce Vita. A circular driveway. Roman statues. Three-story office buildings. Vincent Jacone Laser Surgery. Marigolds, flowers, a basketball hoop. A forest-green truck with a yellow snow shovel. A tow truck: Appalachian. She smelled tires, gasoline. Saw a burned-out restaurant: Bombay Palace. The trees were far taller than the buildings, some of them firs. The Manhasset Fire Department was in a Dutch building. It was a lovely sunny early morning. At the top of the hill, she came to an intersection with a major road. She was breathing. She saw she had reached Northern Boulevard in Great Neck.

54

HE WENT UP THE hill, and when he came out of trees and the court-yard buildings, he passed the lot next to what used to be a drugstore, the broken glass on the asphalt under the amber streetlights. On the other side of the street there was a liquor store and he went into it. The store was a narrow tunnel. There was no door. You just went in, and the bottles went up to the ceiling. They sold McIvor in a gift box and Mr. Boston wine.

The Asian woman behind the Plexiglas had been here since the eighties, and she was nice, sort of a mom. Her large eyelids rose smoothly up to her forehead, uninterrupted by eyebrows, making it look as if she were surprised and delighted to see you.

Which one? she smiled, holding up different bottles of Bacardi. Skinner tapped the glass. That one.

Three old black guys in skullies came in with cigarettes drooping out of their mouths and one was saying, This motherfucker wants Chivas. Who you talkin bout? Softee? And Skinner slipped out past them carrying his bottle and went around the corner.

He went up the street looking for somewhere to drink. The side streets contained complexes of brown brick apartment buildings, a sun deck on every floor, seas of ferns in the alleys. He backed into a U-shaped hideout formed by three buildings and cracked his bottle and started drinking.

Five minutes later, a group of males gathered around a double-parked Lincoln. Skinner put his bottle away, thinking they could be undercovers. He got out of there and walked up the block. On the next corner, there were liquor stores, Chinese restaurants, Salvadoran restaurants, laundromats and a bar. He went to the bodega on the corner for cigarettes. Just give me one. Do you sell them loose? I can't think that far ahead for a whole pack. Under the yellow awning, he lit up and sat on the pavement with the cigarette in his busted-up fingers from fighting, and concentrated on the smoke, his small red ember, the fume of tar in his nostrils, throat.

When his cigarette was over, he got up and crossed the avenue, which looked gray in the streetlights, and turned back onto one of the roads that ran parallel to the railroad—either Franklin or another one, but he did not care enough to tell which. After walking several minutes, he stopped where it was dark and took his bottle out again and started drinking alcohol as if it were spring water. He drank half, about 250 milliliters, in under five minutes. When the liquor hit his bloodstream, it staggered him—he couldn't hold himself upright anymore. But this wasn't enough for him. He drank the rest and then blacked out.

While unconscious, he found his way to a construction site somewhere down a dead-end street. He ripped the caution tape away from the rebar stakes in front of the house and stepped in wet cement. The house was covered in yellow exterior sheathing. He kicked his way through a plywood board that was supposed to keep people out and found the rubble where they were breaking up the old concrete slab. Under the streetlights, he started lifting up the stones and carrying them out of the house and down the road until he had to drop them. He left a scattering of one hundred twenty-pound stones strewn out on the asphalt.

Good to go, he said aloud and jogged away, his hands white with concrete dust, knuckles bleeding.

He had no awareness of doing any of this, or of running around the neighborhood and hiding, taking cover behind parked landscaping trucks. Still blacked-out, he followed the street signs to his address and woke up standing on the corner of 158th Street, still so intoxicated he had no concept that he lived here. He thought he was here for Zou Lei, that she would be waiting for him. He thought he was going to see her standing there on her strong legs in her new shoes ready to run with him. But she was not there.

Rotted sneakers hung from the power lines like game. He focused on the statues in the Murphys' yard. He remembered that he had been arrested here this afternoon. The house was not necessarily empty—there was a light on. Someone could be in there behind all the wood and aluminum, Sheetrock and fiberglass.

Skinner came lurching across the street and walked straight at the house until the waist-high yard fence stopped him. The trash barrels on the sidewalk attracted his attention. He bent his head over one of the barrels as if he were going to vomit in it. But he was not being sick. He was staring at what was in it. After a minute, he reached inside and took out a handful of green camouflage silk and regarded it without comprehension.

He started pulling the rest of the camouflage material out of the barrel like a silk handkerchief from a magician's hat, pulling it out on the ground. His thought and action alternated between drunk and lucid, as if a wheel were turning inside him and a different part of him was coming around on every revolution. By now, he must have recognized his poncholiner. He mumbled something, staring down at it.

Then he picked up the barrel and turned it over, dumping it out on the pavement, and all his gear came out in a slew of trash. Everything came out—jeans, camouflage, beer cans, his expensive clothes, his U.S. Army duffle bag with the American flag patch on it, his magazines. His belongings were soaked in rancid chicken. He dropped the barrel and it rolled away into the street. The reek hit him. Flies flew up and hit his face.

Some things had been reserved from the trash. He sensed their absence. No laptop or cell phone were there. He pawed around in the muck and the bad light and found a sneaker, but it was not hers; it was his own, and he dropped it.

Then his hands touched something that affected him and he started feeling what it was to be sure of it, clutching it, feeling what was in it. He had found his assault pack. He felt for the L-shaped weight of the weapon. It was there. He uttered an exultant sound. Flies settling on his face, he put his hand in the bag and drew the weapon out.

He stood up, and after peeking around the street, went up the driveway to the Murphy's door. He pulled back on and released the part of the pistol called the top slide, putting a round in the chamber. In his drunken state, he studied the pistol closely in an effort to determine that it would work. He looked around the street again and seeing nothing but the whirl of lights, rang the doorbell.

Twenty seconds went by. Subaudible voices emanated from somewhere in the interior of the house. Then he heard footsteps thudding down the carpeted steps inside the vestibule. He held his hand behind his back and waited where he could be seen through the peephole like a suitor bringing flowers. His thumb took the safety off. Floorboards creaked and Jimmy's presence coalesced behind the door.

You better get out of here.

I've got some things I'm missing.

There was no answer.

Look, Skinner said, sounding drunk, You can be a hardass and I'll keep you up all night. Or you can be cool and just give me my laptop.

The silence continued one, two, three, four, five seconds.

The latch popped open. Skinner filled his chest. The door came open. He took a step and raised the gun in Jimmy's face.

Jimmy threw the door shut and Skinner hit it open. Jimmy bolted up the stairs and through the kitchen door. Skinner caught himself in the doorframe, regained his balance, and vaulted after him into their apartment. Jimmy was through the kitchen and down the tunnel of the blue hall. He grabbed a banister and started going up the stairs. Skinner flew through the kitchen, the kitchen a flash of mustard yellow. His boot hit the linoleum. His next boot landed in the hall. Jimmy had disappeared. Skinner's next stride carried him to the end of the tunnel, the shadow-blinders of the walls containing his view. He caught the banister and sprang up the stairs. Two meters away, Jimmy was climbing with all his might, bending over his legs and striding like a mountaineer. Skinner pointed the weapon at the back of Jimmy's undershirt and pulled the trigger.

The boom of the first shot blew out like an overinflated tire exploding in the enclosed space. Skinner heard nothing. He did not hear the scream. A picture fell off the fake wood wall on the landing. Jimmy ran into a room. Skinner ran up behind him and pulled the trigger at the room. There was a dry-fire click. He yanked back the slide. A live round jumped out and landed on the carpet. He pointed into the room again, squinted, and squeezed.

The gunshot boom went through the Masonite to the foundations.

Skinner went into the bedroom. There was a stereo, a poster on the wall. The lamp was on. The venetian blinds were askew. Jimmy was half behind the bed, his long legs in jeans extending out. His chest was inflating and deflating.

Skinner pointed the gun at him and kicked his foot.

Jimmy's head turned sideways on the floor and his jaw moved.

Just go.

Just what?

Just go, man.

In a minute, Skinner said. He leaned down and put the gun to the back of Jimmy's head. Jimmy had soft brown hair of a lighter shade than his own.

Feel that.

Don't, man.

Listen up. I don't know what you did with her.

I didn't do anything with her, man.

Listen to me. I don't know what you did with her and I'm going to accept that I'll never know. Knowing doesn't change anything. I already know.

Listen, man, I didn't do anything.

Sure, I believe that.

No, said Jimmy.

Skinner pulled the trigger from an inch away, and Jimmy's head jumped. The bed got knocked away from the wall. An empty casing fell in the bedclothes. The lamp fell over and cast a cone of light sideways on the white plaster wall.

He backed away from the scene in the room, stepping backwards through an invisible veil of powder smoke, blinking his eyes at the mannequin-body on the floor in the weird light. He backed away from what the light showed. His ears rang. There were no other lights. This floor of the house was dark, the real darkness of where the people lived, and the deeper in you went, the blacker it was. He smelled their house and saw their laundry on the floor.

She told the emergency operator, Help me, there's someone shooting in my house.

Slow down, the operator said. Don't hang up.

Erin, who had run outside and was backing away from the house, was hyperventilating.

I'm scared shit, she gasped.

Skinner thumped downstairs in his boots aiming the pistol at everything he saw. He saw no one. As he crossed above the basement stairs, he wanted to call down to Zou Lei one more time to see if she would answer, but he couldn't stand to hear his own voice. He thought of descending to the basement to look for her again, but he knew that if she wasn't there, he would end his life, so he made the decision to leave the house.

He emerged from the side of the house, hurried down the driveway and started walking fast and innocently towards the corner, stepping over the dumped-out trash, stepping on his own possessions, barely conscious that what he stepped on was his.

As he reached the corner, he broke into a jog because he was hearing sirens.

Sirens were distinctly audible, there was no doubt.

He ran across the open vapor-lit space of the avenue to the black trees and the tracks and rocks on the other side.

A short sturdy man walking on the other side of the avenue stopped when he saw Skinner running at him out of nowhere, backed up and put his hands up.

Skinner ran by without looking at him, the pistol projecting from the end of his heavy forearm, his shins like broom handles going into his boots, picking them up and dropping them down, running, showing fatigue, a lack of coordination as if he might trip and fall. His damp black t-shirt was flapping on him, his close-cropped head turned sideways gazing in the direction of the racing sirens and the red and white sparks that were appearing down the avenue.

After Skinner ran by, the man lowered his hands and made a wide berth around the area of darkness covered over by black trees into which Skinner had disappeared.

The sirens got louder and louder and louder and more powerful until they had ballooned into whooping shock waves, and you could hear the engines and feel the tremor in the blacktop as the police cars climbed nearer along a parabolic arc through the intervening trees. The first speeding cruiser arrived in seconds, its electronic siren deafening, and pivoted and turned on 158th Street. Another cop car came streaking down through the dark from Bayside. More were coming now. Red lights whap-whapped on the houses and the man's face, watching them arrive.

Very soon, the street was full of police cars, too many for them to turn and they began stopping on the avenue. The officers jumped out and ran on foot towards the location, their belt gear bouncing, hands over their holsters. You heard their keys when they ran. Some walked purposefully.

How many were there? someone yelled. Did you see him go?

Away from the epicenter, Mexicans could be seen in doorways looking out, silent faces cast in the red glow, which alternated rhythmically with darkness.

The man standing on the train-track side of the avenue was noticed by an experienced gray-haired cop.

You see something?

The man nodded, Sí, and pointed back into the tracks.

55

THE POLICE MOVED THEIR cars and waved the paramedics in.

The house is clear! Come on! they yelled.

They badly wanted to save somebody's life.

But, upstairs, Jimmy had been found with brain matter outside his skull. The cops who met the paramedics coming up the stairs said, Don't bother.

Really?

As in really.

They turned around and left.

For Jimmy, the detectives were called. Distinguished-looking men, they came in suits and porkpie hats. One wore a lavender handkerchief in his pocket. They made the climb up to the bedroom.

Jimmy had been killed face-down. One of the detectives wanted to turn the corpse over to see him. A digital picture was taken.

If the corpse was a man, he appeared to have been compounded with another life form, turned into a hybrid with some kind of flora. A stalk was growing from the skull as if his head had been abandoned in a field and a tree had started growing through it over the course of many years. But in fact the stalk had grown to its length of several inches in under a thousandth of a second. It was splitting and curlicued like an exploded party popper, like fingernails that have been allowed to grow for decades, forming spirals.

You eat dim sum? the detective said, referring to the slimy white tissue in the blood, which resembled the gelatinous noodles served as a snack by the Cantonese.

Downstairs, a diligent rookie found Mrs. Murphy collapsed on her bedroom floor. She was able to talk and asked if her son was dead. The officers tried to find out as much from her as they could. The paramedics came back, saw her hands turning blue and ripped open the LifePak to restart her heart. They bagged her and rolled her on a board, but because of her size, it was very challenging to move her out and she arrested again in the ambulance before they had even left the scene.

Later, the detectives stood outside consulting their notepads and talking to each other while the refrigerated van arrived, and three big black men in city coveralls and rubber boots went upstairs and put Jimmy in a body bag.

The mother hears the door. The son goes to answer it. She hears them talking, doesn't hear what they say. Then the shots fired. She hears them running in the house.

This is from the mother?

From the mother. She was in her room scared to come out, so she can't identify nobody. She calls to the son, and there's no answer. But she says she knows who did it.

The downstairs neighbor.

Right. They had an altercation earlier.

But the mother is no more.

She's no longer with us unfortunately.

But the daughter could identify him?

That's what she says.

Erin was in the street, surrounded by people from the block, many of them strangers, foreign. A cop tried to talk to her and she walked away from him screaming. She was on the phone, she was sobbing, she was in the center of every question that people had, she was in hysterics. Barbara Gambia's daughter, a broad-shouldered blond girl with a pigtail, ran up out of the onlookers in the red darkness calling Erin! and tried to hug her.

Erin turned on her and screamed, Some fuck just destroyed my whole life! My father doesn't even care enough about us to be here! Everybody else is dead!

Skinner ran six feet up the rocks, dropped to his knees and pawed his way to the top, kicking loose a spray of dirt and gravel that spattered on the pavement. As soon as he was able, he jumped up and charged through a screen of snapping brambles, breaking through into an alley that followed the railroad tracks and ran as hard as he could. The pounding of his boots and his mouth sucking air drowned out everything.

He was in the narrow gap between the back of several old six-story brick apartment buildings that were connected together in a long series and a concrete retaining wall that followed the tracks. It was so dark where he was running that he became disoriented. He could have collided into the side of a building and fired the weapon accidentally.

Out on the avenue, the sirens blasted by casting flashes of red light on the trees and trash in the breaks between the buildings.

He stopped, gassed-out, panicked and staring at the hollows of reflected red. The alley felt protected but it wasn't. There were too many straight lines back here. All the NYPD would have to do is shine a searchlight down here and they would see him.

In a crouch, he darted to the retaining wall, set the pistol on the ledge and jumped up after it, grabbed the weapon and started racing up the railroad embankment, stepping through the mud and leaves and around vines and using trees as handholds.

He ran into a cyclone fence between him and the tracks. The mesh had come detached from the horizontal crossbar on top and sagged backwards when he tried to climb it. Unable to negotiate the fence one-handed, he checked that he had the safety on and tossed the weapon over. It landed with a chunk in the gravel on the other side and he kept climbing. Tree branches got in his way. When he grabbed a wire, a barb punctured his palm. He jerked his hand away. Supporting his weight with his arms, he swung his leg over the barbed wire, wedged his boot toe in a diamond, and brought the other leg over. His shorts snagged, but he got them free. He dropped down on the gravel and fell on his ass. The pistol was lying by a railroad tie. He picked it up and started moving again, perceiving the tracks, trees and sky in different shades of darkness.

He was thinking:

I could just keep going, toss the strap. No one knows where I am. I could just keep going. Go back down and reenlist. I could buy a plane ticket to Iraq. I could go as a contractor. I could go as anything, just go, pick up where I left off. They're not going to come get me out there. I'll go back down tonight and say sign me up, sir, all I want to do is fight, sir, and I'm home free.

And he looked around at the night and it felt as if the war, and the freedom it might have represented, was just outside the boundary of what he could see, as if it were in a suburb of the city.

A half mile later, the tracks had dropped beneath street level. Sheer walls, slanted to create a deep V-shaped channel with him in the center, rose up on either side of him, and twelve-story condominiums projected up still higher from above those walls. The sky had grown farther away, and his view of it had narrowed. Ahead, an overpass crossed the tracks, and he could hear street traffic moving over it. He could not hear police sirens. Directly in front of him, the tracks led into the mouth of a tunnel, a black hole of nothing.

He looked up at the overpass where cars were passing and at the lights of businesses that were hidden from this angle. He could see the halo of Chinese neon in the air. They were working late on a Saturday night, deep-frying chicken wings and french fries for people coming from the bars, couples going home to open a Styrofoam shell in the dark, eat something hot together.

She sucks ketchup off his finger when he puts it in her mouth, the window open to cool the room, the street sounds floating in as she spreads her legs.

She transmogrified into an Iraqi lying on her back in a ditch with her knees apart as if she were giving birth to the flies consuming her or the laughter of his platoon. Images of the war flew from his head and pasted themselves like text messages in the depthless black void of the tunnel. Each scene horrified and nauseated him. They culminated with Jimmy's face pressed to the floor, the Berretta at his head, his mouth asking not to be killed, the comprehension of those words, the decision to fire anyway, the head jumping and blood pouring out his mouth and nose. The body was a plastic man. It became a faucet and blood kept pouring out of his mouth and nose as if that was his one purpose. The inanimate blood rushed loudly like a stream from a hose. It sounded lively, while the body was dead. The unseeing corpse twitched as if it was going to stand up. The eyes looked like those of a brain-damaged zombie or retarded person, like a soldier in the hospital with severe brain damage from an IED.

The fast flow of blood lasted for about ten seconds. Pieces of brain tissue washed out in the foam. The mouth was open but did not breathe. The corpse stopped jerking. The stream stopped coming from the mouth but continued from the nose. Then it became a trickle and stopped entirely and the body lay still like someone sleeping.

He had wondered, Are you okay? Did I hurt you? Are you just resting? Do you want me to call a doctor?

Do you want me to call your mother? A woman who is close to you? Someone you cannot bear to leave?

Or has she gone on as well? Has she run ahead of you? In that case you better chase her and stay with her on the avenues, through the parks. Be prepared for a long run, which will sweat everything out of you, purifying you and readying you for a new beginning. So drink water and a lot of it, friend.

The overpass, he realized, led to the park where he had exercised this morning, which put him no more than two or three blocks from the precinct house on Union Street where he'd spent the afternoon. If he tried to climb up there and look for her in Chinatown, a patrol car would see him, and he knew what his future would look like then. An emotionally disabled twenty-three-year-old with a high-school education and a poor service record, he was standing in a chasm in his basketball shorts two miles from where he had murdered a civilian. Whatever else might happen, she was lost to him and he would never get her back.

The V-shaped walls of the railroad cut were spraypainted with graffiti words, just visible, like a procession of elephants in the night. They had written MS-13 in giant humped fifteen-foot-high letters all down the wall as far as he could see. It was the same behind him, a giant written mega-scream, screamed over and over, all the miles back the way he had come. He heard the eerie howling of combatants who, having broken through its final defenses, are racing into a city.

The tunnel entrance was completely black and he walked into it, gravel crunching under his boots. The graffiti continued in here but he could see nothing except total night, not even where he stepped. He stopped walking and the crunching stopped.

Despite being overcome by grief, he was far from innocent. He had traded her for something else, and while he regretted this, even his capacity for regret was compromised. This was the price of the gift that he and Sconyers had received. They had learned that everything could be destroyed and then they had destroyed it. And they had learned what that destruction looked like. Everything else was gone. She was gone. All he had was what he knew, but this knowing was substantial. Even with his eyes closed as he wept, he knew what was in the tunnel.

He took the safety off, put the pistol to his head sideways, took a breath as if he were about to try for one more rep, and, telling himself there was only one way he was going to see her again, he pulled the trigger.

I am so sorry. How sorry I am I cannot say.

Against the pitch-blackness of the tunnel, a spherical white flash exploded next to his head with a blue ring around it. His head rebounded and his body fell to the ground, knees to face, in very fast sequence. His arm was flung out to the side by the recoil and the pistol tumbled.

He died over the course of two minutes, different parts of him shutting down. His heart stopped pumping. He made a choking or sighing sound that no one heard. She did not visit him or take his hand. Five minutes later his temperature had dropped to 96 degrees and continued to cool throughout the night until it was the same temperature as the gravel beneath his body.

56

She didn't feel like walking anymore but she kept going. There was nothing in her stomach and her energy was all gone. Her legs didn't want to move. During the night she had covered thirty miles, maybe more. She didn't know how much further she had to go, only that it was a straight line. The road led downhill across marsh grass and uphill to a highway interchange, the highway signs reflecting the gold sun: JFK-Belmont Aqueduct, the Throgs Neck Bridge. Just the sight of it was hard to look at, the suspension bridge rising above the grass in the distance, pale against the blue sky—just the sight of the distance was hard for her now. She hobbled slowly at a two-mile-an-hour pace as the sun rose another inch behind her ear. Her feet were damaged, and she was afraid to look at them. If she stopped to rest, she might not get herself moving again. Traffic passed her almost soundlessly. It was a quiet Sunday morning. The SUVs waited at lights and no one crossed the intersection. She was the only person walking on the street. The cars idled at the lights and she drew closer to them, walking painfully, and before she reached them, the lights changed and they took off, and she limped on in temporary silence, passing Korean businesses, automobile dealerships, showrooms. Everything was closed and in the white dilapidated houses down the side streets people were sleeping. Or they were quiet, getting up and going to the refrigerator for milk, their faces screwed up with sleep. But not with panic. They could sit down in their kitchens and drink coffee. They had their yellowing roof over their heads, an electric fan, a shower, a job on Monday, the grocery store this afternoon. She imagined red steak in a plastic package in the refrigerated section of the grocery store, the meat soft and cold and the fat hard under her fingers. Her fat was being drawn off her flesh—she felt it being taken—to operate her legs. I have to rest. She held herself on a parking meter. And the large vehicles hissed by on Northern Boulevard in the sun. There were Greek restaurants and tax and law offices and bus stop signs, a low roof of shadow under the awnings, and a

Korean church the size of a hill on the corner. Behind her the sky was blue and there were puffs of clouds, a glare of white from the sun. Her shadow was losing its legs. She looked ahead up the boulevard where Skinner was, somewhere after all those closed businesses, low roofs going on and on into the uninhabited distance, and she began walking again. There was a cloud line on the horizon, and she was moving towards it.

Her sandals broke when she crossed a street with a high curb. Utopia Parkway. She couldn't put them back together, so she tried to tie them to her feet another way—if only she had some string—but she could not. She tried to walk holding the thong between her toes, but it made it harder. She threw them in the street and walked on without them, curling her feet to keep the blisters off the pavement. The sidewalk was going to take her skin off. She would need medical attention. Her face was drawn. The edges of her feet were ragged and black. She looked at her feet and saw them suppurating. She came to a place where another street began: it flowed off of Northern Boulevard at an angle like a river, and it was Sanford Avenue—among decaying buildings, a funeral home with Korean writing, park benches, small trees, broken glass, and the parked cars like rocks on the riverbank. A furlong ahead of her the railroad tracks crossed the boulevard above the newsstands and flower stands. The graffiti on the metal said DEN RIP.

You've made it, she said and walked on not concerned by the pain. She looked for a hawk in the sky, an airplane perhaps, and saw pigeons. They were roosting under the trestles when she got there. She walked over white guano on her bleeding feet and it felt cool and wet. Now she had reached the gray sky that she had seen. It was warm and it would rain. On a board, someone had written: We Design Funeral Flowers. The Food Mart sold High Grade Cigars. Steve's Coffee Shop. Fratelli's Pizzeria. The 7&7 Deli Supermarket. We Accept WIC Checks. People were sleeping in the apartments up above with the windows open in squared-off brick buildings, pigeons on the ripped awnings. Beer Soda Lotto. Milk Barn Farms. Dairy Deli Grocery. Phone Cards. Metro Cards. A sun-faded ad for Boar's Head meats. Adult males playing arcade games inside by the racks of potato chips. The New Asia Restaurant, here since 1989, the year of Tiananmen. Landscaping trucks. A run of boarded-up, burned-out storefronts. The notice said Victor Han Architects. The graffiti on the boards spelled Blunts. The T was devil's horns. Die 666. Leiser's Liquors. A sweatshirt tied around a broken parking meter. CSNR. Romer. Big Dick Fuck All Day. MS-X3. On the boards, the work order said construction by the Hua Fong Construction Corp. Feeney's Tavern: two green turtles and a little green door, number 2401.

She went down Sanford Avenue past an abandoned house sealed by the marshal, by a notice, and possibly used anyway, the siding covered in soot and graffiti too, the backyard teeming with weeds. Mexicans waited for the bus. Between the four-story ghetto apartment buildings was a sea of weeds, tall grass, tires, road cones, a piece of heavy construction equipment, the houses at angles to each other, everything coming apart. Next door there were Mexican men with engines in the yard fixing the door of a beat-up silver-gold Impala. There was the LIRR. The graffiti on the rocks said GLCS. Pocos Pero Locos. A heart and Brazalhax y Soldado.

On the curb, she saw the strewn trash and the camouflage gear. There was yellow crime scene tape, a long strand of it stretched out in the driveway. She recognized some of her own clothes mixed with his. She made her way to the Murphy's door and knocked. It was a city morning. You could hear both birds and cars. The train from Port Washington roared by through the trees across the avenue while she waited. She tucked her hair back and prepared to speak English.

The daughter came to the door, red-eyed. Help you?

Zou Lei tried to ask about Skinner.

And who was he to you? the daughter asked.

And you are?

Yeah, excuse me, and can I get your information in case the cops wanna talk to you?

Zou Who?

Okay thank you very much.

I'll give them a description of you.

What about Skinner? You mean the piece of shit that lived here? I don't know anything about him.

Epilogue

She discovered a greater desert than any she had previously known. It must have been that she was a great explorer. All of this was barren territory of the most forbidding kind. Mineral formations. No drinkable water. It would probably take more than one lifetime to cross it, she estimated. More time than she would have anyway. Like a traveler in space, she thought. But she had entered it, so she kept going across it in the nomadic way that was natural to her. If she expected to see anything, it was the graves of other migrants, their bodies half interred among the shorn-off tree stumps. The land was so vast she had no hope of seeing anyone she knew, neither mother nor father. The figures she saw were too small to distinguish. No one called out, Daughter I remember you. Where are you going? Stay with us and eat.

Not in this wasteland.

She got off a Greyhound bus in a place where the sunshine forced your eyes shut. She put her baseball cap on—the faded navy cotton was hot—to give her eyes enough shade to see where she was going. She walked among Mexicans in jeans and straw hats, women with wide waists and big bosoms and eyes made up like Cleopatra of Egypt, carrying their bags of clothes, children's toys, rice. They climbed into the cars of sometimes ominous family members who came to meet them in the desert.

She had come, this time, by way of Queens, where she had stepped over the police tape and tried to retrieve his blanket or anything else of theirs out of the trash that could be salvaged. Money had been the last thing on her mind. She had been thinking only of holding onto him somehow. But this was how she found her Asics, and in her Asics she found his bank card, which she discovered still tucked inside the right sneaker, where she felt it with her torn-up foot when she put the sneaker on.

His PIN was something she found she could recall. After she withdrew two hundred dollars, she bought Singapore fried noodles and took a livery cab to the emergency room and sat there eating noodles and watching reality TV until they called out the fake name she had given them and a nurse examined her feet.

This is scary. How'd you do this?

Zou Lei left the hospital a few hours later with her feet bandaged and a blister pack of antibiotics and took another livery cab back to Cromellin Street.

Over the next ten days, wearing her hat down low, she went back to the ATM on crutches and kept withdrawing the daily maximum until she had all Skinner's savings.

When her feet were healed and she could walk without crutches, she took her woven plastic bag, left her key with another of Har's tenants, and headed to the Port Authority, where she bought a bus ticket to Phoenix, Arizona.

In Phoenix, she worked at a Chinese fast food restaurant in a one-floor strip mall. The building exteriors were fashioned of a concrete shell coating sprayed over Styrofoam, which was used to sculpt archways and other Southwestern architectural motifs. The stucco was painted an adobe dried-mud color. It was an efficient, lightweight, if not necessarily eye-pleasing, building style, with the unintended consequence that you could put your foot through any building you wanted to.

She almost tried to see if she could throw her manager through the stucco when he fired her for submitting a falsified social security number. It was the first time in her experience that she had worked for a white American boss at a Chinese restaurant. His remarks about immigrants, whom he called You People, had been exasperating to her. Also she felt he was far too proud of himself for having detected her crime by means of E-Verify, his favorite new tool. But what nearly made her violent was when he threatened to call Homeland on her.

You do that and I'll make trouble for you. I know people you don't want to mess with. Put me in jail? I'll put you in the ground. Try that for size.

Since Skinner, she looked at men and thought: Has he ever killed anyone? Been shot at?

She walked or hitchhiked to whatever work she was able to find, travelling on the shoulder of the long rolling roads while the golden sunrise, an event of galactic stillness, spilled across the desert still cold and blue from the night. Every half minute a Ford F-Series truck would blast by her, a kinetic storm and a rebuke to anyone walking. For a period, she took the bus through the downtown area to a plant that fabricated Styrofoam for use in construction, the bitter industrial burning smell of polystyrene in her clothes, lungs.

She would be seen on foot in the lots in front of the giant clean spacious stores, which were polite and hostile at the same time. There was an edge to everything in the west.

She bought a lifter's magazine at the Fry's Supermarket.

At a horse ranch where she performed day labor, cleaning stalls, she met a different kind of American, a cowboy from North Dakota who had come to Arizona to date a lady rancher whom he had met online. He wore a Stetson hat, a silver-tipped cowboy string tie, and a black silk kerchief at the throat of his denim shirt.

I've seen you work, he said. Are you Mexican or Indian?

All of the above. I'm Uighur.

You'll have to tell me what that means.

And when she had explained it to him, he said he found that fascinating. His own people had come a long way too. Us Grissoms showed up in the Dakotas in 1890. Henry Grissom fought in the Civil War. He brought everyone out here from Tennessee. They made their own whiskey. That was one of the things they did, and they did it pretty well. And then they came west and started ranching. They built their spread in the Black Hills, which is where it is to this day. I worked it all my life. My sons mostly run it now.

Do you have any woman or girl working there?

We do have one. She does very well and we appreciate her very much.

He added, after he had heard why Zou Lei had been fired from her last job, that he didn't think the government needed to be involved in everything it was involved in.

It's not all bad, he said, but there's a lot of red tape now that does more harm than good.

He gave her the ranch's web address—yes, they had email—and told her to contact his son. Or just go up there anytime you want. If you work out there like you do here, they'll take you on. There's a lot of work. It's hard work. And it's pretty cold. But some people really like it.

She shook his hand and he tipped his hat.

The style of a man who is both decent and independent, who knows what he must do.

She caught a ride home with a party of Mexican laborers in a pickup truck.

She ate carne asada, refried beans, yellow rice and picante, now speaking Spanish more frequently than Chinese. Con todo, she told the Mexican women at the roadhouse. A small coffee was a chico.

Naranja fresco ha muchas vitaminas.

Down the road, the Circle K sold a paper called the Pinal County Slammer, carrying color mugshots of everyone who was currently locked up. Sullen American Indian women with unwashed hair, manic skinheads, long-faced cowboys, drifters who had worked across America from the Alaskan fish canneries, to Californian logging camps, to hog farms in South Carolina and been arrested in every state in between.

She kept to a strict schedule, early to bed, early to rise. Not out like others, hunting love.

Late one Saturday night in her trailer court after she had been asleep in her bed for several hours she was awakened by a truck outside her window playing a love song. She picked up her head and as soon as she heard the harmony, that aching sweet pain hit her and she clutched her own mouth and cried out.

In the day, she told him she didn't forgive him for anything—for leaving her in this world without him. Oh sure, she said, when he talked back to her. You had your reasons. So I've heard.

Skinner, she said, I'm eating well. And look at this: you see this sun? This heat? Here I am. I look out over the factory roof and see the Superstition Mountains. Aren't I doing well? Look in my pocket: you see that? It's cash. I'm piss-poor, get paid like shit out here. Your money's keeping me in steak for now. When it runs out, it'll be rice and beans from then on. But aren't I happy, Skinner? Don't I look good?

In the evening, she walked to the strip mall carrying an Adidas bag over her shoulder and went into the green glass-fronted gym. It was air-conditioned and there were complimentary freshly laundered white towels, which she had been stealing since she arrived. Athletes from ASU, bodybuilders and military personnel worked out here, along with a smattering of senior citizens, moms, eccentrics and regular guys mainly involved in the construction trades, retail management or telemarketing. The gym had a fleet of treadmills and a mirrored cathedral of Olympic weights.

She went into the locker room and kicked off her dusty boots and jeans and whipped off her shirt, which smelled like the horses, and threw them in a locker. A lifetime of hard work had given her thick rough hands and since coming out west, her forearms and face had tanned dark red. She had a wild-looking face. She looked older, had gained weight in the bones of her jaws and the muscles of her temples. But when she stood before the mirror wearing nothing, she looked like the frieze of Diana on a temple wall.

She unzipped her gym bag and took out her spandex and her Asics, old bloody footprints on the insoles, and got dressed.

She put her headphones in, locked her locker, went out on the weight room floor, bypassing the smoothie counter and the drink case that contained bottled Isopure in green, orange, purple, and red, like liquid jewels—forty grams of protein, zero carbs, the color and succulence of apples, melons, grapes and plums, the entire bounty that poor people had carried out of orchards. All the protein a weightlifter needed, quicker and cleaner than lamb. You dropped the glass bottle in the recycling barrel and let someone else worry about the refund. You'd just swallowed your feast. The rug in this valley was spread with everything you could ever want as long as you didn't mind the chemical aftertaste.

She spoke to no one as she went to the squat rack, her iPod on in her ears as if she were getting instructions from the leader of a sniper team; she moved with concentration. Even if any of the lone men working out had wanted to speak to her, they would have been reluctant to disturb the focused woman. She loaded the bar carefully, hoisting the rubber-coated plates and sliding them onto the fat cylinders at either side of the bar.

From beneath her hat brim, she surveyed the weight. It was a lot for her.

But you never know if she was leaving town tonight. She punched one hand into the other. This might be your last chance.

A hawk flew over the gym's tarry roof, sailed across the Phoenix valley and alighted on a promontory in the mountains and waited for her to catch up. When she got there, the bird would spring off its perch and into the air again, leading out past the canyons into the open desert towards the faint but growing sound of voices.

She put her shoulders under the bar, said a prayer to him and prepared to lift.